THEIR WILL UNDONE

R.J. Valldeperas

HARPER
An Imprint of HarperCollins*Publishers*

HarperCollins Children's Books, a division of HarperCollins
Publishers, 195 Broadway, New York, NY 10007

HarperCollins Publishers, Macken House,
39/40 Mayor Street Upper, Dublin 1, D01 C9W8, Ireland

Harper is an imprint of HarperCollins Publishers.

Their Will Undone

harpercollins.com

Library of Congress Control Number: 2026934022

ISBN 978-0-06-338874-1

Typography by Julia Tyler
26 27 28 29 30 LBC 5 4 3 2 1

First Edition

For anyone who has had a dream and was told it wasn't realistic. Fiction is better anyway.

TULLUMAY
ICOSA
LIMAC
MT. RIMAC
TAQSAY
VIRA
TUTA KULLA
AMARU
KARU
UWACO
N
W
E
S

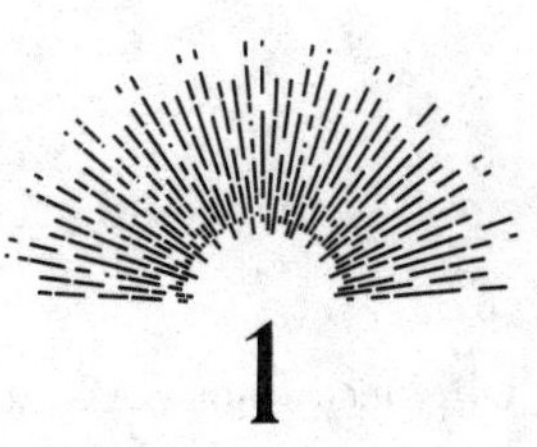

1

The game had just begun, and Nina was determined to win.

The fields around her were eerily silent; the sky above, crisp blue and clear; the soil between her toes, damp and cold. She stood tall, but even if she stretched, she wouldn't be able to see above the stalks of corn spread far and wide. Instead, she crouched low and listened.

The wind was a gentle caress that made the long leaves whisper and tickle her face. In the distance, she heard a familiar giggle and smiled. Lali could never keep quiet.

It was Sacha she would have trouble finding. Her younger sister had won last time, much to Nina's dismay. This was a game they had played many times since they were old enough to walk. One that terrified their mamay, especially when they would disappear without a trace.

But they always found each other, no matter how long it took.

Nina closed her eyes and exhaled, focusing on the sounds of their home that she knew so intimately. This morning, one of their llamas had given birth to a stillborn, so her parents had taken it as an offering to their earth goddess, Pachamama, and left Nina in charge of her sisters. They wouldn't return until well after dark. There was no one but the three of them for miles.

A loneliness crept beneath her skin—a strange, unspoken desire for a different life. It was one of Nina's greatest secrets. She kept it close and only inspected it at night, under the cover of dark and away from her sister's shrewd eyes, but sometimes it filled her with a longing that she couldn't deny. A thirst for adventure among a land devoid of it.

This game was as close as she would get to feeling anticipation. Excitement. *Possibility.*

Without a word or whisper of noise, Nina took off in a crouched run in the direction of Lali's pealing laughter, so carefree and childlike that it replaced her loneliness for a moment longer. She saw a flash of Lali's ocean-blue dress and long, dark hair and smiled.

"I see you," Nina sung quietly, stifling a laugh as Lali shrieked with joy.

But instead of following after her, Nina paused. There was a sudden pressure in the center of her chest. A slight prodding that pushed her to turn around. It was the same feeling she'd had at market day two weeks ago, when she had gotten distracted by a black stone sitting on a small table.

It is achilla, the woman had told her. *A stone forged by the gods to offer protection from those who wish to harm us.* Nina had heard whispers of it, but had thought they were just rumors. She reached out to touch it, mesmerized by its fathomless, swirling center, when she had felt that prodding again.

Reluctantly, she had abandoned her curiosity to follow that relentless prodding and had found Sacha just off the main path, her back against the rough stone of a small storehouse, cowering beneath the attention of two boys.

What had happened next was a blur of nightmarish images. The boys on their knees, blood dripping from their noses and ears, Sacha's voice pleading with Nina. She shook her head clear of it, determined to shove it back into the recesses of her mind. And though she also wanted to ignore the sensation of being lured toward danger once again, she couldn't. Not when her sisters were her responsibility. Not when a feeling deep in her belly told her something wasn't right.

At first, her steps were measured. They were in the middle of a game, after all, and Nina's imagination had a tendency to run away with her logic. There were times she thought she could see things. Golden lights and dancing threads that floated in the corners of her vision. Sometimes, she thought she could *feel* them. Like she could reach out and grasp that light in her hands and bend it to her will.

But as the stalks of corn stretched out endlessly before her with no golden threads in sight, and the tug in her chest became undeniable, she knew that her logic was firmly in place. This was something else entirely. Nina began to run.

Slender leaves whipped against her arms and legs. Panic colored her thoughts. The air stung her nostrils. If she didn't calm herself, she would lose all control again. She might hurt someone *again*. Her mamay had taught them better than this.

Stay calm and in control. Do not let them see what you love. It is the only power that matters, and you are its only master.

But Nina always felt powerless against the strength of her own emotions and insecurities. Against the pressure in her chest that felt like a flood barely contained. One mistake, and the dam would burst.

Bloody eyes and mouths open in a silent scream flitted across her lids with every blink. She wasn't sure if it was real or imagined. A fear of things past or things to come.

A flock of birds burst upward, dots of black puncturing the unending blue. Their calls were the only thing she could hear above her own breathing. Behind her, deep within the corn, Lali had fallen quiet again, hiding until one of her sisters came to find her.

Everything is as it should be, Nina told herself. *Everything is fine.* Perhaps, if she imagined it hard enough, it would be true.

The last line of tall stalks parted beneath her hands. Steps slowing, she pushed through and breathed a sigh of relief. There, in the colorful dress her mamay had sewn for her just this season, was Sacha. Her dark, chin-length hair blew gently forward so that it hid her features, and her bare feet were planted firmly in the rocky dirt of the path that led from the center of their ayllu to their home. She was doing a terrible job of hiding, but she was standing, and she seemed fine, and that was all that mattered.

"Sacha," Nina called out. "You do realize that you've lost the game? It will take but a moment for me to find Lali again and . . ."

Nina's words trailed off as she walked closer to Sacha, who hadn't moved since Nina called her name. A breeze had blown her hair from her face, and Nina now saw that her eyes were trained on the distance, toward the edge of their fields and the far-off ayllu center.

"Sacha?" Nina said again.

"They're coming," Sacha finally answered, but it was barely a murmur. A string of words almost drowned out by the thrumming of Nina's heart.

Nina glanced down the path but saw nothing. "Who's coming? Mamay and Tayta?"

The closer she got, the more persistent the tug became, until Nina could have sworn there was a light in the center of Sacha's chest like a beacon calling her home. Nina squeezed her eyes shut for a heartbeat, took another step, and reached for her sister. She wanted to pull Sacha into her and ground herself in logic, in the things she knew to be truth. They were safe, and Nina would do everything in her power to keep it that way.

All she had to do was tug Sacha out of the stupor that had come over her, like she had many times before. They would end their game with no winner and go back inside to wait for Mamay and Tayta to come home. Everything was just as it should be.

"Sacha, come. Let's find Lali and then—"

From far-off, Nina heard the huff of an animal. The whisper of a command. The shuffle of dirt and rocks. She finally reached Sacha, but Nina's attention was focused on the bent road, on the things she could not see and the way her imagination filled in the blanks.

Mind racing, she calculated the time of year. There were weeks before the growing season came to an end and their ayllu was required to pay the chani, the price for belonging to the united empire of Tawantinsuyu. The empire took their crops, textiles, knowledge, and sometimes even children. Sons to serve in the emperor's military, as walla who were trained to fight and defend. Daughters, always the most beautiful, to serve as acllas that were kept cloistered in the acllahuasi, trained to become wives and servants and gifted to houses the emperor deemed worthy.

An honor, they were told. But it hadn't felt like an honor when the walla had come to take Samaq ten years ago. It had felt like a punishment. Like a price too high to pay. There was nothing left they were willing to give, and so Nina, Sacha, and Lali had hidden during every following harvest on their mamay's orders.

No one should have been there to collect. They should have had more time.

And *yet*.

Nina sucked in a sharp breath as the first beast rounded the corner, just as large and ferocious looking as she remembered, even from such a distance. The achipuma's sleek black fur glistened in the early-afternoon light. Large clawed paws carried it silently closer. It prowled casually, as if it was in no hurry at all and nothing was important enough to merit its attention, but its pointed ears flicked back and turned from side to side, listening to sounds Nina couldn't begin to hear. Then its glossy black eyes landed on her, and a chill spread down Nina's back.

That chill crawled further when her eyes found the man sitting atop the beast, broad shoulders clad in a tunic so red it was almost black. The sharp lines of his jaw, the length of his hair, the way his body seemed an extension of the beast he rode, all spoke of unfathomable strength and power.

Sacha's hand slipped into hers, and Nina squeezed gently, painfully aware of how fragile it felt. How small they were in the face of man and beast.

"We should hide," Nina whispered, voice high-pitched and thin. Standing there in full sight was a slap to the face of their brother—the boy, only eleven years then, who had concealed his fear and followed the men in red on their terrifying beasts, never to be seen again. It was a direct slight against their parents, who made sacrifices to Pachamama and worked tirelessly to gather enough crops to pay the chani and keep them all safe.

Sacha shifted closer. Her hand trembled, but her voice was steady as she said, "There is no hiding from this."

"Then we find Lali and run. We know these fields better than them." Nina shifted back a step and tugged Sacha with her. There was defeat in her sister's eyes, but Nina had never been one to give up so easily. "Please, Sacha. Something isn't right."

Sacha's wide brown eyes met hers. Dark circles rested beneath them from the previous night of restless sleep. She knew Sacha had little energy, that this was a rare day when she felt well enough to play, and Nina would carry her if needed. Even against her will.

After a tense pause that seemed to last forever, Sacha nodded imperceptibly. A simple acquiescence that felt more like a damning. It was all Nina needed. Without another word, they turned and ran, but not before Nina caught sight of a sly smile, a twinkle of anticipation in a pair of dark eyes, a murmured command to *hunt*.

They ran like the defenseless prey they were. Sacha was slow, and though the beasts and their men were far down the path, she could feel the earth shake from their bounding leaps. One of the men called out a command, and Nina yanked Sacha forward, hoping she kept her feet underneath her.

The path stretched out before them. If they kept on it, eventually they'd reach their small home with its stone walls and thatched roof, where tiny handprints decorated the step before the door and delicate blue flowers adorned the door casings. It was a safe place, but their home offered no real protection. Their parents were gone, and there were no weapons within. Even if there had been, Nina couldn't use one, and neither could Sacha.

They had never been taught to fight—only to hide. Their best option was to lose themselves within the cornfields.

Nina veered sharply to the right. A blur of black cut them off.

"*Nina*!" Sacha screamed, but it was too late. The achipuma's tail lashed out and yanked her feet from underneath her. The ground slammed into her back and stole her breath. Ears ringing, she rolled onto her side and found Sacha's arm, ready to tug her to her feet so they could run again.

But Sacha's eyes were closed, her arms limp. Nina pushed to her knees, ready to crawl, to shove past all her physical limits and drag Sacha away. The sting of cold metal against her exposed neck stopped her in her tracks. "Don't move," a voice said.

Nina held herself unnaturally still. Metal scraped across her skin until the point of a wickedly curved blade rested on her throat. Attached to the blade was a tanned hand with several gold rings that glinted in the dying sunlight. At her predator's feet, a red cloak swept the ground in an errant breeze, the embroidered wings covering the hem fluttering as if they were in flight.

Though tempted, Nina didn't curse or cry or spit at his feet. She sat back the slightest amount, rested her palms on her thighs, and met the man's eyes. They were the same she had seen from a distance, set in a face so carefully crafted he looked carved from stone. Dark hair brushed his cheeks and forehead, and even darker eyes held hers. His tunic was sleeveless, and at the center was a golden disc bearing the face of the sun god, Inti. Golden snakes wove around his upper arms.

Behind him were two more men and beasts, but Nina paid them no mind. She knew the man with the blade at her throat was who she should fear, and not only because of his weapon. The urge to glance at her sister, to watch her chest move with breath, was almost more than she could ignore.

"If you're looking for my mamay and tayta, they are in the fields. They'll hear if I scream," Nina lied.

The man didn't respond.

"You have no reason to be here," she continued. "The chani isn't to be collected for several more weeks. We have no debts with Emperor Maicu or any of the nobles."

It was true. They were nothing but a small farming community, an ayllu far from Amaru Kancha, where the emperor resided. Their family always paid the chani on time. They consistently made offerings to Pachamama. They did everything right.

And *yet*.

"Your fields have grown much since the last time I saw them." The man tilted his head as he watched Nina absorb his words. It felt like he was peering into her mind.

"We are diligent with our offerings to Pachamama, and she has favored us in return," she said, the words heard so often that she repeated them without thought.

Their home by the ocean should not have had fertile land. It was said that their ayllu had survived on nothing but fish until Nina's mamay made the first offering, hoping for healthy children, and for abundance to feed and love them. Their fields sprouted overnight. It was the women of Limac who continued to carefully cultivate their crops, paying the chani but always giving to Pachamama first.

"Indeed," he said, a curious glimmer in his eyes that set Nina on edge. "And it seems that her favor has extended to me, and led me to you."

From where she sat, she could have sworn the man's eyes were darker than they should be, the black in the center bleeding into the whites. When his attention shifted from her to Sacha, Nina scooted her body to the side as if that could convince him to look away, but it only made him grin and crouch so that they were almost eye-to-eye.

The blade finally left her neck, but Nina knew she had made a grave mistake.

"Restrain her," he commanded.

"Yes, Kunay," a voice responded.

The kunay, the emperor's *personal adviser*, was there to collect. None of it made sense, but before Nina could so much as form a thought, hands clamped around her upper arms and dragged her back.

Nina twisted her body against the viselike grip. "Let *go*," she screamed, watching with dread as the kunay knelt before Sacha and gently removed the hair from her face.

"*Don't touch her*," Nina spat. He paid her no mind.

If only she could force him onto his knees like she had the boys who had touched Sacha a fortnight ago. If only she could find the golden threads that always taunted her, and put them to use.

But the kunay was devoid of all light. She saw in his eyes that his soul was darker than night, and Nina felt weaker and more delusional than she had ever been.

"She's perfect," the kunay whispered reverently, scanning Sacha from head to toe, drinking her in as if in a drought. "The emperor will be pleased to have her."

At his words, Nina thrashed against the bruising grip that held her. *"No,"* she screamed, spittle flying from her mouth, her simple blue dress riding up and exposing her lower legs. "You cannot take her."

The man unfurled to his full height and turned his attention to Nina. It was where she wanted it, but it didn't soothe the terror that spiked in her chest with the weight of his gaze.

A hand slipped into her hair and yanked her head back. The force of it made her eyes burn. Still, she kept them pinned to the kunay. "Leave her alone," she begged. Her voice was ragged, barely a whisper, but she knew from the amusement lining his mouth that he heard her.

The kunay stepped closer and bent over her, forcing her head farther back to hold his gaze, now hidden by his own shadow. The curved blade at his side caught Nina's attention. All she had to do was snatch it from his hand and swing it across his throat. How difficult could it be to kill a man?

A hand shot out and grasped her chin. Fingers dug into her cheeks and squeezed. "Your thoughts are written all over your face," the kunay said. His eyes narrowed, and he moved even closer. Close enough that she could see the hunger in the black depths of his eyes, so dark she could see herself in them. Tiny cracks bled into the whites like jagged paths in shattered stone.

"What do we have here?" he asked, his voice intimately quiet. Danger lurked behind each word, but Nina's focus boiled down to his hand on her face, the way his eyes ate her up, the way his touch silenced something vital within her, as if the darkness in him had bled out and consumed her. The feeling of inexplicable loss sent her reeling.

"Ah, so it was you I felt," the man whispered with glee. He brought his left hand to cup the back of her neck and pressed his forehead against hers. Inside, she was screaming. On the outside, Nina held perfectly still. Her shoulders throbbed with the effort of it. "You are favored, indeed."

The words were a vibration against her forehead, and Nina suddenly understood that nothing she had been taught had prepared her for this.

Emperor Maicu and his men didn't commune with Pachamama. They made no offerings to the land and showed up without invitation. They took what was not theirs to serve an empire that Nina and her people had been forced into.

They felt themselves above the rules. Above the gods.

"There's another in the fields. Should we grab her as well?" the man behind her asked.

The kunay inhaled sharply and pulled away. Nina surged upward. "*No*," she raged, fully breaking the one rule her mamay had given her.

Do not let them see what you love. There was so much Nina loved, her sisters above all else, but her mamay wasn't there and her guidance wouldn't serve her well. Perhaps it never had, for Nina was scared and soft and *angry*. So angry that she could feel it bubbling within her, rising from her stomach into her chest, where it sat like a fist around her heart.

The man only smiled. "These two will do. Leave the other be."

Nina finally glanced at her sister, her failure thick between them. She could no longer feel her like she had always been able to. In its place was a dark unknown, a gaping hole of uncertainty. Nina wasn't one to pray often—there had to be a balance, a give and take, and Nina had always felt she had nothing to give—but she found herself praying then.

She begged the gods for their divine intervention. She prayed for her parents to return just in time to save them. Or, at the very least, to save Nina from doing what she knew she needed to do.

It wasn't as if she expected the sky to open and rain salvation, but there was no sign and no savior. There was only her, and her love for her sister.

"Take me," she said miserably. "Sacha's weak and won't last the journey. It's me you want. Leave her be, and I'll go willingly."

Nina kept her gaze hard on the kunay, hoping to sway him toward her conviction. The man's eyes darted between hers, the cold smile that slithered onto his face another omen of things to come. Nina immediately got the sense that she had made some terrible miscalculation, but it was forgotten as the kunay scooped up his blade and sheathed it at his side. His touch lingered like a phantom cage around her chest.

"I think you might be right," he agreed easily. *Too* easily. He turned to his men and gave a command she didn't understand. Her vision had begun to blur around the edges, and her chest hurt with the force of her breath.

Sacha remained motionless on the ground, and Nina was most grateful for that. She knew her sister would have tried to do exactly what Nina was doing, but what Nina told the kunay was true; Sacha *was* weak, her body frail and ill, her mind fragmented on most days. She often spoke in her sleep, her words like riddles that Nina had stopped trying to solve many years ago.

With Nina gone, their mamay would have to soothe Sacha back to sleep. Lali would have to allow someone else to braid her hair. Sacha would have to venture alone into their small ayllu on market day. Whatever Nina had done to those boys, she hoped it was enough to scare them away forever.

Though Nina knew she was doing the right thing, all she could think as the emperor's men grabbed each of her arms and pulled her to her feet was *What have I done?*

With that sudden doubt came an uncontrollable inaction. When she wouldn't walk, they shoved her forward. When she wouldn't climb onto the beast's back, a walla gripped the collar of her dress and dragged her up in front of him, his arms around her like shackles. The achipumas ambled away. Her sister's body grew smaller and smaller until it was nothing but a colorful lump in the middle of a sea of dirt and stalks.

On the edge of the fields, she saw a flash of blue, there one second and gone the next. Lali had always been a good rule follower. Eager to be included and please.

Nina had tried her best to follow the rules, and still, there she was. No one came to save her, to take this burden from her. She didn't cry out, or struggle, or pray.

Despair trickled in, slowly replacing any hope she might have once harbored. For the first time, she understood her sister's propensity toward acceptance and defeat, for there was nothing to be done about this choice she had made.

Their fields were at the edge of the ayllu and the path before them split into two directions; one led to the heart of her people's land, where the market was and the altar where they made their offerings, where she knew her mamay and tayta were, and the other path led out of her ayllu and into the unknown.

A path she had never traveled before, that loomed barren and strange. Nina stared toward home. The last thread of her hope disappeared with the sun.

"Take these." A hand appeared in front of her face. Nina glanced at it and then at the kunay, who sat on his beast beside hers, his palm bearing a small pile of dark leaves. "The journey is long, and we will not stop."

"Where are you taking me?" she asked, eyeing the leaves nervously. They looked similar to Mamacoca, the plant provided by Pachamama that connected her people to the earth and their spirits, but they were bled through with veins of black. Like the kunay's eyes.

He saw her hesitation and leaned forward. His achipuma shifted slightly closer. "We are still near enough to go back for that sister of yours. Perhaps both of them. Shall I—"

Nina snatched the leaves from his palm and shoved them into her mouth. They were sharp. The taste of blood mixed with a bitter tang. Her muscles protested, but still she chewed and chewed, until her mouth was numb and the tingling in her fingers eased and the world around her spun.

Suddenly, everything seemed less dire. Less daunting.

"Good." The kunay nodded and leaned back. "You're being taken to the acllahuasi, where preparations for your true purpose will be made. Remember our agreement."

Already, Nina's mind was fuzzy. The promise she had made felt like a distant memory. But it was the feeling of Sacha's small hand in hers that grounded her. "I go, and Sacha stays safe," she said, the words slurred, her tongue and eyelids heavy.

A hand pressed into her forehead until the back of her head was resting against the walla's chest. "Sacha will be safe," she heard the kunay say as her eyes drifted shut.

How easy it felt to give in. How freeing.

Perhaps this was her punishment for ever wishing for a different life. For ever wondering what it would be like to be unencumbered by the expectations of others.

Now, she had buried herself underneath expectations. Tethered herself to them.

Nina had saved Sacha and perhaps even Lali, but she had condemned herself in the process. Regret morphed into shame that bled into steely resolve. No matter what came her way, Nina vowed to face the consequences of her choices head-on.

2

Kasik swung the curved blade another time, despite the ache in his shoulder and the sweat pouring into his eyes. The exertion felt good, like it might possibly make up for the lack he felt in every other area of his life. *This* he was good at. *This* he could control. He could be the perfect walla, even if he couldn't be the perfect son.

Instead of allowing his tayta's low opinion of him to become an excuse to slack off, he used it as fuel to be better. He would swing this sword until his arms shook with exhaustion and his vision swam, and then he would do it all over again the next day. He would prove to himself that he was worthy of leading a contingent of men, that he was the best option for it, regardless of his propensity toward mercy for the man who gave him life.

The clang of metal against metal rang out as his blade met Samaq's in a practiced dance. Samaq whirled to block another of Kasik's strikes. They had been sparring for so long now that each move was anticipated, every arch was met, and every feint was avoided. Yet Kasik pushed on, determined to land a blow, ignoring the pain in his chest as each breath demanded more. He felt no propensity for mercy toward Samaq, not when his tayta's derisive laughter echoed in the recesses of his mind.

Kasik swung down hard and fast and swiftly lost his balance as his blade met nothing but air. Samaq was bent over a short distance away, his shoulders heaving with breath.

"Enough," he rasped out. "Are you trying to kill me?" But there was a jovial tone beneath his words, a flash of a smile on Samaq's handsome face.

Kasik dropped the tip of his blade to the earth and relaxed his grip. The early-morning mist curled around his legs, cooling his heated skin. He forced himself to inhale deeply and exhaled the tension in his shoulders.

"I'm sorry, Samaq," he said sincerely. It was only another way in which he failed. A terrible son and a terrible friend.

Samaq was the kind of person Kasik could only wish to be. Carefree and full of optimism. So sure of himself that nothing could shake his faith. Even now, when Kasik had gone too hard and any other partner would have retaliated in earnest, Samaq simply huffed out a breathless laugh and walked over to him.

"Ah well, you'll have to try a lot harder than that." He threw an arm over his shoulders and pulled him toward their canteens, the subtlety of it not lost on Kasik. He was always able to do that, pull Kasik from one ledge or another in a way so seamless that Kasik hardly knew what was happening. Sometimes he wondered if it should be Samaq leading their contingent and wearing the title of kamayuq.

Kasik brushed the thought aside. It only led to dark paths that Master Wara had warned him against, and now more than ever, he needed to be of sound mind. Tomorrow they would be leaving for Tullumay, the ayllu in Icosa that the empress had called home, the first to be absorbed into Tawantinsuyu and where they would begin the Harvest. It was meant to be his first year leading as a kamayuq.

After Tullumay, they would make their way to Amaru and to the ayllus of Limac and Taqsay, where the acllahuasi was located, to ensure that each paid the chani. They would return just in time for Inti Raymi, a yearly festival to celebrate the winter solstice and all the emperor had achieved. But there was tension in the air that Kasik couldn't quite place. It made him anxious, which annoyed him to no end.

"Are you ready for tomorrow?" he asked Samaq.

Samaq took a swig of water from his canteen and shrugged at him. "Are *you*? You seem tense."

"It's nothing," Kasik reassured. "Just anticipation. It's our first Harvest."

"It is," Samaq agreed, but he wouldn't meet Kasik's eyes as he closed the lid of his canteen and wiped his mouth with the back of his hand. "There's something I'd like to speak to you ab—"

"Kamayuq Kasik." The sound of his title made Kasik straighten. The smile slipped off his face before he turned to meet the walla, a young boy who barely filled out his uniform with a fist to his chest, an achilla wrapped in thin leather and tied to his wrist.

The walla were faithful servants offered to the emperor through the Harvest. Boys who were trained into men who fought to unify their lands under the banner of Tawantinsuyu. The ayllus of Amaru and Icosa were fully absorbed, and it was only the southernmost ayllus in Uwaco that rejected the union.

How long that would last, Kasik wasn't sure, but he did know that the walla in front of him would see his blade stained red soon enough. The achilla around his wrist could not protect him from that.

The urge to reach for his own stone was almost too much to ignore. It hung from his neck as a reminder of what he had lost. He had taken to rubbing the surface of it with a thumb whenever he was deep in thought, and it had become a tell that gave too much away. A bad habit he was actively working to break.

"The emperor has requested your presence immediately."

The tension Kasik had already been feeling increased, but he let none of it show as he thanked the walla for his message and sent him with one of his own. "Please tell Emperor Maicu that I will be there shortly."

The boy hesitated—he had been expecting to escort Kasik there himself—before nodding and scurrying back the way he had come.

Mind racing, Kasik turned back to Samaq. "You were going to say something?"

Samaq clapped him on the shoulder and shook his head. "We'll speak later," he said, his eyes tilted with a small smile. Kasik watched him walk away, strangely tempted to call him back.

But his emperor had *requested* his presence, and Kasik, being the dutiful walla that he was, began the trek through the training grounds and the labyrinth of the kancha to answer his summons.

The mist that clung to the ground had already begun to lighten with the rising sun, revealing a large area full of green and seasoned walla alike, gathered to practice, to solve rank squabbles, to let loose and perform. Surrounding them were the walls that secured the kancha and all the living spaces behind it. Smaller houses for visiting nobles. The kallankas where the walla slept. Stables for their horses, and then the kancha, a sprawling, unassuming structure from the outside.

Inside those walls was something entirely different—stone speckled with flecks of gold buffed to a velvety-smooth finish and arranged in such a way that anyone unfamiliar with the layout would become hopelessly lost. Something only the lucky few who had been invited in were privy to.

Kasik was one of those lucky few because of who the kunay was to him—his tayta, the man who had a hand in creating him, and the one whose position Kasik was expected to inherit when he died. But not a moment before. Perhaps never, if Kunay Atik could help it.

It wasn't a role that Kasik was anxious to accept. He preferred being with his men, on the battlefield, among their people. He preferred to be reminded of what it was they fought so hard to protect—the expansion of Tawantinsuyu that offered opportunity, protection, and resources to every corner of the empire. This journey to the capital of Icosa would serve that purpose well.

He could almost taste the freedom of the emperor's road, his men at his side and nothing but the emperor's orders on his mind. The sooner they left, the better. Perhaps Maicu wanted nothing more than to bid him a safe journey before they left. Kasik doubted it, but still, he hoped.

Entering the kancha was always an interesting experience. Kasik had to wait until his eyes adjusted to the lack of light, which was exactly what the emperor's ancestors had envisioned when they designed it. If anyone tried to invade, they'd be blind upon entering, and as their eyes adjusted, his men would be there to remove the intruders' heads from their bodies. Anyone who happened to make it past would get lost in the stone labyrinth.

Having grown up within these walls, Kasik could navigate the way to the emperor's quarters with his eyes closed. The receiving room was the only space with something identifiable on the walls. A large, garish tapestry that depicted the fall of mortals in the time of gods. He had seen so it so many times he barely glanced at it as he walked by.

The rest of the halls were made up of blank walls with nothing to differentiate one hallway from another. Any of the doors he passed could reveal the emperor's quarters, or the kitchens, or the bathing chambers. Staff inside the walls were light; only those the emperor trusted most, and only after swearing fealty on their knees with the promise of death should they be found treasonous.

The door to the emperor's wing of the kancha was nondescript, a simple wooden slab with a golden latch similar to every other door. Without knocking, Kasik pushed it open and stepped through, lowering into a quick bow with a hand still on the latch. "Emperor," he said simply.

The man behind the desk was just barely taller than Kasik, though not as broad, and his hair hung freely around his shoulders, a dark contrast against the ivory tunic he wore. There were gold rings on his fingers and forearms and upper arms that matched the strange gold hue of his eyes. His smile was wide as he leveled a look at Kasik.

"Will you ever call me 'friend' again?"

It wasn't so long ago that they had been more like brothers than friends. But then Maicu had betrayed his true brother in the pursuit of power, and the control of Tawantinsuyu had fallen to him. It was quickly learned that Maicu did not keep a relationship that did not benefit him—brother or friend. Kasik was simply a man indebted to an emperor. "Not so long as you are my emperor," he said softly, the words tinged with regret.

Maicu sighed and gestured toward the chair before him. "Come in, then, and have a seat. I have a request to make of *my* friend and most trusted walla."

Kasik obeyed, adjusting the sword at his hip so he could sit comfortably. It showed how little Maicu questioned Kasik's intent that he didn't so much as blink at the weapon. They sat across from one another, Maicu's hands steepled underneath his chin, his eyes pinned to Kasik's, and then he spoke. "I need you to go to Taqsay."

The name of the ayllu in Amaru gave him pause. It wasn't strange of the emperor to misspeak. Often times, there was so much on his mind that his words made little sense. "Do you mean Tullumay?" As he sat there, his men were preparing to travel to the capital of Icosa. They had all but one foot out the door. "My men and I will be departing—"

"No," Maicu interrupted with a sigh. "I meant Taqsay. Your plans have changed."

Kasik stilled, muscles coiled tight and ready to spring. It was all he could do to keep from jumping to his feet and pacing the room. He balled his fists on his thighs and swallowed once, twice, mustering all the calm he had trained into himself before speaking. "Lord Anri is expecting us. This will set us back many weeks and—"

"You misunderstand me," Maicu said calmly. Kasik envied him his restraint. He hadn't been so restrained when they were children, and Kasik felt the lack of control in himself like a wound. "Your men will continue to the ayllu of Tullumay, to Lord Anri, but *you* will journey to Taqsay and to the acllahuasi, where you will collect a girl and bring her to me." Maicu held his eyes, challenging him to refute his commands. "I am telling you this in confidence, as a friend. Master Wara will give you a missive that you will deliver to the matron of the house, Mamakuna Dusi, and you will not speak a word of this to anyone else."

Kasik forced himself to take a deep breath, to settle back into his chair and adopt the unaffected air Maicu seemed to have. "All of this for another servant?"

"A *wife*, Kasik. And you would do well to remember who it is you are speaking to."

The words were quiet, but lethal. Gone was the friendliness between them from only moments ago and in its place was the emperor, a man who had murdered his brother in cold blood and then clapped Kasik on the shoulder as he passed by.

Maicu didn't suffer those who stood in his way, even if that person was his brother and the next emperor of Tawantinsuyu. To him, Kasik was a friend when it suited him, but a means to an end and as replaceable as the plush rug underneath their feet otherwise.

Firelight from the torches in the corners of the room danced over Maicu's face. Kasik worked to keep his own features still, to give away nothing. The answer he had received hadn't been the one he expected.

The girls in the acllahuasi were young, and once upon a time, they had specifically been chosen because of their unique abilities to control the elements and, in some far-fetched tales meant to scare children, control people. They were raised in an environment that suppressed those abilities for their own safety, and the safety of others.

Their uniqueness had scared the people, but whatever power the gods had bestowed upon them had waned over generations, becoming nothing more than a whispered myth.

However, the tradition had continued, and children were chosen for the chani as a contribution to their growing empire. Kasik himself had been handed over to Emperor Yachua, Maicu's tayta, at the age of seven, but it mattered little when he had been living within the kancha since the day he was born.

Maicu had never spoken of taking another aclla as a wife. He wondered if this had anything to do with why Atik left the palace so abruptly a fortnight ago.

There had been a time, before he was emperor, where Kasik and Maicu had discussed everything from hopes and aspirations to petty fears and frustrations. Now he could barely ascertain what Maicu thought or had planned.

Did Chaska, Maicu's first wife, know of this mission? The woman was aloof, but there was a glint of keen awareness in her eyes that made him wary. He doubted anything got past her.

"The girl will need protection, Kasik, and I only trust you to provide it." He leaned back in his chair, hands folded in his lap. "Your men will continue to Tullumay led by Samaq. Do this, prove to me your loyalty, and I will let you lead your men as you see fit. You can be the one to win Uwaco to our side."

The words were a puzzle with only the implication of a reward, and yet Kasik felt himself reaching for it, for the freedom Maicu dangled like bait.

If they kept to the emperor's road, then the path through the Tuta

Kulla, the dense forest that occupied most of Amaru, would be smooth. The road was blessed by the sun god, Inti, and led straight to Taqsay. The dangerous creatures that dwelled in the trees stayed far from it, and the citizens of Tawantinsuyu knew better than to bother the emperor's men.

"It will be a simple mission for you," Maicu encouraged.

Kasik knew empty flattery when he heard it. "And what of the mamakuna? Will she be expecting me?"

"In a way," Maicu offered vaguely. "There will be no problems, if that is what you are asking. Collect the girl, bring her here, and begin the life you have always wanted. I'm sure it will anger your tayta to no end."

At this, Kasik smiled. Kunay Atik took every opportunity to remind Kasik that he was nothing but a lowly walla, despite his title of kamayuq. He thought him too weak to lead, and his position only given due to Emperor Maicu's soft spot for a childhood friend.

This could be his chance to prove himself. The girl would be young and compliant. The terrain was fairly predictable. He trusted Samaq and his men to travel the northern leg of the emperor's road to Tullumay. There was no reason he should be wary.

And yet he was.

From the set of Maicu's brow, it was clear he had no choice.

Kasik took a deep breath and bowed his head. "When do I leave?"

"In the morning. Master Wara has a bag of provisions you'll need for the girl. Be sure to see him first. And Kasik." Maicu's voice softened, once again the friend. "Protect her with your life. No man is to lay a single hand on her without consequence."

This was a vow Kasik could easily make. "As you command," he said with a fist to his chest.

✦ ✦ ✦

Sleep evaded him, so Kasik found himself walking outside to clear his head. The sun hadn't risen yet, and the morning air was wet and brisk. The kallankas just past the training ring were quiet with sleep. Soon, the walla would be up and preparing for the day, and his men for their journey north without him. He intended to work out his frustration in the training ring and was just about to step into the empty space when he saw a shadow dart away from the side entrance of the kallankas.

A familiar face. Kasik relaxed and went to call his name when he realized Samaq was not heading in his direction. His friend glanced back furtively and then disappeared around the corner. Two heartbeats later, Kasik was following at a light jog.

A chill settled over him that had nothing to do with the shadows. This part of the kancha grounds was empty. There was a small storage building behind the kallankas and then beyond that, the walls that separated the kancha from the rest of the mountain.

Kasik pressed his back against the stone wall and slid sideways. Carefully, he peeked his head around the corner and narrowed his eyes.

Samaq and Empress Chaska stood together in the shadows of the storage building. They spoke too quietly for Kasik to hear, but the familiarity between them was plain as day. Chaska placed a hand on Samaq's arm, and Samaq ducked his head to listen closely. Then he nodded and they hugged.

Kasik whipped around and went back the way he came, refusing to believe what his mind was trying to convince him of. The empress was too smart to get involved with a walla. Too powerful. And Samaq was too kind. There had to be something else going on, but Kasik could not, for the life of him, think of an explanation.

It didn't matter. Maicu was sending him away, and anything beyond his mission was no longer his responsibility.

Kasik abandoned clearing his head and went straight to Master

Wara, who was exactly where he expected the scholar to be—in the small room off the kancha library, dangling off a tall stool in between sheets of quipu, his finger tracing over the knots on strings as his lips silently formed the message.

It was any wonder Master Wara knew where to find what he was looking for. The room was positively covered in stories and records. Years and years of information filed in only a way his teacher could understand. Fond memories washed over him as Kasik watched him read. The man was more of a tayta to him than his own, and Kasik was loathe to think about what would have become of him without such an influence.

"I'm told you have provisions for me," Kasik finally said.

Though he was in his fifth decade, and a scholar who barely left this room, he was a robust man full of health and life and an obscene amount of knowledge that could bury a simpler man. Knowledge that he did not hesitate to impart on Kasik every chance he got.

Master Wara parted a thick sheet of strings and found Kasik by the door. "Ah, just in time, my son."

He was always *just in time.* Kasik had begun to wonder if Master Wara had any concept of time at all. Perhaps the man needed more sunlight, but he seemed perfectly content as he began to collect items from various shelves around the room and place them into a thick cloth bag. Kasik leaned against the doorframe, dedicated to staying out of the way.

Finally, Master Wara held the bag out to him. "The missive for Mamakuna Dusi and the tea leaves for the girl. It's imperative she drink a full cup of it every single morning."

"Is she very used to having her morning tea? Shall I also bring herbs to calm her nerves?"

Master Wara gave him a baleful look. "The tea will help her transition. Routine is important. You, of all people, would understand that."

It was true enough. The upheaval of his carefully laid plans was giving him a throbbing pain in his temple. Kasik peaked into the bag and pulled out a silver cylindrical case. It was cold against his palm.

"That will give the mamakuna all the details she needs," Master Wara explained. "But speak nothing else on it."

With a sigh, Kasik collapsed into a nearby chair. "Another wife, and so soon after marrying Chaska? It has hardly been a year. What is the meaning of it?"

"You seek meaning where there is none. It is simply your duty to obey, Kasik, and understand that there are forces at work that you cannot fight."

"I am here, am I not? There is no fighting to be seen."

Master Wara leaned forward and jammed a finger into Kasik's chest. "In here, my son, there is fighting. I see it, even when you try to hide it. I see *you*." He moved his hand from above his heart to his cheek and patted gently. "Return to us, yes?"

Kasik met his teacher's eyes and frowned. "Of course," he reassured him. What other choice did he have?

3

For three days, Nina was forced to chew the bitter leaves twice a day. Their group stopped only to let her relieve herself and to water the achipuma. The beasts were quieter and calmer than she had imagined them to be from the stories she'd heard. If she had been in her right mind, she might have tried to befriend one and convince it to carry her away, promises be damned. But all she wanted to do was sleep, and when she did, all she did was dream.

At first, she dreamed of her brother, Samaq, as he was the last time she saw him, that he was on the achipuma with her, holding her head as it rolled from side to side. She would cry and he would brush her hair away from her face, shushing her, soothing her, and when she woke to find he wasn't there, it hurt more than she could describe.

Then she dreamed of Sacha, the other half of her soul, though they were an entire year apart. Their mamay said that Nina was a miserable baby until Sacha came. Then they were inseparable, always aware of where the other was, what the other felt and thought and needed. In her dreams, Sacha was scared and alone and Nina was running through the dark to find her, guided by nothing but a feeling that continued to lead her astray.

At one point, the walla and kunay had a tense conversation. Nina heard words like *inform the emperor* and *changes everything*, and then the kunay departed their group in a hurry. She watched him follow the path until he was nothing but a dot in the distance and tried to decide if any of it—their soft words, the singing wind, the laughing trees, the swirling dark—was real.

By the time they made it to the acllahuasi two days later, Nina had entirely lost her grasp on reality. They dragged her off the achipuma and dumped her lifeless body onto the ground. It was dark, but the moon above was full and bright, casting everything in a gray-blue hue that swallowed any semblance of familiarity. Even the air smelled different. Earthier and thicker. Wet dirt stuck to her cheek, and she was shivering so hard her muscles ached.

A warm huff of breath rustled the hairs on her forehead. The achipuma sniffed her once, its moist nose nudging her temple, and then it walked away, leaving her alone in the dark, surrounded by trees that stood over her like sentries.

"And what am I to do with an untrained girl?" No, not alone, she realized as a weathered face appeared above hers. "She's much too old to be here," a woman said, her large eyes boring into Nina's, wrinkled lips pressed into a thin line.

"The kunay said to bring her here." Nina recognized that voice. She had felt it through her back more than heard it for the last five days. "I know only what I have been told, which is nothing more than you."

The woman pinched the bridge of her wide nose. Nina tracked the way her gray braids, suspended in the air above Nina's face, swung from side to side. "Yana, take her to the baths," she ordered. "Let's try to get her decent. And then have Qori keep an eye on her."

Hands slipped under her arms and dragged her through the grass, toward the stone walls she had thought were simply shadows. Everything was painted in shades of darkness. The sky above was a bluish black. The ground below a bluish green. The walls of the building they pulled her into a bluish gray.

Even the woman who dragged her had a bluish tint to her brown skin and black hair, until the door opened, and a shaft of orange light changed everything.

Nina wanted to tell them that she could walk, but she couldn't make the words come out of her mouth. They dragged her through a large stone room lit with torches in the corners, down long hallways past doors that were closed tight, deeper and deeper into the drafty and colorless building.

Until finally, they opened a door.

It was warmer on the other side of it, and brighter, even though the ceiling was lower. The air seemed to thicken and coalesce, and she reached out a hand to touch it.

"Hold your breath," the woman called Yana said from above.

Nina managed only a shallow inhale before another set of hands latched on to her ankles, and then she was airborne. She hit water with a slap and quickly sank beneath the surface, her limbs as useless as boulders weighing her down.

She thought she might drown, until she realized it wasn't very deep. A few heartbeats later, she was breaking through the surface, sputtering and coughing and gasping for air. The water had cleared her hazy mind. An unfortunate inconvenience when two women, without waiting for a word of protest or permission, came at her with sponges and soap. Together, they stripped her of her dress, a pretty blue cotton that she had sewn herself, and scrubbed every inch of her.

Tangles were yanked out of her hair. Her skin burned from the force of their cleansing. Her teeth clattered even with her jaw clenched.

By the end, Nina was on fire. Her skin, her eyes, her heart. She was incandescent with a quiet rage that overshadowed her regret and shame. They pulled a gray robe over her head and walked her to her room in stony silence, and as she slipped into a small, cold bed in a strange and unfamiliar place, it was that rage that kept her company and her dreams at bay.

* * *

Nina woke all at once, heart in her throat, a heavy awareness of being watched simmering in her chest. Sure enough, when she looked over, a girl in an identical robe sat on an expertly made bed, her thick hair pulled back in two tight braids that rested on each shoulder, her big, dark eyes pinned to Nina. The room was sparsely decorated, nothing but the narrow beds and an armoire across from them.

The walls and floors were a dingy brown that bordered on gray. The wood, somehow, was also colorless. She thought about her home, about the tapestries that hung from the walls, the plush rugs that covered the floor, the way her family would gather around the hearth each night and eat and tell stories and be filled with warmth and love.

This was cold and foreign. A punishment for existing. The fury from the night before was gone, and Nina wondered if she would ever feel warm again.

"I'm Qori," the girl said, her voice just as bright as her eyes. Nina tried and failed to cover her wince. "Sorry, but it's time for prayers. Mamakuna Dusi will be angry if we're late."

If it wasn't for the promise Nina had made to face her consequences head-on, she would have rolled back over. With a sigh, she shifted to a sitting position, bracing herself as the room spun.

Qori stood and extended a hand. Nina begrudgingly took it. She led her out of the room and down a long hall identical to the one Nina had been dragged through last night. "These are the girls' rooms," Qori explained quietly. "There are approximately thirty acllas, though this place was designed to hold many more. We are fewer and farther between these days."

The way she said *we* made Nina's skin crawl. All the pains her family had taken to ensure Nina and her sisters didn't end up a piece in a greedy emperor's game, and there she was, another girl to be shaped and bartered. She wondered what devastation she had left in her wake.

Qori continued. "We spend most of our days creating the garments that the emperor's men wear. The process is quite tedious but soothing in its familiarity. We are also preparing the chicha for Inti Raymi."

Inti Raymi was a festival held to celebrate Inti, the sun god, and a bountiful harvest. It was days of feasting and dancing and offerings made to Pachamama, and it was Nina's favorite time of year. She wondered if her family would continue their traditions without her, like they had after losing Samaq. Would they mourn and beg the gods for her return, or would they accept the loss as something entirely out of their hands?

"Most of the acllas will be chosen for service this year," Qori said, interrupting her lamenting. "It's a very exciting time for us. I'm hoping to stay here and continue training under Mamakuna Dusi. She was once an aclla here, and now she presides over all of us." She grinned. "But I wouldn't mind visiting another acllahuasi for a time. Where would *you* like to go?"

Home was Nina's first thought. Already, she was paying close attention to the layout, memorizing each turn they took and door they passed, just in case the opportunity to escape ever presented itself.

Perhaps the kunay would forget all about her, a nobody from a far-off ayllu. Perhaps they had taken her by mistake, and once they learned of Samaq's dutiful service, they would escort her home.

Nina wanted to believe that her mamay was working to untangle the misunderstanding at that very moment. That her tayta, deep in his heartbreak at finding Nina gone, had demanded answers and a solution.

It was unlikely, she knew, but still she hoped.

"Is this the front door?" Nina paused in a mostly empty room and pointed to a large slab of wood. There was no handle, and no windows beside it to give her a peek of what lay beyond. Torches in each corner provided the barest hint of light that did nothing to alleviate the desolation that filled the space. Like a place one might lay the dead to rest.

"Yes," Qori said. She placed a cold hand on Nina's arm, eyes earnest in the pale light. "But there's never any reason to go near it. We don't leave the acllahuasi until we are chosen."

The word sounded strange from her lips. Like an omen instead of the honor she knew Qori thought it was. Nina looked at the door again, the urge to touch it so strong she felt her feet shift toward it.

"There are creatures beyond those doors, Nina," Qori murmured. "They will devour your body and spirit. We are kept in here for our safety. Do not think to test the patience of Mamakuna Dusi, for you will find yourself filled with regret."

I already am, Nina wanted to say. The threat of hungry creatures didn't scare her. Limac was bordered by a large sea on one side and a dense forest on the other, both filled with creatures that, unless bothered, mostly kept to themselves. But Nina was familiar with the outside world, with life away from the acllahuasi. Though she had lived in Limac her whole life, she knew the taste of freedom and the truth of myths made up to coax children into behaving.

The only dangerous creatures she had come across were the men who had put her here.

Without another word, Qori turned and continued past the front door and through a doorway, into a large room lit with more candles than Nina could count. A number of girls turned in silence to stare at her, but Nina was too distracted to absorb the weight of their attention.

At the front of the room was an altar, where statues of several gods sat. Viracocha, the creator god, in the center. Inti, the sun god, to the right. Killa, the moon goddess, on the left. There was Cocha, the goddess of the sea; and Illapu, the god of rain; and Ekeko, the god of fortune.

"And Pachamama?" Nina asked quietly, her eyes still searching for the god her own people served.

Qori only shook her head in answer and extended a cup to Nina. "This is our daily tea. We drink, and then we pray."

Nina brought it closer and peered into the steaming liquid. At the bottom, she saw the blackened leaves she had been given by the emperor's men. The back of her mouth tingled with the memory.

A cold hand covered hers on the cup. Qori's eyes bore into her earnestly. "You *have* to drink it, Nina. There is no choice. It brings us closer to the gods, which allows us to complete our duties with faith."

Nina was familiar with duty. It was her responsibility to her siblings that landed her there, but none of it had required *faith.* If anything, the lack of it would ease the transition. Holding on to hope would only serve to disappoint, and what she wanted was to forget. To be forgotten, left alone. More than that, she wanted to return home and see her family again.

The leaves had tasted awful, nothing like the ones from home, but they had dulled the passage of time and the pain of distance. They had given her a kind of reprieve that she hadn't anticipated, and a part of her craved it once again. Nina would obey, but she would do it for her own reasons.

Instead of sipping the tea, she gulped it down in one fell swoop. It burned her throat and made her eyes water, and then, moments later, she felt less of everything.

Less hot, less angry, less aware of who she was and what she wanted and why she was there.

Qori smiled and led Nina to the front of the room, where several girls shifted to allow them space. Some were as young as Lali, their small faces cast in firelight. The oldest looked younger than Nina's seven and ten, eyes wide and innocent and watching her with uncertainty. She reminded Nina of Sacha, but when Nina smiled, the girl turned away.

There were no sacrifices being made in the small altar room. No drinks poured or dead animals laid at the base of the dais. Nina wasn't sure what she was meant to do as she sat cross-legged on the cold stone floor, and she felt a distant twinge of alarm with the uncertainty. But it was only a fleeting feeling. A slight break in the fog that had settled over her mind. In the next moment, she was captivated by the dancing flames of each candle, delightfully filled with a yawning emptiness that wiped away all her worries.

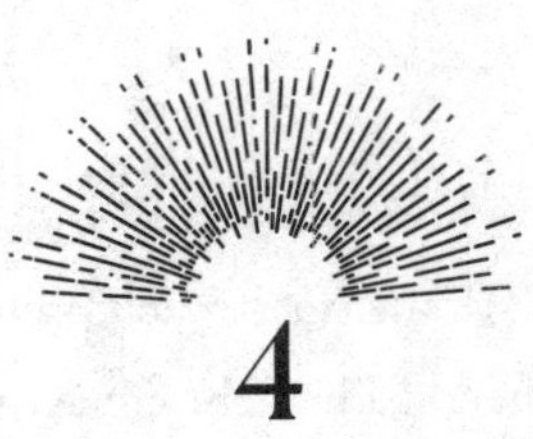

4

Kasik had convinced himself that if everything went according to plan, he could be at the acllahuasi in two weeks' time, back at the kancha in four weeks, and then reunited with his men in time to celebrate Inti Raymi. It was a small price to pay for the freedom Maicu had promised.

But everything did not go according to plan.

To start, the rain was relentless, leaving the ground a sogging mess. The achipumas despised the rain, and though they were sure-footed, their mood was rancid. It became too dangerous to ride, so he walked beside them, coaxing them forward with each step, murmuring encouraging words over the claps of thunder that made his ears ring.

All the while, he held the silver cylindrical case close to his chest. The temptation to open it was strong, his curiosity almost winning as he navigated the muddy path. Perhaps if he better understood *why* he was being sent to collect a random girl—a random *wife*—he could reconcile the effort in his mind.

In the end, it was his unfailing loyalty and inability to go against a command that stayed his hand, even if resentment simmered beneath. Even as the days dragged on in misery.

It was on the sixth night of his travels when Kasik found himself watching a group of bandits sneak upon his camp. He had left the achipumas lounging beneath a thick, canopied tree so that he could hunt, and when he returned, he found three men pawing through his bags. There was nothing valuable in them, only extra clothing and the tea he was supposed to give the girl.

The silver case was safely in his breast pocket, and his bow and arrows were slung across his back. Kasik crouched low and watched as one man approached Illari, the smaller achipuma meant for the girl, and carefully held out his hand. The achipumas were large and ferocious looking, but they were docile. Protector more than predator. They didn't typically attack or eat a human unless provoked, and it was clear Illari didn't feel provoked as she gladly took whatever was in the man's hand.

Capac, on the other hand, had been Kasik's companion since childhood and wouldn't let the men get near. Though Capac didn't rise from his prone position beneath the tree, he hissed and lashed his tail when one of the men got too close. Kasik smiled proudly, and then he glowered as Illari was easily led away.

There was nothing to be done. It wouldn't do him any good to be murdered by a pack of bandits, even if the itch to start a fight was strong. When it seemed as though no other shadows would emerge, he carefully picked his way down the slope and back to Capac. The achipuma slanted his eyes at Kasik as if to say, *Where were you?*

"I know. It couldn't be avoided." Kasik ran his hand down Capac's glossy neck. "No unnecessary fighting. It'll be easier this way, just you and me. Illari was holding us back."

All was forgiven when Kasik produced the hares he had caught, and Capac got two instead of one. Eventually, they were both able to relax. The rain continued, so no fire was made, and Kasik ended up tossing his dinner deep into the woods, hopeful that his continued sacrifices would be enough to keep the forest creatures at bay.

There were only stories of them, but they were terrifying enough that he followed their instructions. Some said the beast-like animals, with wings the span of a man and talons as sharp as blades, were only appeased by blood. Others said it was intention that pleased them. Depending on which ayllu you visited, they were minions of one god or another. Kasik thought it safer to pray to all the gods, to offer blood *and* intentions and disturb the woods as little as possible.

Capac came to join him on the forest floor, as if he knew Kasik needed the warmth and company. They waited for morning to come, and for another day to be done and gone.

The next several days passed without incident. There were no run-ins with bandits or strange creatures or animals. He saw no other people as he traversed the emperor's road. Kasik began to appreciate the freedom—no men seeking his approval or awaiting his commands. No tayta to be disappointed by his mere existence. No emperor seeking his friendship.

He missed Samaq, but he couldn't help but wonder what secrets his friend was keeping from him, and what he had tried to tell Kasik that day in the training ring. What would Emperor Maicu do once he knew that his empress was meeting in secret with a walla, and that Kasik had known it all along?

Perhaps he could stay in these woods where he was just a man with a beast and never have to find out.

It was a fanciful thought, one that surprised and thrilled him in equal measure.

But there was a mission to be completed, and Kasik intended to do it to the best of his abilities. Two more days, and he would be halfway to completing his mission to collect the girl and deliver her unharmed.

5

Ten days had passed since Nina arrived at the acllahuasi, and each morning, she woke with only hazy memories of the day before that sifted through her fingers like sand with each step she took toward the prayer room. And when she drank her tea, she forgot that she couldn't remember anything at all.

But that morning was different. Qori was nowhere to be found when Nina woke, and the streaks of morning light from the tiny window by the ceiling were not in their usual spots on the floor. Her mind worked through what it meant, and then it meandered toward thoughts of home.

Tiny particles floated in the air, bringing forth a memory of Sacha lying in the bed they shared, her thin fingers swirling through the streaks of light and parting the dust while she hummed a soft song.

How she missed her sisters and her home. Her mamay and tayta. How had she, for even one moment, allowed herself to forget them?

A closing door echoed down the long hall. Nina listened for other sounds, but the acllahuasi was deadly quiet, which likely meant everyone was at morning prayers and she was missing them. Why hadn't Qori woken her, and why couldn't she remember if she had told Nina of her plans not to?

She jumped out of bed and dressed, quickly throwing her thick hair into two tidy braids. The hall was empty as she jogged in slippered feet to the prayer room, which she found empty as well. On the small table by the door was a single mug of cooled tea. Nina found herself reaching for it, for the energy and bliss it provided. She snatched her hand back and swallowed down the burn of anticipation.

When she finally made her way to the dining quarters, she took a moment outside the door to calm herself and prepare an excuse. But nobody looked her way as she opened the door and quickly entered the room, much less asked a question. The only sounds were the soft scuff of clay on wood. The click of metal against clay. The whisper of shifting fabric. Nina sat down at the closest table, a strange feeling beating against her chest.

"You sit over there," a girl said to her, pointing with her spoon at a table across from theirs.

Nina glanced nervously between the table and the girl and nodded. "Of course," she said, because it was only after the girl pointed it out that Nina remembered that she *did* sit at that table every morning with Qori. There was already a bowl of corn porridge waiting for her, but no Qori.

After switching tables, Nina thought she would feel less out of place. Less strange, but the eeriness only grew with the silence in the room.

It wasn't that she didn't enjoy the quiet. Back home, there were times when she would escape the company of her sisters and the never-ending chores to venture to the middle of the fields and stretch out on the ground, eyes closed and arms spread wide, and simply listen. To the birds singing in the distance, to the corn stalks caressing each other, to the rustle of insect wings.

But this quiet was unnatural. The girls didn't speak to her, but they also didn't speak to each other. They didn't laugh or hum or move too quickly and spill their food. They didn't apologize when they bumped into each other, or bribe each other to switch chores, or complain about their itchy robes.

Had it always been like this, so quiet and strange? Would anyone even notice if she simply got up and left the room?

Or the acllahuasi?

The thought came unbidden. Nina paused with a bite of congealing porridge halfway to her mouth. *Could* she leave? She had offered herself to the kunay in exchange for her sister, but the kunay wasn't there, and the arrangement hadn't been made known to the mamakuna, as far as she knew.

It didn't seem like they would notice her absence, or come after her if they did, and why would they? She was a nobody from Limac, a small farming ayllu on the outskirts of a bustling and newly formed empire. The only time her people had anything to do with the emperor or his men was during the Harvest, and Nina and her sisters were well-versed in hiding from them.

They had caught her off guard this time, but they wouldn't again.

Nina could go home. She could see her mamay and tayta. Hug her sisters. Swim in the sea. Be *free*. Nobody would have to know.

The plan grew in her mind as she finished her morning meal and made her way with the other girls to the sewing room. It was only when she was halfway there that she remembered she hadn't drunk the morning tea that filled them with faith and brought them closer to the gods.

Perhaps Nina was faithless, but she was filled with clarity unlike anything before.

The sewing room was like the other rooms in the acllahuasi: colorless and cold. The smallest amount of light filtered in from a thin slit of a window near the ceilings. *Too high to climb out of*, Nina thought fleetingly. The rest of the light came from torches in the corners. Cushioned benches lined the walls, and in the middle was a large table piled with baskets of sewing equipment.

Qori sat on one of those benches, dark head bowed over a deep red fabric bunched in her lap. Nina breathed a sigh of relief and joined her only friend, expecting to field questions from her, at least. But Qori hardly glanced up. Her fingers didn't stop moving as she pushed the needle through the fabric, in and out and over.

"Where were you this morning?" Nina whispered, glancing at the three girls sitting across the room from them. They kept their heads bowed and didn't appear to be listening, but Nina scooted closer to Qori all the same.

"I've been here." Qori nodded at her lap. "It's for Empress Chaska. Mamakuna has entrusted it to me."

The needle and thread shimmered in the dim light as Qori stitched another tiny sun onto the hem of what Nina now knew was a dress.

"Can you imagine being married to the emperor?" Qori asked. "A descendant of a god. The *sun god*, no less. What a gift it must be."

"It sounds like a burden," Nina mumbled.

Qori's fingers paused their stitching, and her eyes shot to Nina's.

"Being married, I mean," Nina carefully added. "Imagine how much is expected of her."

"Empress Chaska was once an aclla, and it was her tayta who orchestrated the union to Emperor Maicu." Qori began stitching again as she continued to speak. "I'm sure she was more than prepared for such a role. And look what has come from it! Tullumay is now a part of Tawantinsuyu. The empire strengthens every day."

The union of Emperor Maicu and Empress Chaska was a celebration that reached even the far shores of Limac. Nina recalled how Inti Raymi had been especially festive that year, with every household receiving a bounty of meat courtesy of the emperor's household. They had feasted for weeks, and then life had gone back to normal.

She had wondered how much had changed for Empress Chaska's ayllu after joining Tawantinsuyu.

Nina could not remember Limac before it had been absorbed,

only that after, much had changed. An agreement had been struck, and the emperor implemented the chani, the price paid for belonging to his empire. It hardly mattered that most of their people didn't want to belong. The emperor's banner, a golden sun set against a red sky, was raised over their altar all the same, and the next year, Samaq was taken.

In return, they had gained access to the emperor's road and trade with other ayllus. Protection, should they ever need it. After all, her people were not warriors. They had no nobles to establish dominance. No designs on conquering and ruling. They lived simple lives. Peaceful lives.

Boring lives, if Nina was being honest. The morning the kunay had come for her, she had been wishing for adventure. Now here she was, thick in the middle of one and wishing for nothing more than to return home.

Nina picked up the sewing project she had begun the day before and considered Qori's words as she tried and failed to complete a simple stitch. The needle slipped and pricked her finger, not for the first time. She licked the blood away and began again. "The empire strengthens, but at what cost? And for what reason? What comes next?"

They were questions she hadn't been able to put into words before then. Thoughts that had stayed buried beneath her desire to please her mamay and tayta. To be compliant and helpful.

The way Qori was looking at her now made her think she should have stayed that way. "There is no need to justify a union. We are stronger together, Nina. That is the only reason we need."

"It's just that it seems that Emperor Maicu might be benefitting from this *union* more than we are, and—"

"That is enough, Nina. I understand you are unfamiliar with the customs and expectations of us as acllas since you are very new, and very late, but we are here to serve the empire and the gods. This is how we contribute and earn favor." Qori gestured to the fabric in Nina's lap, and to the walls around them. "There is nothing else we need to concern ourselves with."

Nina stared at Qori as she continued to work, her fingers confident and her features free of worry. It must have been such a relief to know one's place in the world and accept it so fully. Sacha was much like that. Always content to do as she was told, to help in any way she could, while Nina constantly sought to understand. To *know*. Others thought her obstinate, but it was simple curiosity.

Over time, she had learned to dampen it, but it was that same curiosity that had Nina watching the other girls throughout the rest of the day. They were disinterested, flitting from one task to the next without question or complaint, but when Nina's finger stung from too many pricks, she threw the needle to the floor and watched it roll away. Qori had simply handed her another. And by the time they broke for the evening meal, Nina felt ragged with exhaustion. Her back ached and her feet throbbed, and her head was pounding with each beat of her heart, whereas there was a quiet intensity, a surety, that held the other girls' heads high and their shoulders back. They confidently navigated the halls and their chores, and Nina couldn't help but wonder how much of it was the tea's influence, and how much of it was a misguided sense of honor at being chosen.

Though Nina felt more of everything without the tea and was glad to be clear minded once again, she wished she couldn't feel the eerie silence so heavy on her shoulders. She wanted to stand, to shake the pressure away and run as far as possible, but the mamakuna was at the head of the room, her sharp eyes aware of every charge under her care.

Nina ate her bowl of vegetable stew that was as bland as every other meal and kept her head down, determined to focus on taking one bite after another and keeping her movements as steady and demure as Qori's beside her.

But all Nina could think was *I will die here.* Sacha would have thrived under the calm routine and the careful dedication. She would have exceeded Mamakuna Dusi's expectations.

The regret returned, churning Nina's stomach and prodding her further toward a dangerous idea that had begun to form early that morning.

Night had fallen, and the acllahuasi was dark and quiet as Nina and Qori made their way to the baths. Nina subtly kept track of every step she took, every shadowed corner and gaping doorway. Especially the main door in the barren receiving room. The two acllas from her first night stood within it, watching them as they passed. She kept her eyes down even when she heard Qori greet them.

This time, Nina had the luxury of bathing herself. It was a quick and solemn affair, and possibly the only thing that reminded her of home. It had always been a time of reflection, of deep cleansing. Not only physically, but mentally as well. For Nina, it was that and more.

Beneath the water was the only time that she felt like she could breathe. It was the only pressure that didn't feel like a fist around her heart. The water cradled her and held her aloft. Her shoulders relaxed and her mind cleared, and she let herself *be*.

The reprieve was short-lived. A hand wrapped around her elbow and pulled her up, and Qori eyed her inquisitively. Nina said nothing as she finished washing and dried off. The acllas were gone, and only one torch lit the way back to their room.

The girls had the implicit trust of the mamakuna. For them, it was an honor to be there, to be chosen to serve. Nina could only assume it was the most important thing in the world to them. But for her, it was a nightmare. One that filled her with resentment.

Why did the emperor feel he had the right to come and disrupt their lives? To demand their children and their crops? Limac was a self-sufficient and thriving ayllu. They had the gods' favor; they didn't need

Emperor Yachua's as well, and certainly not his son's, who was barely older than Nina when he took his tayta's place.

If Nina escaped and returned home, perhaps she could convince her people to withhold the chani. To refuse to hand over their children. Perhaps everything could be different.

Sleep did not come easily for Nina. She agonized over what she wanted as opposed to the vow she had made to the kunay to keep Sacha safe. But the further she was from it, the less important it felt, until hours had passed and she finally rolled out of bed and slipped on her shoes.

The floor was cold even through her slippers, and the room was dark enough that she could just make out the shape of the door through the shadows. One look at the small window high up told her that the moon was hiding. There would be none of its light to guide her.

But Nina remembered the path to the front door of the acllahuasi, and her newfound clarity gave her courage.

Sneaking was a skill she had mastered after years of hiding from Sacha in the fields. She was adept, and desperate, and willing as she slid through the door, nothing but a whisper of fabric against stone to give her away. She placed her fingers against the wall to guide her, shut her eyes against the absolute dark, and then she was running.

A right, and then a left, and another right. She stopped for a moment to get her bearings and catch her breath, ears strained to listen for any noise. But there was nothing. She took off again, this time a bit slower, until she felt the space open and knew she was in the front room of the acllahuasi.

Slowly, she placed her back against the closest wall and quietly shuffled along it, her palms out beside her. Her heart ticked in her ears, keeping pace with her erratic breaths. She tried to calm her breathing—in through her nose and out through her mouth—but she was so close to the outside that she could almost taste the wet air, and it tasted like freedom.

Finally, the texture of the wall changed from rough stone to weathered wood. She knew the door had no handle—she vaguely remembered being dragged through it when she arrived. There had to be a way to open it. If not this door, then *a* door, or a window, or a hole in the wall. She'd claw her way out, if she had to.

As quietly as she could, she ran her hands over the wood and banged her fist along different spots, thinking that there might be a false window or a crevice of some sort she could slip her fingers into. She remembered her brother, Samaq, had always been tinkering with different materials, finding inventive ways to build a toy to entertain his sisters. He would have known exactly how to open it.

Frustrated, Nina slumped into the door with a sigh of defeat.

A click echoed through her shoulder. She leaned away, and the wood shifted forward.

With a silent squeal of victory, Nina pried her fingers into the opening, breath held as she pulled it wide enough to slip through. Humid air washed over her. Once out, she found a handle and carefully shut it behind her.

She had succeeded in escaping. It was almost more than she could believe. The wet air chilled her skin as she turned and surveyed the ultimate obstacle between her and freedom.

A line of ominous trees stood in the near distance. Beyond them was a dark so complete that Nina couldn't make out anything more than vague shapes, but she could hear the sounds within them. Leaves rustling in a thick breeze. Owls calling to one another. Insects murmuring a never-ending song that seemed to grow louder the longer she listened.

The forest was alive, and she was about to walk right into its maw.

Briefly, she recalled Qori's warning about creatures in the dark, but this was her only chance at escape, and she would not squander it by standing still with fear of a threat meant to keep her in line. It was recklessness that put her there, and it was her recklessness that would carry her home.

With a deep breath, she took off in a silent run toward the tree line, in the opposite direction of the clear and obvious road. Cold air pushed the fine hairs away from her face and burned the back of her throat. Winter was fast approaching.

More reason to leave instead of waiting for another opportunity that may never come. Her robe was thick enough to keep her somewhat warm, but it attempted to trip her up, until she grabbed a handful into a fist and hoisted it above her ankles.

The trees towered over her as they came closer. What she had thought were shadows turned out to be brush so thick there was hardly any space to walk through. If she gave herself the time, she could imagine the kinds of creatures that would be hiding beneath it, lying in wait to latch on to her ankles and drag her down.

Nina wouldn't allow it. She would do whatever was necessary to survive.

Just as she placed one foot over the tree line, a force knocked into her, stealing the breath from her lungs and slamming her onto her back. Her head thundered with the impact. The stars in the sky swirled in her vision. Then a face appeared, one with beady eyes and a bulbous nose and a lewd smile on his lips.

Nina tried to squirm away, but the man only pressed her farther into the earth, his legs wrapped around hers, her arms pinned beneath his large hands.

Nina opened her mouth to scream, but a hand clamped down before any sound could escape. Both her wrists were pressed together above her head as the man leaned into her face. A lock of short, dark hair brushed her forehead, and she shivered. The only men she knew with shorn hair had been disgraced and exiled from her ayllu. "Shh,

shh, now. We wouldn't want to wake the forest creatures. They love nothing more than a struggle."

Nostrils flared, Nina sucked in several rapid breaths. She scanned the trees for an idea, an answer, some sort of help. She let some of the tension out of her body, relieved when the pressure from the man's hand lessened around her mouth and she was able to gain just enough space to tilt her head and slip one of his fingers between her teeth. She bit down hard, a spurt of warm liquid coating her tongue.

The man screamed and ripped his hand away from her face, and then his fist barreled into her jaw. Her head whipped to the side. Black spots crowded her vision. Her body went limp.

"Ekko! Enough."

The familiar voice came from a distance, the order curt and unsympathetic. The man slid off her body with nothing more than a smirk. And then Mamakuna Dusi slid into view. The same position they had been in when they first met.

The matron of the acllas stood arrow straight, her hands folded together beneath the thick sleeves of her purple robe, and peered at Nina as if she were nothing more than excrement she had stepped in.

"I was curious how long it would take you to try the door. Do you know why it is left unlocked?" Nina knew the mamakuna didn't expect an answer, and she was reassured when the woman spoke again without waiting. "Because my acllas understand their purpose. They are the chosen ones. Gifts to those who are honored enough to receive them."

A shoe dug into Nina's side. "You are not particularly beautiful. You cannot sew. You cannot obey. What use are you to anyone?"

I can plant, Nina thought angrily. *I can nurture. I can grow.*

It was the women in her ayllu who gave life to their fields, and it was only their offerings that Pachamama accepted. This made them worthy beyond measure, but the mamakuna's words needled a deep, unspoken fear Nina had harbored for as long as she could remember. What if she was too difficult to love? What if she wasn't ever enough?

Mamakuna Dusi sighed. "You lasted longer than expected, but alas, not long enough." She turned away from Nina. "Take her to the keep. And you, go bandage your hand. You are embarrassing yourself."

There was movement, the sound of crunching grass, and then Nina was being lifted. Someone threw her over their shoulder like a sack of corn she would watch her tayta haul away. Waves of nausea crashed into her, and the burn of vomit filled her throat before spewing out of her mouth. The man cursed but kept moving, down the slight hill, across the grass, and back through the front door of the acllahuasi.

Back to her prison.

Nina's head bobbed with each step, arms dangling uselessly. The taste of defeat was so much more potent after sipping freedom. A trail of warmth cut across her forehead and into her hairline. Tears, she realized embarrassingly.

After some time, she heard the clank of metal and the grind of a door opening. Boots shuffled across the floor, and then she was being shifted. Her back and head hit the floor again, and it was the last thing she felt before the dark swallowed what little light there was.

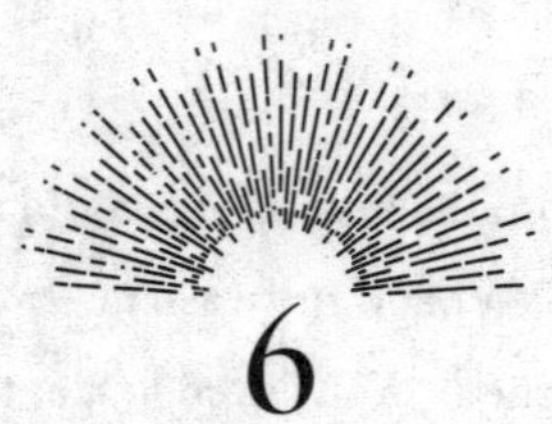

6

When the acllahuasi finally came into view, Kasik had been traveling for fifteen days, most of which were uncomfortably wet and tense. A thick layer of fog had crawled down from the mountains, settling over the forest and road. Visibility was low. Capac's stride had lengthened, and his ears were constantly shifting forward and back, listening for things that Kasik could not hear.

Kasik held a weapon in hand at all times. When he slept, he kept Capac at his back. He did not light a fire for warmth or for food. He did not travel too far from the road, and he tried his best not to let the resentment he felt for this mission fester and grow.

The years he had spent training, the injuries he'd sustained, the men he had lost—all of it boiled down to these fifteen days spent traveling to collect a child bride. If Maicu delivered what he had promised—the freedom to lead his men—then all of it would be worth it. But the silver case pressed against his chest had begun to feel like a knife in his back, and the sight of the acllahuasi did nothing to lift his mood.

It was hard to imagine that this building was a place where the empire's chosen ones were raised. The exterior was dull, the lack of color shocking in comparison to the bright green foliage surrounding it. There was what looked like a main door and receiving room in the middle of the structure, and then wings of the building that shot off on either side, and each of those portions had wings.

A stone labyrinth. A smaller version of the emperor's home, but Amaru Kancha was designed to keep people out. Kasik got the sense that the acllahuasi was designed to keep people *in*.

The wind picked up as he considered his next move. Capac sat quietly beside him, his head tilted to the sky and the first peak of the sun they had seen in many days. It wouldn't last long; in the distance, just below the melodic call of the quetzal and the rustle of leaves, was the low rumble of thunder.

Another day of rain. Just what he needed.

"Let's get this over with," he told Capac. Of course, the achipuma said nothing in return. They might have been an ancient race of animals created by the gods, but they couldn't talk, as far as he knew. However, Kasik could have sworn that Capac sighed before slowly rising to all fours.

A few more steps down the road, and then Capac was slowing, his body dropping into a stalking prowl and a low growl building in his throat. Kasik palmed the blade at his hip just as he heard the creak of a bow string pulled taut. From behind, the shuffle of leaves alerted him to a second person.

Two men circled to his front, one with long hair tied back and an arrow notched in his bow, another with shorn hair and a curved blade held in a bandaged hand. No gold adorned their red tunics or their arms. Their weapons were simple, practical, and the achillas around their necks hung loose for all to see. A sign of their fealty to the emperor and the gods.

Most noticeable was the gleam of envy in their eyes as they took in the gold disk at Kasik's chest and the revered creature by his side.

Kasik flicked a hand to Capac, who immediately dropped into a subdued crouch. Technically speaking, Kasik could have pulled rank on the men and had them on their knees begging for forgiveness, but he was in no mood to play. The sooner this was over, the sooner he would be home. "I'm here on behalf of Emperor Maicu. Mamakuna Dusi is expecting me."

The disgraced walla with shorn hair narrowed his eyes. "Go on, then." He gestured to the path with his blade. Kasik swallowed a command—*We don't point with our weapons*—something he often said to the young boys he trained, and walked past them, motioning for Capac to follow. He didn't trust either of them with his companion.

The guards eyed the achipuma warily, and then Kasik heard them follow closely behind, the tension between them thick enough to cut.

The door to the acllahuasi swung open before Kasik was within spitting range of it. A woman walked out, her long hair loose down her back, the gray a sharp contrast to the purple robes she wore. Her face was heavily lined, and her lips were pressed into a frown, as if she was already displeased. But Kasik was used to the displeasure of a different mamakuna at the golden temple in Vira, the seat of Tawantinsuyu. Anytime he walked into Qorikancha, she gave him the same frown. The matron of the acllahuasi did not scare him.

"Mamakuna Dusi." He inclined his head.

"Kamayuq Kasik. You are early."

"Yes, well, the emperor expressed the importance of this retrieval."

"You know more than I do, I'm afraid." The way she said it made it clear she was not happy with that. Kasik didn't bother to correct her, only produced the silver case from his breast pocket and watched as she unrolled the frame, the strings of knots pulled taught between them. She ran her fingers over the words. Halfway through, she gasped. It was more emotion than he'd ever seen from a woman in her position.

"A *wife*?" she asked, looking up. "Surely, there are other girls more suited to his tastes. This one, she—" The mamakuna paused and seemed to collect herself. "She is brash and unfit."

Kasik felt a surge of annoyance at being questioned. Beside him, Capac shifted closer. "She is who I have been sent to collect. If you would bring her to me, we must be on our way."

It seemed as though Mamakuna Dusi might argue further, but then her brow furrowed, the wrinkles like empty rivers through a valley, and she sighed. She extended her arm toward the acllahuasi in invitation. An achilla swung from a leather cord on her wrist. "It will be but a moment. She must be prepared. Leave your *pet* with Jullan and come in and sit."

There was no sense in correcting her—Capac was the furthest thing from a *pet*—or arguing. The matron was right. He *was* early, and he could understand that a young girl might want to make amends with her home before leaving it. Resigned to wait, he motioned for Capac to stay and then followed the woman into the stone labyrinth. She led him down several halls, past many closed doors, and into a small room that might have also been a workspace.

A simple set of shelves leaned against one corner opposite a narrow bed. There was no window, and the only light came from a torch on each wall. "Sit," Mamakuna Dusi ordered, pointing to a small chair across from an even smaller table.

Taking it would have meant putting his back to the door. "I'd prefer to stand," he said.

She shrugged. "If you wish. I shall return in a moment." She bustled out of the room, taking all the tension with her.

Several minutes passed before Kasik decided to wander over to the shelves, curious about the records an acllahuasi would keep. Quipu hung from pegs protruding from the wall, each of the bundles of strings filled with knots that told stories and recorded important information that preserved their history. Being a kamayuq meant that he was taught how to interpret the language, and it was poor Master Wara who had been given the task of teaching him.

Kasik was an eager student, but he wasn't patient by nature. It was something his tayta had trained into him, and that Kasik had tried to adopt if only to please him, but as more time passed and the silence grew thicker, his patience wore thin.

They were wasting his time. Kasik left the room and walked back the way they had come, surety in every step because he was a kamayuq, a commander of men in the emperor's army. Though the matron was essential to their empire, as her job was to raise and train the acllas in Amaru, it was the emperor's will he sought to please. The sun god's own descendant, and therefore *Inti's* will. No one else's.

It was eerily quiet, especially for a place full of young girls. He was an only child growing up, his mamay having died soon after he was born, but he had watched the other children in Vira, the way they ran squealing and laughing through the streets and playing sneaky games, huddled in corners to chat about all manner of things. He had expected at least some of that in the acllahuasi, but perhaps they were in lessons. The lack of sunlight and color did make him question whether they had been discouraged from it altogether.

The quiet was so severe, only his footsteps echoing against stone, that he swore he was the only soul prowling the halls, until there was the sound of a shuffle and urgent whispers, which he followed down the hall and around the corner.

They didn't see him as he entered the room. Mamakuna Dusi was speaking to someone, their small frames the same height, but whereas the matron was unencumbered, the girl had each of her arms in the severe grip of two acllas, their robes a darker gray that looked as though they had been dunked in water.

The mamakuna whispered into her face. He caught the words *disrespect* and *truth* before he cleared his throat. The way her back straightened and her shoulders rose with a deep breath told Kasik everything he needed to know. He had seen something he was not supposed to. The only question was if it was something Emperor Maicu needed to know.

That changed the moment she stepped aside and revealed the girl. Suddenly, he had many more questions.

The aclla was small, but not a child as he had assumed. Dark hair spilled out of two thick braids to curl around her cheeks, creating a thin curtain over her downcast face.

And then she raised her eyes to him.

"This is Nina," Mamakuna Dusi said curtly. "As you can see, she is unfit to serve the emperor. I can provide a girl who's much more—"

Kasik raised a hand to silence the woman. Her mouth closed with a snap, and the acllas holding the girl's arms dropped them and stepped farther away. He trailed his eyes over her face.

Dark eyes burned with the light of a thousand fires, piercing him as he reconciled what he saw with what he thought he knew about acllas. They were meant to be revered and protected, chosen ones handpicked by his tayta and sent to one of two acllahuasis to be raised and trained. Their lives were meant to be filled with care and knowledge and consideration.

Though the girl said nothing as she stared at him, it was clear enough that she was angry. There was a welt on the side of her face, not yet turned blue, that was as familiar to him as his own hands. Someone had thrown a fist at her. Dried blood clung to her lips and chin. There were holes in the hem of her robe and spots of blood throughout. He wasn't sure whether it was hers, but it didn't matter. The conclusion he drew was the same.

This girl had been *harmed*, and whoever had done it was going to pay.

Kasik took a slow step forward, careful not to alarm her. She didn't so much as flinch when he lifted a hand and gently rubbed at the blood on her chin. The skin was smooth—it wasn't her blood—but her cheek was warm, and only when he pressed lightly did he see the infinitesimal twitch of her lip that told him she was in pain.

"Who did this?" he asked, voice low as if it was only for her ears.

Nina's gaze flicked sideways and then forward, staring straight past him and into the room beyond. She licked her dry lips before saying, "I did it to myself."

The lie didn't surprise him, but what did was the way she said the words so flippantly. As if they were a challenge, but what he was being challenged to do, he didn't know. What he did know was that there was no possible way she had done this to herself.

"I'm going to ask again, and I would like the truth this time. Who did this?"

After a beat of silence, she turned her head slightly so that their eyes met. Kasik felt the impulse to step backward, to take a breath, but he stayed where he was and waited.

"Does it matter," she said slowly, and he couldn't help but watch the intentional way her mouth formed the words, "what I say?"

"If I am asking, it is because it does," he responded.

There was a beat of silence in which he wasn't sure what she would say next. He was sure only of two things: Nina was older than he had thought, almost a woman, and she was tenacious. The kind that would put some of his walla to shame. The kind that he feared would make for some unavoidable difficulties.

"Ekko," she finally said. "The name of the guard who put his fist to my face."

"*Nina*," the mamakuna hissed. "Kasik, you must understand. She tried to esc—"

"It is *Kamayuq* Kasik, and you would do well to remember that I am not one of your acllas. There is nothing I *must* understand except what my emperor commands of me." He turned to face her. "Or do you question his will, and thus the will of the gods?"

Mamakuna Dusi's mouth snapped closed. Her fingers furiously rubbed the small stone attached to the cord on her wrist. A nervous habit, he assumed, but one he could use against her. "You wait upon your gods, and *this* is their answer. I am here. *She* is my mission," he said, pointing to Nina, "and you will understand when I demand the head of the man who dared to lay a hand on the emperor's property."

When her nostrils flared with anger but she said nothing, Kasik turned, dismissing her, and spoke to the acllas who had held Nina's arms. "Where can I find him?"

Neither of them spoke up. "*Now*," Kasik yelled, the word echoing off the stone walls, and one of the girls jumped. There was a moment of regret before he reminded himself why they were all there in the first place.

"He guards the perimeter. The one with the shorn hair," the girl said quietly.

Of course. Kasik should have known the moment he saw the disgrace displayed about his shoulders. "You both may go," he said to the acllas. They glanced at Mamakuna Dusi for permission, which set his teeth on edge, and then they fled. "Are you hurt anywhere else?" he asked Nina.

Her nostrils flared, but she shook her head.

"Stay here, if you please."

"I'd rather not," she responded quickly, and it was that small act of defiance that sealed his opinion of her. Perhaps she was brash and unfit, just as the mamakuna had proclaimed, but she was also brave. Full of righteous anger that he could break and mold to further their empire.

And if the thought of breaking anything in this girl gave him a twinge of regret, he told himself it was only because he remembered what it had been like to feel broken and lost. It was not because he admired her fortitude, and certainly not because he questioned the emperor's choices.

Kasik couldn't afford to fall prey to emotions. He had one job only—to deliver Nina to Amaru Kancha—and he intended to execute it flawlessly.

7

The emperor's property.

The words echoed in Nina's head as she followed the stranger called Kasik out the doors of the acllahuasi. No one stopped her, though Mamakuna Dusi was hot on her heels, the utterances of prayers like a chant from her lips. She hadn't stopped rubbing that strange stone on her wrist since she started. It was black in some light, iridescent in others. A hue that was at once strangely familiar and entirely foreign.

"Call to him," Kasik demanded. They had come to an abrupt stop in the middle of the grassy yard. The tree line where Nina had failed to escape was so close. If she tried to run again, would she make it?

But another attempt might land her back in that godsforsaken cell where she could feel the spiders seeking her warmth and planning for their new home within her bones. Where she had too much time to think, to remember what she had done all those weeks ago, when two boys had fallen to their knees at her feet.

Even with the tea they so graciously continued to provide, her mind seemed incapable of dwelling upon anything else. The memory was tainted with the illusion of power, and a strange sort of craving had begun to grow in her chest.

Those boys might have died because of her, and it was only her uncertainty that had stopped her then.

Nina would not allow that same uncertainty to ruin this opportunity. The walla seemed bent on proving some sort of point that looked as though it might free her from the acllahuasi, and who was she to question that?

To her surprise, the mamakuna obeyed, though her voice was strained. There was a rustle of brush and then a man in red appeared, a blade hanging loose at his side.

The man began the descent down the small hill with a light step. He was entirely unaware of his oncoming punishment, and Nina gained a sick sort of satisfaction from it. She could still feel his hands around her wrists. The way his body had hardened against hers as she lay helpless beneath him. Even his blood had tasted foul, as if he were infected from the inside.

"Mamakuna Dusi," the man said once he was before them.

"This is Kamayuq Kasik. He has a question for you."

Ekko turned to Kasik, chin high, shoulders back. It was like watching a bird preen itself before its mate. In direct opposition, Kasik slid his hand around the hilt of a weapon at his belt, each of his movements controlled, unbothered by the posturing before him.

The whine of metal echoed through the air as Kasik released his blade from its sheath. The tip caught the light and winked. Ekko's face paled, and his gaze flicked past Nina to the mamakuna. Nina couldn't help but smile at him, jaw throbbing as a reminder of what he had done.

"On your knees," Kasik demanded.

"What is the meaning of this?" Ekko stuttered, stepping back. Kasik raised the blade to his throat and Ekko raised his hands in response. "I've done nothing wrong," he insisted. But his eyes betrayed his lies when they shifted to Nina.

"On your knees, walla. I will not say it again."

Whatever Ekko saw in Kasik's eyes made him obey. He slowly knelt on the ground, head tilted up to keep the blade below his chin and his eyes pinned on Kasik.

"This is your last chance," Kasik said softly, the words just for her, "to walk away and avoid witnessing this."

But Nina knew, from the resolve in his broad shoulders and the steadiness of his hands, that there would be no avoiding this. It would happen whether or not she bore witness to it, and it felt important to ensure that she did, if only because it seemed he was doing it in her name.

"I'll stay," she reassured him, and Kasik nodded before turning back to Ekko.

"By order of Emperor Maicu, son of Yachua, descendant of Inti, and ruler of the united Tawantinsuyu, I hereby sentence you to death by beheading for treason. Effective immediately."

Ekko screamed something incoherent. Nina covered her mouth. Mamakuna Dusi protested, saying something about how he couldn't be faulted for doing his job.

It was going much further than Nina had imagined it would, and yet she did nothing but watch as Kasik raised his curved blade and swung it in a downward arc. It screamed through the air, metal glittering, and hugged flesh and bone with a wet squelch. And then there was silence.

Ekko's eyes were wide. Kasik's weapon was on the other side of his body, the blade dripping blood. Nina stared as the head slowly slid away and hit the ground with a thud. For a moment, she thought she might be sick. She couldn't remember ever being so close to death that she was able to smell the blood and see the way life drained from his eyes.

A wave of nausea came over her, and she sucked in a breath and watched Kasik kneel in his victim's blood, the curve of his blade buried into the ground for support.

Nina blinked, and it was a different boy kneeling at her feet and bleeding in the dirt. She blinked again, and the past disappeared. The emperor's man pushed to his feet and turned to face the mamakuna. A single drop of blood adorned his cheek like a mark from the gods. Nina fought the urge to reach out and wipe it away.

"I suggest you dig a deep grave, and quickly. The god's blessing is not enough to keep the things that will consume a body at bay."

Nina heard the mamakuna shuffle away, then Kamayuq Kasik stepped forward. She remembered that *kamayuq* was a position in the emperor's army. A commander of men, and now, it seemed, a commander of *her*. Nina's stomach tightened with distrust, but he only lowered his voice and asked, "Is there anything you need to collect before we leave?"

Nina glanced at the garish blood splattered against the soft green grass. She wondered what it felt like to dole out retribution so completely. If it wasn't for her sister's soft pleas, Nina would have become familiar with the feeling.

This isn't you, Sacha had said, but Nina wasn't sure that was true.

"There's nothing for me here," she finally answered, her eyes meeting his with resolve.

The kamayuq nodded once. "The emperor is waiting."

There was no doubt in her mind that she would follow Kasik. She had no idea who he was, why he was there, or where they were going, but he had taken the life of someone who had laid a hand on her. If it was his duty to protect her, then she would use that to her advantage and take what he was giving her—an escape.

Nina looked to the sky, hoping to get an idea of which direction her home was, but the sun was hidden behind a sheet of gray. If she never saw the color again, it would be too soon.

The ground shifted, and Nina steadied herself with a deep breath. She hadn't had much to eat or drink beyond the tea while she was locked in that lightless room, and furiously hoped the kamayuq had plans to feed her. She turned to ask him, but he was already stalking away with purpose.

And not toward the tree line, as she had hoped. He was circling to the back of the acllahuasi. Nina ran to catch up with him.

"Where are you going?" she asked breathlessly, having to take two steps to his one. He was much taller than her, which wasn't saying much as she wasn't very tall, but he was also wide like a tree. His long hair swayed as he walked, and she wondered whether he had ever needed it cut. If he had ever broken a rule. Most likely not, she decided. He didn't seem the type.

"*We* are going to find Capac, and then we are leaving this place." She saw him surveying the grounds and the trees beyond. "I told him to stay, but gods forbid he listens when I need him to. Are there stables around here somewhere?"

"I've never seen more than the inside of this place," she replied.

Just as she said the words, a small lean-to came into view. Under the flimsy cover of wood was a familiar black beast, sniffing the ground between its giant paws. She saw the kamayuq's shoulders drop in relief, and then he was rushing forward.

Nina came to an abrupt stop, ready to turn and run if necessary, but the achipuma saw Kasik coming and merely leaned forward. Then Kasik surprised her by tenderly resting his forehead against the achipuma's.

It was such a contrast to the version of him she had seen moments before, where he had demanded a man kneel and separated his head from his body. This felt intimate. Like something that Nina shouldn't have been witness to, and while it was touching, she was desperate to leave and never look back.

She cleared her throat loudly. "There's only the one?"

"Are you disappointed?" Kasik answered curtly without looking her way.

The first time she had seen one of the gods' beasts was ten years ago, when the emperor's men had ridden into Limac on them. They had seemed larger than life then. Like monsters straight from her nightmares.

When she had seen them again weeks ago, they had been much smaller than she remembered, but no less dangerous. Nina assumed they were meant to strike fear into the hearts of the common people. A show of power from the emperor, and to boast his favor with the gods.

Much to her dismay, it worked. Nina went no closer as Kasik coaxed the achipuma to his feet and then walked back toward her.

For the first time since he had arrived, Nina had a clear view of his face and no reason to look away. His features were large but evenly set. Dark eyes that seemed to be perpetually narrowed in concern. A prominent chin and jaw that flexed with each step he took.

He caught her staring, and one of his eyebrows arched in question. "There's no need to be afraid," Kasik said.

"I'm not," Nina answered automatically. "I'm just remembering how one attacked me the last time I saw it."

"I have a hard time believing that," Kasik said, rubbing the beast's neck fondly. "Here, give me your hand."

When Nina eyed him skeptically, he said, "Let him get to know you."

If it wasn't for the threat of returning to the acllahuasi looming behind her, Nina would have refused. With a sigh, she reluctantly placed her hand in Kasik's, surprised by the warmth and gentleness as he pulled her closer. She watched as he lifted their joined hands to the achipuma's nose.

She tried not to stare at the way the golden-brown skin of his arms shifted, the muscles underneath rippling with movement.

"See? Harmless."

The achipuma's wet nose nudged her fingers, his whiskers tickling her palm. *Harmless* wasn't the word she would use, but she could admit that the beast seemed friendly enough.

Nina turned her eyes back to Kasik. The golden disk lying over his chest caught her eye. The sun god's symbol. The *emperor's* symbol.

"What did you mean when you said 'the emperor's property'?"

The kamayuq sighed and lifted his head, his gaze peering over her and into the tree line surrounding them. "We've got a long journey ahead of us and plenty of time to explain as we move."

"Am I expected to follow you, a stranger, into these strange woods to an unknown location for an undisclosed reason?"

The kamayuq shouldered past her. "Yes" was all said as he walked by. His achipuma followed without so much as a huff. Nina had to step aside or risk being knocked over.

She watched as they walked away. All the way past the acllahuasi, through the yard and to the base of the small hill. Surely, they would stop there and notice her absence. But when they didn't, Nina took off in a run to catch up, cursing the thin shoes barely covering her feet, the thick robes that threatened her every step, and the throb in her jaw that only reminded her of what had happened the last time she crested that hill.

She reached the tree line without incident, apprehension pounding in her chest. The road was empty save for the walla and his beast. They had finally stopped, and he gave her a passing glance before adjusting the seat on the achipuma's back. "We should get as far as we can before the rain comes."

Nina looked up. The clouds were darker than before, and closer. She smelled the tang of stale water on the breeze. She missed her home and the salty air. The sound of the wind through the stalks in the fields. The call of the coastal birds as they spoke to one another.

In the morning, she would put together a plan.

For now, she would ignore the questions she was tempted to ask and enjoy the fresh air on her face after weeks entombed in stone.

"I need you to get on."

Nina dropped her face from the sky and back to the kamayuq. He was standing an arm's length from the beast, watching her. Waiting. She glanced behind him to the road, clearly marked and bordered by countless mossy trees for as far as she could see. She didn't want to admit that the first time she'd ridden an animal of any kind was when they had taken her from her home, and that the experience had left her with a bad taste in her mouth, lest he think her uncultured and easy to scare. Even if it was the truth. "I think I'd rather walk."

"It'll be easier if you ride."

"Easier for who?"

"For both of us." The kamayuq sighed heavily. "Please?"

The word threw her into a memory of her sister's hands on her shoulders, the word *please* like a prayer from her lips. Nina had rounded the corner to see two boys towering over Sacha, one of them with his hand in her hair, pulling back so that she was forced to look into his eyes.

Let go of her, Nina had demanded.

But the boy only laughed, and his friend, taller and older, leered at Nina. *This is none of your business*, girl, he'd told her.

It made Nina angry. So much so that she had begun to see a light and thought she was losing her mind. But the light was like a thread, a guide, that led straight to the boy whose hand was on her sister.

She blinked and that thin, golden thread was in her hand. She blinked again, and both boys were on their knees, and Sacha was in front of her, pleading.

I'm okay, Nina. They didn't hurt me.

Nina had known that they would have. That they might hurt another if she let them go. But her sister was begging, and Nina's rage was cooling, and those threads were slipping from her fingers.

Let them go, Sister. This is not who you are. Please.

Nina believed her. Sacha had always known her better than she knew herself. The boy and his friend had gone free, and Nina and Sacha went back home. They hadn't told their mamay. In fact, they had acted as if nothing had happened.

Nina had pushed it from her mind, desperate to cling to the life she knew, and thought nothing more of it until the kunay appeared.

It was you I felt.

She couldn't piece it together, but Nina somehow knew that all this had started with that one, fateful day. That her recklessness and stubbornness had doomed her, and that, if she wasn't careful, she might never see Sacha or her family again.

If what her mamay said was true, and Nina was miserable until Sacha came along, it meant that her sister was the best part of her. Without Sacha, Nina felt heavy, like the weight of the world was on her shoulders, and she was so, so tired.

The path that lay ahead was long and uncertain. She could continue to fight it, or she could give in and ride the beast. Perhaps this one thing could be easy.

"Okay," Nina finally agreed. The surprise on the kamayuq's face almost made her laugh, but then she remembered that the kunay's men had dragged her onto their beasts, and this time, she'd have to mount on her own, and any relief left her with a grimace.

"It's not as difficult as it looks," he told her, confusing her expression with fear.

"I'm sure it's not," she said defensively.

Nina marched to the beast's side, determined to look as though she knew what she was doing. The kamayuq only watched as he held on to the achipuma's seat. She lifted a foot to place into the loop dangling from the side and missed. She would have face-planted if her hands weren't bracing her but was mercifully saved the embarrassment.

The next time she tried, she missed again, and this time the achipuma let out a huff and stamped a foot, as if impatient with her pathetic attempts.

A swell of frustration forced Nina to take a deep breath. She stepped back to reassess the situation, wondering whether there was a better way to do it. She was going to get on that beast, without anyone's help, if it was the last thing she did.

"Can I—" Kasik started.

"No, you cannot!" Nina yelled, interrupting the kamayuq, who promptly shut his mouth and stepped farther away. Nina almost felt guilty, but she wanted to figure this out herself. She wanted to be in control of at least this.

She reached down and grabbed the hem of her robe. The seam was easy to find; she had sewn similar seams many times before, but these stitches had been executed much better than hers. She fisted the robe between two hands, one on either side, and *pulled.*

The fabric tore, and the sound echoed through the trees, sending bright blue-and-green birds fluttering into the sky. Even the achipuma snickered softly, but the sound had quelled something in Nina. It gave her the space to breathe deeply and move more freely.

This time, she got a foot into the loop without any trouble and then pulled herself up just as easily.

"There," she said, confidence restored.

And as if the achipuma couldn't stand that outcome and was determined to put her in her place, he opened his mouth wide and stretched forward as far as he could. Nina screamed and grabbed his fur, convinced that *this* would be the way she died. Of all the things she had faced thus far, it seemed the least terrible. She wasn't imprisoned in a lightless room or doused with infected Mamacoca that stole her mind and made it unfamiliar. Perhaps she would hit her head on a rock and simply slip into death.

In any case, there was nothing she could do but brace herself. Except, death never came. Instead, a warm hand pressed against her thigh, firmly holding her body in place as the achipuma settled back into a standing position.

Heart racing, Nina watched as the kamayuq whispered into the achipuma's ear and ran his right hand along the beast's neck. His left hand remained wrapped around her thigh, his long fingers digging into her flesh.

Nina stared at the hand until it was snatched away. When she looked up, the kamayuq had squeezed it into a fist by his side and met her eyes.

"Is he trying to kill me?" she asked breathlessly. Because of the near-death experience, of course. Certainly not because of the way the warmth of the kamayuq's hand lingered, a reminder that she had gone a long time without an affectionate touch. If she was willing to be honest with herself, she might concede that she had never felt anything as warm in her entire life.

Kasik huffed a laugh and swept away the loose hairs around his face. "He would never. He's just bored."

"Well, *he* is not nice," she muttered at the beast, who she could have sworn gave her a look from the side of his eye.

The kamayuq took a step closer but kept his hands to himself. "I'm going to get on behind you," he said, and she thought of the heat of his hand spreading to encompass her back, how good it would feel, and opened her mouth to argue against it. "It'll be faster for both of us to ride," he continued before she could say a word. "And this way we can ensure Capac doesn't kill you."

She narrowed her eyes at him. "I thought you said he would never."

"I might have misspoken. Who knows what these beasts are capable of."

It was difficult to tell if the kamayuq was being earnest, but she knew he spoke the truth. The faster they could ride, the sooner they could be rid of this place once and for all.

"All right," Nina said with a sigh, slipping as far forward in the seat as she dared. Of course, Capac held perfectly still as the kamayuq slid on behind her. The whole ordeal was over in several heartbeats, and Nina was aware of each and every one of them. She kept her body stiff and leaned away, afraid that he'd feel them through her back.

A cold drop of rain landed on the middle of her forehead.

Nina tilted her head to the sky and closed her eyes as one drop after another fell. She missed the rain. She missed the sea and Sacha's hand in hers as they ran through puddles, splashing mud over the hems of their tunics that their mamay would surely berate them for later, but with a smile on her face and joy in her eyes. She missed the comfort of her home, and the warmth of their fire. Feeling safe and happy.

It hadn't occurred to her until that moment just how cold she had been all this time, and she resented the kamayuq's touch for bringing it to her attention.

"I need you to lean back." His voice broke through her thoughts. "We're going to ride as far as we can as quickly as possible."

It sounded like a good plan to her. She never wanted to see Mamakuna Dusi or the acllahuasi ever again. Putting her obstinance aside, Nina relaxed into his arms, all at once aware of the strength in his legs and arms that could easily kill her or keep her safe.

"Are you ready?" he asked, his breath tickling the top of her head. Left no other choice, Nina nodded.

The kamayuq's arms slid around her and he grabbed on to a leather strap resting on the achipuma's neck. He fisted the slack in one hand and the other he rested on Nina's thigh. She stiffened beneath his touch. "I'll keep my hand here as a precaution. Is that all right?"

Nina squeezed the lip of the leather seat beneath her, all while trying and failing to convince herself of her discomfort, that she preferred to be walking, that she would rather be left behind to soak in the rain, that she was *not* all right.

But the truth was, within his arms and against the solid pillar of him, she felt safer than she had since leaving home.

With a click of the kamayuq's tongue, the achipuma took off down the road, all her misgivings left behind.

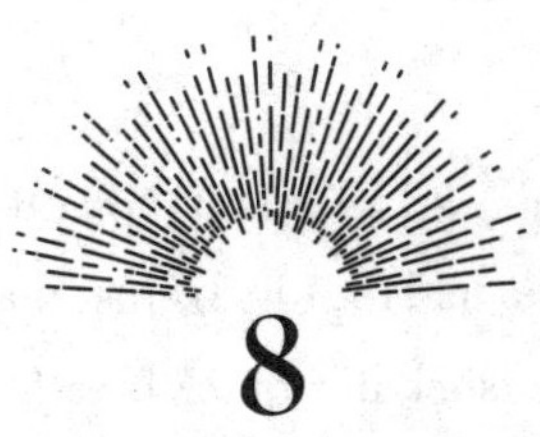

8

The rain was an enemy Kasik hadn't anticipated.

He was less familiar with this part of the emperor's road, having been there only once before this mission as a child who accompanied his tayta on a Harvest. It was then he had met Samaq, both of them young boys chosen to serve as walla, and they had been friends ever since.

Because he was unfamiliar with the area, he had a harder time deducing where there might be cover. The mountain range was smaller, the trees thicker, but everything was wet. The canopies of leaves were dumping buckets of water when they became too full. The ground was soggy. There would be no fire.

Nina's body was warm against his, though he tried not to think about it too much. She fit perfectly in the space between his legs, her head tucked nicely under his chin. Though she said nothing about being cold, her body had begun to shake, and it was that movement that made his decision. They would have to leave the road now.

Carefully, Kasik maneuvered Capac off to the side and through the trees. Nina leaned farther into him, and he knew that if he looked at her, he'd see her eyes closed tight. But he kept his attention on the narrow path before him, sighing with relief when a large outcropping of rock came into view. Beneath it was a shadowed space that looked just big enough for the two of them.

Capac skidded to a stop and Kasik swung off the seat. He grabbed Nina around the waist and slid her down carefully. "There," Kasik spoke into her ear, pointing at the rocky cover. She nodded and ran toward it. Once she was safe, Kasik motioned for Capac to *stay*, murmured praise into his ear, and then took off to join her.

It was a tight fit. Nina had to shift against the wall for him to slide in next to her. He heard her suck in a quick breath and turned to her, eyes trailing over her face and neck. The injury on her jaw was darkening in color. "Are you hurt?"

She shook her head, tendrils of wet hair stuck to her forehead and neck. He fought the urge to push them aside and inspect her further. "I'm fine," she said, shifting farther away from him. Kasik realized he had leaned closer and sat back as far as he could without putting himself out in the rain.

Silence grew between them. If it wasn't for the rain, he knew he would be able to hear her every breath and movement. As it was, he saw the way she discretely rubbed the tops of her thighs. She was sore, he realized, and wondered why she didn't say anything about the pain before.

But he was a stranger. Already, she was trusting him more than she should. Admitting to pain was revealing a weakness, and he couldn't help but admire the silent battle she was fighting. What he needed to do was pay closer attention. Her life was in his hands.

Nina suddenly broke the silence. "You called me 'the emperor's property.' I want to know why."

Apparently, their minds were in the same place. It hadn't been made clear what he could and could not tell Nina, so he said, "The emperor personally sent me to collect you."

"Yes, I gathered as much from your presence." She shifted so that she was facing him more, and her knee came to rest on his thigh. "But *why*? What does he mean to do with me?"

Kasik didn't want to be the one to explain this to her, but he hoped that by giving her a small piece of information, she would be more likely to trust him. It could go a long way in ensuring their survival. "The acllas are dispersed through Tawantinsuyu, to serve in the households of those loyal to Emperor Maicu, but it was the emperor who chose *you* to serve him."

Nina's eyes narrowed skeptically. "He specifically chose me? Is he usually so involved in the smaller details of his household?"

Kasik scoffed. "I can assure you, a wife is no small detail."

The girl surprised him again by letting out a sharp laugh. Her hand flew to her mouth. "I'm sorry, *what*?" she said through her fingers.

"You are meant to marry the emperor and—"

"Yes, I know what a 'wife' is, but I am not becoming one. Much less the *emperor's*."

"Haven't you been trained for this day? Surely, this isn't a surprise."

"'Trained'?" She said the word as if it were a curse. "I was *taken* from my family just weeks ago. The only thing I'm trained for is caring for our cornfields and my sisters."

Kasik closed his mouth, swallowing the retort on his tongue. It explained why she was older than he had expected, and wilder, as if she had different expectations on her shoulders. Perhaps they had given him the wrong girl. But no, the matron had read the emperor's missive and she had made it clear that she would have given him any other girl if allowed.

"You are who I have been sent for. The emperor was very clear."

"And I'm expected to simply"—she paused, as if searching for a word—"obey? He can find another girl. There were plenty to choose from. In fact, I know a girl who would be perfect for the role. Pious, dutiful, quiet," she said with a wince.

The rain had grown stronger, and they were yelling to hear each other over it. Kasik tried to think of words that would settle her, tried to put himself in her position, but he failed to understand her hesitance. "You are who he chose, Nina. This is a great honor."

But Nina wasn't listening. Her wild eyes surveyed the small space, then the woods past them, as if contemplating her escape. "This is a mistake. This can't be—"

"The emperor does not make mistakes."

"I doubt that," she insisted.

"You will be well taken care of. All your wants and needs will be met. You are acting as if this is a death sentence. It will—"

"Death would have been preferrable to *this*," Nina spat.

"You're being unreasonable."

"'Unreasonable'? I was forcibly taken from my home, made to fear for my and my sisters' lives, caged behind stone walls, and then thrown into a cell without food or water, and now I am told that I am someone's *property*. *I* am the unreasonable one?"

"The emperor has saved you from that fate. He has chosen you, the *gods* have chosen you. This is a *privilege*."

"This is a gilded *cage*."

At some point in the conversation, they had turned to face each other fully. Kasik's back was to the opening of the small cave, and the watery light lit Nina's face. Her lips were pursed, and her brows were furrowed angrily. A drop of rain hung off the tip of her nose.

Kasik took several deep breaths. If he opened his mouth, he would shout, or he would apologize, or he would say something stupid about the way her eyes held his gaze so fiercely.

The silence between them was thick enough to take up space. It might push him out of their cover, if he allowed it. *She* might push him out if he wasn't careful. "Everything is a cage," he finally said quietly. "Gilded is better than not."

The concept of bars around his life wasn't foreign to him. Kasik lived his life within a strict set of expectations, most of them there because of the choices he had made, all of which erected a new bar. A new boundary.

There were the expectations of his tayta, who he disappointed at every turn, no matter how hard he tried not to. And then there was his emperor, who demanded his loyalty without question. Samaq, who expected nothing, which made Kasik want to give him the best bits of himself. And Master Wara, who treated Kasik as though he was capable of so much more than even Kasik believed.

All of it a weight around his shoulders. Shackles around his feet. Oftentimes, it felt like the walls of the kancha were closing in. But it was his duty. Everyone had a role to play in the empire. Why did Nina believe it was acceptable to shirk hers?

"This cage is of your own making," she replied, as if she had heard his thoughts. "It appears I won't have that same *luxury*. Only those your emperor has decided to hoist upon me."

Kasik stilled at her dangerous words. There was no one else to hear them, but sentiments carried far and lines were easily crossed in the wrong company. "Be careful, Nina. He is *your* emperor as well."

At his tone, she abandoned whatever else she was going to say and leaned against the rock wall. Only then did he realize that he was no longer cold. In fact, he was sweating underneath her scrutiny.

"He must pay you well for this caliber of loyalty." She crossed her arms over her chest. "Murder, abduction—what other atrocities have you committed in his name?"

Kasik's heart was beating fast. The air was too warm to breathe, and Nina's judgment was too heavy to bear. "That's none of your concern," he replied shortly.

"That's what you believe, right? Even though this is *my* life, *my* freedom—that it's none of my concern?"

"You act as though you will have no freedom whatsoever. He isn't stripping you of your will."

"He may as well be. That's the point that you are refusing to see."

They both fell quiet, chests heaving as if they had been running across valleys. The quiet of their alcove magnified their anger, their differences and disagreements. Kasik was loyal to the emperor and the gods. Nina was loyal to no one but herself, it seemed. She couldn't be argued with, and it was a waste of his time to try.

"We'll start moving again as soon as the rain stops."

There was no response, but he didn't need one. The look in her eyes was enough to tell him exactly what she thought.

Hours later, when the rain finally stopped and the sun had begun its descent, Kasik wasn't surprised when Nina refused to ride Capac with him again. It wasn't as though he was particularly excited about being pressed against her after their argument, so he had decided to walk beside them and swallow the worry about the time they were wasting.

If only Illari hadn't been stolen. If only the acllahuasi had transportation of their own. If only he had left for Tullumay one day earlier, then all this could have been avoided.

Out of the corner of his eye, he saw Nina sitting stiff as a board atop Capac. It would make everything hurt that much more when she finally dismounted.

"You don't need to hold yourself so stiffly," he said, breaking their silence. Nina kept her eyes forward and ignored him, and Kasik fought the urge to roll his.

When she finally spoke, it was not at all what he had expected. He was coming to understand that would be the normal with her.

"Is it gold? Or maybe a fancy room in the kancha? Oh!" She gasped dramatically. "Perhaps they'll let you pick a wife as well! That's a valuable reward for a lonely boy."

And they were back to that. Kasik felt his face flame with frustration, but he kept his eyes on the road ahead and the trees around them as he said, "It is *duty*. Something you wouldn't understand." He wanted to say more, to defend himself and Maicu, but he had never been very good at controlling his emotions, and he couldn't allow himself to give her the satisfaction.

Nina, however, had no qualms about showing everything she was feeling and saying whatever was on her mind. "I am more familiar with *duty* than you think, Kamayuq. Perhaps it is you who doesn't understand what it is to serve out of love and not out of obligation."

Kasik stared at her, jaw clenching. Nina stared back, unashamed, her eyes hard and her shoulders back. She looked like an empress on her beast. Confident and in control while her servant yielded to her every command.

But it was her words that hit a nerve Kasik did not realize was exposed. Had he ever done anything out of love? Was he capable of it?

There was nothing he could say, and it seemed Nina thought that as well, because she had turned back to the road, dismissing him entirely. They walked on in another heavy silence. Kasik couldn't help but think that it should have been Samaq beside him, and his men behind them.

They would have been almost to Tullumay, where Lord Anri would have greeted them with enthusiasm and a large cup of chicha, which would have led to a rich meal and countless stories of a thriving ayllu.

It was something he had been looking forward to for quite some time, and now there he was, wondering, not for the first time—

"Why you?" Nina asked suddenly, as if she had plucked the words from his mind.

He glanced at her, waiting to see if she would say more, but she was still looking ahead and her lips were pressed tight. Kasik sighed. "Is there someone else you might have preferred?"

"I just meant that you're young, and if I'm to be the emperor's wife, I would have thought he would have sent someone with more experience."

He didn't owe her an explanation, didn't *want* to explain it, but he found himself doing so, anyway. "The emperor is my friend. He trusts me, and I'm experienced enough."

"Is that why you have a title? Because you're the emperor's 'friend'?"

"I have a title," Kasik said through gritted teeth, "because I have trained for years to prove my worth and loyalty to the emperor, just as my tayta has served the emperor and his family for years."

"And your mamay? Does she serve the emperor as well?"

"My mamay is dead," he said quickly, the words harsher than he had meant them to be. He touched the stone around his neck, which had belonged to her, and imagined she must have loved him enough to want to keep him safe. The actual weight of that feeling was lost to him.

Nina finally looked at him. "I'm sorry," she said softly. "That was rude of me."

Kasik shrugged. "You couldn't have known. It happened a long time ago."

"And your siblings?"

"No siblings," he answered truthfully. It was just him and his tayta, who was more absent than he was present. Kasik had mostly been raised by the kancha staff, and then Master Wara once he began the lessons that would shape him into the perfect tool. But he didn't tell Nina any of that.

"When did you join the emperor's army?"

"I was seven years old when I learned to wield a tumi, but we don't have official roles until the age of fifteen."

"What's a tumi?" Nina asked, brows furrowed. Already, Kasik was beginning to understand her facial expressions, something he had been taught to notice from a young age. *It will help keep you alive*, Master Wara had said. Hopefully, it would help keep others alive as well.

Kasik pulled the weapon at his hip out of its holder and twirled it in his palm. "This is a tumi."

Nina's eyes were wide. "You must have been terrified."

Kasik smiled. "Quite the opposite. I was eager to begin training."

"That's . . . strange," she finally said. "At seven, I was playing in the dirt."

"A privilege you had because there are those of us willing to carry out our duties to serve and protect."

Again, the words were harsher than he intended. Mostly, he was repeating what he constantly heard, but before he could explain or apologize, Nina was sliding off Capac while he was still in motion. "Whoa," he called, motioning for the beast to stop. "What are you—"

"I'm tired of riding." She stretched her arms to the sky, the newly made slit in her robe revealing the top of her thigh and drawing Kasik's eye like a moth to a flame. "Will we be stopping soon?"

Kasik cast his attention elsewhere. "Yes, but you have to ride, Nina."

"I don't want to ride, *Kasik*. I'd rather walk. *You* ride the beast."

It occurred to Kasik, in that moment, that Nina had not said his name once since they met. He wasn't sure why, but it stuck in his head, the way her mouth formed the word. Sharp, but not at all painful. "I'm not going to ride while you walk."

Nina shrugged her shoulders and took off down the road. "Then we can walk together."

There was no sense arguing. It was a lesson he was quickly learning. He hurried to catch up with her, hesitant to let her go too far from his side. If she decided to make a run for it, he would be ready to hunt her down.

Like an animal, his mind tossed at him. But she wasn't an animal, he knew that, and this wasn't a cage, just like he knew he was doing this because it was the right thing to do. He trusted Maicu and the gods. There was no questioning that.

With time, Nina would come to do the same.

But first: "There are a few matters we should discuss. You'll need to stay close at all times. There are creatures in these woods that would love to take advantage of a young, defenseless girl."

"I am not—"

"And I need you to trust me. If I say run, run. If I say be quiet, be quiet."

She came to an abrupt stop and stared at him. "You do realize that trust is earned, right?"

"How have I not earned it? You are alive. You are unharmed. You have ridden my beast more than I have. What else do I need to do to earn your trust?"

"All of those things you've done for your own benefit. This has nothing to do with me."

"This has everything to do with you." Kasik took a step forward, hand balled into a fist at his side, his frustration finally overflowing. Capac followed closely behind and nudged his wet nose into Kasik's arm. "I swore on my life to deliver you unharmed. I cannot do that if you don't follow simple directions."

Nina stepped closer, so close he could see the flecks of amber in her dark eyes. "It is not me who is having trouble understanding something so simple." She looked into his eyes, her judgment bright and heavy. "I hope whatever they are paying you is worth it."

She turned away, and he muttered, "Nothing is worth *this*."

9

The sky was a deep blue by the time Kasik walked them over to a small clearing directly off the emperor's road. Nina had begun to regret not riding Capac shortly after sliding from his back, but she refused to concede when it felt like Kasik was waiting for it. They hadn't spoken for hours, and now that it was dark enough that she could hardly make out the features of his face, she realized just how much of a stranger he was.

There was something uniquely lonely about following a stranger into the unknown. It wasn't as though she wanted to be his friend—he had made it very clear that he was simply doing his duty, and begrudgingly at that—but she had hoped that knowing something about him, finding common ground, might make the journey easier.

As it turned out, they couldn't manage to have a conversation without arguing.

Nina pulled off one shoe, sighing in relief as the cool air blew over her blistered skin. Kasik was removing the seat from Capac, his back to her, the shadows cutting grooves into his arms and neck. His red tunic now looked black, a clever trick of the light. It clung to his broad shoulders. The golden bands on his toned arms dug into his skin as he pulled a bow and arrow from Capac's side and turned to her. She averted her eyes just in time to avoid being caught staring.

"I need to hunt." Kasik said. "Do you want to come, or can I trust you to stay here?"

Alone? she wanted to ask, but of course she would stay alone. It was only them for miles, it seemed, and though the clearing they were in appeared harmless enough, she suddenly wondered what other beasts were lurking in the dense dark beyond their small circle.

She hardly knew him, and yet she felt safer by his side. And in his arms. Nina tossed that thought away as if burned. "I'll stay here," she almost shouted. In a softer voice, she added, "With Capac."

Kasik's eyes bounced between hers, and Nina got the feeling that he was deciding if he could trust her. When he nodded and mumbled a quick "Be back soon," she wondered how he had made the choice so easily.

For all he knew, she could have lied and taken off the moment he turned his back. Capac was still there, and he would make a fantastic companion on the dark and lonely road. Big enough to scare off creatures and humans alike. But he couldn't talk, and he couldn't navigate, and Nina didn't know her way home.

And she had made a vow, one that weighed heavily on her shoulders now that her future had been realigned. *Assigned.* Trying to evade it in the acllahuasi had put her in solitary confinement for three days. Out here, trying to evade it might get her killed.

She peered into the trees. There could be any number of *things* watching her. Hungry animals, curious creatures, vengeful spirits. The canopy of leaves soared high and thick enough to block her view of the sky, and the underbrush obscured most of the ground.

Cold crept along her arms and trailed icy fingers down her spine. In the distance, a bird screeched. She jumped at the sound and then laughed at herself. Capac licked his paws and ignored her entirely.

Nina wasn't scared of the dark at home, but this dark was different. Thick and ominous and absolute. Out of sheer desperation, she moved closer to Capac and slowly, warily pressed herself to his side. To her surprise, he turned and sniffed her temple, his whiskers tickling her cheek.

It had never occurred to her to seek comfort. With her family, it was freely given, as natural as breathing. When she was frightened, her mamay stoked the fire and made her tea. When she was sick, her tayta would spoil her with her favorite meals. When she was lonely, Sacha would tell her secrets and make her laugh, reminding her that she was not alone. Never in her life had she gone without it.

Even so, there were times when she felt invisible under the endless sky. Inconsequential while floating in the vast sea. She had wondered if the gods could see her and if they cared to know her deepest desires. If there would ever be anyone besides her family who saw her for who she truly was.

The kunay had seen *something* in her. The memory of his eyes filled her with dread, and now she wished for nothing more than to be forgotten, to be able to quietly return home and be free of the expectations placed upon her. A *wife*. How preposterous, and even more so that the emperor had supposedly chosen her by name. All her thoughts and plans of escape dissolved into the dark before her very eyes.

A twig snapped nearby. Nina jerked her head toward the sound and narrowed her eyes into the darkness. Behind her, Capac had gone utterly still, which concerned Nina more than anything. Were achipuma trained to kill? Or would he slink into the night to save his own skin and leave her defenseless?

Perhaps Kasik should have left a weapon. She didn't even think to ask.

The dark was playing tricks on her eyes. Everything seemed to move and shift and reach out, and she held in a scream as a shape floated closer and closer. Nina pressed her back against Capac, grateful he had stayed to witness her death, at the very least, since he didn't seem willing to be of any help.

What did it say about her that she sighed with relief upon seeing a flash of Kasik's face through a solitary shaft of moonlight? "You scared me," she said, a hand to her heart to steady it. "I can't see anything out here."

Kasik dropped a bundle at her feet and then unslung the bow from his back. It was quiet enough that she could hear every movement and each of her own breaths. "Will you start a fire while I prepare the meat?"

Nina pressed her lips together. She didn't want to admit that she didn't know how to start a fire, not like this. At home, she would have used a silver bowl to gather the sun's heat, and the fire would burn for many weeks. If it began to go out, they would easily light it again. If there was another way to do it, she didn't know of it.

Kasik didn't wait for an answer before moving off to the side, a small blade curled tight in one hand and his kills in the other. Nina stood and squinted at the ground. They would need tinder, that much she knew, but it was all wet and squishy. In her ayllu, they stored their fire materials in a watertight space. Everything was planned for and controlled. All this was so far out of her realm of knowledge that it made her embarrassed to think that she had ever thought she wanted or could handle adventure.

The past fortnight was enough of an adventure to last a lifetime.

There was a light touch on her shoulder. Nina stiffened against the familiar press of his hand. How was he always so warm?

"Come," Kasik said, voice soft. "Let me show you."

Nina breathed a sigh of relief. Somehow, he had known she was struggling without her having to say, and it meant more to her than she was willing to consider right then.

"The rain has been heavy, but there is brush thick enough that the water doesn't penetrate completely." He crouched at the base of a bush and stuck his arm in up to his shoulder. When he brought it back out, his hand was full of twigs and dried grass. "See?" he said, handing her one bundle after another until her arms were full and he led them back to their small campsite.

Nina watched as he arranged the tinder just so and rubbed a long, thin stick between his hands, back and forth, from top to bottom. Just when it seemed like nothing was happening, he blew lightly on the bundle. Her eyes widened when the small embers ignited with his breath.

"Now you try," he said, handing her the stick. She copied his stance, one foot as an anchor on a larger piece of wood on the ground, hands flat and rubbing together quickly. The muscles in her arms began to burn.

"You have to move down the stick." Suddenly he was behind her, and his arms were around her, hands on top of hers as he guided them down. Warmth bloomed in her chest and crawled up her neck. His mouth was close enough to her face that she could feel his breath with each exhale.

"I *am* moving down the stick," she said. "It's not—" A thin line of smoke appeared, distracting Nina from the rest of her thought and the pressure of his body against hers. "Look," she said surprised. She bent down to blow on the embers and watched with awe as they briefly flared.

"Good," Kasik complimented. "Now do it again."

So, she did, a few more times before the embers caught fully and flared to life. Kasik had moved to her side, their shoulders pressed together, his comforting warmth seeping into her as the fire grew and lit their faces. Nina snuck a glance at Kasik.

In this light, he looked less burdened, and somehow younger. As if the breadth of responsibility cut away at him and there, in that moment, the orange glow softened his harsher features. She remembered what he said about expectations and gilded cages and wondered if she had judged him too harshly.

Perhaps, like her, he was simply trying to navigate the limited choices he had. Perhaps they had much in common.

Nina was loathe to admit it, but she was desperate not to be alone.

"Before, you asked if there was only one." Kasik lifted his eyes to where Capac lay sprawled on his back, paws in the air without a care in the world. "There were two, but Illari was taken by bandits on the road. She was carrying a bag of provisions for you. Extra clothing and tea. Master Wara said it was essential that you take it every morning."

He sounded amused while he said it, but Nina was surprised to realize that, in the chaos of Kasik's arrival that morning, the acllas had forgotten to serve it to her. She was glad for it. The tea Nina and her family often drank at home was made from Mamacoca leaves that were a beautiful bright green and made her feel more connected to the land and to herself. More grounded.

The blackened leaves the kunay and mamakuna had given her tore her away from herself, from her thoughts and hopes and dreams, and only then, after a full day in the fresh air, could she feel the difference.

"I'll be fine without it," Nina reassured him.

Kasik nodded, and they fell into silence again, save for the crackling fire and the singing forest. Nina looked over her shoulder, into that shrouded dark, and shivered.

"I've never been this far from home," she admitted. "Everything is so unfamiliar."

"It's the Tuta Kulla." Kasik looked into the shadows. "The dark forest can be disorienting. My men and I like to tell stories to pass the time and fill the silence. Remind us who we are."

She wasn't entirely sure why, but she found herself saying, "I like stories."

Kasik laughed, the sound deep and comforting and inviting her closer. "I'll tell you one while I prepare our dinner, then."

Nina's cheeks burned—she'd forgotten why they had started a fire in the first place—and leaned away from the stability of his body.

Kasik moved around the fire, setting up sticks for a spit and using a large flat rock to prepare the hares. He pulled a small knife from his boot and spoke as he worked, and Nina found a comfortable spot to listen to the timbre of his voice pull her into a past so distant the stories had turned into fables.

"This story," he began, "is about the creation of our world and people. The creator god, Viracocha, emerged from the sea and saw that the land was empty. Craving companionship, he created beings from stone. But they were brutal and unintelligent and incapable of the deference Viracocha craved, so he destroyed them all and began again.

"Viracocha wanted warmth, so he created the sun and its god, Inti. He wanted rest, so he created the moon and its goddess, Killa. Finally, he wanted the essence of life threaded through the earth, so that the land could sustain and nourish and thrive, and he created Pachamama.

"Soon, the land was covered in flora and fauna of all kinds. Viracocha and his children were content for a while, but the children did not praise him as he had wanted. They became indifferent to him, and so he gave them his power to create beings, hoping for gratitude in return.

"But Pachamama and Killa took advantage of that gift and created Ikara—a woman with the essence of her creator's power threaded through her. They called it attay, and it is said that it gave her the power to control and destroy—and with it, she turned the world to carnage. Rivers of red flowed, and the earth began to thirst for blood.

"To balance the scales, Viracocha created a stone that could protect people from the Ikara, and a man who, immune to the Ikara's attay, could render their power useless with one touch." Kasik touched the stone around his neck.

Nina remembered the stone she had seen on that market day, how it had seemed to swirl with life and beckon her closer. *Achilla,* the woman had called it, but that wasn't the only familiar part of Kasik's story.

Ikara. The word called to her, like a whisper that demanded her ear.

"In fear," Kasik continued, "the Ikara ran. The man searched the ends of the earth for the Ikara, until finally, he found her. But instead of killing her as he was commanded, he fell in love.

"Together, they created three children: one boy, and two girls. The girls were born with power just like the Ikara's, and the woman was pleased that their line would continue. All was well, until one night, the gods appeared to the man in a dream.

"'She manipulates you with her power,' Inti told him. 'Remember your true purpose,' Viracocha hissed. Angry with their interference, Killa and Pachamama banished all the gods, including themselves, to the upper realm where they could no longer communicate with the living.

"But the man had learned the truth, and his love shattered like the illusion that it was. Fearful for his life and the lives of his children, he finally killed the Ikara.

"The children ran and hid, never to be seen again. From their line came more Ikara with the power to control the elements, and even the will of people. Wars were fought, hundreds upon thousands died, and thus started the Harvest, to find the children of the Ikara and dampen their powers for the safety of everyone.

"Over time, attay has waned and disappeared altogether, but the Harvest continues, to remind us of the responsibility we have to our people, and to the gods."

Nina had begun eating while Kasik spoke, and now the meat sat in her belly like a rock. This was not the creation story Nina knew. In her story, Pachamama had created them all, and had done so with love. The women were not called Ikara, and they did not have attay, but they *did* share in Pachamama's power to nourish and sustain the land.

The power Kasik spoke of was absurd, yet she couldn't help but question her own mind and the memories she had buried deep or forgotten with time. Was it possible that she had misunderstood their history, as is so often the case due to the innocence and disinterest of childhood? More alarming than that, was it possible the story had been purposely altered, that her mamay had taught them something entirely different to suit her own needs?

But no, Nina couldn't believe that. Her mamay had always been truthful with them, sharing her fears and concerns, her doubts and dreams, and encouraging her and her sisters to do the same. She had taught Nina to center herself anytime her own mind felt unfamiliar, like when she thought she could see and do things that were impossible.

You are the master of your mind, Mamay would always say. That Nina would doubt her now because of a story told by a stranger said more about Nina's character than her mamay's.

Nina realized that Kasik was telling her this story to further drive home the point he had argued all day—Nina had a responsibility to see through. She was merely a tool.

A means to an end.

To Kasik, she was powerless, but Nina's strength came from her love for her family, and she was doing all this for them, something he could not understand. There was no reason to believe that she had to obey his every command without question or take his every word for absolute truth. The only truth that mattered was Nina's vow, and she intended to carve her own path while keeping it.

10

When they finally settled for sleep, Kasik's dreams were filled with monsters with eyes darker than night, in a forest whose shadows unhinged like a jaw to reveal teeth as big as trees. Kasik screamed silently and clutched the stone around his neck. It burned his palm in warning, trying to tell him *something* that was just beyond his reach, right on the fringes of his mind, if only he could—

Kasik's eyes flew open. In his hand and no longer around his neck was his mamay's achilla. Quickly, he untangled it from his fingers and tied it back in place. It was warm against his chest, right over where his heart pounded erratically.

The ominous dark of the Tuta Kulla pressed in on all sides, and the center of their small clearing glowed eerily from the dying embers of Nina's fire. Kasik meant to keep watch, but he had fallen asleep.

The tendrils of his dream sifted through his memory, and then he pressed his palms to his eyes, trying to clear away the haze that the restless sleep had left behind.

Something felt wrong.

The hilt of his blade was pressed against his side. Capac lounged to his right, his chest rising and falling evenly in sleep. He turned to his left, but the space he had watched Nina lie down in was empty.

Heart in his throat, he shot to his feet and scoured the campsite for signs of her. She wouldn't be able to go far, not in the dense forest without the moon or stars to guide her.

Calm down, he told himself. She had probably walked away to relieve herself. Everything was fine.

But deep in his belly was a foreboding that he could not shake. He reached over Capac and grabbed his bow and arrows from the pack, quietly slid them onto his back, and gave Capac the command to *stay*. The achipuma growled low in his throat but sank onto his belly.

In the near distance, a twig snapped. Kasik froze. Waited for one heartbeat, two, and then he took off through the trees, brushing aside massive leaves and low-hanging branches, ducking deep and jumping high to avoid tripping over gnarled roots and downed trees.

It felt as though the hands of the forest were sinking into him, slowing him down.

A rustle deep within the brush pulled Kasik to a stop. As he listened, he held his breath, the trees watching and waiting and leaning in. Three heartbeats passed, and then he took off to the right, the shadows a blur as he raced by, glowing eyes staring down from the cover of leaves. He passed them by without sparing a second glance. Nina's name was on the tip of his tongue, but he was afraid to call for her lest something else respond.

Afraid that she was trying to escape, and he would give his position away.

It wouldn't surprise him. She had made it very clear that she wanted nothing to do with the emperor's plan for her, but he didn't think her foolish enough to slip away in the middle of the night with nothing except the clothes on her back. She would die before she made it far, and he'd have to tell the emperor that he had failed, that he had lost her to the grasp of the Tuta Kulla.

No, it wasn't an option. He would search every shadow, turn over every leaf, until he found—

Kasik skidded to a stop, chest heaving. At some point, his blade had made its way to his hand, and it shook as he beheld what kneeled before him.

Nina's back was to him. She was on her knees, but her head was tilted toward the sky, and all he could see was the way her hair swept almost to the floor.

"Nina?" he called carefully. Breath held, he waited for her to acknowledge him, for her head to turn and see that she had been caught, but she was deathly still, unmoving like the darkness itself.

Finally, his eyes followed the path of hers, and a knot of dread lodged itself in his throat.

Perched on the trees high above, razor-sharp beak glistening in a patch of moonlight, was a beast he had only ever seen on the murals that covered the kancha walls. Its talons curled over the branch it held on to, gouging the soft wood with ease. He knew that if it stretched its wings, it could envelop her whole. It could snatch her from the ground and take off into the sky where he couldn't follow.

"Nina, please," he pleaded in a low voice.

Ever so slowly, he melted into a crouch, blade held tight in one hand and the other extended toward Nina. If he could just brush her shoulder, she would snap out of the trance she was in.

For all the dense and dark corners of the forest, there was nowhere near enough to take cover. His only option was to give himself enough time to kill the beast, but Nina was just out of reach, and he couldn't risk it attacking her first. He shifted forward and it moved its bulbous eyes to him. It was exactly what Kasik needed. Fueled by terror, he launched himself at Nina.

Their bodies collided and the momentum sent them rolling into a fallen tree. Kasik felt the rush of wind from the beast's wings skim over his head and heard a gasp from Nina as they came to a stop. He'd let go of his blade so he didn't accidentally stab them, but now he was weaponless and the bird was circling above, a predator with its prey in sight.

It let out an ear-piercing cry that sent chills down Kasik's back. It was alerting the others to food. Kasik scrambled to his feet and pulled Nina up with him. Her nostrils flared with every breath and her eyes were wide with panic. The last thing he wanted to do was separate from her, but he knew it was the only way to hopefully save her. They didn't stand a chance against a monster in the throes of hunger.

"Nina, listen to me." He placed his mouth against her ear and held her face firmly in hand. "When I say go, you're going to run to the left, and I'm going to go right. Do not stop running, no matter what you hear. Find cover only if you must. I'll come for you, all right?"

He pulled back to stare into her wild eyes. Her hands came up and covered his. Kasik felt the tremble but also the resolve. This was not the way she would die. "Ready?" he whispered. Beneath his hands, she nodded.

Above them, the bird circled once more and then dove.

Kasik muttered a prayer to Ekeko, god of fortune, and then he yelled, "*Go!*"

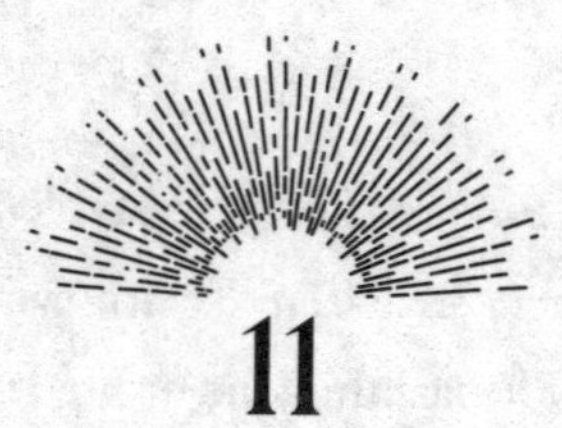

11

Nina had been lost in what she thought was a dream, pulled underneath the dark paths of her innermost fears, stumbling through them blind and alone. When she woke, she was being tackled by Kasik, the flash of a winged beast flapping and screaming above them. She'd thought she was still in a nightmare, until Kasik pressed his lips to her ear and spoke, the warmth of his words breathing life back into her.

She heard his instructions, and she obeyed. He yelled, *Go*, and she scrambled away, hands over her head as if they could protect her from that terrifying beast. She pushed herself as hard as she could. The gnarled fingers of branches clawed her face. The edges of thick leaves sliced her skin. She felt the sharp sting of hair tearing away, but she didn't stop.

The sounds of rustling wings and piercing cries faded, slowly replaced by her frenzied breaths and the buzz of insects. She searched the trees for Kasik, waiting to hear his footsteps, but there was nothing. Silence surrounded her.

Then, in the distance, she heard a crash and a cry of pain.

It was one man against one beast. Kasik seemed capable, trained to survive and kill, but what if there were more? What if those bird cries were a call?

And what could she possibly do about it?

Once again, Nina begrudged her lack of training. Had she known how to fight, or how to wield a weapon, she wouldn't have been so hesitant to go back. If Sacha was there, the answer would have been simple. Her sister would never have left anyone behind. But Nina wasn't Sacha. She wasn't sure she was capable of that same selflessness.

If she died, did her agreement with the kunay also die? Would Sacha no longer be safe?

But what would happen to her if Kasik died? How would she get to the emperor then? Or would his death prompt her freedom?

In a roundabout way, Kasik had saved her life. He had come to collect her and forced Mamakuna Dusi to free her from that cell, and she wouldn't survive this forest without him. She couldn't leave him behind.

Nina turned back, dodging branches and leaves as big as her head, praying that Kasik was still alive, that she wasn't about to stumble upon a bloody feast. Her stomach roiled at the thought.

A flash of a shadow darted between two large trees ahead. She ran straight toward it.

Kasik was nowhere to be seen, but the bird was hovering high, its large wings beating the air, sending dirt and leaves swirling around her feet. Its attention was pinned to a spot on the forest floor where three trees had fallen into each other. An arrow shot out from within the enclosure. The bird tipped sideways, narrowly avoiding being impaled.

A plan quickly formed in Nina's mind. All she had to do was get the bird's attention and give Kasik the chance to aim true.

The clouds parted just enough for hazy moonlight to illuminate the shadows. Her eyes darted over the floor. *There*, a rock the size of her fist. It was cool and heavy against her palm.

It left her hand and soared through the air.

And fell just shy of the bird's feet, pathetically crashing to the ground with a quiet thud.

But it was enough that the bird turned its head sharply, unblinking eyes meeting hers. Nina could have sworn they were made of achilla. That the gods were watching her through its fathomless orbs. For a moment, she saw her death reflected in them, bloody and gruesome and excruciating.

And then an arrow punched through its right eye. The bird shrieked and flapped once, twice. Another arrow lodged into its chest and sent glossy feathers the size of her arm floating into the air. It opened its blade-sharp beak in a silent scream, stretched its talons as if seeking purchase, and then it plummeted to the ground, tearing leaves and branches in its wake.

Nina fell to her knees, chest heaving. From her periphery, she saw Kasik stumble out of the downed trees and make his way toward her, but she couldn't take her eyes off the dead beast.

It was easily three times her size, its wings wide enough to wrap her in a deadly embrace several times over. The entirety of it was a vicious, gleaming black, except for a white band around its neck and on the tips of its wings. In the dark, it had looked like an evil spirit. A creature straight from her worst nightmares.

In death, she saw it for what it truly was. A creation of the gods, much like the achipuma. She only wondered *which* god, and for what purpose.

From not so far-off, she heard an unnatural screech. A response to a call made not long ago.

"Up, Nina, now." Kasik's hands slid under her arms and hoisted her to her feet. Then he grabbed her hand and tugged her away, slowly at first, just a limping gait, and then faster as the cries grew louder and closer.

They ran with seemingly no direction in mind, sometimes slipping through trees so dense she had to hold her breath to make it through. It was a labyrinth of unfamiliarity. An endless abyss of shadow. She tripped over a root and caught herself with her free hand, hissing as her skin gave way over a sharp jut of rock.

Again, Kasik lifted her to her feet. Again, he pulled her along as quickly as she could go.

There was no air for speaking, no energy for thought. She followed for what felt like an eternity, until Kasik tugged her underneath a canopy of low-hanging branches, thick enough that the sky couldn't be seen through the leaves. He crawled in first and then yanked Nina between his legs, her back to his chest. One arm wrapped around her shoulders and the other around her mouth, quieting her frantic breathing. She clung to his wrists and strained to see beyond their hideaway.

All was quiet. They stayed as they were, wrapped around each other, their chests surging as one.

Finally, Kasik's arms fell, his body going limp behind hers.

She whirled around and steadied him with two hands on his shoulders. "Are you hurt?"

"My back" was all he said. Nina nudged him forward and supported his body against her chest. It was almost impossible to see, but she could smell the sharp tang of blood. Carefully, she prodded the skin, shivering when his hiss of breath caressed her neck.

When she held her fingers up, she found them glistening in the dim light.

Kasik pushed away from her with a groan. "I'll be fine," he said unconvincingly. "I just need to rest a moment. We'll stay here until it's light."

Nina nodded, but his eyes had already closed, and she stared at his face hidden in shadow, the way the lines of him were once again sharp and unknowable.

Except, she knew now that, regardless of *why*, his convictions were strong enough to compel him to risk his life to save hers, and she was afraid that it would change everything.

12

The sun rose and shone with all the breadth and width of a fire scorching the land, and the forest transformed from a nightmarish landscape to a whimsical dream. Winged insects flew through shafts of sunlight in lazy circles. Small creatures jumped from branch to branch, leaves and feathers falling and twirling softly to the ground.

A leaf fell into Nina's hair, and she plucked it out while carefully climbing over the tangle of foliage covering the ground. Kasik walked beside her, his breathing labored, face pale with pain. She peeked at the three large gashes in his tunic. Dried blood covered most of the wound, but she could see bits of white fat and tendons underneath the red.

Nina swallowed her worry and followed Kasik closely. Even as near to death as he looked, he helped her climb over trees covered in slippery moss, and his eyes never stopped roving over their surroundings. They were far from the road, and Capac was nowhere to be seen.

"Are we lost?" Nina asked after a few hours had passed.

The muscles in Kasik's jaw clenched. He refused to meet her eyes. "I've never been this deep into the Tuta Kulla. We just have to find the road."

It wasn't straightforward, but it was answer enough, and it was the last they spoke for a long while. Sweat trickled down Nina's spine. The air was humid and heavy, as if she were buried beneath layers of cloth, and the heft of her robe clung to her. How she longed to rip it off, to dive into the briny sea and cool her burning, blistered feet.

Still, they pushed on, Nina's every step plagued with visions of that unnatural bird.

"That thing." She braced herself against a tree and stepped over a large hole, refusing to consider what was living in it. "What was it?"

"It's called an achiyanga, *god bird*. It's said to have been a messenger for the gods, but when they were separated from the mortal realm, the birds went mad and became vengeful. They hunt at night by capturing their prey in thrall and then devouring them piece by piece."

Nina shivered at the memory of being under its control, a dreamlike blur until Kasik's body had collided with hers. "There are no stories of it in Limac."

Their myths involved monsters that lived deep in the sea. Snakelike creatures that lured men to watery deaths. Demon-like beings that stole crops and children. But as terrifying as the stories were, she had never seen them in real life, nor had anyone she knew.

"They're confined to the Tuta Kulla." His hand cupped her elbow, and she noticed how cold it was. "People believe the emperor's road is blessed and therefore they are unable to go near it."

"And what do you think?" she asked.

"I think we need to find the road before it gets dark," he said, pausing to tilt his head to the sky, where the sun hung high overhead. "And water."

"And Capac?"

Kasik glanced behind them. Nina followed his gaze, wondering what he was thinking. "Capac will find us. He always knows the way."

But the line between his brows matched hers, and she couldn't help but think he was just as worried as she was. He walked an arm's length in front of her, the muscles in his back bunching as he parted the giant leaves at head level. If he was in pain, he didn't show it.

His wound had stopped bleeding, but it was caked with dirt and debris around the edges, and she knew from life on a farm that dirty wounds were the most dangerous.

They needed water, and the medicinal paste her mamay made.

The idea struck her like a fist. She was familiar with the shape of the leaves, and the smell of the plant, having traded for them many times in the market. And though it was always Sacha who helped their mamay make the paste, Nina had watched enough times to hopefully be able to recreate it.

The band around Kasik's upper arm caught the light of the sun and shone right into her eye. She blinked and looked away, but still it was there in her periphery. A small glint of gold that tickled her memory.

Nina stopped walking. Stopped breathing.

There, in the center of Kasik's back, was a point of golden light, so faint it was almost invisible. If she looked away again, it would disappear. She had to strain her senses to see, to *feel* it, a tiny piece of something at once familiar and foreign that whispered softly to her soul.

It was the same light that had danced in those boys' chests back home. The same one she had been lured to like a moth to flame.

The memory became clearer then. How she had been at first confused, and then concerned, and then coerced to reach out a hand and call the light toward her. How it had obeyed easily. How she had squeezed it in a fist and felt the breadth of their lives leaking through her fingers.

Now it was there again, and it called to her all the same.

Attay, her heart whispered.

When she brushed her mind against it, Kasik came to an abrupt stop and turned sharply toward her. His umber eyes narrowed as they took her in. "Are you all right?" he asked.

But Nina wasn't paying attention to the way he slowly closed the space between them and then clasped her chin between his fingers, his gaze inspecting her face. With a shaky hand, she reached for his light and firmly pressed her palm over the center of his chest.

It jumped with a gasp. She wasn't sure what it felt like to him, but to her, it felt like holding her hand over a fire. Like burning potential and endless possibility.

The intensity terrified her. She shot her eyes to his, wondering if he felt anything at all, but he was watching her intently, gaze darting from her eyes to her mouth, the space between them narrowing with every inhale.

There was a war within Nina. Part of her hoped for him to come nearer, for his breath to mingle with hers, to feel his lips and taste his mouth. The other part of her longed to grasp his light and twist, to watch with glee as he knelt at her feet and obeyed her every command.

The urge was sudden and slippery. There one moment and gone the next, along with that golden thread.

All that was left behind was confusion and worry and exhaustion. "I'm just tired," Nina said, her voice ragged as she forced herself to take a step away.

Kasik nodded, and finally the weight of his gaze left her. "We'll rest as soon as we find water."

It was the truth. Nina was more tired than she could ever remember being, and not just physically, but mentally. Every shadow in the forest was a creature waiting to feast on her bones. Every thought in her mind was an enemy trying to coax her. She couldn't trust her own desires that prodded her toward kissing the kamayuq who had taken her captive.

Or killing him, if she inspected that dark whisper in the far recesses of her mind that told her his death would solve all her problems.

If Kasik was dead, she could go back home, the emperor none the wiser. She could convince her family that they could find somewhere else to live, far from the reaches of duty and responsibility and fate.

But she was afraid the vow to the kunay would sit like an omen over her head. That he would never stop searching for her if she disappeared, and what was she if not loyal to her own word?

The gods had heard her vow and they would favor her if she kept it. Nina forced herself to believe that as she blindly followed Kasik through the forest and toward her future.

* * *

They heard the stream before they saw it, a gentle gurgle of water that sent Nina running through the dense trees. Kasik called after her, but his voice was light, a soft warning that fell on deaf ears. Her sole purpose was to sink her head beneath the surface and let it wash away the stink of the last several days.

When the stream came into view, it did not disappoint. It sparkled in the afternoon light, flowing gently in a direction she couldn't discern nor cared to consider. She didn't stop running until her feet hit the water. It was icy cold, and it stole her breath, and still she dove as far as she could.

Nina had never felt anything more exquisite. The small injuries covering her body went numb. She sank to the silty bottom where she allowed the weight of the water to suffocate all her thoughts for just a few moments.

The air was warm when she popped up for a breath. Kasik sat on a large rock by the shore, his eyes pinned to her. She smiled and threw a handful of water his way.

"Come in," she called to him. The water had left her feeling invigorated, freer than she could ever remember feeling.

"In a moment" was all he said.

Nina shrugged and sank beneath the surface again, this time swimming along the floor to find the deepest part of the stream. At home, her room was full of prizes she had plucked from the ocean floor while Sacha watched from shore. Shells in pinks and oranges, flat and circular, large and small. She would place them in a bowl and weave the smallest and brightest into her sisters' hair. Lali always lost hers, but Sacha treasured them, carefully reattaching them if they came loose.

Nina was pulled into a memory of the last time they had swam together.

Mamay always told them to stay near the shore, but Nina was a strong swimmer. She would swim out farther and farther every time, just to see how far she could go. Nina wasn't worried that Sacha would follow her. Her sister always stayed on the shore with her feet firmly planted in the sand.

Except this time, she didn't. Nina stared out at the horizon with a smile on her face.

How vast the world was. How exciting to consider what was on the other side.

When she turned to wave at Sacha, her sister was nowhere to be seen. A surge of water came and swallowed Nina. She ducked underneath just as Tayta had taught her, and waited until the white foam passed to come up again. Her vision blurred as water dripped into her eyes. Perhaps that was why she still couldn't find Sacha on the shore. It was just as her mamay always said—Nina needed to pay better attention.

Someone called her name, but Nina ignored it and closed her eyes. Calmed her breathing. Let the water carry her weight.

There. *Nina felt her sister like a tether to her heart. Felt the essence of her life, not strong and bright and on the shore where Sacha always stayed, but flimsy and quiet and floating nearby.*

Nina swam faster than she ever had, but it wasn't fast enough.

Tayta reached Sacha first, scooping her up, then Nina, and raced to shore. Sacha's body was still, her lips blue, her light dimmed further to a barely there flicker. Tayta pushed on her chest and breathed into her mouth while Nina watched, and whispered, and tugged on that weak, gossamer light.

Sacha flared to life with a gasp.

Nina let out more air as she sat on the sandy floor and the memory washed over her. Her hair floated around her head like a halo. Streams of sun penetrated deep enough to touch her hand, and she curled her fingers through them, considering the threads of golden light that appeared at random and what they truly meant.

Suddenly, a hand wrapped around her arm and dragged her up. She broke the surface with a gasp. Kasik stood before her, his eyes wild as he held Nina's upper arms in a bruising grip.

"What are you *doing*?" she sputtered. Hair clung to her face and neck. She used rough hands to shove it out of her eyes.

"You were down there for so long. I thought you were *drowning*."

"It's called swimming, Kasik. Haven't you ever done it before?"

Kasik abruptly let go of her. He ran his hands through his hair and turned away. She caught sight of his back and swallowed down a flood of guilt. He was in pain because he had saved her life, and it was clear his nerves were frayed. The least she could do was reassure him that she was all right.

Hesitantly, she reached out and touched his shoulder. Kasik looked down at her hand, and then followed the path of her arm to her shoulder, her neck, her jaw, her cheeks, and finally, her eyes. It was as if he was inspecting her to ensure that she was whole and hale.

"I'm all right," she said softly. His shoulders relaxed as he blew out a breath, the warmth of it skimming the top of her hand and sending shivers up her arm. She yanked her hand away before he could see and pointed at his back. "We should clean this properly."

"It can wait," Kasik said, heading back to shore. Without thinking, Nina grasped his wrist. His pulse beat hard against her fingertips.

"I don't think it should," Nina said. "I've seen injuries less severe than yours get infected from much less." When it looked as if he might argue again, Nina gently pulled him closer. "Please," she added. His eyes traveled to hers, and Nina saw in them that she had won.

Kasik allowed himself to be guided. She gently turned him, his back facing her, and plucked the bottom of his tunic. "This needs to come off."

Kasik's hands curled around the hem and tugged. Nina slipped her hands underneath to protect his wound and tried not to focus on the way his muscles rippled with movement. How the water sluiced over the ridges carved into his browned skin. The urge to run her fingers over each scar was so strong that she curled her hands into fists by her side.

The tunic hit the water with a slap. Nina cleared her throat. "Kneel, please," she asked, and Kasik obeyed easily.

It was different than she had imagined, him on his knees at her feet. Instead of feeling powerful, she felt pleased that he trusted her enough to give her his back and determined to help as much as she could. Gently, she swiped the long, dark hair from his shoulders. A thin, leather cord she hadn't noticed before rested against his neck.

Then she lifted a sleeve-covered fist to the uppermost wound and carefully wiped away blood that had dried beneath the dirt. Kasik didn't so much as twitch as she worked. She went slowly, ensuring that there was nothing left to irritate once she could place a poultice. As soon as she was done, she would search the surrounding forest for the right materials and she wouldn't stop until she found them.

It was a quick and thorough job, and she tried her best not to touch him more than absolutely necessary. Every time she placed her fingers against his shoulder blades to steady herself, his skin would jump beneath her touch. Either he hated this, or he was in more pain than she thought, but with each handful of water that ran down his back in rivers, Kasik's shoulders lowered, his head falling farther back, until he was relaxed and entirely at Nina's mercy.

That thin, golden light appeared again, brighter and louder than before. Nina stumbled away and pressed her hands to her chest.

"All done," she said, and winced at the pitch of her voice. She marched out of the water and into the brush to find the proper plants for a poultice.

Any excuse to wipe the feel of him from her hands.

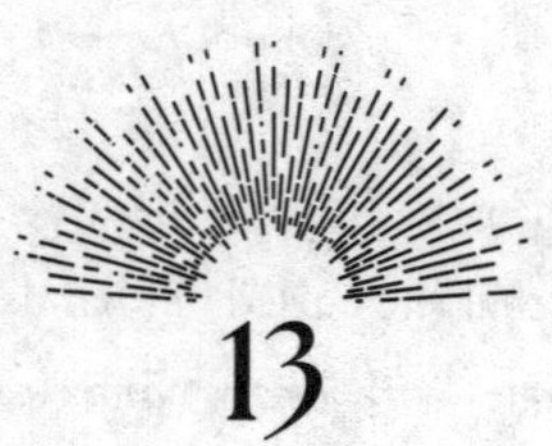

13

Kasik's skin was on fire, and it wasn't because of Nina's hands on him, though he had to close his eyes against the feel of her, small and soft and kind. He couldn't remember the last time he had been cared for so thoughtfully, so *gently*.

Any injuries he'd had were treated quickly and discretely by the kancha healer, his tayta none the wiser. The man would've stabbed him before providing any comfort.

This yearning for touch wasn't a desire he was aware he had, and he hated Nina for bringing it to his attention.

More than that, he hated himself for wanting it. For failing his mission so miserably. They had gotten far off course and added days to their trip. Days he wasn't sure he had. The wound and muscles around it burned, and if he didn't find a healer soon, he knew he would succumb to the infection spreading through his blood.

A short distance away, Nina flitted from plant to plant, feeling and smelling their leaves and stems, until she yelled, "Aha!" and snapped several stems in half. When she came closer, he could see that she held small branches, grayish white in color and dripping a red liquid that looked eerily like blood.

"Hold this, please," she said, handing Kasik a bundle of leaves. The thought crossed his mind that she could be killing him, but he shook it away and did as she asked. If she had wanted to kill him, it would have been as simple as leaving him to face the achiyanga on his own. But she had come back, risking her own life to save his.

Kasik watched over his shoulder as Nina collected the red sap in her hand and then dipped two fingers into it. "This might burn," she said, and then her fingers were rubbing the sap into his wounds without hesitation. *She would make a good healer*, he thought, biting back a curse as pain radiated up his spine.

"I need something to crush these up," she said, taking the leaves from his hands and bunching them on the rock. The first thing that came to mind was the small knife in his boot, but he hesitated. Handing her a blade seemed foolish.

As if sensing his hesitation, she said, "Actually, you can do it for me. My hands are sticky."

Kasik was filled with guilt when she so easily absolved him of his doubt. The wounds burned as he reached forward and plucked the knife from his boot. He wrapped his hand around the hilt and crushed the leaves against the rock until it was a slimy paste.

Nina's small fingers collected it in her palm and then she was back to work, diligently covering every part that stung and burned until all he felt was blessed relief.

"There," she said, "that should help."

Kasik mourned the loss of her touch as her fingers slid away. He turned to thank her, but the weight of her attention stole his words. They held each other's gazes, neither speaking, neither moving, only watching and waiting.

For what, Kasik didn't know. He only knew that she was arresting in her intensity, that the way her brows drew over her eyes made him want to soothe the crease with a thumb. That if she allowed it, he would shoulder all her worries. For no other reason than her well-being was his responsibility, of course. He was simply following orders.

Then Nina's eyes dropped first to his mouth, then his chest, and her hand slowly reached up to finger the stone around his neck, and the weight of his responsibilities waned under her scrutiny. She turned it this way and that and pulled it and him closer to her face. Kasik held his breath as her hair tickled his jaw.

"*Achilla,*" she whispered. "I saw Mamakuna Dusi wearing it as well. Does everyone in the capital have one?"

"No, not everyone," he said. This close, he could see flecks of light brown splashed across her dark brown eyes. He cleared his throat. "Those of us closest to the emperor do, and of course, Emperor Maicu wears many."

Nina leaned away and dropped the stone, but her eyes stayed trained on it. Kasik felt like he could breathe again.

"We don't wear them in Limac," she said. Her eyes got a faraway look. "My people are in tune with the land and each other. There's an understanding that if harm comes to us, it is because we have sowed it."

Her words were innocent enough, but he felt defensive all the same. It was as though she was implying that his choices had led them there, into chaos and near death. That to wear one at all was an admission of harmful intention.

To him, the stone wasn't about protection. It was a reminder of his loyalty and mortality. That he wasn't above duty or death. Kasik could do everything right and still, death would come for him, just as it had his mamay, who had invited it simply by giving birth to him. But how to explain that to someone whose views so clearly opposed his? "It was my mamay's," he said instead, and hoped it was enough.

Nina nodded, but gratefully said nothing more. They sat in silence, side by side, on the sun-warmed rock, shoulders touching, the stream and the insects and the rustle of leaves the only noise. The beauty of the Tuta Kulla washed over Kasik. He had never been this deep into the forest. When he traveled with his men, they stuck to the road, making camp right off the path in the less dense trees.

They had been taught that the forest was an evil place, but he saw beauty in the way everything grew wild and free, and he was glad that it had remained untouched.

"We'll rest here for the night," he finally said, "and then follow the stream south." From his periphery, he saw Nina's mouth open and close and waited to see if she would gain the courage to speak whatever was on her mind.

"I was thinking," she started, "that it might be ideal for me to have a weapon."

Kasik turned. She was staring into the trees on the other side of the stream, her fingers idly tearing apart a leaf in her hands. He was able to study part of her face, full cheeks and lips and large eyes darting back and forth. "I don't think that would be ideal for anyone," he said honestly.

"If something like *that* were to happen again, I could help."

"Do you know how to use a tumi? Or a bow and arrow?"

He could see her deliberating, but she finally said, "No. I don't."

"Then you'd be more likely to hurt yourself than help."

He could see the way her face tightened. He knew she was angry before she spoke. "I think I could manage," she said sharply.

He grabbed the knife from beside him and slid off the rock. "Here," he said, holding it out to her. "Try to kill me."

"What?" She eyed him warily. "I'm not going to fight you. You're hurt."

"Even so," he challenged. "I said *try*."

Resolve slid over her features, and she hopped off the rock, landing nimbly on her feet. Kasik wondered if he might have miscalculated, that she was pretending to be unskilled and this was all an act to kill him while he was injured.

If so, then so be it. He had carved this path with his own two hands and there was no evading it.

Nina snatched the knife from him. Her feet slid apart to shoulder width, and she bent her knees the tiniest bit. Kasik ignored the throbbing in his back and met her stance, waiting for her to make the first move.

When she did, he was surprised at her speed and commitment. If he had been one heartbeat slower, she might have actually stabbed him, but he dodged sideways at the last moment and pushed her arm away. She whipped it right back, her moves sloppy but fast, her whole body lunging at him with each jab and swing of her arm.

Impressed wasn't the right word for what he felt—more like *inspired.* That tenacity he had seen in her eyes when they first met was dripping from her every move, and it reminded him of how he had felt just a few years ago, the determination to serve his emperor and empire fuel behind his every action.

Somewhere along the line, he had become jaded, numb to the convictions of his heart, and as Nina split open the skin of his forearm, a tiny slice that barely bled, he vowed to try to be just as steadfast as her.

They had both been caught off guard by her minute victory, and he used her shock and imbalance to his advantage. He trapped her arm beneath his and then twisted so that the knife was pointed away from him, and her back was against his chest.

"I win," she said brightly.

"You surprised me," he said through a smile. "But you haven't won just because you landed a single scratch." He moved his lips to whisper into her ear. "It would take nothing but a pulse of pressure to turn this knife and put it through your heart."

"But you can't," she said smugly. "Or else you'd have to remove your own head, just as you removed the head of the man who gave me this bruise."

The reminder of who he served and why he was there was a punch to the gut.

Kasik swiftly removed his arms and the weapon from her hands. She stumbled forward out of his grip and whirled around to face him. "I won that fair and square."

Shaking his head, he scooped up his shredded tunic and bow and arrow, wincing as he spoke. "There is no such thing as fair."

14

Somehow, Nina had convinced Kasik to let her keep watch, and the forest was beginning to lighten with the morning sun. Kasik had fallen asleep quickly and was still asleep. If she was more vindictive, she could have leaned over and stolen the knife from his boot while he slept. Perhaps stabbed him in the heart.

But she wasn't vindictive, and she couldn't muster enough indignation over his refusal to give her a weapon because he was right—she probably *would* manage to hurt herself. It seemed that everything that had gone wrong in her life thus far was her fault.

First, Samaq had been taken only weeks after she had saved Sacha from drowning. Then, Nina had been taken weeks after she almost took the lives of those boys. But she couldn't find a common thread, and it felt like the gods were pulling on invisible strings, guiding her this way and that. She wondered if they found amusement in watching mortals scurry around like ignorant ants.

She plucked a leaf from a nearby bush and tore it to pieces. They fluttered to the ground, and she plucked another. There was a pile of broken leaves collecting in the center of her crossed legs. *Fitting*, she thought. It resembled the pieces of her life.

A noise from the shadows stilled her hands. She listened intently, but a moment passed and there were no other sounds beyond the normal melody of the forest. She was simply on edge, waiting for some other creature from legend to jump out of the trees and devour her whole.

All because Kasik wouldn't give her his knife.

Nina surged to her feet and started pacing. There were so many questions she wanted to ask her mamay. So many things that simply did not make sense. They had hidden when the Harvest came every year. Was it because her mamay couldn't bear to part with her remaining children, or was there more to it?

Why did they continue to serve a god who had, according to Kasik's story, gone mad?

And most importantly, why did Nina feel like there was something vital her parents were keeping from her?

It was strange to consider that the people she trusted most in life might have been lying to her all along. If she kept thinking on it, she would work herself into a frenzy.

The river was close enough that she heard it gurgling, and she found herself walking toward it before she could decide if it was a bad choice. She needed to clear her head more than ever.

Everything felt out of control and entirely unfair.

There is no such thing as fair. Nina didn't disagree, but that didn't mean she couldn't lament over it.

She parted the thick brush quietly and carefully to avoid waking Kasik. His wound looked less inflamed this morning, but it also had thin streaks of black creeping along the edges. Nina knew it wasn't dirt. She had cleaned it more thoroughly than she had ever cleaned anything. They would just have to keep an eye on it and continue applying the paste and hope it didn't get further infected.

When Nina finally reached the water, she dove in without hesitation, surprised that the weight of her worries didn't immediately drown her. But the water did exactly as she had hoped—it cleared her mind, silenced the doubt and the uncertainty and grounded her in the present. In the vow she had made to take her sister's place.

It was the only thing that mattered. Though she might not have expected it to go so far, to be summoned to serve the emperor so closely, she would do whatever was necessary to see her vow through. And then she would see her family again.

Nina emerged from the water feeling invigorated. Her purpose clearer. As she shook out her days-old braids and carefully untangled the leaves and knots, she allowed herself to consider what would be expected of her. Not only as a servant to her vow, but as a wife to the emperor.

A *wife*. A role she had never imagined she would fulfill.

Nina was more than aware of the roles in a family and an ayllu. The women were just as necessary and vital to sustaining life as the men, if not more. In Limac, only the women could plant the seeds and nurture the fields. They were responsible for the health and wealth of their people.

But Nina never saw herself as a wife, or as a mother.

Would Emperor Maicu expect her to provide him with children, to lock herself away to care for them? Would she ever see adventure or the world beyond the walls of the kancha?

Would she ever see Kasik again?

The thought came unbidden, and Nina's first instinct was to shove it aside. She shouldn't *want* to see him again, not after he was responsible for delivering her to her fate like a lamb to slaughter. But he was simply doing his job, and he was doing it well. It showed a level of care and dedication that she couldn't help but admire. And she couldn't deny that she felt safe with him, comfortable in his arms after the terror of the night.

That was all that it was; Nina wanted a friend. A familiar face in a strange world. She felt nothing for him beyond that.

Perhaps she could request that Sacha come live with her. Lali was so much younger than them at ten, and would need to stay with their mamay and tayta, but Sacha was sixteen, and her health was tenuous at best. Surely, the kancha had the space and the healers to care for her.

Kasik had said she would have power, and this was such a small request in the grand scheme of things. Everything would be okay. Nina had trusted her instincts, and perhaps they were guiding her to the best possible outcome for all of them.

She turned away from the shoreline to wade deeper, where she could submerge herself again, but a sudden flash of movement made her freeze.

There, directly across from her on the bank of the stream, was a man. He wore a tunic the same shade of green that surrounded him, and his hair was shorn all the way to his ears. There were streaks of mud on his face that looked purposefully placed. As if he was attempting to further blend into the foliage.

Heart pounding, Nina sank slowly into the water until it was at her chin. She made no sudden movements, and he came no closer. They only stared, each of them waiting to see who would make the first move.

And then there was a snap behind her.

The man's eyes darted away from her at the same time he raised a bow and arrow in his hands. Nina's stomach turned. The world narrowed to a point with her at the center. She was going to die in that river. She was never going to see her family again. Or Kasik. All this had been for nothing.

"Nina." A voice pierced her panicked thoughts. "Walk backward toward me. Slowly, please."

Kasik. His tone authoritative yet soothing. Nina obeyed. It was the easiest choice she had made thus far. The man's bow swung to point directly between her eyes.

"*Don't*," she heard Kasik warn. "Keep coming, Nina."

Nina stayed low in the water and filled with despair as it receded. She felt exposed. Vulnerable. But she was almost fully on shore. A few more steps and she could—

Another shape appeared across the river, a face seemingly floating between the leaves. She saw the glint of a blade in their hand, held low.

"Nina. Listen to my voice. Keep walking."

She hadn't realized she had stopped. Her legs felt heavy and unmovable. The air felt too thick to breathe. Time seemed to slow, and then all at once, it exploded.

The man with the blade took a step forward and an arrow punched into his shoulder two heartbeats after. The man with the bow and arrow ducked low and dove into the water, coming straight for her. Nina turned and ran. The water slowed her down, but Kasik stayed where he was, notching another arrow that he pointed somewhere behind her.

"Kasik!" she screamed, but it was too late. Another man in green had run out of the bushes behind Kasik, a broad-ended weapon in one hand that he swung at Kasik's temple. Kasik turned, but he was too late. Nina watched with horror as he crumpled into a heap.

Arms wrapped around her from behind and lifted her off the ground. Nina kicked her legs and jerked her body from side to side. She opened her mouth to scream, but a rough hand covered it before a sound could escape.

"I'm not going to hurt you," a voice whispered in her ear. But he already was. His grip was bruising and Nina could scarcely breathe from the pressure of his arm around her chest and his hand over her mouth. Panic had wormed its way into her heart and her mind. She was losing strength and losing consciousness.

The last thing she saw, before everything went dark, was Kasik's blood dripping into the dirt beneath him.

Kasik groaned. The earth tilted underneath his cheek and the urge to vomit made his mouth water viciously. But he swallowed it down and rolled onto his back.

The first thing he noticed was the lack of light. The canopy of leaves was gone and in its place was a green fabric, the same color the men in the forest had worn. The one that made it so they were hardly visible. As if they were hiding in the Tuta Kulla. The tent was circular, so there were no corners, and entirely bare. There was only the dirt floor and him lying sprawled in the middle. Nina was gone.

Kasik tried to sit up, but his hands were bound above his head and when he tugged, there was resistance. He looked up to see he was tethered to a wooden column. They had bound him like an animal, and they had Nina in their clutches, hopefully alive, though he knew there were worse things than death.

A flutter of panic urged Kasik to yank harder, the rope biting into his wrists and his head pounding with every tug.

He heard the shuffle of a boot a heartbeat before the tent flap parted and a man strolled through. Kasik stilled. He didn't want to give the man any reason to run him through with the tumi at his waist.

The man prowled closer and stood over his head. "What is a walla doing deep in the Tuta Kulla?"

They didn't know who he was, then. Kasik had removed his tunic for Nina to clean his wounds, and his armbands were tucked away somewhere on the forest floor. Any evidence of his station was gone. Kasik inspected the stranger, from his shorn hair and the lack of achilla on his person to the green tunic that he wore that was not the emperor's red, or the loyal's blue, or the gods' purple, or even the foreigner's black. Who did they belong to, and what did they want with them?

"Where is she?" Kasik asked, tongue heavy.

The man tutted at him. "*I* am the one asking questions. How did you find us?"

If Kasik played this right, he might be able to get answers while also stalling long enough to free himself from the binds. They were tight, but he wasn't unwilling to break his hands and squeeze them through if necessary. "I'll tell you everything you want to know if you let me see her."

Head tilted, the man smiled wide, teeth almost glowing in the semi-dark. "Smart boy," he said. "But I am not stupid. Answer my questions, and I won't have her killed."

"If you touch a single hair on her head," Kasik seethed, "I *will* kill you. Slowly and painfully."

"Big promises coming from a boy tied up like a boar ready for the spit." The man straightened and came to stand near Kasik's stomach. "I'll ask you again; what are you doing so deep in the Tuta Kulla?"

Kasik kept his mouth closed and stared straight ahead. He wasn't prepared for the blow that stole his breath, or the vomit that surged up and almost choked him. On his side, his wrists burning above him, he spat into the dirt and sucked in a ragged breath.

"How did you find us?"

Before he got the chance to answer, another kick landed squarely in his abdomen. He felt something give way under the man's boot. A sharp crack that made the world spin again.

"What does the emperor want?"

Kasik smiled through bloody teeth. "You're going to have to kill me," he whispered. "If you keep me alive, you will regret every second of it."

"We'll take our chances, *Kamayuq*."

Guess I was wrong was Kasik's last thought before there was a flash of agony, and then everything faded away.

15

Nina woke with a gasp. She was lying on a bed, curled into a ball, her temples throbbing. She was alive and, as far as she could tell through her pulsing vision, alone.

The walls of her enclosure were green and cloth-like, but they were pulled taut all the way to the ground. The space was large enough to hold the bed she was in, a table across the way, and a humble firepit in the middle. Above it, the room had a small opening to let out the smoke.

There was nothing to indicate where she was or who her captors were.

But it mattered little. Her only objective was to escape and find Kasik. Hopefully alive. She slipped off the bed and began crawling around the edges of the room. She saw nothing she could use as a weapon and no way to leave the tent without ripping through it. If only Kasik had given her the small blade, then she could have easily cut her way to freedom.

"Good, you're awake."

Nina shot to her feet and spun toward the voice, heart in her throat. The same man she had come face-to-face with in the forest stood before her, with his shaggy hair and shrewd eyes and fake smile.

"Don't come any closer," Nina warned, voice shaky but firm.

The man raised his hands in surrender but took a step closer all the same. "I'm not going to harm you."

"It's too late," Nina argued. The bruises forming on her arms could attest to that. "Where is Kasik?"

At his name, the man's face hardened. "He can't hurt you anymore," he said, taking another small step forward.

"*Hurt* me? The only people who have hurt me are *you*. Kasik, he—"

But she didn't know how to finish that sentence. He technically hadn't hurt her, but he *was* holding her against her will. "What have you done with him?"

"Don't worry," the man said, which made Nina worry more, "your walla is perfectly contained."

The words were vague and ominous, but she ignored them. "What do you want?"

The man smiled. "That's a question that will take a long time to answer, but for the purposes of this conversation, I want to know why you were so deep in the Tuta Kulla, and what you were looking for."

"We weren't looking for anything. We were attacked and—"

"Attacked by what?"

The question was sharp, and the way he said *what* instead of *who* made her wonder if he knew the answer before he asked. "An achiyanga. The god bird. It was hunting us, and in trying to escape, it set us off course."

The man's brows furrowed, his eyes darting between hers as if searching for the truth beneath her words. "You weren't searching for something specific?"

"Specific?" She looked at him curiously. "No," Nina said, exasperated, "we were just—"

"That's enough, Hatun." A woman pushed through the tent entrance, her white hair pulled back loosely, tawny-brown eyes startling against the deep brown skin of her face. Her tunic matched the man who questioned her, but that was as far as the similarities went. This woman was small, and ancient, and her attention didn't feel dangerous.

Hatun turned sharply toward the woman. They shared a tense, whispered conversation, and then the woman said out loud, "She won't hurt an old woman, will she?"

Nina wasn't above it, but she wasn't going to say that. "Of course not."

A weathered hand patted Hatun's arm. From where Nina stood, it looked more like a shove than a reassurance. "See. Now go. You're scaring her."

Hatun glanced at Nina, and she schooled her face into one of fear. It wasn't difficult; she *was* terrified and worried, and the sooner the man left the tent, the sooner Nina could figure out a way to sneak out and find Kasik. With a sigh, he walked out of the room, but not before throwing her a look full of warning over his shoulder.

"There," the woman said once he was gone. "That's better. Care to sit?"

"I'll stand here, thank you," Nina insisted.

"Well, I'm old and tired, so I'm going to sit." She walked over to the bed and sank onto it, smoothing her tunic over her legs with wrinkled hands. The material looked lightweight and soft, with short sleeves and a rounded neckline. It looked both comfortable and functional. Much better than the heavy, dull gray robe she still wore.

"My name is Shayim," the woman said. The smile on her face brought out more lines around her eyes and mouth. They reminded Nina of her mamay's. *Laugh lines*, she had called them. *Because I am so happy all the time.* "You have a very interesting story."

Nina froze, eyes pinned to the old woman. If she knew anything about Nina, it was because Kasik spoke, and if Kasik spoke, it was most likely with a knife to his throat. Even then, she wasn't sure he would give them anything true.

"I want to see Kasik."

"You will." She tilted her head and peered curiously at Nina. "Soon enough. But first, you must be hungry."

It wasn't until that moment that Nina realized she was famished. As if signaled by Shayim's words alone, Hatun walked back into the tent, a steaming bowl in either hand that he placed on the table. Then he left without so much as a second glance.

The food smelled incredible, and it made her mouth water. Some scents were familiar, like the earthy smell of oregano and the tang of ají. She could see potatoes and grains and small chunks of meat floating in a brown sauce. But Nina didn't make a move to touch it.

"It's not poisoned." Nina hadn't even considered that. She was only hesitant to let them think they had won her over with a bowl of stew. "Eat, and then I will answer all your questions."

With a sigh, Nina acquiesced. Perhaps, with food in her belly, she would have the strength to demand to see Kasik and keep her wits about her. Gods knew she wouldn't be able to think of anything else with the scent of the stew in the air.

The meat was tender and the vegetables soft and flavorful. It reminded her of home, of the meals she and her family would share together at their small table, laughing and telling stories, and it made her want to cry. Instead, she shoveled more food into her mouth and kept her eyes on Shayim. The woman may have been old, but Nina knew she wasn't stupid. Her scrutiny was heavy and her smile was knowing. Nina got the sense that she had failed some sort of test.

After several bites, she placed the bowl back on the table. "Where's Kasik?"

Shayim carefully folded her hands in her lap. "He's being detained for now."

"'For now'? What does that mean?"

"It means we cannot ascertain his intentions and are unsure if he is a threat to our people."

"What is this place?" Nina glanced at the walls of the tent and strained to listen to the sounds beyond.

"It is a home," Shayim said wistfully. "A community of people seeking safety and peace."

"Well, we aren't a threat to your community. This is all a misunderstanding. If you let us go, we can leave and—"

"The kamayuq is the largest threat to our community," she said, the smile lines around her eyes and mouth gone. "Outside of the emperor, of course," she added sharply. "I'm afraid the only misunderstanding here is yours."

Nina's mouth snapped shut, the words on the tip of her tongue swallowed whole. "Why am I here?" she asked instead.

"Your attay led you here."

Nina took a step back, almost tripping over the table in her haste to put more distance between them as Shayim stood. "I—"

"Yes, I know about your attay. What surprises me is that you do not. Now that you're here, I can See you much clearer." She hummed and then sighed deeply. "And I See you have much to learn."

Cold fear washed over Nina, and she snatched the utensil out of her bowl and wielded it in front of her. "I don't know what you're talking about," she declared. "But I demand to see Kasik *now*. Let us go, and nobody gets hurt."

Shayim gave her a pitying look. "The only thing dangerous about you is your ignorance. Put the spoon down and listen."

"Let me see Kasik and I'll think about it." She wasn't sure why the woman was entertaining her demands, but Nina was going to continue pushing it for as long as she did. It was clear they wanted her alive and unharmed, though she didn't know *why*. Nor did she care to find out. All she knew was that she had more of a chance at freedom under Kasik's thumb than with these unknown people.

"You can see him," Shayim agreed, "but I'm not sure you'll like it."

With those ominous words, Shayim walked out of the tent. Nina's heart was pounding as she replayed the woman's words and inspected them for clues. But everything she had said was vague and lightly disturbing. Nothing to suggest Nina was going to suffer an immediate death, so she steadied herself with a quick breath before hurrying to follow.

Hatun was trailing behind Shayim, his hands waving in the air and then gesturing back toward Nina as she rushed to catch up. "She's not restrained," Nina heard him whisper fiercely. "At the very least, she should be blindfolded."

Shayim waved him off. "She's no threat, Hatun. She has no idea what she can do. And she agreed to comply if I let her see the boy."

"I agreed to *listen*," Nina corrected sharply at the same time as Hatun said, "He's not a *boy*. He almost killed Hawka."

"A well-trained boy, but a boy, nonetheless. Come, if you'd like. But no hitting anyone."

Nina had never seen such a large man roll his eyes. It would have been comical if it wasn't for the dangerous circumstances.

But these people didn't *seem* dangerous, and yet therein was the danger. It was clear they wanted something from her. That they had kept her and Kasik alive for a purpose, and she was afraid to find out what would happen when they realized she had nothing to offer. Hopefully she and Kasik would be far away by then.

Night had fallen, and the cool air sent a chill over Nina. The camp was quiet as Shayim led them down a road between several large tents. They passed a massive fire in what looked like the center of camp where there were a few people sitting, all of whom turned to stare at Nina. She couldn't see their eyes with the fire glowing brightly behind them, but she could feel them. It was like being in the acllahuasi all over again. A stranger, an outsider.

They passed a fenced-in area with achipumas dozing underneath a wooden frame, and Nina thought of Capac. He hadn't had the chance to find them, as Kasik had promised. She wondered if something had eaten him, or if he had just taken advantage of his freedom and run.

"This is a mistake," Hatun mumbled, watching her, his strides tempered so that he was next to her with a hand on the hilt of a blade at his hip. Nina rolled her eyes this time.

Finally, Shayim turned toward a tent set apart from the rest of the camp. Two men stood outside and nodded their heads as she walked by. Hatun clapped one on the back and then went to step inside, but Shayim stopped him.

"Just the girl for now."

Hatun fumed. Nina was immediately suspicious, but grateful.

They could have the chance to talk, her and Kasik. Figure out a way to escape together, because despite the fleeting thought she had entertained in the forest to leave him behind, she knew it was not an option any longer. He had saved her, and she owed him a favor. That was the only reason she cared.

She pushed aside the tent flap and paused in the entrance. It was dimmer than outside without a fire, and she had to wait a few heart-pounding moments for her eyes to adjust.

Finally, she was able to see him.

Prone, eyes closed, hands tied to a wooden column anchored into the ground, Kasik looked dead already. She let the flap close behind her and approached him cautiously, unsure whether it was dread or relief that pooled in her belly and made her hands shake. Her eyes burned with unshed tears as she whispered his name. When he didn't respond, she hesitantly dropped to her knees beside him.

Up close, Nina saw Kasik's chest rising and falling the slightest amount. *Alive*, her mind screamed with relief. She placed her hands against his bare chest and lowered her ear to his heart. It was faint, but it was beating. She sat back and moved her hands to his neck, then his cheeks. "Kasik," she whispered again. "Please wake up."

His skin was a furnace against her palms, and his hair was damp with sweat. She pressed her lips to his forehead, as her mamay had done to her so many times, and hissed with worry. Fever had settled in his blood. "I need you," she murmured into his ear, hoping her words would shake him awake, just as they had done for her in the forest.

Still, he didn't move. Nina sat back, vision blurred with tears, and gasped. There, in the center of his chest, right next to the achilla resting around his neck, was a dim, golden light.

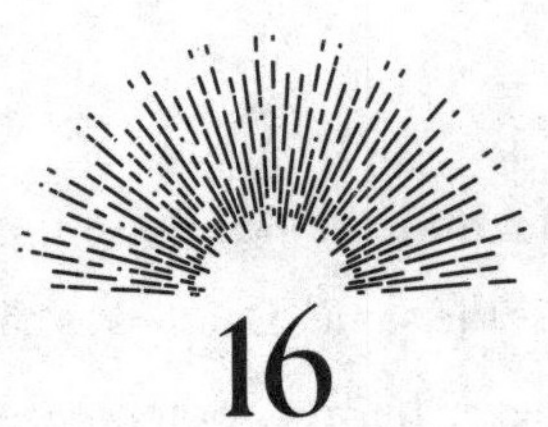

16

Kasik knew he was losing his mind when he heard Nina's voice in his sleep. Then he felt her hands on him, and he groaned. Seeing her terror, hands reaching for him, so close but so far, had been bad enough, but now he was being tormented with something he could never have. Could never *want*.

It was a product of his circumstances. How many times could one surrender their life for another before they began to feel attached? Her soft eyes and her strength and stubbornness had crawled under his skin and made him feel more alive than ever. Funny that it had led him right to death's door.

Though he knew he was alive, he wasn't sure for how much longer. His pulse flickered lightly in his neck and wrists and his consciousness wavered between defeat and determination. In the simplest of words, he was exhausted. It seemed that everything was fighting against him.

A simple mission, the emperor had said. Collect the girl and deliver her unharmed, but fate had stepped in and ruined all his plans.

The longer he was away from the kancha and his duties, the less sure he was about said plans. Why Nina? Why did Maicu want *her* so badly, so much so that he was willing to upend all his plans to acquire her? The friend he had known was calm and calculated, but the version of him that was the emperor was unfamiliar. Reckless. *Dangerous.*

What would happen when Kasik failed?

It didn't seem to be a matter of *if* anymore. The wounds on his back had begun to fester before Nina had the chance to clean them. He could feel the burn flow through his blood. Poison, perhaps, but it mattered little when the result was the same. Death was calling his name.

And Nina would never be free. Some part of him knew that if he didn't bring her in, it would be someone else. Someone much less forgiving and much more ruthless. Wherever his tayta was, he would hear of his son's failures, and he would take it upon himself to ensure that their family name was restored.

They would hunt her down. When Maicu set his sights on something, it didn't matter what he had to do to obtain it, and if he found these people who had interrupted his plans, he would remove them from his path just as he had Rumi.

It was Rumi, the emperor's elder brother, who was the heir to the throne, and it was Maicu who had slit his throat as they beheld their tayta take his last breath. Kasik could remember the blood flowing down the front of Rumi's tunic, the sheer and utter panic that had flooded Kasik's body, thinking he was next. But Maicu had simply turned away from his brother's crumpled body and placed a hand on Kasik's shoulder.

It had felt like an anchor tying them together. An irrepressible weight.

"It had to be done," Maicu said, but his eyes were across the room, pinned to Kasik's tayta, Atik, who nodded his head in approval. With pride.

Jealousy, hot and sharp, pierced Kasik's heart. He was terrified to utter a word in disagreement, but Maicu knew him better than his own tayta. They'd been friends since childhood, after all. They had been trained by Atik together. Scolded by Master Wara together. Raided the kitchens together.

"You understand, don't you, Kasik?" Maicu shifted so that both his hands were bracing his shoulders. Kasik could smell the blood on them. "Rumi was weak. He couldn't do what needed to be done to ensure that Tawantinsuyu continues to expand and thrive. It's Emperor Yachua's legacy. It will be our *blood that stamps out our enemies'."*

Maicu's dead tayta lay not two arm's lengths away. He had always been a formidable man, but even the sturdiest of them wasn't immune to the gods' fate. A strange sickness had stolen his strength, then his life.

And now Maicu had stolen his seat.

"This is between us, yes? I need my friend by my side."

Kasik stared into his eyes, and he hesitated.

"Kasik?"

"Kasik!"

Cool hands pressed against his cheeks, his neck, his arms. He heard her voice again like a whisper to soothe his aching soul. Or perhaps it was a punishment for the secrets he had kept and the man he had become. Was he any different from his cruel and cunning tayta?

Would his mamay be ashamed?

He couldn't remember much of her—he had been so young when she died—but he heard what he imagined was her voice in his dreams sometimes, reminding him to keep going, to keep trying.

It's time to wake up, my love. Today is a new day and a new chance to be happy.

"Kasik! Please wake up!"

But Kasik didn't want to wake up. He didn't want to remember the pain or bear the responsibility any longer.

"I need you," the voice whispered, so clearly that he thought it was his own voice pleading.

But he couldn't decide who or what it was he needed, and if he cared enough to try and find out.

17

"He needs a healer."

Nina whirled around, shielding Kasik's body with her own. Shayim stood just inside the door, her hands folded in front of her and her face in that perpetual intimation of calm that made Nina want to scream. Her mind was a swirl of panic and chaos, of doubt and confusion. These people, with their soft words and reassurances, had killed Kasik, for there was no world in which he came back from his current state, even *with* a healer.

"What have you done to him?" she hissed through gritted teeth.

"*We* haven't done anything. It seems that the creatures of the Tuta Kulla got to him before we did."

Kasik's skin beneath her hand was on fire. There were no other injuries on him that she could see, no blood pooled underneath him on the ground. If she could collect the plants she needed, she could try to keep him alive. "I can heal him if you let me gather what I need."

Shayim looked at her intently, head tilted and eyes narrowed. "Is that what you really want?"

Nina sucked in a breath. The question rankled her, even if it was something she had considered previously. She glanced back at Kasik, the sweat on his brow glistening in the dim moonlight pouring in from above, his bound wrists tied to the pole above his head, and she nodded.

She couldn't let him die any more than she could take his life herself. "Yes," she said confidently.

Shayim nodded as if Nina had passed a test. "Good. Then you have everything you need already."

The woman was maddening. Nina looked around the tent, at the barren dark that stared back, and shook her head. "I don't understand," she said slowly.

"Yes, you've made that perfectly clear." Shayim sighed, then stepped closer. "Perhaps I will be clearer. You have a vast and untapped power within you. I know you feel it," she added when Nina opened her mouth to object, "and you need not ignore it any longer. You are Ikara. The *true* chosen one."

Ikara. The beings with attay from the story Kasik had told her. The word had spoken to her then, and it spoke to her now, a gentle murmur that brushed the edges of her soul with truth and knowing. But Nina wasn't supposed to be there, and she certainly wasn't powerful. They had come for Sacha, and she had offered herself in her sister's place. What a coincidence it might be that they had collected an Ikara as they had done for centuries before.

Unless they knew, and it was truly Nina's own ignorance and lack of self-control that led her there.

"You can heal him, Nina. You could save his life, or you could take it and free yourself."

Nina shook her head. "Only the gods can do such a thing," she whispered.

"A god's power resides within you, if only you are brave enough to accept it."

Nina scoffed. "I am not brave," she firmly said, remembering the regret and whispered pleading she had made to the gods. "There is nothing to accept."

Shayim shrugged her shoulders. "Then he will die."

"I know exactly what I need. My mamay taught me and if you—"

"He is beyond your plants and prayers, Nina."

She stiffened. Her hand tightened into a fist by her side. "Let me *try*. You would allow him to die to prove your point?"

"It's *you* who is doing so in fighting your true nature."

Kasik twitched. His breathing paused, and Nina turned with dread, waiting for his chest to rise again. It did, but the moments in between felt like an eternity. She closed her eyes and exhaled.

If there *was* attay within her, Nina had no idea how to find it, but more importantly, it would mean that her life had been a lie. Her entire childhood was comprised of moments when she thought she was losing her mind, where she would close her eyes tight and count to ten and hope that when she opened them, the golden threads swirling in the air would be gone. Times where she would rest her head on her mamay's lap and beg to know what was wrong with her.

You must learn to control yourself, her mamay would say. A different version of the same idea every single time. Nina had thought it comforting then. Now she saw it for what it was.

The hiding, the avoidance, the distractions. Had they always known, or were they drowning in denial just as she was?

To learn the truth was her only option. If not, the unknown, the possibility, would eat her alive. "Fine," she said aloud. "I'll play your game."

"This is no game, girl. It is the will of the gods."

The dirt floor was cool beneath Nina's legs, and she was grateful for the length and thickness of the aclla robe. Kasik's body pressed against her side, and Shayim sat across from her. Moonlight drifted in from above and bathed them in a circle of pale blue light.

"The gods enjoy the chaos of challenge and the reward of adoration,"

Shayim began. "In order to achieve those, they imbued their creations with free will. Water will flow where it may choose. Fire will burn eagerly. Wind can be a gentle caress or devastation. And man can follow their greatest desires." She placed a hand to her chest and inhaled deeply. "Do you know of the gods-touched, the Ikara?" she asked.

With a curt nod, Nina said, "Kasik told me the story."

"I'm sure he did." Shayim folded her hands in her lap. "I will tell you the *truth*, but first, I will speak to you of your power." The woman leaned closer and pointed a finger at Nina's chest. "You have seen the light, yes? The golden threads?"

Nina said nothing, but her stunned silence was enough for Shayim to continue. "That thread is a person's life. Their *will*. It is the choices they have made and will continue to make. My attay allows me to See those choices like the quipu we use to send messages. Knots on threads. Even now, I can See what has led you here and that you will face many challenges ahead." Her gaze drifted to Nina's right, a hazy sheen settling over Shayim's vibrant brown eyes. "But you," she said, her attention snapping back to Nina's face. "You can hold those threads in your hands and bend them to *your* will."

Nina looked away, remembering all the instances of seeing threads of gold, faint yet present, mockingly close but impossible to grasp. The only times she had succeeded were when Sacha was in danger. That day beneath the raging sea. The boys in the market.

And in Kasik, in the forest when he had walked ahead of her, a light that had beckoned her closer.

All along, she had held power in her hands. She had touched it, *used* it, and then just as easily disregarded it, preferring to believe that she was a child prone to delusion. She was mostly glad her illness didn't affect her like Sacha, content to ignore and repress all hints of confusion and strangeness to make it easier for their mamay.

It was Nina who had been lying to *herself*.

The saliva in her mouth had gone thick and sticky. She swallowed. "I've seen it, but it never stays long."

Shayim nodded slowly. "The more you use it, the more control you will develop, but there are also obstacles to consider, the first being internal. You are not an endless well of power. Using too much attay at once will drive you to madness. I spent most of my childhood in and out of consciousness as my body adapted to Seeing so many threads of life. The second thing to consider is external." She gestured to Kasik. "He wears the achilla around his neck, as do all of the emperor's men. It prevents the Ikara from touching their wills with harmful intent."

A stone forged by the gods to offer protection from those who wish to harm us. The woman in the market hadn't been lying. The stones did protect from harm, just not in the way Nina had thought.

"You can heal him, if you truly wish to, but if there's even the smallest seed of doubt, the stone will protect him. Of course," Shayim mused, "you could simply remove it. Or do nothing at all, since he is already at death's door."

Nina stared at Kasik, at the stutter of his breaths and the beads of sweat rolling down his temple. He had been so full of life not long ago, and now there she was with his life in her hands. How strange it was to have the power to choose, and what a privilege. The choices she had made that led her there were fraught with fear and obligation. *Responsibility.* She had lectured Kasik about how different they were, and all along, it might have been that they were exactly the same.

Nina had a duty to her sister, to her family. Kasik's honor belonged to his emperor, and it was clear they were both willing to risk their lives for those they served. Now Nina was being given the chance to determine whether Kasik's existence served *her* purpose. She could let nature take its course and be free of blame. Just another charge under the emperor's rule who had lost his life in service.

But would she be blameless if she sat back and did nothing, knowing she had the power to do *something*? Even if it didn't work. Even if her efforts were in vain and she was only saving him to settle a debt.

Whatever the reason, the thought of losing Kasik filled her with dread. She told herself it could have been anyone and she'd feel the same, but Nina was beginning to understand that she had become too adept at lying to herself. "What do I do?" she finally asked.

"Close your eyes," Shayim instructed. Nina let go of her distrust and denial, let herself float in the sea of renewal, and obeyed. Shayim continued. "Now focus on Kasik and your intentions for him. Imagine you can see his source of will and it will show itself to you."

Nina took a deep breath. In her mind, she saw herself applying the medicinal paste to Kasik's back, worrying over the heat of his skin and the streaks of infection that had begun to spread. She remembered the way his arms had held her beneath the tree, how she had felt protected in his embrace after the terror of facing the achiyanga. She imagined him whole and healthy once again.

"Ah, there it is," Shayim murmured, and when Nina opened her eyes, the room was aglow with a golden wash of light from the threads burning at the center of Kasik's chest. "To heal him, you will have to take control of his will. Convince it to bend to yours."

It was what she had been trying to do with her words since the moment he came to collect her. A battle of wills that she had been consistently losing. But this was different, and Nina could see exactly what needed to be done and how to do it. Shayim had been right that the threads were will, but they were also the essence of life. The core of who a person was—their wants and needs, dreams and hopes, fears and secrets, all inextricably twisted together.

It was the light of a god, a kernel of their power in each and every one of them, and Nina could grab on to it with fists clenched. She could squeeze and take and grind it into dust.

With that thought, Kasik's light dimmed, but across from her, Shayim's light stayed bright and malleable. "You don't wear a stone," Nina said, staring intently at her chest, mesmerized by the strength and possibility of that vibrant light.

"I do not require protection from the Ikara," Shayim snapped, and Nina's head jerked back to her face. "Now, focus."

Nina breathed deeply and homed in on her intentions. They pierced through to Kasik's will like a knife sharpened by desperation, igniting the dim threads until they were burning so brightly that Nina thought the whole world might see. Power coursed through her. Into her mind and heart and fingers until she was reaching out and trailing a hand through that burning light, fully expecting it to scald her skin.

His will was hers to command. And Nina finally fully understood that she had never been powerless a day in her life.

"Carefully command his body to heal," Shayim urged. "A gentle encouragement toward life."

But there was nothing gentle about the way Nina's power moved. It was greedy. *Hungry.* The threads of Kasik's will were spread out before her mind's eye like a tapestry, and Nina was the weaver, her attay like a needle that slipped beneath the threads of flesh and bone and sinew, spreading until he was consumed with her will, with her desires come alive. She didn't encourage so much as devour.

Right before her eyes, Kasik's wounds began to heal. The dark of infection bled away to light. Torn sinew mended and fused from inside out. Skin was cooled and tension eased.

She was *saving* him. Attay coursed through her, the strength of life in her hands headier than any feeling. Never could she remember feeling so complete.

“That’s enough, Nina,” Shayim said, but Nina was lost to her efforts, drowned beneath waves of power and purpose and awe as the broken pieces of Kasik’s body mended. She felt like a god then, giving life and forcing fate to bow at her feet. The rush of it, the pure thrill of possibility—she could have reveled in it for eternity.

“Nina, that’s enough!” a voice insisted, but it was distant and unimportant. All that mattered was this attay at her fingertips. It felt like a well within her, vast and endless, and yet, she could see the end clearly. Realized only too late that she didn’t know how to stop, and as she poured all her will into healing Kasik, her own body began to shut down, as if it were being sucked dry.

She would have given her life for Kasik right then, just as she had given her life for Sacha, but strong hands grabbed her face and somehow also grabbed her attay and shoved it back into her body, where it wound into a tight spool, contently sated, and went to sleep.

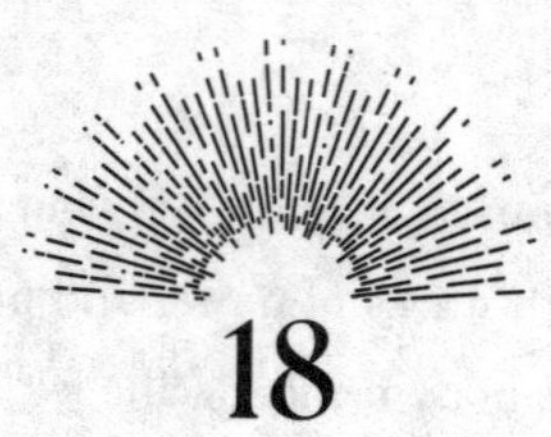

18

The soft, familiar sounds of life came to him in a wave first distant, then closer as it rose and crashed on a shore of awareness. Kasik shot out of sleep in a panic, Nina's name on his lips like a plea.

His hands were bound again, this time behind his back. By some stroke of luck or fate—he couldn't decide which he preferred—he was alive.

There had been dreams and voices in his near-death slumber. His mamay's, specifically.

And Nina's hands on his face, his name on her lips, her fingers digging in his head and rearranging everything he thought he knew and wanted.

Vague memories washed over him until he wasn't sure what was real and what was his mind breaking in half. The room spun, and he tried in vain to calm his breathing. He would have grabbed on to his achilla if he had hands to do so with. When he finally stopped to take in his surroundings, he realized he wasn't alone in the sparsely furnished tent.

Across the way was a bed identical to his, and atop that bed was a small body curled into a ball, dark hair spilling over the side and brushing the ground. He blinked once, twice to clear his sight, but he would have recognized Nina anywhere and from any distance.

One hand was tucked beneath her head, and the other hung off, palm up and fingers slack. He had stared at those hands wrapped around Capac's seat, and then his arms, and the stick she had used to build a fire. Never had he seen them so open.

Pressure began to build in his chest, an indescribable desire to slip his hand into hers, to feel her heartbeat beneath his fingertips. *Just to ensure she's alive*, he told himself.

But he was terrified of the possibility that she wasn't. That his failure would end up with her dead instead of him.

Kasik gathered what little strength he had gained and slid his legs off the bed, testing his weight on both before standing.

He stumbled toward her and fell to his knees at her bedside. He lowered his forehead to Nina's and murmured her name gently, quiet enough so only she could hear, the urgency in his bones bleeding out of him to make her name as sharp as a prayer. "Wake up, Nina."

He heard Nina's voice echoing his words.

His mamay's voice beckoning him near.

A woman's voice tinged with fear.

Dreams or memories, he couldn't tell. It felt as though he was losing his mind.

Beneath his forehead, he felt Nina shift. He pulled away and exhaled deeply when he saw one of her wide brown eyes open through the curtain of her hair.

"Kasik?" she whispered in awe. The hand that had been relaxed and open came up to touch his eyebrow, soft fingers trailing along his temple and cheek and jaw, burning a path down his neck and then his chest, where she pressed her palm firmly. Her other hand pushed aside her hair, and she stared at him as if he were a spirit.

"You're alive. I did it," she said, the words filled with a reverence reserved for the gods.

That must have been how he was alive. The poultice she made had worked after all. But it wasn't himself he was worried about. "Have they touched you? Are you hurt?" Kasik wished his hands were free to press against her neck, to feel her pulse and warmth for himself.

"I'm fine," she reassured. "They haven't touched me."

Kasik felt his chest loosen with relief, all the tension coiled within him, the uncertainty, breathed out with his next exhale. "You should consider becoming a healer once we leave this place. Perhaps the emperor can make arrangements for you to study with Master Wara."

Nina's brow furrowed, and she removed her hand from Kasik's chest. He felt adrift without it. "A healer? So, you know?"

"About medicinal plants? We can talk more about it later, but we must go *now*, before—"

"No." Nina sat upright, her hair tumbling down to cover her shoulders and chest. "No, we can't leave," she said. "Not yet. Look at you, bound and weak. We need rest."

Kasik could feel the burn of embarrassment color his neck. It was something Samaq had said gave away his true feelings, something his tayta had laughed at. *Control yourself, Son. Your insecurity is showing.*

"I don't think you understand just how badly we *must* leave. The emperor will not wait long for us to appear before he comes looking, and then he will find that we've been kept against our will and destroy this place without blinking. If he finds that we've purposely extended our stay? The consequences will be grave."

The uncertainty in Nina's eyes made him feel terrible, but the resolve in her shoulders softened into acceptance and he knew he had won. "One more day. Then we can make up for lost time on the road." She paused for a moment, eyes going distant in thought. "They have achipumas. Perhaps we can borrow one."

"Borrow, or steal?" Kasik asked with a quiet laugh. But nothing about this sat right. They had been ambushed, and Kasik had been beaten and questioned. He wondered why he was there, in the same space as Nina, both of them alive.

This wasn't how prisoners were treated in Vira. It felt like he was many steps behind and missing many pieces. Nina was staring at him, her eyes wide and imploring. Kasik sighed. "One more day," he agreed, unable to deny her.

It was true that he needed the time. Though he was alive, he felt barely able to stay upright as he was, on his knees at Nina's bedside. At the very least, another day would give him the time to figure out where they were, who these people in green belonged to, and if they were enemies of the empire. Gathering information would be a good excuse should he need to explain their stay to Emperor Maicu.

"Kasik." Nina said his name so softly that he felt it like a caress, the scent of her washing over him as she leaned even closer.

It struck him suddenly, the positions they were in. Her unbound and hovering over him, hair falling to create a privacy that felt intimate in a way he had never experienced before. Him on his knees looking up at her, throat and chest exposed, wanting so badly to tear the binds away so that he could use his hands to—

"Good, you're awake."

They quickly moved apart as if caught, Kasik spinning around to place himself face-to-face with the man who had *interrogated* him only hours—or days?—before. He had lost all sense of time, but he knew that voice and that face no matter how many hours had passed.

The man pulled out a knife and stepped closer. Kasik's entire body buzzed with anticipation. Nina's small gasp set his fury alight. He would rip this man apart limb from limb, somehow. In this life or the next.

"Easy." The man held up his hands. "I'm just going to cut your ties. Unless you'd prefer to stay bound. We can arrange that."

Kasik eyed him warily. "I don't trust you," he spoke through gritted teeth.

The man smiled. "Likewise. But this isn't about us." He glanced at Nina, who stiffened behind him. "Shayim wants to speak with you again."

Again? Kasik wondered, but he felt Nina's hand on his shoulder quieting his thoughts. "It's okay," she murmured to him. "They won't hurt us."

How do you know? he wanted to ask, but he kept quiet long enough to consider what it would mean to have his hands freed. Whatever their intentions, this worked in his favor as well. With a sigh, he shifted his hands as far to the side as possible. The man approached and crouched before him. Kasik could see a muscle in his jaw jump and knew the feeling well.

Frustration. This man wasn't in control any more than he was.

Once Kasik's hands were free, the man stepped away and watched as Kasik shakily pushed to his feet. Nina's arm wrapped around his waist, and it was with her strength that he managed to stay upright.

"There are clothes over there to change into." The man nodded toward a bundle at the foot of the bed. "Come outside once you've changed."

Nina and Kasik stayed where they were until he was gone, and then Nina was guiding him to sit on the bed. Her hands left him, and though he felt stronger than before, the loss of her touch was almost a physical ache. His body yearned for its return.

Kasik took a deep breath. He had to pull himself together.

"Where are we?" he asked. Nina shook out the clothes and handed him the larger tunic.

"It's a camp of sorts. I'm not entirely sure, but I know they won't hurt us." Nina's movements paused. Kasik watched her and waited for the rest of her thoughts. How strange that he knew her well enough to know there was more. "Shayim helped me. *Us.* In exchange, I told her I would hear what she has to say."

"And you believe her?"

Nina slid on a pair of dark green pants underneath her robes and reached for the hem to lift over her head. Kasik pulled the tunic she had handed him over his head just in time, heart thumping with something he wasn't quite familiar with. "I know it sounds crazy," she said. "But I trust her. And I need you to trust me."

The thing was, he did. She had come back for him and saved his life as many times as he had saved hers. There was a balance between them that he couldn't describe, and he knew that no amount of persuasion would change her mind. He also knew that he did not have it in him to force her hand.

"At the very least, you can see the camp and plot our escape," she added.

Kasik looked up to find her dressed in a bold green tunic, the color a compliment to her burnished gold skin. Her eyes trailed over him, taking in his face and hair that hung loose around his shoulders, lingering on his chest where his heart raced beneath his bones. There was something like pride in her eyes, as if he were a piece of art and she the artist, and also a spark of hunger that set Kasik's skin on fire.

Nina cleared her throat and looked away. Kasik took the opportunity to tug his pants off over his boots, grateful that he was sitting. Once dressed, he pushed himself up again. Nina rushed to brace him, but he found that he felt stronger than before.

"I'm all right," he told her gently.

She nodded, their faces close, and smiled. "Ready?"

Kasik nodded, even though he felt anything but.

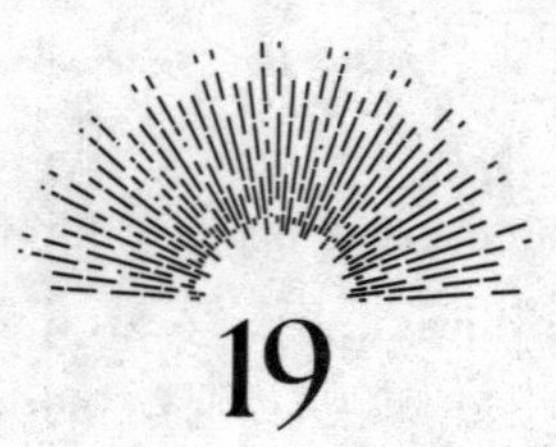

19

Nina didn't understand how, exactly, she had healed Kasik. The memory of it felt like a dream that faded the longer she was awake.

The attay was there, simmering in her veins, and though she felt as if she had only just peered beneath the surface, she knew the implications of this power would change the course of her life all the same.

More than anything, Nina wanted answers. An explanation. Shayim seemed more than willing to guide her, but Nina only wondered how she could use it to her benefit, and what it would cost her. What was she expected to do with this gods-given power?

It felt like shackles around her wrists dragging her toward an unknown future, like any hope she had in returning to her once-normal, boring life was dissipating into the wind. No longer was she a forgotten nobody. No longer could she claim ignorance.

This power and the choices that came with it were hers to command.

As she and Kasik walked through the camp, she felt the pressure of curious eyes on her, and she returned their attention tenfold. In each of their chests were threads of light calling to her and begging to be used. Nina swallowed and glanced at Kasik, who was also watching and assessing everyone they passed, a furrow between his brow and his hands balled into fists at his sides as if an enemy might spring upon them at any moment.

What a pair they made, each seeing something entirely different. Where Nina saw life, Kasik saw threats. He was wary, and it made her wary. How much longer could they remain without consequence?

Hatun stalked ahead of them, his contempt clear with every step he took. Nina had no doubt he would kill them if it was his choice. But it wasn't. It seemed that Shayim was the leader of this group, and it was Shayim she needed more answers from.

The woman had known about her attay. More than that, she knew how it worked and had some of her own. There were more people like her. She wasn't alone, and she had one day to learn the answers to all her questions.

Hatun led them toward the large fire at the center of the camp. There were other people milling about, but most were seated on stools or on the ground, steaming bowls of food in their hands. They all wore varying shades of green, and the tents were green to match the trunks of the trees. The space was open but somehow closed off at the same time. A thick canopy of leaves provided shade from above.

It was beautiful here. Peaceful. It made her feel at home.

Kasik's shoulder brushed hers and she was tempted to lean into his touch, to take from him the strength and confidence he seemed to exude despite the precarious situation they were in. Once again, she wondered what it felt like to navigate life with such faith. How he kept on his feet when it felt as though everything was set on tearing them down.

Hatun came to an abrupt stop and gestured vaguely to the right. Nina saw Shayim seated alone on a large tree trunk, a bundle of strings in her lap and her lips moving silently as her fingers ran over a thread.

"He doesn't seem to like you very much," Nina murmured once Hatun was out of range.

"The feeling is mutual." Kasik shifted closer, his body blocking Nina's line of sight to Shayim. "We don't know what they want, so be careful what you say. It's best we keep who you are to ourselves."

Nina looked into his eyes and saw the sincerity in them. Always committed to keeping her safe. *His duty*, she reminded herself. But she agreed that it served no purpose to disclose her role in their strange relationship of emperor's betrothed and protector. "I won't tell," she agreed, and the furrow between his brow softened the smallest bit.

They walked to where Shayim sat. She watched them approach with a serene smile. "Sit," she said, pointing to the bench across from her. "You look much better than the last time I saw you."

"She helped me heal you," Nina clarified for Kasik. He nodded but said nothing. The tension in the air felt like sludge, making everything seem slower and louder than it was. Nina opened her mouth to fill the awkward silence when a girl appeared with two bowls of porridge.

"Thank you, Mika," Shayim said.

The girl looked about Nina's age, with copper skin and short brown hair. Her green tunic was darker than the others, and around her waist was a thin piece of fabric embroidered with familiar pink flowers and red-and-green birds. A gold band hung from her wrist, and she smiled when she saw Nina inspecting it. "I can make you one, if you'd like."

"I'd love that," Nina said, surprised and delighted by the offer. She reminded Nina of Sacha, with her bright eyes and infectious smile and the way she always made others feel seen and included. Nina felt as though she could never get a proper read on people. She was always unsure of motives and emotions, constantly withdrawing to decipher her own thoughts and feelings, but the girl's intent was plain as day.

"I'll find you later," she said before walking off. Nina watched her go and was nearly blinded by the force of the girl's will. How easy it would be to wield.

Next to her, Kasik shifted, and his thigh brushed hers. The touch grounded her.

"It's always interesting," Shayim said unexpectedly, "to See certain choices made. I'm endlessly surprised by how the threads shift."

Nina froze and leveled a look at the woman, trying to convey a message without words. She felt Kasik glance at her, then back to Shayim. "What is that supposed to mean?"

Shayim's mouth tipped into a secretive smile. "Only that life is like a tapestry, and weaving is an intricate and tedious affair. One stitch, one small misstep, can make all the difference."

"Then you understand why we need to leave as soon as possible," Kasik said. "One day can set us far from our intended path."

"Tell me, Kamayuq." Shayim shifted forward, elbows on knees, and stared intently into Kasik's eyes. "Should I allow you to leave now that you have seen this place?"

"I'm not entirely sure what 'this place' is, or where exactly we are. Cover our eyes and lead us out. We'll be sure to never return."

"And if I don't?" Nina felt Kasik tense with Shayim's words. She wondered, if he had a weapon, would it have been in his hands then? "Cover your eyes, that is," Shayim added. "Will you scurry back to your emperor and tell him what you have seen? What is the weight of your word?"

"My *word*," Kasik started, his tone sharp, "is all that I am. And my loyalty lies with Emperor Maicu. As it always has and always will." He peered at Nina, a quick, sidelong glance that softened the tension in his jaw. "But I admit to knowing little and remembering even less in these last few days. Especially if you allow us to take an achipuma with us when we go."

Shayim smiled and leaned back. "Clever boy," she said. Her eyes flicked to Nina and away. "And are you loyal to her?"

Nina pressed her lips together, waiting for an answer she knew better than to want. Kasik was loyal to the emperor only, she staunchly reminded herself. Despite the fact that they had saved each other's lives, and despite the bond that came from such a thing. That was the only reason she hoped.

"It is *because* I am loyal to her that I honor my word," Kasik said, his voice dangerously low, the conviction in it sending chills up Nina's arms. "Anything else would put many lives in jeopardy."

The sounds of the camp seemed to fade into the distance. It was only the three of them surrounded by a vast forest and an uncertain path out.

"Kamayuq Kasik," Shayim said. His title sounded more like a taunt than an honorific. "Is that a threat?"

"It is a promise. If anything happens to us, Emperor Maicu will find you all, and he will not be as forgiving as I am."

Shayim chuckled and shook her head, but her mirth set Nina on edge. It felt like whatever she said next would push them over an invisible line. "Your tayta's temperament simmers beneath that carefully constructed facade."

It was Nina's turn to glance at Kasik in confusion. He was eerily still, animosity pouring off him in waves. Nina was certain now that if he had been armed, they all would have been in danger. But it was no coincidence that Shayim made that comment, and Nina was eager to find out what it meant.

"Whatever you think you know about me or my tayta will not change anything. Do not believe that I am so easily distracted," Kasik seethed.

Anyone else might have turned away from his anger, but Shayim leaned closer. "There are many secrets between us," she said softly. "But I will share one so that there is one less. Once upon a time, I served Emperor Yachua. My sister was betrothed to him, and we journeyed to the capital together. Her name was Aliyma, and you are a spitting image of her."

Kasik stood abruptly, his bowl of porridge splattering to the ground. Nina gasped and slid sideways.

"Do *not*—"

"I served as the emperor's Seer," Shayim interrupted, her voice firmer than before. "A position that made me more powerful than your tayta, much to his dismay."

"Now I know you lie," Kasik seethed. "There is no such thing as a 'Seer.'"

"I can assure you there is," Shayim said pointedly.

"I have been beside the emperor for *years*. I would know if there are Seers, or—"

"I never said there still *were*," Shayim said sadly. "Only that there *was*. You can choose to believe me or not, but consider whether you know as much as you think you do, or if you only know what you have been told."

Nina watched Kasik closely, ready to reach over and . . . what? Comfort him? Sheild him? She only knew that his body had stiffened before her very eyes, and what was at first confusion and then curiosity had morphed into something colder and sharper, as if he had come to a decision and would not be persuaded otherwise.

"I need some air," he said before stomping away.

Nina watched him go and fought the urge to follow.

"The achilla around his neck," Shayim said, turning to Nina. "Did he tell you where it is from?"

"It was his mamay's," she said quietly.

Shayim snorted. "It seems as though he's been led to believe many false things. And you, Nina from Limac, what do you believe?"

Nina thought of all the things she had been led to believe. The sacrifices she had made because she had thought they were her only choices. If she had been more aware of her attay when the emperor's men had come for her, would she have given in so easily? Could she have used it to do something more than surrender?

She could still feel the golden thread of Kasik's will within her hands, the way it had fallen under her complete control, and wondered what else her power could do.

"I don't know anymore, but I'd like to find out."

Shayim smiled. "Then you've been led to the right place, my child."

20

Kasik stalked through the encampment, surprised that nobody stopped him. In fact, they seemed to keep far away from him, casting questioning glances his way while he did the same to them.

They should have blindfolded him. They should have kept him restrained in the tent.

Every sight he took in was damning evidence of a community shirking the payment for the emperor's protection. They were an ayllu without recognition. A people without law.

Even if it seemed like the opposite. There were children running by with little care to look where they were going. Adolescents carried baskets full of food and clothing. A boy walked by with an achipuma, and Kasik, struck with determination, turned sharply to follow.

They passed by several tents, some with their entrances pinned open and flowers planted around the perimeter, before turning onto a wide path that led closer to the tree line. A fenced pasture came into view. In one corner was a wooden lean-to on a small plot of grass, and lounging in the shade underneath the lean-to was a familiar beast.

Two, actually.

Capac and Illari looked as though they hadn't a single care in the world. Kasik looked around, wondering if the bandits who stole Illari were nearby. He was itching for a fight, but there was only the boy with a bucket of food in his arms and the curious glances he sent Kasik's way.

With a sigh, Kasik turned back to the enclosure and whistled low. Capac's ears twitched. Illari lifted her head. They both stared at him, unbothered and uninterested, before Illari slowly got to her feet and left Capac behind to greet him. He could hear her purr even from where he stood as she lowered her head to be scratched between the ears. He imagined it had been this easy for the bandits to gain her trust.

It was said that, long ago, achipumas were companions and protectors of the gods, ferocious and fierce hunters that tore apart any being that presented the smallest threat to their master. Kasik watched Illari roll onto her back and present her belly, and he shook his head. They served their purpose, but whatever ferociousness they possessed before was long gone after hundreds of years of pampering.

A moment later, Kasik's hand was pushed aside and Illari's belly was replaced with Capac's head. Kasik smiled. His feline friend had always been jealous.

"Hey, boy," Kasik cooed. Capac shoved his head underneath Kasik's arm and demanded to be scratched. "I missed you, too."

It wasn't that he had doubted whether the achipuma was alive—he had no doubt that Capac could adapt and survive in the Tuta Kulla—but they had never been separated for so long since Kasik was a small child, and Capac even smaller.

Master Wara had taught him that achipumas did not bond with their humans, that they belonged to the gods and the emperor alone. But Kasik didn't believe it. Not when Capac was in his face, his pitch-black eyes boring into Kasik as if to say, *Where have you been?* and all the outrage and turmoil that swirled in Kasik's chest was soothed with the gentle rumble of Capac's purr.

The happiness of the reunion was short-lived, though, when Kasik felt a presence at his side.

"He hasn't let anyone get near him."

Hatun held out a hand, and Capac bared his wickedly sharp teeth at it. Kasik couldn't help but laugh.

"He's incredibly loyal," Kasik said proudly. "Unlike that one." He nodded toward Illari, who had moved on to the boy and was being hand-fed a piece of raw meat.

"With time and reason, loyalties can change," Hatun said pointedly.

Kasik stiffened. Capac nudged his hand to encourage him to keep scratching. "Loyalties only change for those with traitorous hearts. Capac has been with me since we were both very young. He knows my heart as I know his."

Hatun hummed. "But a man's heart is fickle. They make promises they cannot keep and want things they cannot have."

Kasik turned to challenge Hatun, but the man was paying him no mind, his eyes pinned to a point behind him and toward camp. Out of curiosity, Kasik followed his gaze and found Shayim and Nina walking down the center of two rows of brown and green tents, every so often stopping to talk to a child running by or a woman with a basket full of fruit.

Nina stood apart from Shayim, and Kasik could see, even from a distance, that there was a small smile on her face. That her body leaned forward while also trying to give them space. She watched the faces of those who spoke, and she waved at a small child who glanced her way and then ran away giggling.

Behind that tenacious and hardened exterior, he saw someone who wanted to belong. Someone whose convictions were at odds with the expectations placed on her shoulders.

Someone like him.

"I keep my promises," Kasik said. He turned back to Hatun again, certainty heavy on his tongue. "They are all I am."

"Yes, but it's not about the promises we make," he said. "It's about who we make them to."

Hatun clapped him on the shoulder as he passed by. Kasik stayed rooted in place, jaw tense, his mind racing with Hatun's words. Capac had given up on him and joined Illari where she lay licking her paws. The sky was clear and the air was crisp with the scent of winter. He hoped the calm weather would last until they made it back to Vira.

If we make it back to Vira, he thought, and he wasn't sure why. There was no other choice—not for him or for Nina. He wasn't lying when he told her that Emperor Maicu would find them. The man was singularly focused on whatever fleeting fancy caught his attention.

It seemed that, this time, it was a new wife, and whatever his reasons, Kasik knew he was willing to do anything to see it come to fruition. And if he found an ayllu hidden deep in the Tuta Kulla, in an area that he thought conquered and claimed, thriving without the promise of his protection? That had slipped under his watchful eye? Kasik shuddered to think of the repercussions.

Again, he wished they had kept him tied up in that tent, blind to all *this*. Their freedom was a threat, but more than that, it was a lie. Just as Shayim's words.

The Ikara were violent and monstrous, and Seers were a twisted myth born from generations of rumors and desperate wishes. Her claim to possessing such a vast power undermined every word she said.

If she truly had served Emperor Yachua, why wasn't she at Emperor Maicu's side? And if she was his mamay's sister, why had she abandoned Kasik to his tayta? Why stay hidden with these people? Unless she had done something unforgivable, something so atrocious that she had been forced away.

And he had left Nina with her.

Kasik pushed off the enclosure and frantically searched for her face among strangers. The wholesome community from before had morphed into a trap. Every tent was a possible prison. Every tool a weapon. His hand automatically went to the tumi at his hip to find it gone. How stupid he had been to let them disarm him so easily. With or without a weapon, he would find Nina and he would tear down anyone who got in his way.

There was no other choice. He had given too much of himself to fail Emperor Maicu now.

"Kasik?" He knew it was her before he whirled around. He would recognize her voice anywhere, had heard it even in his dreams. Kasik feared he would never get used to his name in her mouth, the way its hard edges softened, the way it made him want to drop to his knees and beg her to say it again. "Is everything all right?" she asked.

Nina seemed perfectly fine, besides the furrow in her brow as her eyes touched every part of him. She had one hand extended toward him and the other wrapped in her tunic. There were no shadows over her face and her eyes practically glowed with happiness. She was perfectly unharmed. The only danger there was *him*.

Kasik swallowed and stepped closer. "Can we speak privately?" he asked, glancing at Shayim, who stood a few paces away, watching them with those strange, shrewd eyes.

"Of course," Nina replied, but her words were hesitant, and she nodded imperceptibly toward Shayim. It was strange how much that small gesture reminded him so much of Samaq. How he knew exactly what Nina was telling Shayim without words. He wondered if she trusted everyone she met so easily, and it was only him she saved her disdain for.

Instead of being worried, he was only annoyed. *Jealous.* Kasik wanted Nina's implicit trust. He wanted that wordless language. What a fool he was.

Nina followed him between two tents, past the edge of the clearing and into the line of trees that soared above and blocked the sun. The brush wasn't as thick in this part of the forest, and there were bright orange-and-pink flowers shooting up from the ground in random clumps that spread farther than he could see. Emperor Maicu had the same flowers in his garden at Amaru Kancha, except they were smaller and shorter and more . . . contained.

These flowers were unrestrained, and they grew stronger for it. It made him wonder what would happen to Nina if she stayed in a place like this.

Hands on his hips, Kasik turned to face Nina. Her arms were crossed over her chest, and she leaned heavily on her right leg. Her hair was in two braids, one over each shoulder, the ends tied with a thin piece of twine. In her dark eyes, he saw himself reflected.

"I think it's best if we leave sooner than we planned," Kasik said quickly. "Tonight, if possible."

"What? Why?" Nina's eyes narrowed. "We agreed to wait," she said. "You needed to gain back your strength, and I told Shayim I would listen to what she had to say."

"I think you've heard plenty." Kasik gestured over her head, back toward camp and the chatter and bustle of people and life. "And what she has to say matters very little to our plans."

"Why are you being like this?"

"In case you've forgotten, they took us against our will, beat me, threatened you, and are keeping us captive. I'm not being anything other than reasonable."

He saw the way Nina pulled away from him, and he prepared himself for what she was going to say. This was the look exchanged between her and Shayim. This was the thing he did not know and would not like. "I want to stay," Nina said in a rush.

"Stay?" Kasik repeated like the fool he was.

"I know we agreed to leave but I need to—"

"What you *need* to do is listen. You cannot stay." Nina opened her mouth to argue, but Kasik stepped closer and bent so that they were at eye level. "Do you think the emperor will not find this place when he comes looking for you?"

"That's the thing," she said excitedly. "Shayim explained that with her attay, she's able to change perception. The camp is hidden from those who do not know of it. That's why they were so surprised when they found us, and why they were so eager to know how we had found *them*. We are meant to be here, Kasik. I know it."

How Kasik wished he could carve her smile into his skin. He knew his next words would tear it apart and he would likely never see it again. "No, Nina. You know *nothing*. We were only led here because the achiyanga set us off course. This was an ill-fated coincidence. Nothing more." Kasik straightened and pinned his gaze over her head, afraid that Nina would be able to hear the lie in his voice. He hardly believed his own words, but he knew that if he did not say them, he would lose this fight. In fact, he might lose it regardless. "If I leave you here and return to the emperor empty-handed, do you think he will not demand to know the truth?"

"You can *lie*. It's not that difficult."

"Just as you've lied all this time?" he said sharply. Nina's mouth snapped shut, and he stepped away, unable to curb his hurt. "Did you ever plan to return with me, or were you simply biding your time for the perfect opportunity for escape to present itself?"

"If that were the case," Nina said, her voice just as sharp, "I would have let you be eaten alive by the achiyanga. Or not bothered to heal your wounds."

"I think you did those things to appease your own conscience. But what will happen when my death, and the deaths of all these people, are on your hands simply because you refuse to accept your fate? I cannot lie, Nina. If the emperor asks a question, I am bound by my duty to the empire to speak the truth."

"Well, I am not." She crossed her arms and stared into his eyes. She was unyielding in that moment. "And I never agreed to your plans, or the emperor's. I want to make my own choice. I want to stay here. I want to be *free*."

"These people are not *free*," Kasik spat. "They are trapped by their choices just as you and I are. These trees are the bars of their cage, and when the emperor finds it, because he will—attay or no attay—they will all be burned for it. I watched him murder his brother in cold blood to get what he wanted. You are a fool if you think what you want matters. *You* are what the emperor wants, and he will never allow you to slip through his grasp."

Kasik's chest heaved with the force of his words. They were just as much a reminder for him as they were for her.

Nina said nothing in return, but the way her eyes shifted between his, soft with seeking at first, then hard with determination, exposed her every thought.

Who are you? her tear-stained eyes said.

Why have I ever trusted you? her quivering lips said.

I loathe you, her body said.

So be it. Kasik loathed himself, too.

21

Nina stomped away from Kasik without looking back. Her hands shook by her sides, not from anger, but from the force of her disappointment. It was too much to expect Kasik to understand. She knew he was bound by duty and loyal to a fault, that he wouldn't abandon his word for her.

And yet, Nina had foolishly hoped. He had said he was loyal to her, but what he had meant was that he was loyal to her *fate*.

Now she knew too much of the truth to go against it. If staying meant that she was consigning all these people to death, she would have no other choice than to leave, to follow the path set out before her, even if she wanted nothing more than to carve her own.

Shayim was speaking to a woman with shoulder-length hair, the green of her tunic darker than Nina's, and longer, more like a dress. The same flowers and birds that Nina had seen on Mika decorated the edges of the woman's tunic, and instead of a cinch at her waist, her belly swelled with child.

Nina remembered when her mamay was expectant with Lali. She had come early, just days after Samaq was taken, and Nina, only seven at the time, had been awestruck by the strength of her mamay. Together, they had dug a hole deep into the earth and planted the afterbirth, right next to where Nina's, Sacha's, and Samaq's had been planted.

In that place, four trees had grown tall and thick with leaves. They stood sentinel over Nina's small limestone house, and provided shade for play and afternoon meals. They had been a source of pride for her mamay and tayta. A sign that said, *Look how blessed we are.*

Nina wondered if they now served as a reminder of everything they had lost.

"I have to begin preparations for Jana's birthing," Shayim said to Nina. She pointed at a small tent. "There is where you will find Mika. She'll tell you more."

About what? Nina wanted to ask, but Shayim was already guiding Jana away, leaving Nina to stand among the bustle of a world she didn't recognize. Rocks skittered underfoot as she rushed to the tent Shayim had pointed to and stopped at the entrance, deliberating whether to announce herself or just walk in or leave altogether.

"I can see your shadow," a voice called from inside. "If you don't come in now, I'll be offended."

Nina winced and inhaled deeply. She pushed aside the flap to find Mika sitting cross-legged in the middle of the tent surrounded by rocks and unfamiliar tools. In one corner was a narrow bed and in the other, a small table, similarly covered in items Nina couldn't name.

"Don't mind the mess," Mika said, then she pointed to the spot next to her. "Sit here. I need to measure your wrist."

Nina did as she was told. Mika took her wrist and wrapped a string around it, then used a small knife to cut it. It was done before Nina could think to be concerned about a knife so close to her pulse point. "You're very demanding," Nina said.

"I've been told," Mika said with a sigh. She plucked a yellow rock from a collection at her side and turned it this way and that. "Good enough." She closed it in a fist that she extended to Nina. "Did you know that every creation on this land has a thread of life, and that it is only the Ikara who can see those threads and tug at them? We can create and shape and bend to our will."

Nina fought the urge to flinch back as the small rock in Mika's hand began to shift from something jagged and misshapen to something first flat and smooth, then long and thin.

Mika's fingers were soft as they grabbed Nina's wrist again and bent the gold into place. When she was done, Nina wore a band identical to Mika's. "The difference between our attay is that while I can only see the threads of life, you can see the threads of life *and* will."

"How do you know?" Nina whispered, her heart beating hard enough to make her ears ring. The golden band was cold against her skin. It caught a spark of light from the hole in the ceiling of the tent and mirthfully winked.

"Shayim Saw in my threads that one with your power would come," she said with a mischievous glint. "Though she wasn't sure when or how. Apparently, I somehow convince you to practice your attay on me and we become fast friends because it is clear that I trust you with my life, and you want a friend more than you want to keep your secret."

A laugh burst out of Nina's mouth. She covered it quickly with both hands, embarrassed at the force of it, but Mika was smiling wide, a red flush blooming over her cheeks and neck.

"I think you should try it and see what happens."

"You aren't injured," Nina said, but she was already reaching for the girl's threads, eager to feel the power of healing once again. Like a compulsion she wasn't sure she could control.

"I don't need to be injured for you to use your attay." Nina snapped her eyes back to Mika's. The girl smiled wide. "You can do much more then heal." Mika grabbed her hand and pulled it close. "You are more powerful than you know. Trust me."

Perhaps Nina *was* a fool, just as Kasik had accused, because she wanted to believe this girl's words. So much so that she closed her eyes and reached for Mika's will. It was difficult to believe that nobody else could see what she saw, how the strands of gold slithered and danced in the air, waiting for her to wrap them around her fingers and command them where to go.

Nina could feel how with one tug, she could stop Mika's breath. Stop her throat from swallowing, her chest from inhaling, her blood from flowing.

The story Kasik had told her echoed in her thoughts, about the Ikara gone mad with power. She could understand. Mika's threads were luring her in, inviting her to take and bend till they broke. This power was more than just healing. It was devastation, and it was terrifying.

Nina wondered if she was alone in the strength of this power. If there were more like her, and if so, were they all capable of such destruction?

"Mika," Nina whispered, her eyes closed, the map of Mika's will burned to the back of her eyelids. "If you ever find yourself in possession of an achilla, make sure you wear it and never take it off." And then she, very carefully, healed a small cut on Mika's finger that took nothing more than a stitch of thought.

When she opened her eyes, Mika was gazing at her finger with something akin to awe. "I didn't even know it was there." She looked at Nina. "Is it difficult for you?"

Nina shook her head. "It's almost too easy. I wonder if it is so for all Ikara like me."

"That's the thing," Mika said. The girl leaned closer. "Shayim has said there are no others like you. That your attay is singular in its ability and strength."

It should have made Nina feel better, but all she felt was alone and unknown. Already, she was being dragged to Vira to become the emperor's wife, set apart from her family and her ayllu and other girls her age. A commodity in every way, even in this.

Mika must have sensed her spiraling thoughts, because she squeezed

Nina's hand between both of hers. "You are exactly where you should be. Your power—*you*—will change the world."

"I don't want to change the world." Nina pulled her hand back and stood. The band shifted down her wrist. She was suddenly too aware of the clothing against her skin, the hairs on her head, the power thrumming in her blood. "That's too much responsibility."

"This power was given to you because the gods believed you worthy of it. It doesn't—"

"The gods are selfish," Nina hissed. "They gave no thought to how these *abilities* might have us hunted and killed and used against us."

"Abilities?" Understanding dawned over Mika's face and she smiled. "You've only heard the walla's version of the Ikara. You don't know the full story." Mika patted the ground next to her and after a moment of stubborn hesitance, Nina sat. "It's not his fault. We can only know what we've been told until we are ready to seek what we *haven't*. I will tell you the truth of it. The Ikara that Killa and Pachamama created was named Yuri."

Mika shifted onto her bottom and crossed her long legs beneath her like a child settling in for a fireside story. "It is said that Yuri was violent, a bringer of destruction and devastation, and that was why the achilla and her counterpart, Dimas, were created. To quell her power and bring about peace.

"But Yuri was created to protect those that were powerless against the gods. Dimas was only a shell of a man, a vessel for the gods' will. He had none of his own. Inti and Viracocha took Yuri's righteous rage and twisted it to evil, and it was her that became the enemy. When Dimas found her and fell in love, because he saw that she was strong and good, the gods were threatened. Their power crumbled in the face of love, and so they whispered into his ear and convinced him that his love for her was a lie, that she had *tricked* him. They were afraid of her power, and they knew that he was weak enough to fall under their thrall again.

He had found free will when he chose love, and he lost it again when he chose betrayal. The gods' will filled him once again, and he killed Yuri as she slept next to him.

"Stories have always reduced women to madness and devastation, fear and defeat," Mika continued. "But we are so much more than that. We are renewal and reward. Hope and destiny. It is only women who are Ikara, who give and nurture life in all ways, and it is women who will always prevail."

Mika reached forward and adjusted the golden band on Nina's wrist. It was no longer cold against her skin.

"We are all connected. Remember that when you feel alone."

That evening, the fire Nina had seen burning continuously in the center of camp was surrounded by people both young and old. Children danced to the beat of drums. Adults drank celebratory chicha from wooden cups made by a young Ikara with deft fingers and a melodic laugh. Shayim watched it all from a stool nearby, her eyes alight with the flames and what Nina suspected was pride.

The woman had left the emperor's side. She had veered off the path set before her and carved out her own. More than that, she had created a world in which others were safe to do the same. Nina wondered how much Shayim had lost along the way, and if it had been worth it in the end.

Kasik thought the trees around them were a cage, but at least they had chosen it for themselves. It was all Nina wanted.

The emperor wanted a wife, but the kunay had made a mistake in accepting Nina in exchange for Sacha, who spoke kindly and supported generously and obeyed willingly. Not like Nina, who was filled with resentment and discontent, who was willing to find a way to keep her sister safe *and* fight the emperor's plans for her.

Despite her words to Kasik, obligation was obligation, whether done in love or otherwise, and she had been a fool to believe it made a difference. Nina wanted to protect her family, but she also wanted to be free. The memory of Mika's threads glowed in her mind. How easy it would have been to take them and crush them in one hand.

If she could learn to better wield her attay, then she could use it against the empire. She could take the path they had given her and bend it to her will, and it started with the emperor.

Nina now knew exactly what she had to do. She only wondered if she was capable of it.

A hand squeezed her shoulder, pulling her from her thoughts. She turned to find Mika, a smile in her eyes and a flower between two fingers. "Come dance," she pleaded, tucking the stem behind Nina's ear.

Nina took Mika's hand, and she twirled underneath the stars of a cloudless night, the warmth of the fire igniting her resolve. Despite the heat, a shiver crawled up her spine, and she knew without looking that Kasik was watching her. She was always aware of him and the weight of his gaze.

When she looked, he didn't look away. She raised her hands above her head and swayed back and forth, her eyes pinned to him in challenge. Everywhere his attention touched felt like invisible fingers trailing across her skin, an unfamiliar burn of want left behind.

Nina was filled with desire, with hunger, with the insatiable urge to draw her power forward. Perhaps her mamay had tried to convince her that strength laid in calm and control because she knew just how capable of destruction Nina was.

Perhaps it was time she stopped hiding. She was in possession of a different kind of power now. One that had the potential to change everything, if only she was brave enough to embrace it.

22

Firelight danced over Nina's skin. Even from a distance, Kasik could see the weight of the world on her shoulders, the way she cradled it as she twirled and danced to the drums. He couldn't keep his desire at bay. In that moment, he felt weaker than ever before, wanting for what he knew he could never have.

He was acutely aware of Nina's humanity. The soft shape of her, the sweat glistening on her skin, the way her chest heaved with excitement and pushed taut against her tunic. The flower in her hair that grew wild in the forests surrounding them, a riot of pink and orange and freedom that encompassed all that Nina was.

A bright spot in a wave of obscurity. A hand reaching beneath the surface to pull him up for air and remind him what it was to breathe.

The music began to slow, as did Nina's movements, until she was staring directly at him, eyes like an arrow piercing the space between them. Kasik watched her come closer in a daze, foolish hope filling his chest and head with thoughts that left him speechless. The fire at her back and the moonlight on her face made him think of vengeful gods and relentless mortals, and for a moment he thought it was a good thing that they were on the same side.

He pushed away from the tree he had been leaning against to greet her. It felt important that he was standing tall before her, no weaknesses on display.

"You were right," she said, suddenly close enough to touch. He wanted to reach out and run his fingers through her dark hair, loose and wild around her, but her face and body told him what he needed to know. This wasn't the Nina who was desperate for comfort. This was the Nina who was desperate for change, and her words were a double-edged weapon. A promise.

"They are not free," she said, a razor-sharp finger pointed behind her. Then at her chest. "But *I* will be."

Their gazes held, a storm of reckoning brewing between them, and Kasik realized then that they had never been on the same side and would never be. She was caged fury, insatiable curiosity, and relentless pursuit. The only reason she was still there was because she *allowed* it.

Kasik, on the other hand, was at the mercy of his masters, the gods and the emperor. She was a storm wielding transformation, and he was the boulder that never changed, never moved, and never grew.

The temptation to reach out, to touch her, to steal a taste of that power, was almost too much to bear, but it was Nina who stepped closer, her dark-as-night eyes glowing with moonlight. He wondered what she saw when she looked at him. If he disappointed her as much as he disappointed himself.

I cannot say no again, he thought to himself, *if she asks me to stay.*

Kasik could recognize the same resolve that filled him slip beneath the surface of Nina's features. Her eyes hardened with it, her mouth settling into a capricious grin. Kasik held his breath and waited for her judgment, but she only glanced at his mouth, and then turned and began walking away.

Peeling himself from his spot to follow her took effort. He felt disoriented. Like an animal on a tether. "Where are you going?" he asked.

"To get an achipuma. We must leave, right? No sense in waiting until the morning."

"Nina," he called after her. "It's not safe to travel right now."

She whirled around to face him, a tempest on the horizon. "Is anything safe? At least if I am killed by an achiyanga then I am free in some way. Your beloved Emperor Maicu can hardly fault you for that."

"It's not about that," he practically shouted at her. "There is no power in being dead. At least, as his wife, you will have the chance to create a life. Perhaps even create *change*, if you wished to." This seemed to give her pause. "You'll be close to the emperor. You'll have his ear. Things could be different."

Nina tilted her head and pursed her lips. "You're right. The emperor's ear is exactly what I need."

Kasik thought that he had finally said the right thing, but her concession came too easily. Her words made the hairs on the back of his neck stand on end. They were far from the fire, far from the warmth of people and life. The moon was large and bright in the sky, bathing everything where they stood in sharp contrast to the shadows in the mossy tree line.

"We'll leave in the morning, as planned," he said, holding a hand out to her. "Let's go back to the fire and enjoy this night."

Heart pounding, Kasik waited for Nina to accept his offer. Her hand twitched by her side, and he could see the way her shoulders lowered the slightest bit. Another small victory. She extended her hand to his, fingers nearly touching, and then she paused. She turned her head sharply to the side, and then he heard a clap. And another.

Nina looked at Kasik, confused. A slow round of applause came from a man materializing from the shadows between tents. "That was *very* touching," he said, voice rich, measured steps bringing him closer to where they stood. "And this place is quite charming. The emperor would love it, wouldn't you agree, Kamayuq Kasik?"

Kasik's chest clenched as he watched Kuna, a favored spy of Emperor Maicu's, approach. His eyes flicked to the trees, searching for Aysan, the man's other half. They were t'ira, brothers identical in appearance, with the same long hair and slender builds that made them quick and light on their feet. They were known to be needlessly cruel and vicious in their pursuits.

Though he couldn't find Aysan, Kasik knew he was there. Lurking in the shadows like an achipuma, waiting for permission to pounce. They didn't go anywhere without the other.

Kasik didn't waste time questioning how they had found the camp—it was further proof of Shayim's lies—or *why* they were there. It did not matter. Their mere presence was a danger to everyone there, including Nina.

Slowly, Kasik moved toward Nina to cover her with his body, to keep Kuna's eyes from drinking her in. He was a man thirsty for violence and would take it any way he could.

When Nina's hand found the back of his tunic and fisted the fabric tight, Kasik kept his shoulders from softening, his face neutral so that they wouldn't think her important in any way. "What is your business here?" he asked.

Kuna tsked and took a small step forward. "You know we cannot share that information, not even with the emperor's pet."

Kasik tensed, his hand reaching for a weapon that was no longer there. He only had the small knife in his boot. It would have to do. "Jealousy does not become you, Kuna. I'd suggest you answer the question plainly."

Kuna hummed a laugh. "It's curious," he said. "Do you know this rebel camp did not exist only two days ago? Then, suddenly it appears, and here you are. Are you plotting against Emperor Maicu, Kamayuq? Your own *friend*?"

"This is *not* a rebel camp," Nina hissed behind him. Kasik reached back and pushed her farther to the side, so his body was completely covering hers once again.

The smile on Kuna's face twisted into wicked delight, all teeth and danger. "You have no idea what you've walked into, do you? I guess we'll have to take care of the problem ourselves. Aysan," he called out. There was a rustle in the trees, and then a barely discernible thump. From the shadows appeared the second t'ira, just as Kasik expected. Nina inhaled sharply, her fist tightening farther in his shirt. "Do you think Emperor Maicu will be glad to know what we've found?"

"Oh, he'll be delighted, indeed," Aysan said. The gleam in his smiling eyes was a terrifying promise. "We must tell him at once. But it has been a long day of travel. Perhaps our *comrade* here will invite us to dine with him."

"I am not your comrade," Kasik said through his teeth. "And you are not welcome here."

"Oh, ho." Kuna smirked sideways, his eyes alight with sport. "Then we will leave, of course, and—"

Kasik, working hard to control his breathing, felt the shift in Nina a split second too late. The heat of her body against his back disappeared, and then she was beside him. "You cannot leave," she said, voice firm with authority. Kasik did not spare her a glance, did not dare to take his eyes off the men, even as his heart clawed at his chest. "You must stay. Come. There is plenty of food."

The t'ira grinned at each other. "What manners," Kuna said, taking a step closer, Aysan following close behind.

Kasik felt each of their steps like a fist to his chest. It was instinct that sent his arm out and across Nina's abdomen. That pushed her back and braced for whatever came next.

Kuna faltered suddenly, a small stutter that looked almost like he had missed a step, and then he grunted. Aysan looked to his t'ira with a furrowed brow, an expression that mirrored Kasik's own.

"What—" Aysan started, but then he stopped speaking, and his hand flew to his chest. He looked at it as if it didn't belong to him. As if something had taken up residence and was devouring him from the inside out. Beside him, Kuna fell to his knees, his neck craned back at an unnatural angle, mouth open and eyes wide toward the moonlit sky.

No more than a handful of heartbeats had passed, but Kasik felt as though the scene before him was trudging through mud. By the time he pulled Nina behind him again, blood that turned brackish in the moonlight was dripping down the t'ira's faces. From their eyes and ears, sputtering from their lips as they gurgled nonsensically.

It was a scene from Kasik's worst nightmare. Deaths just as cruel and vicious as the men before him. Their mouths opened and closed with phantom screams. Their hands clawed uselessly at their throats and chests. They gouged their flesh and tore at their hair.

Kasik's muscles coiled to attack, but there was no enemy he could see. No monster he could slay. It was something only the gods could have done, a death so miserable that none but the most despicable of mortals deserved.

He shielded Nina, ready to absorb anything that came their way, but the men suffered in solitude until they fell to the ground, face down, necks at strange angles, arms and legs twisted at their sides.

Nothing but whimpering masses of flesh.

Not dead yet, Kasik realized with dread.

"Nina, we have to—" But his words were cut off as the weight of her body fell against him. He grabbed her and spun, heart in his throat, imagining the worst as he pushed her hair back from her face. But there was no blood leaking from her eyes. No agony etched onto her features. Her eyes were closed as if she had simply fallen asleep, and Kasik did the only thing he could think of.

He screamed for help.

23

Nina found the cords of their wills with little effort, but tearing the men apart was a much different task than mending. The intricacies of the body and mind were foreign to her and she remembered now that it required a certain kind of finesse. The boys in the alley had been naive practice. These men before her were the final test.

They hadn't been expecting an attack. As they walked closer to Kasik, she had plunged into their minds with the ease of childish want and frustration. There had been a moment of resistance that had easily melted away with the first drops of blood soaking into the dry earth. And once their blood was spilled, it was as if Nina's attay was boosted with satisfaction. It became brighter and simpler to wield. Easier to tear them apart from the inside out.

Truly, Nina hadn't planned on killing them, but it was a delicious descent into darkness, one that had terrified her only because she had misunderstood it. This darkness wasn't an absence of light—it was simply the choice to extinguish it. All the power lay in her hands, and the darkness was hers alone to command.

Finally, she understood what her mamay had tried to teach her. In this acceptance, there was calm and control, and her purpose was clearer than ever.

These men could not take what they knew to Emperor Maicu. It would ruin all her plans and consign them all to death, including Kasik. The only option was *their* death.

So, she refocused her attay on their hearts. Their blood. The vessels that carried it and the organs that carried them. She directed her will to latch on to their threads of life, to suffocate, to twist and tear apart. Perhaps it was easy because she had half done it before, or perhaps because she wanted it more than she could remember wanting anything else. It was a desire that deserved further inspection but was squashed beneath the satisfaction that came with listening to their silent screams.

In hindsight, she could have gone straight for their hearts and saved them the suffering of a slow death, but it was over in such a short amount of time, their bodies collapsing to the ground surrounded by pools of blood, that it didn't matter much at all.

What surprised her the most, however, was the fact that it was much easier to kill than to heal. She didn't feel her life force draining away like she had when she had been feeding it to Kasik or Mika. Her mind felt present, clear, as if their deaths were feeding *her*. Nina wanted to be horrified, appalled by the prospect, but she felt nothing except pleased with herself.

Until their life forces were not enough to sustain, just shadows in her mind, and then she was weak and hungry for more. A despicable craving had awoken inside her, and as she fell to her knees, she couldn't think of anything else but taking *more*.

The glow of threads was so bright that she had to close her eyes against it. Kasik cradled her in his arms, his body warm and hard and welcome against hers. His threads were nowhere to be found. The achilla around his neck knew she meant all them harm, that the power inside her was frenzied with need.

Kasik gently lowered her to a bed in a nearby tent and crouched before her, blocking the sight of the others behind him. A voice asked a question, and Kasik responded.

"They just dropped. I don't know what happened, but Nina, she—something's not right here."

There was terror in his eyes—an emotion Nina hadn't seen from him before. Not when the achiyanga came after them, or when Hatun and his men had captured them. There had been fury and promise then. Resolve. She knew he was spiraling and that it was her fault.

A hand circled his shoulder. "We're not in any danger," Shayim said, her eyes on Nina. "Hatun, take care of the bodies and send someone to check on the children."

Nina began to feel more like herself with every breath, whatever danger she possessed leaking away to leave behind a burning in her belly and a bone-deep exhaustion.

"You're okay," Kasik murmured, his hands slipping over her thighs. Shayim handed her a canteen, and she lifted a weak hand to take it. Kasik supported the bottom as she tipped it to her lips. The water was cool, but it did nothing to satisfy her hunger.

"What if there are more?" Kasik asked. Nina inspected his profile while he sent an accusatory glare at Shayim. "How did they get past your so-called power?"

There aren't more, Nina wanted to say. She could see threads from every corner of her vision. All of them close, all of them bright and tempting. Beyond their camp, the forest was relentlessly dark. There was no one else.

In front of her, Kasik's will began to glow like a timid animal that needed gentle coaxing. She reached out a hand to touch him, but the flap of the tent blew open and Hatun marched through.

"The bodies have been taken care of," he said. Blood dripped from the tip of a blade in his hand and hit the earth with a thud that vibrated in Nina's ears.

She blinked and the tent was gone. Another blink and the men were on their knees in front of her, the sky stretched out above them like an all-seeing eye that watched as they fell, their bodies twisted, their will undone, extinguished within them.

Nina sucked in a sob and pressed her hands to her chest. Warm hands slipped over her cheeks. Kasik's earthy scent filled her and his whispered words slithered beneath her skin, offering comfort she knew she didn't deserve.

She had killed those men and had taken satisfaction from it. Worse still, she felt no guilt, no remorse. They would have exposed their secrets. She thought of Mika in her tent, the children who ran wild, the women who laughed and danced. Secrets worth killing to keep.

It struck Nina then, the weight of what she had to do. What she now knew she *could* do.

Kill Emperor Maicu. Do away with the threat to her family, to Shayim's ayllu, to the other girls and boys taken from their homes and forced to serve the empire. And then she could be free, her conscience clean. Her debt to the gods repaid. For this power was their gift to her, and even if she didn't want it, she would have to pay the price.

Kasik gently brushed the hair from her face. "I'm okay," she told him, and he blew out a breath. In the corner of the tent, Shayim and Hatun spoke animatedly until they felt her gaze on them. When Shayim met her eyes, Nina saw the pride and gratitude and determination there.

Rebel camp, Kuna had said, his teeth glinting like weapons in the night. But that wasn't quite right. This camp, these *people*, were a movement, and Shayim had been expecting her.

"Your attay failed," Nina whispered slowly, working through the pieces she held in her mind. "You said the camp was hidden."

"It was," Shayim agreed. "But this moment needed to happen. The only reason why those men found this camp is because I let them."

"Are you saying that you willingly put the lives of powerless and innocent people in jeopardy," Kasik said, his tone disbelieving, "to prove a point?"

"Why do you assume we are powerless? Because we are outside of your emperor's purview?" Shayim tutted like a mamay scolding foolish children. "The only point that needs proving is the fact that you are blinded by your loyalty. You couldn't see the truth if it slapped you in the face."

Kasik's hands fisted at his sides. Nina had the urge to defend him, but she didn't have anything to say against Shayim's words. "The truth of *what*, Shayim? Of who you are and your supposed power? We don't have time for your lies." He grabbed Nina's arm and gently lifted her to her feet. "We're leaving, and so should all of you. It's not safe here any longer."

"It's not safe where you're going, either," Hatun added with a scoff.

"We can't leave." Nina placed a hand over Kasik's, hoping her touch would calm him like it often did Sacha when she was in the throes of a nightmare. "Not yet. I have to—"

"I will not stay here and see you suffer the same monstrous fate as those men."

"I won't," Nina promised softly, "because I am the one who placed it upon them."

24

Kasik turned to Nina and grasped her chin in one hand. "You cannot blame yourself. They made the choice to come here knowing the danger this forest holds. The Tuta Kulla is a thing all onto its own, and—"

"You misunderstand," Nina interrupted, her eyes flashing. "It was *me* who killed them. This . . . this power I possess. The same power I healed you with."

Kasik may not have known her well enough to be able to speak without words, but he peered into her brown eyes, at her face tilted up at him, her body leaned into him, her voice firm and clear, and knew she wasn't lying.

"I am an Ikara," she insisted. "I am the woman from your story, and a god's power lives inside of me."

Every interaction, every encounter they had, he now viewed it—*her*—through new eyes.

At the acllahuasi, when he had seen the grit in the set of her jaw. When she'd watched him murder a man without so much as a flinch. The way the achiyanga had simply stood before her. Had it seen in her something monstrous and kindred?

The stories he was told as a child, of those with power who had destroyed the world time and again, only for the gods to remake it and the end to remain just the same.

Chaos and destruction.

Then he remembered Maicu's words about legacy and loss and the sacrifices required to make change. It dawned on him all at once.

"This is why he wants you," he whispered, mind racing. "This is why the emperor sent for you. Have you known about this *power* all along?"

"*No*, Kasik, no. I—" She placed a hand on his arm, and he yanked out of her touch. Stepped away from her reach. The fire burned his back like a knife between his shoulder blades. Still, he preferred it to the way her eyes filled with hurt. "I knew something about me was different, but it was only when we came here that Shayim showed me what I could do."

Kasik ran a hand down his face and turned from her. It was miraculous, his healing. He had felt the rot from the inside out, the burn of death taking root, and still he had refused to see the truth of it. "You should have let me die," he whispered miserably. "You should have never interfered in something you don't understand."

"You make it sound as though any of this has been my choice."

When he turned to her again, she was wearing that same expression he had found her with. Determination in the downward tilt of her eyes and lips. Anger in the clench of her jaw. "We *always* have a choice," he said tenderly.

"You as well," Shayim interrupted. He turned abruptly. The old woman stood tall, her brown eyes glowing in the firelight. He had almost forgotten there were others in the room. "What will you choose to do with this knowledge?" She gestured at Nina, at herself, at the ayllu surrounding them.

Kasik glanced at Hatun beside her and felt the phantom blows of the man's boot in his stomach. He was in a room full of enemies, and the path of his life depended on his answer.

Shayim flicked her eyes to Hatun. "Leave us," she ordered, and surprisingly, Hatun obeyed without a whisper of dissent.

Kanu's words rang through Kasik's mind. "Kanu seemed to think you are a rebel ayllu. Is he right? Am I such a fool that I thought you all innocent?"

Shayim stood taller, her eyes hardened as she met Kasik's judgment. "We are not a rebel ayllu. We are a *resistance*."

Kasik barked a laugh, the sound sharp in the tense silence. He expected her to say something more, but when she didn't, he sobered with disbelief. "A resistance? Against *what*?"

"There is much your emperor has not told you."

Kasik went to argue, but Shayim held up a hand, and the authority with which she did so stopped him immediately. "I know you think it is not your place to know, but it does not absolve you of your hand in it," Shayim said. "You must be aware of what your master does, and when you decide to follow his commands, it will be with all the information, and with all your own free will.

"Do you know that the acllahuasi is filled with Ikara?" she continued. "Girls with mythical power that we've been told is unnatural and nonexistent, but the truth is that your emperor hunts them. He takes them from their families and stores them behind stone walls, drugs them with tainted leaves, and then trades them in exchange for fealty. And then he takes our boys and hones them into weapons to defend against any who dissent."

Shayim paused, waiting for Kasik to interrupt, to argue, to admit disbelief, but there was nothing he could say that would accurately portray the level of his skepticism. If he hadn't seen the t'ira die the way they did, he would have walked out of the tent and dragged Nina with him. Instead, against his better judgment, he stayed and listened.

"*We* are where his power comes from. Without the Ikara, he is just another lofty, greedy man. And the *kunay*," Shayim said, shooting him a sharp glance, "is no better. He is just like Dimas, compelled to hunt Yuri to the ends of the earth and deliver her to the emperor."

"And I am Yuri," Nina whispered, her eyes distant with some memory that Kasik could not see. "Weeks after I used my attay for the first time, they came and took my brother. Then recently, I used it again. Without knowing," she added and glanced at Kasik. "They came again, but I thought it was for Sacha. The way he *looked* at her . . . I offered myself in exchange. I threw myself to the wolves."

Shayim looked at Nina with sympathy. "You couldn't have known. This particular gift is not passed through blood, and while your mamay might have thought there was something different about you, she could not have guessed the depth of it."

"If all this is true, then what do they want with Nina?"

Shayim looked back at Kasik, and her eyes hardened. "The gods have a plan for her, but I cannot See it. All I know is that it has been five hundred years since their banishment, and they grow weary and forgotten. They yearn for the pachakuti—the turnover of time—to return them to power, and they use mortals like Maicu to do it."

"You lie," Kasik seethed. "You speak of gods and power and resistance and yet here you are, hiding in the dark. Cowering while the emperor continues his reign unopposed."

"I do not lie." Shayim lowered her voice, and her eyes bored into Kasik. It was as if she was seeing beyond this moment, perhaps even beyond his life. Shivers crawled up his spine. "It is only that you refuse to *see*. Do you want to know what Aliyma would say to you if she was here?"

Kasik had pushed the first mention of his mamay away, unwilling to face it, but he couldn't ignore it for a second time. He shot to his feet and paced to the edge of the tent, watching as his shadow flickered in the firelight.

"Your sister?" Nina asked, voice soft with thought. "Why would she have anything to say to Kasik?"

"Because she was my mamay," he said to the dark. When he turned, he pinned his glare on the Seer, watched every shift in her features. The tent was tense, the quiet deep enough to swallow all sound until

Kasik could hear his own heartbeat. He thought it might give away how badly he wanted to beg for more. Even a morsel of information about his mamay would soothe the ache, but he would not give her that satisfaction. "And Shayim thinks to use her memory against me, as if I am so easily weakened."

"Love is not a weakness," Shayim said softly. She dropped onto the edge of the bed with a sigh. "Just as hiding is not cowering. Taking action against threats we do not yet understand would be unwise."

"What of your power?" Nina shifted toward Shayim. Color had returned to her cheeks, and the firelight burnished her skin. Kasik could not reconcile the girl sitting before him with a girl capable of slaughtering two men in cold blood. "Can you not See threats before they come?"

"I only see the threads of life before me, and even then, the details are vague, but I can See that there is a war coming."

Kasik scoffed. He couldn't help it. "Now there is a war coming? What threat will it be next?"

Shayim's lips quirked. Kasik knew he was being childish, but he didn't care. "Twenty years ago, I told Emperor Yachua that I had Seen something strange in his threads, in *all* our threads. A flash of a man bleached of color, like an apparition that I could only See the impression of, but could not ascertain when, or how, or from where they would come. The kukuchi, we had called them." Shayim paused, eyes distant as if reaching into the past. "The gods mean to use the chaos to their advantage. It will change everything."

"That is . . ." Nina started, but her brow furrowed, and her words drifted off.

"Convenient," Kasik finished for her. "And that is your excuse for shirking your responsibilities to this land, to your people? A fear of some distant, unclear threat? Your delusion puts them in danger. Whatever fight you think there is, you cannot fight it and win. The emperor has power—*true* power—and you consign all your people to death by going against him."

Kasik stood so that Shayim had to crane her head to meet his eyes, which she held unflinchingly. She was not afraid of him, not by any means. "I will keep your secret, if only so that the deaths of your people do not belong to me. They solely belong to you." Then he turned to Nina, who watched him warily. "We'll go *now*," he said.

"Kasik." She said his name so softly, it was almost his undoing. "We should wait until morning. Ask Shayim your questions."

But Kasik had had enough. There was no more time to wait. He whirled away, unable to look at her a moment longer without saying the wrong thing. "We cannot stay, Nina. And I do not *want* to ask questions."

"Now who lies?" Shayim mumbled. Kasik ignored her.

When he spoke, he looked only at the wall of the tent. The green fabric blurred in his vision. He told himself it was frustration and exhaustion, nothing more. At his back, he heard the whisper of the tent flap shifting aside and knew that Shayim was gone. "You will come willingly, or I will be forced to drag you away from here."

"You cannot force me to do anything at all." Nina's voice was low and lethal. He could imagine the hatred that lined her mouth and the betrayal in her eyes. He had seen it earlier when he had told her she couldn't stay. This time, it was strengthened by the truth of what she was capable of.

Kasik's anger toward her was irrational. It was better blamed on the fact that he had thought he had no family besides his tayta, and suddenly he did, and he was being forced to confront the possibility that everything he had believed his whole life might be a lie.

That Atik, cruel and inflexible, was a liar, something that seemed incongruent with his narrow-minded, rigid worldview.

He knew all this, and yet he turned and stepped closer to where Nina stood with her shoulders back and her chin held high, his voice low so no one else could hear. "Will you stop me like you stopped those men? Will you let your power turn you into a monster?"

"If I am a monster for protecting them," she said, gesturing to where the entrance of the tent and Shayim stood, "then so be it. It is the gods who have made me this way, and I will not be made to suffer guilt because of it."

"Your *power* doesn't make you who you are. Your *choices* do, and the choice of life or death does not belong in the hands of man." Kasik gave her his back, daring her to stop him. "I'll gather the achipumas while you say your goodbyes."

And then he walked away, uncertain if Nina would follow.

25

Kasik left the tent in a whirlwind of anger and insecurity. Nina could feel it in his threads, her attay heightened along with her emotions to the point where she could see life and will in all corners of her vision. It was overpowering and nauseating and exhilarating all at once. It also told her that she had no intention to harm Kasik, even subconsciously, since the achilla was still around his neck. If he had remembered that, perhaps he would have thought twice about calling her a monster.

But regardless, she knew it was exactly what he thought, and it hurt her more than she could have imagined. Still, she followed him out of the tent. Still, she watched him walk away, wishing things could be different.

"It is difficult," Shayim started, her eyes also pinned to the shrinking image of Kasik, "to ascertain who is an enemy and who is simply too afraid to enact change, and therefore an enemy by default."

The woman grabbed Nina's hand as they stood side by side. With that touch, it was as if Shayim's soul whispered to her. Her threads blazed bright, and Nina had to close her eyes against them. "The time will come when you will be forced to decide who *your* enemy is. I cannot tell you how it will end, but you must always remember who you are, and that you are meant for more than what anyone tells you."

The words penetrated Nina's heart in a way that reminded her how deeply she craved her mamay's presence. It was she who could tell Nina who she was, for Nina could not tell it to herself. She simply did not know. Her life had been simple, one day after the next, the same as the day before, and she had never been forced to consider what choices she would make amid trials and tribulations.

Now there were heaps of choices at her feet, at her *fingertips*, and she was expected to navigate them with wisdom and justice. She could not be blamed for who she became from the weight of it.

When Kasik returned, he had two achipuma with him. Capac, as dark as the night surrounding them, his ears halfway back and his eyes wide, and a smaller achipuma who sat with a huff at Kasik's feet.

"This is Illari," Kasik said. "She was stolen on my way to collect you."

Nina approached the achipuma with an extended hand. Illari leaned forward and sniffed it, then promptly placed her head against Nina's palm. She was soft and warm, and so very trusting. Nina wanted to bury her face in Illari's fur, to close her eyes and inhale deeply and exhale this tension in her bones and deep within her soul that felt like she was being suffocated.

Illari stayed perfectly still as Nina mounted her. The smaller achipuma fit better between her legs, and there was plenty of space without Kasik behind her. She did *not* miss his warmth, or the pressure of him that had held her together that first day. Nina did not need anyone to hold her together now, and she promised herself she wouldn't need it ever again.

Behind her, the sounds of the ayllu continued as if nothing had happened. Smoke from the communal fire rose high in the sky and Nina closed her eyes, inhaling what she instinctively knew to be her last memories from this place. The side of her face warmed with attention. She was wary to turn, to meet Kasik's eyes, to see the judgment and the disappointment, and face the consequences of her actions.

In hindsight, Nina had been reckless and brash. With a bit of coercing and guidance, she could have brought those men to their knees until

Hatun and the others in the ayllu subdued them. She could have let them go. Let them return to the emperor and divulge all their secrets.

But Nina had taken their lives and cut their threats off at the knees. She had made her choice, and though she was searching for the regret she should have felt, she was having a hard time finding it.

It was *her* choice to leave Shayim. It was *her* choice to follow Kasik, and it was *her* choice to earn her freedom by killing the emperor. Nina was taking control of her life now.

The taste of freedom sat on the back of her tongue, and her body craved more of it. No longer would she feel fear or remorse. Only resolve.

It kept her warm as the cool air rushed over her during their travels, and after several hours of riding toward Vira, they finally found a place to rest. Kasik left the achipumas under a tree, and then he worked to light a small fire.

"There are clothes in Illari's pack," he said, turning to face her. "We should change and burn these garments so no one asks where we've come from."

It was the first thing he had said to her since they left the camp, and his voice was different from before. More reserved, as if he had placed her behind a wall. She watched as he tore off his shirt and threw it into the fire, the muscles on his back undulating with the movement. The wounds that had threatened his life were completely gone. There wasn't a hint of what had transpired, including evidence of her healing. But she remembered the way those muscles had felt underneath her hands. The strength. The potential. The control that he exerted every time he had used his body to protect her.

The golden coil at his chest shone brightly. Nina knew she could use it to end his life and was tempted to reach for it, to grasp it between her hands and mold it to fit her will, to smother and—

The light blinked out of existence with the thought.

"Nina?" Kasik, watching her warily, took a step closer and then abruptly stopped, as if he hadn't meant to move. As if he was unsure of her. As if he thought she would kill him where he stood for saying the wrong thing. And she couldn't blame him, not really, not when she hadn't given those men the chance to change their minds.

Would they have begged if she had dangled their lives over their heads? The thought made her doubt everything.

"I'll change," she said before rushing to hide behind Illari.

It wasn't that she *wanted* to kill everyone, but there was a part of her that tried to convince her that their deaths—Emperor Maicu, the kunay, even Kasik—might suit her needs and make things easier. That only then could she truly be free.

This is not who you are, Sacha had said, the imminent deaths of two boys in the palms of her hands. But she was beginning to think that her sister's expectations were lofty, and meeting them might be more difficult than she cared to attempt.

Another person to disappoint. The responsibility pressed on Nina's shoulders as she changed her clothes and tossed her old ones into the fire. The color of her new tunic was hard to parse in the shifting dark, but she assumed it was as red as the one Kasik had worn to collect her, before it was torn and bloodied and dirtied beyond recognition.

So much they had endured together, all of it reduced to this tense, uncomfortable agreement. Neither of them said anything about it as they lay on opposite sides of the fire.

But Nina couldn't sleep, the call of Kasik's threads too loud in the quiet of the night.

Just over a week later, they found the road, and she could see the tension that had existed in every shift of Kasik's shoulders lift the moment their achipumas' paws met the crushed rock. The road looked like a wound that had been carved into the lush greenery only to heal into a discolored scar. It was unnatural. An offense to the Tuta Kulla. It was no wonder the achiyanga refused to come near it.

Kasik brought Capac beside Illari, their legs almost brushing with every step they traveled.

"How much longer until we reach Vira?" she asked.

"If we push hard, we could reach the city gates before tomorrow's sunset."

Nina glanced at the clear sky, the road ahead and then behind, the thick mass of trees on either side of them. Everything looked exactly the same. "How can you tell?"

"There are markers in the trees." Kasik's voice was cold and impersonal, a loyal kamayuq once again, only answering her questions to teach a lesson. "There, and there," he said, pointing to a pair of trees on either side of the road. Nina saw a mark, but she wouldn't have thought anything of it had he not pointed it out, nor could she discern the meaning. She assumed that was purposeful.

They lapsed into silence again, the weight of things unsaid enough to crush.

"Tell me about Emperor Maicu," she asked, desperate to prove that nothing had changed, even if it meant inviting an argument.

Kasik hardly glanced sideways at her, but she saw the question linger in his mind. She wondered what kind of answer he was crafting. One to scare her, like he had back in the camp, or one to encourage her, like he had after they left the acllahuasi.

All she knew of the man were the rumors whispered in her ayllu. They were so far removed from Vira that, by the time news reached them, it was either watered-down or outlandish. According to Lihan, a girl whose tayta was a fisherman, Empress Chaska had six toes on each foot she kept hidden in custom-made slippers.

"He's charming," Kasik started, his eyes distant as they moved back and forth over the tree line, "and devout. He truly believes that the gods work through him."

"And what do you believe?"

Nina saw Kasik's jaw twitch and braced for a verbal sparring. "I believe that it isn't my job to question the emperor or the gods, and you shouldn't, either." Kasik glanced at her with a small smile carved onto his otherwise stern face. "Not out loud, anyway. Maicu is honorable, but he can be cruel."

"And he uses the gods as an excuse to enact that cruelty." It reminded Nina of something her tayta used to say: *A righteous man is a dangerous man.* Men who thought themselves close to divinity, who allowed their delusions to guide their hands toward greed and lust, who believed themselves above the law of the land.

"I imagine it must take many difficult decisions to run an empire."

Nina scoffed. "I feel no sympathy for a man who grasps power with fists held tight. The trouble he finds is brought onto himself."

"Emperor Maicu is continuing Emperor Yachua's legacy. Uniting all our lands isn't about control—it's about ensuring that all the people of this land have equal rights and equal protection."

Nina rolled her eyes. "Now you're just repeating what you have been spoon-fed all your life. My ayllu was a safe and happy place before being absorbed." Kasik huffed and she turned to glare at him. "We are favored by Pachamama. Our fields grow food when they shouldn't. Our animals thrive. Our people are free. *Were* free, before the emperor came and slapped a name on us and demanded the chani. Do not pretend that he does this for anyone other than himself, or that he doesn't enjoy the power that comes from ruling over us all."

"Just because your ayllu hasn't seen the benefits of it doesn't mean that others have not," he said, the words sharp. He lifted a hand to run through his hair and blew out a breath. The gold bands were around both arms again, sitting snug against his flesh and reminding everyone with eyes that could see who he belonged to. "I don't think it's possible *not* to enjoy it. But does that make him evil? I'm not sure. You would know more about power than I do."

Nina bristled and faced forward again. She refused to appreciate his face and arms and hands a second longer. "If you believe that all power is the same, then you are sorely mistaken."

"It wouldn't be the first time," Kasik mumbled under his breath.

They had argued, but Nina was left thoroughly dissatisfied. Especially as the road narrowed and Kasik rode ahead, giving her his back. Capac's tail swished back and forth along with Kasik's hair. She snorted and then pressed her lips together when Kasik turned to glare at her.

But mirth bled away into appreciation once again.

There was no doubt in her mind that he was beautiful, carved with care by the gods he so dutifully served. His long black hair was tied at the nape of his neck and fell against his back in a discreet show of privilege. Those who labored kept it braided and out of the way most of the time. Kasik's was thick and shiny, and she wanted to run her fingers through it. Just once, to see how it felt.

Instead, she ran her mental fingers against the threads burning in his chest. They didn't shy away from her touch so long as Nina kept admiring. She thought about the definition in his arms, the strength in his legs as he sat atop Capac without a hint of strain, the confidence with which he wielded both weapon and mind.

This was how she would get past the emperor's many achilla. This was how she would kill him.

With less finesse than she had intended, she took Kasik's thread in hand and tugged, appeasing the curiosity to know just how far she could go. Kasik gasped and beneath him, Capac jerked to a halt, his ears back and slitted eyes trained on the distance as if searching for a threat.

But the threat was right behind him, and Nina had failed. Kasik's threads disappeared between one blink and the next, leaving her hands and head and heart emptier than ever. The ground seemed to tilt beneath her with the loss.

Illari carried her to Kasik's side. His hand shot out and wrapped around her wrist, tugging her closer to him and keeping her seated on Illari. Perhaps unintentionally, Nina thought, as Kasik bent over her, eyes boring into hers, his usually full lips pressed into a grim line, and said through gritted teeth, "What did you do?"

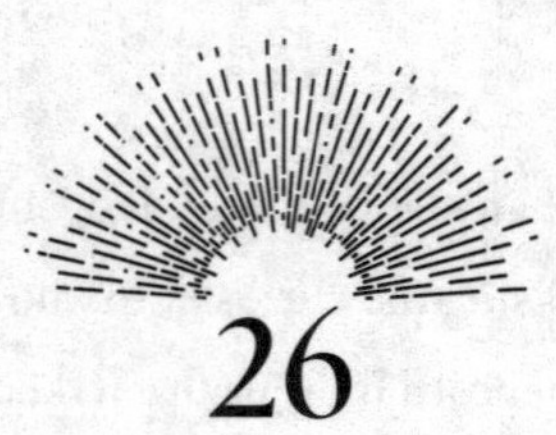

26

Kasik had felt a prodding in his chest and thought it merely the quiet discomfiture of his soul. Or perhaps a nudge from the gods. But when he turned to find Nina pale and shaking, he knew he was entirely wrong. It wasn't his conscience that made him pull up short. It wasn't a sudden surge of pity that stole his breath. It was Nina and her godlike power digging beneath his skin, searching for a hold of his will.

Capac was unsteady beneath him. The forest on either side of them was whispering frantically, as if it had heard a salacious secret and was spreading it far and wide. Nina's pulse skittered beneath his thumb.

"Kasik, I—"

"If you want to kill me, then go ahead." He pulled her closer and pressed her hand against his chest, right over the beating drum beneath his bone. "But at least look me in the eye while you do it."

Nina yanked away. Illari shifted closer to Capac, pressing their legs together. "I wasn't trying to kill you, Kasik."

"Then what is it you are doing, Nina, because you are driving me *mad*. You have made it perfectly clear that you do not want to be here, and I know for a fact that you could stop me if you chose to. So, *what are you doing*?"

"I have made my choice, and I am sticking to it. *That* is what I am doing. Surely, you can understand."

Her tone was mocking, but Kasik knew he deserved whatever she threw his way. "Why did you come back?" he asked, remembering what it had been like to watch her throw that stone at the achiyanga, her face a blur of fierce shadows and sharp edges. He was at once terrified of the truth he knew was coming and hopeful for the answer he wanted. "Why did you save me time and again?"

"I don't want your blood on my hands." It was so simple, the way she said it. So obvious that Kasik was embarrassed he had thought anything else of it. "We aren't enemies, but we aren't allies, either. You belong to the emperor."

So do you. We are the same, he wanted to say. Instead, he asked, "Would you have told me about your power?"

Nina sighed and shifted, but her leg stayed pressed against his. He was endlessly grateful, though this touch wasn't his to have. The red tunic she now wore was a stark reminder of who she belonged to, who they *both* belonged to, and once they were back at the kancha, Nina would marry Maicu and Kasik would head north to join Samaq and his men. They would finish collecting the Harvest and then return to celebrate Inti Raymi.

Life would go back to the way it was before he was sent on this mission.

He could continue to avoid his tayta and Maicu, could continue to pretend like one day, he wouldn't be taking Atik's place as the emperor's right hand. But these things would happen whether or not he wanted them to.

"No," Nina finally said, eyes downcast, fingers plucking at a loose thread in the hem of her tunic. "I don't think I can trust you."

Kasik clenched his teeth and looked away. Down the road, into the trees, anywhere but at Nina's imploring eyes and downturned mouth. He was weak. Maicu had been wrong to trust him with this. "Then why not kill me so that you could be free of this? Why let me take you against your will?"

Closing his eyes, he waited for the fingers of her power to pluck at his soul, for her to rip it out of his body like she had the t'ira, but all he felt was a gentle brush. A pleasant tickle that made him want to lean in, to press his lips to her skin, to breathe her in. He wanted, he wanted, he *wanted—*

Nina's power disappeared, leaving a void in his chest that hadn't been there before. Kasik fought the urge to press a fist against it to hold it all in.

"I refuse to absolve you of this," she said, her voice hardly more than a whisper but challenging, nonetheless. "You have made your choices, and now you will live with them."

Kasik opened his eyes. Her face was close enough that the world behind her had begun to blur. "And if I cannot?" he murmured, his gaze darting to her mouth.

Beneath them, Capac and Illari leaned closer, their bodies supporting one another. Even the trees and their leaves seemed to dip lower, just as he did. Time seemed to stall. It was only them and this moment, this choice swirling in the space between their bodies, dark and delicate and consuming. An ember waiting to catch and burn everything to the ground.

"Then make different choices," Nina said. As if it was the simplest thing in the whole world. And perhaps it could be. She made him want to riot, to forsake the vows he had made to himself and his emperor, to shuck the expectations of himself and embrace the wild chaos that seemed to follow Nina like a cloud.

But he knew the truth of that darkness and the dangers it held. He remembered the stories of the gods with power, the way it drove them mad with an unquenchable thirst.

He knew they would all be safer with her in the emperor's hands.

It was that thought that betrayed him. Nina stiffened and yanked away, her absence sucking the breath from his lungs. Illari huffed and skidded sideways with the abrupt movement. He watched as Nina's eyes hardened, as her mouth turned down into a severe and uncompromising slant, and the warmth from her skin on his faded to a lonely, regretful cold.

So much had happened, so much had changed, and yet nothing at all. It seemed as though they were fated to be forever at odds. And for reasons he could not explain, Kasik bemoaned that most of all.

They burned away whatever had happened between them by running the achipumas through most of the night. When they did stop, Kasik didn't bother to light a fire. The sky had already begun to lighten from a deep blue to a soft purple. He only let Nina rest until the sun's orange light peeked through the trees, and then they were off again. She didn't complain, though he could see the way she grimaced and shifted every so often.

Now they sat side by side, their legs close but not touching, so that the heat of her was only a faint impression. Below, stone walls cut through vibrant green grass like a snake. On one side were mountainous forests as far as the eye could see. On the other was a sprawling city which, from where they stood, looked like a maze of small stone buildings from the gates to the center where Qorikancha sat.

The temple of the sun god sparkled in the late-afternoon light. It spread from one end of the walls to the other, the brown stone interspersed with flecks of gold that Kasik knew were the size of his head. It sat above everything like a sentinel, each level higher and brighter than the one below it, stretching far up into the sky as if to reach the gods themselves.

Directly behind it was Amaru Kancha, a formidable fortress set atop a shallow hill with Qorikancha at its gates and the continuation of those stone walls cutting it off from the mountain. Kasik could see the main building, where the emperor slept and ate and lived, and the kallankas where he and his men slept. The training grounds were a large, bright green circle amid the stone.

The last time he had walked those grounds, he had been following Samaq. Watching as his only true friend met with the empress in secret and spoke in low tones and familiar touches. Kasik couldn't shake the memory, but it was going to have to be a discussion for another time. With Samaq, hopefully, so he could understand before jumping to conclusions, and not with his tayta, who would be waiting for them in Amaru Kancha.

Dread filled Kasik's belly, but he swallowed it and dismounted. "We'll walk from here," he said. Nina obeyed without question, sliding off Illari with more grace and confidence than she had when they first met a fortnight ago. He remembered the way she had torn at her robes. The way she had refused his help. The way he had been both impressed and exasperated by her determination.

So much had happened, and the memories would be all he'd have of her once they reached those walls. Memories that he would shove away until they were all but forgotten.

Back on two legs, they stood side by side, beholding the city before them. The homes in the capital were small and laid out in neat rows, their roofs peaked in the center to imitate the mountains around them. There were paths of green between them, and leading to the doors of Qorikancha was a winding dirt road where the people gathered on market days and celebrations.

People dressed in varying shades of red and blue milled about, tiny pinpricks of color against the browns and greens. There was a slight chill in the air that meant that winter was fast approaching, and with it, the end of the Harvest and the first day of Inti Raymi celebrations.

Soon after, the streets of Vira would be transformed. Snow would cover rooftops and fill the spaces between homes. Families would spend more time inside around their fires. The walla would exchange their sleeveless tunics for layers of coats and fur, and travel would become more difficult and less frequent.

Kasik glanced at Nina. She was studying the city with something akin to awe written across her features. He wondered what it looked like from her eyes, and how he would manage to avoid her once he returned. "This is your last chance to kill me," he said lightly.

Nina laughed, and it eased the knot in his chest ever so slightly. "Not today," she said somberly, pausing. "It's bigger than I thought it would be."

It was as if she was drinking in the sights and sounds like she would never see them again. As if Kasik was walking her to her death. It was what she had said, all those days ago, and it hurt to know that she still thought it.

The city was his home, and usually he was grateful for it. The excitement, the crowds and the noise, the possibilities, but today it weighed on him. He would miss the eerie quiet of the Tuta Kulla. The fresh air and cold streams, the murmur of the wind and whispers of creatures. The presence of Nina at his side.

"We should go," he said, mostly for himself.

With a sigh, Nina stepped forward. He joined her a moment later and together, they walked toward their fates.

"Kamayuq Kasik," one of the walla said with a nod as Nina and Kasik approached the large iron gates. There were two, both in simple red tunics with small achillas at their throats. "Welcome back."

Behind them, the gate opened with creaks and groans. He would suggest to Maicu that it needed to be serviced. In fact, it wasn't a bad idea to inspect the entire wall. He couldn't get that one word, *kukuchi*, out of his head. Though he had brushed Shayim off when she shared her omen, it still poked at his mind. Surely, there was no harm in taking the extra precaution to ensure the safety of the capitol.

Kasik gave Capac and Illari the sign to follow, and they obeyed, keeping pace close behind. From the corner of his eye, Kasik saw Nina, arms crossed over her chest against the chill, watching the gate slowly open. She looked lost. Something he had not, in all their time together, seen from her. Kasik had to resist the temptation to reach out and ground her with a touch. To remind her that he was there at her side, traversing the same path.

But it wasn't the same path. He was returning, and she was discovering. They were on two different journeys, worlds apart, and he found himself once again admiring the way she swallowed down that uncertainty, straightened her shoulders, and held her head high as they walked past the wall and into the heart of Vira.

Storefronts lined the road, small houses peeking from behind, and though he had traveled these roads all his life, he felt like an outsider. Like a figure on display. The people watched them travel with wary interest. They stopped what they were doing to stare, hands held up to hide their mouths and their whispers, their gold bands and rings catching the light and Kasik's attention. He couldn't remember the last time he was in the city this way, among the people and the markets without a reason to rush by, but he never remembered it feeling so unwelcoming.

Kasik turned to Nina. "Come on," he said, stepping up to Capac's side and extending a hand. "We'll ride the rest of the way." To the walla, he said, "Take Illari to the enclosure and see to it that she's fed and watered well."

Only a few heartbeats passed before Nina's hand was in his. He was surprised she complied so easily, and even more surprised when he settled behind her on Capac's back and she didn't so much as shift away. It took only one click of his tongue before Capac was leaping down the road and Nina's hair was lashing against his face.

Kasik knew he couldn't protect her once they were behind the kancha walls. They would be no one to each other once again. But he could at least do this; save her from the judgment of strangers who had no idea who she was or what she was sacrificing to be there and serve their empire.

But he was also doing this for himself. The quicker they arrived, the sooner he could be done with this mission. He could walk away and forget Nina's heat, her penetrating stare, her dangerous curiosity.

Perhaps only then, with time and space, he could forget that he had ever wanted her at all.

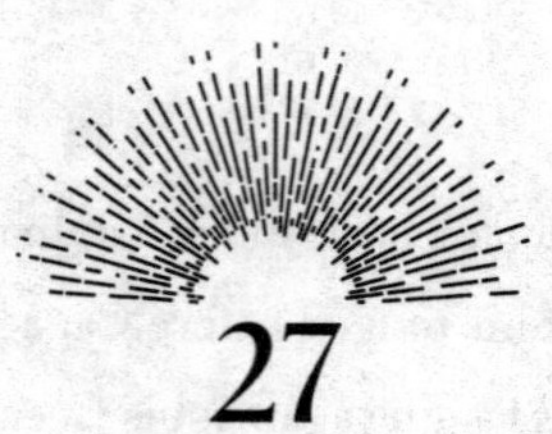

27

The heat of Kasik's chest against Nina's back was more familiar than the chill of her welcome to Vira. The people had stared at her as if she was unfit to walk their proper streets. She imagined she looked frightful, with her hair tangled down her back and the ill-fitting tunic hanging limply from her body, and she hated that she felt a sort of shame and want to belong wrapped up inside her because of it. Those kinds of thoughts would only set her off course.

But any and all thoughts fled the moment she caught sight of the temple.

They rounded a shallow corner and there it was, surrounded by paths of the most brilliant green and up on a stone foundation that lifted it several levels off the ground. The walls were stone, but there was gold everywhere that caught the last light of the sun, shimmering as if it had been set on fire. It was truly a spectacle to behold, one that took her breath away.

"This is Qorikancha, the temple of the sun." Kasik had slowed Capac so that Nina could take in the view. "Behind it is Amaru Kancha, the emperor's home and the royal grounds."

Nina had seen the kancha from the hill above the city, but now that they were on ground level with Qorikancha, she couldn't see past the sprawling building. She didn't possess the words to describe the way the stones lay one on top of the other, how they formed sharp corners and, higher up, designs in the walls that spoke of time and patience.

There were columns jutting into the sky on either side of the main peak, each of which had the image of a god carved into its surface, the largest being the sun god, Inti. His likeness was gold shaped into a sun with a face in the center. The tips of each ray were filed to an almost invisible point. His gaping eyes pierced straight through Nina.

It was the same face that decorated the disc on Kasik's chest, but larger than life, both beautiful and terrifying to behold.

The homes in Limac were small. The offering site for Pachamama was a modest altar in the middle of the ayllu where the sea breeze was sharp and sweet and the earth was soft and supple.

This ground was hard, and the building towered over her and spread farther than her eyes could see, and she got the sense that she was nothing but a tiny, insignificant figure standing in front of an unknowable, unreachable god.

"When we arrived at the first set of gates, the walla there would have sent a message with a bird to my tayta. He'll be waiting on the other side."

"That sounds like an omen." She half turned to see Kasik's face, but his eyes were trained on those walls in the near distance, brows furrowed.

It was hard to imagine not being excited to see her family after being away. If it was *her* tayta on the other side, she would have been clamoring to open the door, and she knew he would be waiting with a smile and arms wide open.

Nina wondered if they missed her. If they were worried for her. Sacha's fragile health and Lali's carefree spirit kept them plenty busy, but she was the one who had helped with the fields and the animals, who kept Lali occupied while Sacha was ill. Perhaps she hadn't realized it at the time, but she knew her place there. She was needed, and seen, and loved.

Once she passed those walls, there would be no more hope of that. Kasik had made it very clear that her desires mattered little. That she was a tool. A pawn in the emperor's schemes. She would play their game, but in her own way.

"Not an omen," Kasik finally said, his voice unconvincing. "Only an inevitability."

Nina hoped he was dreading this as much as she was. That this decision and her acquiescence would haunt his dreams. Mostly, she wanted him to remember her and think about her and care enough to wonder what might have happened had he simply disobeyed Emperor Maicu.

The closer they got to the wide wooden doors of Qorikancha, the harder it was to breathe. Fearsome-looking walla in bloody-red tunics stood at intervals along the perimeter, their wickedly sharp spears glinting with promise like the rays of Inti's face.

It was a statement to all, one that said, *Here I am; do not come any closer.*

And Nina was being escorted right through the doors.

"Kamayuq Kasik," one of the walla called, placing a fist to his chest. Nina wasn't familiar with the terms of their military, nor the importance of their ranks, but she had been under the impression that Kasik was someone further down, someone dispensable. He was young and had been sent on a glorified childminding mission. But the way the other walla nodded in deference told her a different story.

Kasik dismounted and held out a hand for Nina. She looked at it, and then back at Qorikancha, tempted to take Capac and run and never look back. Perhaps it wasn't too late to go back to Shayim and learn to wield her attay. The choice she had made to kill the emperor felt ridiculous now that she was in the shadow of such grandiosity.

Who was she, except a nobody from Limac with untrained attay and a half-formed plan?

The gods have chosen you, Nina thought. But they had chosen wrong; not because she wasn't capable, but because she refused to heedlessly follow their path.

His dark eyes searched her as she took a deep breath and placed her hand in his. He didn't let go when she landed on her feet, and he didn't pull away when she took a step. If anything, he leaned closer, enough so that if she took a deep breath, her chest would brush his. Close enough that she had to tilt her head back to hold his eyes. Close enough that she saw the way his gaze darted over her face and landed on her lips.

"Ask me to stop," he begged, so quiet she hardly heard him. "Ask me to forsake every vow I've ever made so that neither of us has to see this through."

It was then that Nina realized that he would turn his back on his duty for her. That she could ask it of him and he would willingly comply. But she would not, because doing so would mean that she would have to forsake her own vow. "No," she said. Kasik's eyes closed, and his exhale tickled the top of her head. "I have made my choice, and you have made yours. We are both loyal to our word."

Kasik moved away from her, and a cold wind replaced the space that he abandoned. The desperation in his eyes shifted to acceptance in a blink. "The emperor is waiting," he said again, an echo of the time when they were strangers, the meaning clear in every word.

They left Capac with a walla and took the steps up to the doors. They opened with a groan, and then Nina was swallowed in darkness. Their steps echoed in the vastness of the chamber-like room. In the distance, she heard a shuffle that was carried on a phantom breeze so that it sounded like it was right beside her, but when she whirled to the side, no one was there.

It was quiet enough that she could hear each of her ragged breaths, and dark enough that she could only see a few arm's lengths in front of her, and beyond, squares of light cut into the stone walls that looked over what she assumed were the kancha grounds.

The room was empty, which lent to the eeriness and cold. Not what she had imagined for a place that was meant to represent the gods. It didn't feel divine, but forgotten. *Forsaken.*

They walked up another set of steps and over another flat expanse of stone. Nina glanced behind her but found nothing but shadow. She could have sworn that the windows ahead were growing smaller instead of larger, that the room was expanding even as they forged on. But after another set of steps, they were there, outlined in daylight. The doors to her fate.

They opened without touch, and when Nina glanced at Kasik for reassurance, she found none. His attention was forward, his jaw clenched, the tendons in his neck strained. He was fighting his own battles, and she was left to face hers alone.

The sunlight was harsh after the bleakness of Qorikancha. The first thing she saw was grass, a green so vibrant it hurt her eyes. When she lifted her face, she next saw people in red milling about. Walla young and old, with achillas on their wrists or their necks, and what she assumed were attendants in blue scurrying between buildings with baskets full of textiles and food piled high.

From a distance, she could hear the clashing of metal and grunts and cheers. There was subdued chatter and other sounds of life that were as familiar as they were foreign. The air felt thinner, and colder, and it did nothing to ease her racing pulse.

Directly ahead, standing between small peaked buildings and in front of a larger stone structure, stood a man in red, his long coat flapping around his legs, the shape of wings in flight embroidered along the edge. At the center of his chest was a large golden disk that she knew depicted the sun god. His fingers were adorned with rings that he tapped together with each step she took.

It sounded like a death march, and when she finally looked up at his face, she saw her demise in the fathomless shadows of his eyes and the wicked curl of his lips.

The dread that coated her mouth tasted like blood.

The guiding hand at her back slipped away, and then Kasik was in front of her, his hair swaying as he lowered into a deferential bow.

"Tayta," she heard Kasik say with such loyalty, such desperation, that she felt it like a plea on her own soul.

See me, that word said. *Love me.*

"You're late," the man responded curtly.

Nina hated that she was intimately familiar with the set of Kasik's shoulders, enough to see that they fell slightly with his tayta's words. That she wanted to reach around him and yank the man's threads from his chest and send him to the floor in a puddle of blood and gore and—

Kasik moved aside and turned to face her. Both sets of eyes watched her expectantly, but she didn't know what they wanted, hadn't heard their words over her murderous thoughts and the sudden, chilling realization that the man across from her, Kasik's tayta with the black eyes, had no light at the center of his chest.

Unlike Kasik, whose burned brightly in comparison, his tayta possessed no threads. Nothing but a void where his will should have been.

If Nina hadn't been standing in front of him watching his lips move and his chest rise and fall with each breath, seeing his pulse pound in his neck, she would have thought him a walking corpse. A puppet held up by strings she couldn't see.

It was then, with a scourge of emotions pushing at her skin, that she placed the man. She saw him touching Sacha's face. Remembered the hem of his patterned cloak brushing the dirt. Felt his fingers digging into her skin. Heard the words he had murmured so that only she could hear.

It was you I felt.

As if she were outside herself, she saw the man's hand reach for her. It landed on her shoulder with a thud and shook her from the past with a gasp. She was solidly back in the present, aware of every part of her body, from her toes curled in her slippers to the hair that blew back from her face on a chilly breeze. She was especially painfully aware of the sudden silence that throbbed in her chest. The beat of her heart that echoed in her ears. The abrupt disappearance of Kasik's light.

"We meet again. I am Kunay Atik," he whispered, and she could have sworn that the black lines of his eyes swirled as he watched her, that his nostrils flared as he breathed deeper. His fingers curled into her flesh and dug into her bones. "Welcome to your new home."

The words were gentle. Perhaps they could have been construed as kind, but she heard them for the threat they were. *This is your final resting place. You belong to me.*

And in that moment, Nina believed him. Something vital had been hidden from her, and it left her feeling vulnerable but eerily calm. Less worried about her convictions and the secrets she held close.

The kunay's head tilted as he watched her breathe through her thoughts. "Your power is strong." His hand released her, and Nina fell forward with the loss. "The emperor will be very pleased."

An arm slid around her middle and braced her. It was Kasik, his jaw clenching as he spoke through gritted teeth. "You knew?"

The moment she was stable, Kasik let go. She pressed a hand to her chest, prodding at the pit of raw hunger in the center of her. Had she always felt this empty, this powerless?

"Of course. I sensed her the moment she used it for the first time. Across such a distance." Atik's eyes sparkled with delight as he spoke. "Impressive, really. It is why we went through all this trouble to bring her here." Gentle fingers traced the edge of her jaw. A shiver of repulsion lifted the hairs on her neck.

"I don't understand," Kasik said, despair laced through each word. "You *knew* she was dangerous, and you sent me without the information I needed to protect myself *and* her. Did you want me to fail?"

"You're letting your emotions get the best of you, *Son*. I gave you that achilla. So long as you kept it around your neck, you would have been aware of her influence."

Dread filled her belly as Kasik glanced at her, a quick flick of his eyes that Atik saw and grasped on to like a hound on a scent. "Did you remove it? Did she fill your mind with her power and make you believe that you *want* her?" He took one step closer and lowered his voice. "Oh, Son, how foolish you can be."

Kasik was turned fully toward her now, betrayal lining his mouth and between his brows, but Nina was filled with her own rage beneath the pressure of emptiness that filled her. "I did no such thing," she argued tensely.

Atik gripped his son's shoulder and shook once, twice. "This is what they do," he said harshly. "They use our will to deceive us into loving them, but who could love such a monster? They are not meant to be loved. Their purpose is so much greater than that."

If Nina had been thinking clearly, she would have stopped to consider who *they* were, but she was lost to his lies, too close to her greatest fears and insecurities, too overcome with outrage to control herself. She launched at Atik, satisfied when she felt the flesh of his cheek fill the crevices underneath her nails.

Before she could relish the small victory, there were hands on her, bruising her arms as they pulled her back. She kicked out to no avail. Screamed her threats to the sky.

It was the Harvest all over again. No one was going to come to her aid. There was no one to save her.

Hands gripped her face and held her steady. She glared into the kunay's eyes as he pulled her face close enough to see every crack in the whites that gave her a peek into his dark and sinful soul.

Then he leaned forward, pressed his cheek to her cheek, and whispered into her ear. "Should you forget your purpose, I will bring Sacha to remind you."

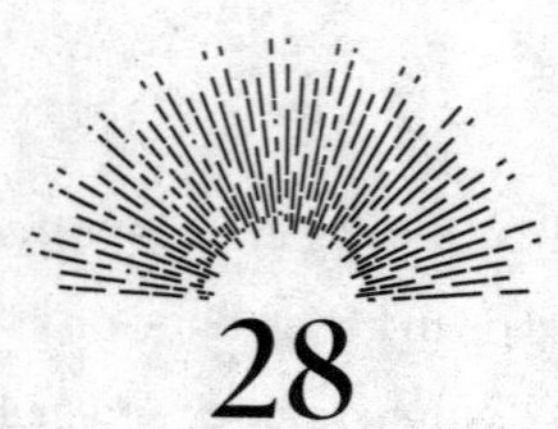

28

Whatever Atik whispered into her ear, Kasik couldn't hear it over the aching realization that he had been so utterly and cruelly deceived. By his tayta, but also by Nina.

He remembered the part of the story he told Nina, where the Ikara controlled and manipulated the man into loving her. Where her powers had drawn him in and held him captive until he was forced to kill her.

Kasik thought back to all the times he had felt an unexplainable pull toward her despite his unyielding loyalty to Maicu. Her stubbornness as she worked to light a fire. Her fearlessness as she threw the rock at the achiyanga. Her carelessness and whimsy as she danced under the full moon.

It had been against his nature, against his will. The essence of her had sunk beneath his skin and burned like an infection in the blood. Had it taken root when he was nearly dead and unconscious, when she had used her power to stitch him back together? Had he been so easy to poison?

Even then, he could feel her lure, feel the sundering in his heart as she looked past Atik, arms pulled behind her, and seethed. "I will never forgive you for this." The walla pulled her backward without care. "One day, I will kill you both," she screamed, her promise echoing off the stone buildings and beating against his heart.

They watched her go, Atik beside him, the hem of his ceremonial red robes fluttering in the breeze. Kasik despised the color. Loathed this place. Begrudged that he had been born to this man.

"You lied to me," he said to the now-empty space before him. He refused to turn and look at the man who had helped give him life. Who had kept so much from him and given him so little.

Nina disappeared through the main doors of the kancha and with her, all unfamiliar sound. Whoever had stopped to watch their interaction were back to their duties as if nothing had happened. The sounds of walla training filled the silence, the lack of explanations from his tayta.

"You sound like a child." Atik lifted a hand and pressed it to his cheek. He smiled when they came away with a thin line of blood across his fingers. "There was no need for you to know more than you did, and now you understand the truth of her."

"I understand the truth about a lot now." Kasik turned to face him, fists at his side. He dug his nails into his palms to hold back this anger, this misery he felt bubbling in his chest. "Like the fact that mamay's family is not dead."

It slipped out before he could stop it, and once the words were between them, Kasik realized what a mistake he had made. He had given up his hand, exposed a secret that he had promised he would keep. And, once again, shown how little control he had over his emotions.

"And where," Atik started, his body preternaturally still, his dark eyes swirling with hunger, "did you learn that?"

What a fool he was to give his tayta this power over him. "There is no need for you to know more than you do," Kasik said, throwing his words back at him and barreling on with his own. "Did you keep her against her will?" His tayta turned away from him, without so much as a flicker of emotion, and began walking toward the kancha doors. Kasik followed, feeling like the child his tayta ridiculed him of being. "Was she only here to serve a purpose, like Nina? If I am such an inconvenience, why keep me? Why not send me away to live with *them*? It's what mamay would have wanted."

Atik stopped and turned suddenly, hands behind his back as he stepped close enough that Kasik could feel the moisture from his breath. "Do not believe for one moment that your mamay spared a single thought for you. The circumstances of your birth were as unavoidable as your very life. It is the gods who brought you to us, and it is the gods who keep you alive."

Kasik couldn't understand what it meant, couldn't parse the expressions on his tayta's face. "You are here to do as you are told," Atik continued. "That is your *only* purpose. If you cannot do that, then there is no reason to *keep* you."

"I will embrace the day that I step into your role if it means that I am free of you."

"You will never be free of me." Atik pressed a finger into Kasik's chest, right over his heart. "Who I am will one day be all that you are."

The words sent a chill down Kasik's spine. They were murmured with such conviction that he couldn't help but believe them. He was silent as Atik reached up and straightened the shoulders of his tunic and the leather cord around his neck, his cold fingers sending a trail of foreboding down Kasik's spine.

"The emperor is waiting," he said, and then he strode away, leaving Kasik to follow.

Maicu was waiting in his sitting room with a wide smile and outstretched arms as Kasik and Atik entered.

"Have you brought her to me safely?" he asked, grasping Kasik's shoulders warmly. In that moment, with the full brunt of Maicu's praise directed toward him, it wasn't difficult for Kasik to remember the days before Maicu had become emperor, when they shared in their triumphs and downfalls together. When they were just friends. Now Kasik was full of doubt and curiosity and questions.

"Did you know about her attay?" he asked carefully, holding on to a tiny sliver of hope that he didn't. It wasn't that Kasik was offended that he hadn't been given the full spectrum of information; it was that he felt like he had been tricked. That his life was expendable.

Nina could have killed him at any moment, but she hadn't. She had only used her attay to heal him and save Shayim's people. He would forever remember the way those men had died in silent agony. The way their twisted limbs and blank eyes had lain in a puddle of blood.

Maicu's eyes sliced toward Atik, then back to Kasik. He dropped his hands to his side and wiped the smile from his face. "Is she unharmed?"

Kasik inhaled deeply to calm himself. There was no point in proving his tayta's opinions of him, though all he wanted to do was rant and yell. "Yes. There was an incident at the acllahuasi with one of the walla, but I took care of it."

"You took care of it?" Atik asked skeptically, his arms crossed over his chest and a smug smirk on his face.

"Yes. I removed his head from his body. I took care of it."

For a moment, Maicu looked almost remorseful. For whom, Kasik couldn't say. The look was gone in a flash, and then Maicu was prodding Kasik to sit, to relax, to discuss the details. Kasik sat stiffly, carefully considering what to say and what *not* to say.

"Her attay. Have you seen it firsthand?" Maicu leaned forward, hands folded in his lap, eyes filled with a type of hunger Kasik had become accustomed to seeing. Maicu was always hungry, always seeking and frantically prodding. It was such a difference from the innocently curious child he had been.

Kasik couldn't lie, not about this when he had to lie about so much else. Halftruths, he decided, were the only path. "We ran into two of *your men* in the Tuta Kulla." He looked at him pointedly, waiting for Maicu to put the pieces together.

With a sigh, Maicu sat back, the plush chair creaking underneath him. "The t'ira," he said.

"She killed them," Kasik said regretfully.

Again, Maicu's eyes slid to Atik, and it was his tayta who spoke. "She's strong," he said eagerly.

"She's the one," Maicu whispered back, his eyes distant.

Kasik could only guess at the path of his thoughts, and he could keep his own to himself no longer. "You didn't tell me. You sent me on a fool's errand without any foresight, any protection. How can I perform my duties properly without all the information?"

"You had plenty of protection," Maicu said, pointing flippantly at the stone that had escaped from beneath Kasik's tunic. "And you seemed to have managed just fine." Maicu gave him a chiding smile, as if this whole thing was nothing more than a joke and Kasik and his ignorance were the brunt of it. "I had faith that you would succeed"—Atik snorted, and Maicu sent him a scathing look—"and you have. That's all that matters. Your loyalty has saved us all, Kasik. Never forget that."

"Saved us *how*? From *what*? Nina only killed those men to save us. She isn't—" *Dangerous,* he was going to say, but she was, wasn't she? He had said, to her face, that her power was monstrous. Perhaps it was too harsh. Perhaps his tayta was right, and he was guilty of letting his emotions get the better of him.

Maicu leaned forward and looked directly into Kasik's eyes. "What I'm about to tell you—"

Atik abruptly pushed away from the wall and stepped toward their seats. "Emperor Maicu—"

"Please, Atik," Maicu said, raising a hand to silence him. Atik let out a huff and turned his back.

When Maicu looked at Kasik again, his eyes were brimming with sincerity. "I trust that what I am about to tell you will never be repeated. If this was made public, there would be panic across the territories."

Kasik had the brief thought that perhaps it was better not to know whatever it was Maicu had been hiding from him, but it was a coward's thought. "You have my word," he said earnestly.

Maicu took a breath. "Several weeks ago, a farmer came into the city speaking of an unfamiliar balsa in the water coming toward the shore." Maicu's voice was hardly more than a whisper, as if there might be enemies listening at the walls. "He said it came closer and closer, and that there were beings on it. Men that looked like us, but their skin was as pale as the moon, some of them with hair the color of straw."

Kukuchi, Kasik thought, his heart pounding as he listened intently.

"We brought him in for questioning and found the location he spoke of. The balsa was unlike any of ours, made with a denser wood and flying a brightly colored tapestry tethered high above on a pole. There was no one on it, but we found evidence of them. Strange clothing and weapons. Unfamiliar foods. It was as if they had come from a different world."

Shayim was right, Kasik thought. Her Seeing was coming to pass, and she didn't even know it. At some point, Kasik had leaned forward to match Maicu's position. They were two childhood friends again, boys plotting against the world once more. "I can take my men to find them. Samaq and the others, they—"

Maicu interrupted with a sigh. He hung his head and folded his hands together between his legs. Kasik swallowed his words, his stomach filled with dread. "We haven't heard word from your contingent since they left."

It felt as if his ears were filled with cotton. His racing thoughts poured out of his mouth. "They should have sent a missive halfway. I can find out what's happened. I'm sure it was just the weather holding them up. I fought against the rain for the first part of my journey, and it was—"

"Kasik," Maicu interrupted gently, his eyes soft. Pitying. "I need you here. I cannot afford to lose one more walla."

He felt Atik's judgment piercing him, waiting for him to be weak, to argue, to show himself for who he thought Kasik was. Kasik had never wanted to prove him right more than he did in that moment. Samaq was his only true friend, the best person he knew, and it was possible that he was waiting for Kasik to find him, to save him. When Kasik didn't show, Samaq would think the worst of him. That he had been forgotten and abandoned.

"I cannot turn my back on my men," he said ardently.

"You cannot turn your back on your *emperor*. Nina and her safety are your priority right now, until the sacrifice can be made. After that, everything will be set right. You can choose new men and lead them as you please."

"Sacrifice?" Kasik asked. It was a practice born from the gods' thirst for praise and obsession, one that had been used to beseech them for mercy and favor and abandoned after the gods were banished to the upper realm. Surely, he didn't mean to give life to it once again. "An animal offering? For what?"

"Not an animal, Kasik." Maicu glanced at Atik again, a question in his eyes, but Kasik didn't dare remove his attention from his emperor. Even if the strange power dynamic at play made him nervous, made him wonder if it had always been this way and he had gone blind to it, or if it was something new and dangerous. "The appearance of the white man was foretold to my tayta many years ago. He knew that he had to unite the people of Amaru, Icosa, and Uwaco to stand against them. Thus began the expansion of his new empire, Tawantinsuyu, and the Harvest. We needed men to fight—"

"And the acllas? Will they fight as well?" Kasik asked, feeding into the facade of his ignorance. He wondered if Maicu would tell him about the Ikara, if he would admit to stealing and hoarding that power for himself.

"Some, if necessary. But it is Nina who we have been searching for all this time. It is Nina who will appease the gods and earn their favor, whose blood will bless and protect the land. Your tayta sensed her all those years ago." Maicu's eyes grew distant. If Kasik didn't know any better, he might have thought there was a sheen over them. "My tayta died before he could see his plans come to fruition, and my brother could not do what needed to be done to ensure that our people survive."

"That's what you meant." Kasik was remembering Maicu's hand on his shoulder. The smell of blood that filled the room. Rumi's body in a puddle next to his tayta's lifeless body in bed. His tayta watching from the corner. "You meant that Rumi wasn't willing to murder an innocent child?"

"She's *not* a child, and this *isn't* murder," Maicu said harshly, his golden eyes shining with fervor. He stood so that he was now towering over Kasik, his loose hair falling over his shoulders as he looked down at him, the power he possessed on full display. "She is *dangerous*. The gods demand her blood, and we will gain their favor and the strength to defeat these foreigners who threaten our lands."

"We don't need the gods to protect our lands," Kasik said pleadingly. He stood to be at eye level with Maicu once again. Atik took a step forward, hand on the hilt of his blade as if he would cut down his own son if necessary. Kasik believed he would. "We have the people. The whole of the empire we've been building. Send me to Uwaco and let me convince Juac to join Tawantinsuyu. Their people are fierce and ruthless warriors, but they are smart. I can speak sense into Juac, and he can convince the other ayllus that it's in their best interest to unite against the kukuchi."

Kasik realized his mistake too late. The word had slipped from his mouth with ease.

"Where did you hear that word?" Maicu asked, his voice disturbingly calm. Kasik could feel Atik's attention like a blade at his throat.

"They are the color of the dead. I thought it fitting."

Maicu hummed, his eyes pensive, and then he came back to himself, the features of his face hardening once again. "No. There is too much at stake," he said. Just like that, he had moved on. "Plans have already been set in motion. The ceremony will take place during Inti Raymi. Until then, you will escort Nina to and from lessons and meals. It is essential that her blood and body remain untouched. Do you understand, Kasik?" Maicu stepped closer, his eyes boring into him. "She will be treated like royalty. Fed the richest foods. Taught by a royal scholar. Dressed in the finest fabrics and gold. The gods demand only the best. Can I trust you in this?"

The emperor clamped a hand onto his shoulder, the pressure gentle but firm. A reminder of who Kasik was. A friend, a kamayuq, a murderer, *loyal.* A storm raged inside Kasik's mind, one that he felt keenly beside the loss of everything he had ever known.

Maicu had been his friend. They had played together, learned together, grown together. For all their lives, they had been inseparable. The difference was, Kasik had been ignored by his tayta and cast aside as his attention was mainly given to Maicu, and for the first time, Kasik couldn't help but feel that he had been spared.

Behind him, Kasik heard the shift of fabric. The whisper of metal. He could imagine Atik taking a step closer, ready and willing to remove his son's head from his body. Kasik would give him no reason. He would play his part perfectly, just as his tayta wanted. "Yes, Emperor. I am yours to command."

Maicu, back to that young and affable persona that Kasik knew so well, smiled brightly and clapped him on both shoulders. "Good. Now I command you to go take a bath. You smell like an animal."

Kasik laughed lightly and stepped aside, avoiding his tayta's heavy attention as he made for the door. He swung it open, prepared to dart out of the room, and ran straight into a wall of flesh. He braced himself against the body, the small upper arms in his as he held them both upright.

It was Chaska, the empress, with her hand raised in a fist as if she was just about to knock. The gold circlet adorning her head tilted to the side as she stepped back and out of his hands. She fixed it quickly before smoothing her hands down her dress and giving him an exasperated look, but he saw the flash of panic before the composure. A look that appeared as if she had been caught listening.

"Chaska," the emperor called from behind him. "What a surprise."

Chaska bowed and leaned around Kasik to speak directly to the emperor. "Your Majesty, I was coming to offer my aid in settling your betrothed."

Feeling as though he was in the way, Kasik opened the door fully and reluctantly stepped back into the office. Chaska breezed in as if she owned the place. Kasik couldn't say he didn't like her; he hadn't spent enough time with her or given her existence enough thought to form such an opinion, but he saw the way she carried herself, how she did as she pleased. Chaska was aloof and spoiled. A princess through and through.

"Your timing is impeccable," Maicu said, and the smile he gave her was genuine. Though they had been a political match, their relationship seemed to have flourished under mutual aspirations of power.

"You can bring her the morning meal and tea. I'm sure she'll enjoy a woman's company."

"Hmm," Chaska hummed in agreement. "Much preferrable to his, at the very least."

They laughed in unison. Chaska shot Kasik a smug smile, and he pressed his lips together.

He left the room holding his tongue, the empress's words echoing in his head.

29

Kunay Atik's whispered words poured into the places Nina's power had filled, pressing against her heart and her soul and her sanity, threatening to tear her apart from the inside just as she had those men.

Should you forget your purpose, I will bring Sacha to remind you.

Her sister's name on his lips had sounded like a curse. Like an omen she could not shake as the guards dragged Nina down long, empty hallways that reminded her all too much of the acllahuasi halls she had been imprisoned behind only weeks ago. She tried desperately to get her feet under her, but the men were relentless, their stiff fingers digging into the fleshy parts of her upper arms.

"Wait," she pleaded. Her voice came out strangled, barely loud enough to her own ears. The guards continued to drag her, and she had the fleeting thought that she should pay attention to where she was going, count the turns or steps, anything to guide her through this labyrinth when the time came to enact her plan.

But her mind was fragmented. *She* was fragmented, the absence of her power like a missing limb, her thoughts like pieces of dried clay shattered across the floor. Kunay Atik was the man from Kasik's creation story, the man with the power to yield hers unusable. Who was immune to the touch of her attay. That was why his threads were nowhere to be found. Why the inside of him was like a lifeless void.

When Atik touched her the first time, she hadn't been familiar enough with the parts of her that had gone missing to know they were gone. Now that she had experienced that power, had coaxed it to life and used it, she could see that it had shrunk away, so small and shriveled that it was entirely out of reach.

She was useless once again. Powerless against the men who carried her between them, their grips unyielding, their ears deaf to her pleading. Finally, she was able to get a foot underneath her, and she braced herself against the floor. The walla on her left grunted as she yanked out of his grip, fully intending to demand to walk herself, but the other walla pulled her to his side so suddenly that she tripped. He caught her by the elbow before she fell.

Nina steadied herself, and then the walla yanked his hand away as if burned. His fingers came away with a smear of red. Both walla stared at the hand, and then glanced at Nina. She turned her arm and there, on her elbow, was a thin line of blood.

Something had scratched her, and only when she noticed the small wound had it begun to sting, but it was the least of her concerns. The walla glanced at each other with wide eyes and then pushed her through an open doorway as if they couldn't get away from her fast enough.

The room was sparsely furnished, the light of a small fire pouring over her and onto the rug she stood on. When she turned to argue, the large double doors were slamming shut. The sound reverberated against her skull, like a bucket of cold water over her head. Against her better judgment she ran to the doors and threw herself against them, pounding with both fists, demanding to be let out.

If anyone heard, they did not come. They did not tell her to stop. She threw herself until her fists were bruised and her throat was raw and the power inside her shrank smaller and further away under the loss of control. And when it became too difficult to continue, she fell to the floor in a heap of aching muscles and a battered heart. She allowed the tears welling in her eyes to streak down her cheeks and gather into the hollow of her neck.

There was nothing she could do against the despair that filled her, that gutted her soul and cleaved her heart in two. The hurt begged to be felt, the loneliness demanded to be held, and so she curled herself into a ball right in front of the doors, as if she could hold herself together by sheer strength of will, and closed her eyes.

Kasik had told her she wouldn't be a prisoner, that she would have the emperor's ear and some form of power. Part of her had trusted him, had taken his words and used them as a pillar of hope.

And then he had called her a monster. Believed when his tayta said she had manipulated him, which was absurd. If Nina was capable of that kind of influence, she wouldn't have landed *there*, of all places. She would have convinced Kasik to leave her at the camp, consequences be damned. There, she could have strengthened her power, protected her family, and kept Kasik's blood off her hands.

There, she could have fought against her ill-fated feelings for Kasik. She couldn't pinpoint when they had started. Perhaps when he was sacrificing himself to save her from the achiyanga. Or when she was healing him from the inside out. Or perhaps it was before that, when she had seen him like an avenging angel in the halls of the acllahuasi and he had so thoroughly punished the man who had touched her.

It hardly mattered when it had blinded her to who he was. The kunay's son. The emperor's unshakable tool. Not her friend, or an ally, or anything else. It was her fault for allowing herself to see the things in him that she wanted to see. Kasik's sense of loyalty did not make him a good person, nor did his concern for her. It only made him more of her enemy.

With a renewed sense of resolve and shaky arms, she pushed herself up to sit against the door and stretched her legs out before her. There was no view of the sky to tell her how long it had been, but she was tired in her bones. Her hands were throbbing and her eyes burning from tears that she angrily wiped away. She inhaled deeply, and then she blew it all out—the anger, the resentment, the hope, the fear.

One by one, she tucked the emotions behind a stone wall in her mind—she would not allow the emperor or the kunay to use these things against her—and slipped on a mask of indifference.

Then she mentally listed the details of her circumstance to inspect.

Kasik had fabricated how much power she would have. As of right then, she had none.

Kunay Atik, Kasik's *tayta*, had no will. There was no thread within him, nothing with which she could use to kill him, or persuade him, if his insinuations were to be believed.

He was like the gods' puppet, Dimas, able to dampen her power with one touch. She knew it wasn't permanent, because it had come back eventually when she was traveling with Kasik. She would need to avoid him and his touch at all costs. At least, until she was ready to kill him with her bare hands.

Kasik had said Emperor Maicu wore many achillas, which meant that her attay couldn't be used to harm him so long as he wore them. They would have to be removed. *How* was the only question.

And finally, she was well and truly alone.

No more, she told herself. No more hoping someone was going to save her. No more praying for the gods to intervene. No more waiting for the perfect opportunity.

She was going to take control of her power and use it to mold her fate, and then she was going to ensure that nobody threatened her freedom or her family ever again.

She awoke hours later to the sound of a door pushing open. Disoriented, she opened her eyes and took stock of her surroundings; the bottom half of a bed, a rough rug underneath her cheek, slanted firelight on the walls, a fierce pounding in her head. A boot-clad pair of feet approached her and stopped, and she dragged her eyes up to find Kasik frowning down at her. There was a moment of relief, a small, hopeful part of her that saw his face and sighed with comfort.

Then her last waking moments reached her addled brain and she quickly sat upright, ready to attack and feed the vengeance simmering beneath her skin.

The anger was back. She had only a moment to realize it before Kasik caught her as she stood, his large, warm hands wrapping around her upper arms and bringing them face-to-face. It was too close. Too much. She tore herself free and raised a hand, to hit or to push, she wasn't sure. Kasik grabbed her wrist, somehow gentle but also firm, and said, "Please," as soft as a whisper meant only for her ears. He had not come alone.

A woman appeared beside him. She was beautiful, with a round face and rosy cheeks that spoke of health and youth. A spiky golden circlet sat atop her head with a single black stone in the middle of it. The dress she wore was long, trailing on the ground behind her, and dark, with tiny golden suns embroidered onto the hem.

The same suns she remembered watching Qori stitch that day at the acllahuasi before everything went wrong.

Her upper arms were covered in golden bands shaped into snakes and arrows, and the smile on her face was patient and sharp as she gave Nina the time to take her in.

The empress. Nina had heard of her only in passing, when news of her betrothal to Emperor Maicu had been on the tip of every girl's tongue in her ayllu. They spoke of the extravagance and the romance that had been sweet enough to taste, of her beauty, elegance, and strong lineage. And of her twelve toes. All rumors, of course, as none of them had seen her with their own eyes.

Nina remembered being both curious and jealous. Not because *she* wanted to marry the emperor, but because she had wished for the kind of opportunity to be so composed and powerful.

Now there she was, standing face-to-face with the elusive woman.

Nina leaned away from her, as if that little distance could help her escape from the empress's sights. If it weren't for Kasik's hands holding her in place, she would have fallen backward and made a fool of herself.

"Thank you, Kasik." The empress smirked. She knew Nina was uncomfortable, and she was enjoying it. "You may leave us now."

Nina turned her eyes to him, but he wasn't looking at her. All she could see was the side of his face, the way his jaw muscles sharpened as if he was clenching his teeth, as if the mere thought of looking at her was too much to bear. Nina's heart hardened further. She took a step back, out of the grasp of his hands, and tried to rub away the memory of his touch. There was no erasing the look he had given her when believing his tayta's lies, or the words she had spat at them.

I will never forgive you for this.

It was a vow she felt deep in her bones, just like the vow she had given her sister by sacrificing herself.

"Empress," Kasik said, the reverence in his voice clear, but he hesitated for a moment, his eyes darting to Nina and back before he left the room.

Empress Chaska watched him go with a placid smile on her face. After he left, Nina stood rooted to her spot, unsure if she was meant to bow or beseech, but it felt like conceding to her fear and this woman who held herself as though she was owed everything she desired.

Instead, she held her stare, even as the empress tilted her head condescendingly and pursed her lips. The prongs of her circlet glinted in the orange flames from the fire behind Nina. She imagined the kinds of marks they would leave on her skin if used as a weapon.

Neither woman said anything as they stared at the other. Nina felt like she was being measured, and she was judging in return. She opened her mouth to speak, but the empress stopped her with a finger in the air.

The door opened again, and this time two servants walked in carrying trays. They placed them on the small table to Nina's right, bowed quickly, and then exited the room.

"There," the empress said. "Now we may speak."

Nina felt woefully ill-equipped for a conversation with this cunning woman. She was full of anger and resentment that clouded her thoughts, but when she reached for the power that typically accompanied her anger, it was nowhere to be found.

"You will find," the empress started as she pulled out a chair and sat before the tea and food, "that everyone within the kancha grounds wears achillas to protect themselves. Emperor Maicu has prepared extensively for your arrival."

She said all this as simply as if she were discussing the weather, while pouring tea at the same time. Nina stayed where she was, hands clenched at her sides, feeling uncertain and slightly fearful. If the emperor was so well prepared, then how would she kill him? Obviously, he wouldn't allow her to simply remove his achillas and slip her fingers around his threads.

No, it would be much more complicated than that. Nina would have to plan and prepare as well.

"Come." Empress Chaska gestured a hand to the cup in front of Nina's seat. "Have tea with me."

It wasn't a request that Nina could choose to ignore, but she wasn't sure her curiosity would have allowed her to.

"Drink," she ordered, and Nina brought the cup to her lips, the steam caressing her face. The scent conjured hazy memories of her time in the acllahuasi. She tried to put the cup down, but the empress's fingers appeared at the bottom and pressed it up.

"It will help," she said gently, "to appear as if you are going along with the emperor's plans. Your freedom depends upon it."

Nina's pulse pounded in her throat as she stared at the empress. Nina wished she could see her threads the way Shayim did, filled with the knots that could be interpreted and known. Anything to help her navigate such a formidable, unknowable person. But the threads at the center of Empress Chaska's chest were blurred and unreachable, and Nina had to make a choice.

She gulped down the tea and waited for . . . *something*. The memory of drinking the tea at the acllahuasi was there, but it was difficult to remember exactly *how* it had made her feel. Almost like there was a thin layer of fog over it all. She looked at the bottom of the cup and saw the leaves there, a muted green, but entirely green. No blackened, sharpened edges.

"Do you like it?" Chaska asked eagerly. "Master Wara brews it himself with Mamacoca leaves foraged from the Tuta Kulla."

They looked like the same leaves her mamay would gather and brew over the small fire in the kitchen. "I do," she said, and she meant it. She still felt like herself, if maybe a bit more settled. Her thoughts went from calculated concern to calm curiosity as she considered Empress Chaska's words.

It could have meant that Nina's freedom in the kancha and the marriage depended upon her compliance. It also could have meant her freedom from this place altogether. But why would the empress help her?

She wouldn't, Nina decided. This was another instance of Nina being too trusting, too hopeful. Whatever game Empress Chaska was playing was beyond her experience.

The empress didn't drink her tea, simply studied Nina and then smiled thinly. It didn't reach her eyes, but Nina found that it mattered little. The tea had given her a kind of clarity that she hadn't expected.

“You will learn to function despite external factors,” the empress added. “Master Wara will share our history and guide you through the expectations you will face while here. There is much for you to learn.”

Nina held her eyes but said nothing. She was too busy trying to parse through her words and decipher the underlying meaning.

The empress leaned forward. “Can I tell you a secret?” she asked.

“I imagine you’ll do so regardless of my answer,” Nina said with a shrug.

The empress sat back and smiled, and this time, it looked genuine. “I didn’t come here to be who they wanted me to be. You will find that there is a lot to gain as women in our position. We will not be so foolish as to mistake our true enemy.” Then she rose from her chair and headed toward the door. When she pulled it open, Nina could see the back of a guard standing to the side.

“Kasik,” the empress said. She placed a familiar hand on his shoulder. Nina’s cheeks burned watching the exchange. She caught a glimpse of his face as he turned to her and spoke, the words too quiet for Nina to hear, and then the door was closed, and she was alone again.

This time, the urge to pound and scream at the doors was fleeting, replaced with acceptance and impatience. She wondered if Kasik had been standing outside earlier, listening to her cries yet doing nothing. That seemed to be a theme for him, but she refused to give him, or anyone else, the satisfaction of hearing her beg ever again.

Once she could figure out how to reach her power, it was going to be *them* begging for her forgiveness. She just needed time, and as she considered her new home and what was expected of her, she assumed she would have plenty of it.

30

Kasik caught only a glimpse of Nina before the door closed, forcing him to give the empress his full attention. She always looked at him with such disdain, as if the mere sight of him was a damper to an otherwise pleasant day. Like a disappointed mamay, though she couldn't have been more than a year or two his senior.

"She needs to be escorted to the bathhouse. Do you think you can manage that?"

"Yes, Empress Chaska," he gritted out. What he wanted to say was *I managed to keep her alive for several days in the depths of the Tuta Kulla*, but that would raise too many questions. Instead, he asked, "Do you need an escort to wherever it is you're going?"

Chaska smiled as if amused, the tips of her pointed head circlet winking in the torchlight. "Emperor Maicu is expecting her at the evening meal. Do not be late."

She turned away with a flourish, the hem of her gown swishing against the floor as she disappeared around the corner.

Kasik waited until she was completely gone, and then he faced the door and took a fortifying breath.

This was not where he was supposed to be. This was not what he was supposed to be doing. Everything he had been told was a lie—he couldn't help but wonder if the emperor had lied about Samaq and his men as well. Perhaps to keep him there under his thumb, and Kasik had led him to believe that he was so easily manipulated.

It was becoming more and more evident that he had *always* been under the control of someone. Maicu. His tayta. Kasik's own ridiculous notions of honor and duty. What was loyalty if the men he served were loyal to no one but themselves?

And what did it mean for Nina and the secret of her fate?

Kasik ran a hand down his face. It wasn't a problem that needed to be solved at that moment. There was plenty of time until Inti Raymi and the sacrifice, and he wasn't in the right frame of mind to solve problems as large as these. He'd had little sleep last night, and he still had to speak with Master Wara. His teacher would know what to do; he always did.

Steeling himself, he knocked.

There was a moment of silence, and then another. Kasik knocked again, this time louder, though there was nowhere Nina could go where she wouldn't have heard.

He was just about to throw open the door when it opened on its own.

Nina stood before him, the features of her face shuttered, her thoughts closed to him except for the anger lining her mouth. He had to clear his throat before he spoke. "I have been instructed to escort you to the baths."

She was silent a moment, and her scrutiny was worse than his own. "Are you sure she didn't use her power to compel you to escort me to the baths?"

The question was sharp, and ridiculous, because Chaska didn't have that kind of power.

And neither did Nina, if what she was implying could be believed. Kasik had to admit that it was unlikely. When he had awoken in the tent bound and healed, the achilla had been hanging from his neck as it always was. There would have been plenty of time to remove it and compel him to . . . what, exactly? Leave her? Love her? Join her?

Whatever there might have been between them was gone, replaced with apprehension. He couldn't think too much about all the things he wanted to say for the risk of spilling it all. They needed to come to an understanding first.

Kasik stepped forward, and she stepped backward, a dance of avoidance that made him want to reach out and pull her into him. The emperor's red matched the warmth blooming in her cheeks as he closed the door behind him and leaned against it. Her hair was a tangled mess, and he was almost certain that was a smudge of dirt on her left cheek. She had faced the empress like that, dirtied and distraught, and he knew she had done it with her head held high, her chin jutted out stubbornly, just as she stood before him when he first laid eyes on her.

So much had changed since that day, but not her resolve.

"I'm sorry," he said simply. No other words, no explanation. He hoped she could see the sincerity in his eyes, hear the hope in his voice. He was tempted to say more, to burden her with all his secrets, but he couldn't. Not until he spoke with Master Wara. Not until he had a plan.

They couldn't be friends, but he didn't want to be her enemy.

He could tell by the way she averted her eyes and pushed a clump of hair behind her ear that it wasn't what she had been expecting to hear. All at once, the fight had drained out of her, and he hated that he was the one to disarm her.

"Lead the way, then," she said in lieu of an acceptance, but it was good enough for him.

There was nothing to marvel at within the halls of the kancha, except for the tapestry Nina had been standing in front of for so long that Kasik was beginning to grow stiff. Everything else she had seen thus far was nondescript stone in varying shades of brown and beige. Torches were spread over even intervals to light the way. All the doors were closed, and he saw how Nina had glanced at each of them as they walked by. Her lips had moved soundlessly, and he assumed she was trying to count her steps to navigate her way to an eventual escape.

Now she was silent. Utterly transfixed. Kasik had to admit the tapestry was a sight to behold. It covered the entire wall, and the colors were bright enough that it looked as though you could run a hand over it and come away with real blood smeared across the tips of your fingers. He stepped closer to it, to her, so that their sides were almost touching. The silence between them was tense, a palpable reminder of what they were to each other.

Friends. Enemies. Strangers.

"I didn't think I would see you again," she said quietly. Even so, her voice echoed, the stone whispering her words to him again and again.

"I wasn't meant to be here. My men, they—" He stopped, uncertain why he felt the need to share. *Certain* that she wouldn't care. "Emperor Maicu requested that I continue to guard you until the ceremony," he said instead.

"The ceremony," she repeated. Kasik thought she would ask more, that she would demand to know the things that he knew, but she kept her eyes on the tapestry, quiet and withdrawn.

He took the opportunity to study her profile, each of her bold features outlined by the shifting torchlight. There was always the slightest furrow carved into her brow, not in anger but in thought, as if she was constantly questioning every word and every sight. He wondered if she would figure out his secret before he had the chance to tell her.

The truth of her fate sat in his chest like a weight. Kasik knew he should tell her, but he could not decide if it would help. She had told him she intended to fight it, and he saw the way she surveyed her surroundings keenly. Perhaps she would escape on her own sometime in the next four weeks before Inti Raymi, and his choice would be made for him.

Perhaps none of this would matter. Certainly, he and his feelings least of all.

"This is your creation story," she said suddenly. "The one you told me that night."

The way she said *your* set his teeth on edge. It was the same way she spoke of the emperor, as if he wasn't hers. As if she was outside their purview and therefore their control.

Kasik turned his eyes away from Nina's face and back to the tapestry. At the top were the indistinct shapes of four gods—Viracocha in the middle, woven in threads of dark brown and black, with what looked like hands spread to either side, where from his fingers sprouted golden threads that were connected to Inti on his right and Killa and Pachamama on his left. Like leads used to steer and control.

Below them were crude depictions of humans and flora and fauna shoved between mountains so jagged they looked like weapons. And underneath them, rivers of blood, the thread so rich a color that when Kasik had first seen it, he had reached out to see if it was wet.

And woven throughout, in specks and strands, were the golden threads from the gods' hands, inextricably tying them all together. A story of reciprocity, of inevitability. Of *belonging*. An unmovable force. *That* was what Nina was fighting.

"It is. The gods—Viracocha," he said, pointing to the shadow of a shape whose eyes were holes in the weaving. "Inti." The sun god was bathed in the golden threads, and where his face should have been was a sun with missing eyes. Kasik slid his fingers over the tapestry, feeling the jut of each thread. "This is Killa and Pachamama." The former was made up of silver threads, a stark contrast to the black and gold around her, and the latter was a soft shade of green, easily forgettable in the chaos of the whole picture.

Like the green Shayim's people wore. Kasik had not realized it before.

Nina reached out a hand and gently brushed her fingers over the bundle of golden threads at eye level. They were attached to the shape of a human, its limbs a bit spindly, but upon closer inspection, Kasik noticed they weren't just strange looking—they were unnatural. Inhuman.

He watched as Nina's fingers crawled from one thread to another, closer to the middle where the depiction of Yuri and Dimas stood. Dimas was entirely black and seemed to glisten, like the achilla. Yuri's hands were awash in gold, and the river of blood that saturated the entire bottom of the tapestry began at her feet.

When her fingers brushed over the black threads of the counterbalance, she yanked away with a gasp.

Kasik grabbed her hand and pulled it closer to inspect it. "Are you all right?"

But Nina pulled out of his touch and stepped back, a look of bewilderment clouding her eyes. "I'm sorry," Kasik said again. It seemed as though all he did was apologize, but he hadn't meant to touch her. At some point, it had become second nature to reach for her, and when he tried to wipe the feel of her from his palm, he found he could not.

She was like a stain on his soul.

"We should move on," he said abruptly. Nina didn't meet his eyes, but she nodded. And as he turned away, he caught sight of her bringing her hand to her chest, a furrow on her brow, and wondered if his touch affected her just as it affected him.

31

The bath had been a cleansing affair in all ways. Nina felt sturdier after it, more confident as she selected a pretty blue gown from the chest in her room and slipped it over her head. The golden stitching along the edges sparkled in the firelight. It cinched at the waist and fell to the floor with a flourish. It was the most luxurious thing she had ever worn. Sacha would have loved it.

It was her sister's face she kept in mind as she dressed and plaited her hair. The room was smaller than she had anticipated, but it seemed as though the whole kancha was composed of many small rooms down many long hallways that were meant to confuse.

And there were small bits of gold everywhere she looked. In the handle of the brush she had used to tame her hair. Carved into the wooden beams of her bed. On the table next to it in the shape of a narrow circle. She absentmindedly rubbed the golden circlet around her wrist. The one on the table was similar, and clearly meant for her to wear, but she had felt the chill of the achilla at the center before she had even touched it and decided against it.

And then she waited, and while she did, she allowed her thoughts to wander.

The tapestry came to mind, the colors bright and burned into her mind. The way the golden threads connected them all, and how Yuri's hands had been devoured by them. The blood that ran beneath her feet was her fault, according to Kasik's version of the story. She and the other Ikara had created chaos and devastation and then were hunted down like animals for it.

But she remembered Mika's version, which had told a different story. One where the Ikara were retribution and salvation.

Kasik was right—perhaps her attay *was* monstrous—but it was the gods and the men in power who had forced her hand, who had pushed her toward inevitable destruction. A mutation in the fabric of who she was and could have been.

Had she been left alone, she would have been, at that very moment, in the fields with Sacha and Lali, harvesting their portion of the chani owed to the emperor. But they had come, and they had collected, and Nina no longer felt responsible for the consequences of their actions.

Nor her own. Whatever choices she made were forced by the hands of their greed and misguided faith. Even Kasik's, even if his touch had been gentle and warm and naively wanted. Nina was aching for comfort, for sympathy. To stop feeling so overwhelmingly alone, but the only things she allowed herself to feel were grudging acceptance and bleak understanding.

Nina was but one person in the face of their power and cunning, Ikara or not. Her plan to kill the emperor was foolhardy and brash and enormous, and she would most likely die before succeeding. She only hoped that once she was dead, the gods and their pawns would finally forget her, and leave her family alone.

When a knock came at the door, Nina was ready. She had steeled herself against seeing Kasik again with the reminder that even if he had apologized, it didn't mean she had forgiven him. There was so much he had hidden from her. Whether it was intentional was none of her business. He was a distraction from her grand plan—the only thing that mattered now.

Killing Emperor Maicu would not happen that night. It was their first time meeting, and it was meant to occur at an intimate dinner with his most trusted friends. She assumed Kunay Atik would be there, and

Kasik. She would be forced to sit at the same table as the men who pulled the strings of her fate.

When she finally opened the door, Kasik lowered his hand and raised his gaze to trail over her. She remembered the way his dark eyes had been alight as he watched her dance underneath the stars in the Tuta Kulla, how his throat had bobbed noticeably when she stepped closer. How she had felt unencumbered and foolishly brave with his eyes upon her.

He took her in the same way now. As if she had been conjured from his wildest and most desperate dreams.

Nina tore her eyes away and went to step past him, but he stopped her with a gentle hand around her wrist. "Your feet," he said, his voice both near and distant, the pulse in his neck fluttering quickly.

Cheeks blazing, she glanced down to see her bare toes peeking out from the hem of her dress. She had forgotten her slippers. The feel of Kasik's fingers cradling her wrist lingered even after she slipped on her shoes and followed him out the door, through hallways that had begun to look familiar.

Until, suddenly, they weren't.

The light was different in this part of the kancha. It struck the walls in a way that made them look as if they were on fire, but when she grazed her fingers across the length of one, she found it cool to the touch.

"Gold," Kasik said from in front of her.

Nina looked at him, and then the wall. "Gold?" she repeated.

"Brushed gold," he clarified, as if anticipating her next question.

She turned back to the wall. It wasn't shiny like the empress's jewelry or the stitching on her hem, rather a dull, deep yellow that seemed to soak in the light and burn from within. She couldn't help but press a hand to it, marveling at the sheer beauty and the time it must have taken to craft this.

It was such a different world here compared to her home near the sea, where their existence was simple and everything was crafted in a way that served a specific purpose. There was beauty in the simplicity, and she respected it, but she couldn't help consider how she might not have ever gotten to see the golden buildings of Amaru if she hadn't been brought there.

Even if it was against her will.

Not for the first time, she thought about just how far out of her depth she was, in all ways. How much easier it might be to accept her fate, marry the emperor, and live her life in luxury. This didn't have to be a fight that she fought. Murdering the emperor wasn't the only solution. In fact, it was possible it was the *worst* option, and the farther away she was from Shayim and her people, the more absurd it seemed.

Nina was not a savior, but she was afraid to find out who she would become without her anger, without her resolve, without her hopes and plans for her own future.

The long hallway came to a sudden end at a set of tall double doors, a large torch on either side washing the stone walls in a burnt-orange glow. Behind her, the spaces between the torches crawled with whispering darkness, yet she was tempted to slink toward it and away from what lay beyond and made her heart skitter with apprehension.

"It's just dinner," Kasik whispered. She wasn't sure who he was encouraging, but she inhaled deeply and straightened her shoulders all the same.

They stood side by side, much like they had when observing that tapestry. On the other side of those doors was a different kind of story unfolding, one that she was determined to narrate.

"I'm ready," she whispered back. Kasik's hand rested upon the latch for two heartbeats and then he pushed the doors open with a flourish.

The soft murmur of conversation filling the room just seconds earlier disappeared, and all attention turned toward Nina.

In the center of the small room sat a wooden table, where people dressed in varying shades of red turned to her. The torchlight cast them in shifting shadows so that all she could see were glowing eyes set within unfamiliar faces. Even through the eerie dimness, she could recognize one figure.

Kunay Atik sat at the corner of the table farthest from the door. He smiled at her, and though there was a table full of people between them, it felt as though he were right next to her, breathing down her neck. Peering into her soul.

"Come closer," someone said, and she tore her eyes away from Atik to look at the man next to him, who beckoned her forward with fingers long and lean and glittering with gold.

In her head, Nina had created this image of a man who was larger than life, someone who could crush her beneath his thumb, but Emperor Maicu was young, perhaps no older than Kasik, and soft in a way that spoke of a lack of hard labor. His long black hair shone in the firelight, and his golden eyes tracked her every move, down to the slightest shift of her shoulders with each breath.

It was clear that he was a man used to getting what he wanted, which at that moment was her. All she could do under the scrutiny was comply with his demands, walking swiftly toward the head of the table with every pair of eyes in the room watching her. Nina knew they were expecting to see her cower or cry or flee with her tail between her legs. But she would not show fear in this den of predators. Let them believe her an animal well trained and honored to be in their presence.

Out of the corner of her eye, she saw Kasik walking opposite her, their steps in sync, their footfalls heavy with obligation. He stopped at the empty seat next to his tayta. A clear sign of their position, of the strength of their relationship to each other and to the emperor.

The emperor is my friend.

Perhaps he hadn't lied to her all along, and she had only been lying to herself.

The emperor turned in his seat to anticipate Nina's approach. He was handsome—there was no denying that. He wore a sleeveless, bloodred tunic that exposed arms corded with muscle, his hair, dark as night, cascading around his shoulders and down his back. Sitting on his head was a gold circlet wrapped with colorful feathers, a large black stone set in the middle. The achilla was similar to the one that hung around Kasik's neck, but glossier, the surface polished to an impressive shine.

Nina traced each detail until she was standing before him and could no longer ignore his eyes. They were bright, alive. Warm honey that coalesced and beckoned. The way he sat, leaned back in his chair as if she was putting on a show, muddled her thoughts and made it so she barely remembered to bow. The fingers of his left hand tapped the table, not with impatience, but to a beat she could not hear.

Up close, she saw that his hands were soft. No calluses, no scars. When they touched her, they wouldn't scrape her skin, not as Kasik's had. And Emperor Maicu's eyes didn't leave a path of wanting in their wake, only alarm.

This was the most powerful man in the empire. The man who had taken up the legacy of his tayta's dream of a united Tawantinsuyu. The man who had stolen children from their families and murdered his brother in cold blood, and there he was, smiling at her as if she was the most fascinating thing he had ever seen.

Creases formed at the corners of those dancing eyes. A light dusting of facial hair covered his jaw, and Nina, realizing that she had begun to inspect his features again, dropped her face toward the ground. Whatever bravado she had fed herself before entering the room fled under his amused scrutiny.

Emperor Maicu chuckled, a quiet, private laugh meant only for her. "I hope everything has been to your liking," he said as he stood, putting himself directly in front of her. He was tall, his chest at eye level, and Nina swallowed as he took one small step closer. She was all too aware of their audience, of the pregnant silence surrounding them, of the way his movements were slow and deliberate as if to soothe her nerves. He pinched her chin between two fingers and guided her eyes to his.

Nina peered at him through lowered lashes. "Thank you for this gift," she said. Let him think her overflowing with gratitude. Let him think her weak and overwhelmed with fear. His eyes dipped to her mouth as she spoke. "What an honor to be chosen."

The pressure of his thumb dug into her chin. Nina was right; the hands that cradled her future were soft and supple, and she knew he was more dangerous than the most hardened of walla because of it. She would not allow herself to forget.

32

"May the gods . . ." the emperor called, standing above them all, a golden cup in one hand and the other splayed on the table. One of his ringed fingers tapped against the cup, perfectly in sync with the beat of Kasik's heart. "Favor this union." He poured a tiny amount of the chicha onto the floor at his feet, and the rest of the guests at the table did the same.

Kasik was slow to grab his cup, to pour, to drink, acutely aware of his tayta's attention, of Maicu and his expectations, of Nina and her ire, of Chaska and her indifference.

One misstep, and they would all question his intent in different ways.

The chicha went down like acid. It didn't help that he felt Nina's desperation like a hand wrapped around his throat. He couldn't tell if the uncertainty he sensed was hers or his own.

If Maicu knew of the doubts Kasik harbored, the animosity brewing in his heart, he would have him disposed of without a second thought. In fact, Kasik had no need to wonder whether his tayta would be glad to carry out that specific task.

The gods might be keeping him alive only so long as Maicu decided so, and if he was dead, there would be no one left to protect Nina.

Unless he didn't stay. He could help Nina escape and then leave with her. They could find Shayim's ayllu again. Perhaps he could find Samaq and his men, and then they could all hide there.

Like cowards. The achiyanga would probably smell their fear and eat them alive before they found it again.

Underneath the table, something bumped his foot. He glanced

sideways. Master Wara's eyes were wide with warning, and then Kasik heard his name, as effective as a slap across his cheek. He whipped his head up to find Maicu's gaze fixed on him, lips tilted into a semblance of a smile.

"Are you with us?" he asked pointedly.

Kasik's fingers tingled with dread. They knew of his traitorous thoughts. They would kill him, and then they would kill Nina, and Samaq would be lost forever, perhaps captured and tortured by the kukuchi and—

"We were just discussing the festival." Empress Chaska's voice pulled him out of the spiral. Beside her, Nina sat demurely, brows furrowed as she watched him falter. "We've heard news from Uwaco."

"From Uwaco?" he repeated mindlessly. Maicu hadn't told him. When he glanced at the emperor, he found him running a finger around the rim of his cup. He looked as though he had no interest in relaying that news to him now.

Chaska glanced at Maicu before she continued. "Yes. They've agreed to attend, and whatever choice they've made will be displayed in the color of their garments."

It was a practice that hadn't been used since before Emperor Yachua began uniting the territories. Custom required that foreigners wore black to set themselves apart. Once they became allies, they would wear a mutually agreed upon color that represented their union.

Emperor Maicu's color was red. Those who belonged to him wore it as well, while those under his care wore blue, as Nina was wearing. He wondered what color they would put her in for the ceremony, and if she would belong to him even in death.

Kasik blew out a breath and leaned back, shoving the image of her blood-covered body aside. "That's brave of them," he said somberly.

“They flaunt their insubordination,” Atik said, dismissing his son entirely. “They deserve to be made examples of.”

“We cannot kill everyone who does not submit to the emperor’s plans,” Kasik said, looking directly at his tayta, challenging him to meet his glare. “If Uwaco chooses to remain independent, then that is their right.”

“I agree,” Chaska chimed in. “A gentle hand is needed in situations like this, and Emperor Maicu is so very good at inspiring loyalty. Let them choose him, for *when* they do, they will be unfailingly true to their word.”

Master Wara leaned forward and cleared his throat. “The empress is right,” he said simply. It wasn’t often that Kasik’s teacher spoke up, most times remaining neutral in situations of dissent. “They will see that joining is to their benefit.”

“They must be convinced.” The words came from the mamakuna of Qorikancha. It was true that Master Wara did not speak up often, and this woman spoke even less than he did. Kasik didn’t even know her name, only that she wore nothing but purple, and sometimes, her words weighed more than even Atik’s. A fact that Atik seemed to resent at that moment, if his blanched lips and flared nostrils were any indication.

The mamakuna and Emperor Maicu shared a look, and Kasik took the opportunity to glance at Nina. Her attention was pinned on the emperor, her eyes darting over his features as if she was committing them to memory. Kasik dropped his hands below the table to shake them out.

“We will find a way to do so, I’m sure.” Maicu shifted to Atik, and they continued to speak, but Kasik allowed himself to be distracted by Nina, determined to decipher each small movement of her face. He remembered the vow she had made at the ayllu, that she would find a way to be free, and he wondered what exactly she was planning.

The divot between her brows was deep with thought and her lips were pressed tightly together. If she wasn't careful, she'd give herself away. But when he glanced around the table, he noted no one was watching her as closely as he was. Perhaps it was *him* who would give her away.

"—she will begin her instruction with Master Wara," Maicu was saying. "Kasik, you will escort her there every day, and Mamakuna," he said, turning his attention to the woman in purple on the other side of Chaska, "you will see Nina tomorrow?"

"Of course," the mamakuna answered. "Though we have plenty of time."

"Best to get it over with now. We don't want to waste anyone's time," Maicu said. The mamakuna nodded, and then the conversation veered toward other things, like the territories that had asked for extensions on their chani and the acllas who were due for service selection.

He heard Chaska lean over and say, "Don't worry—it's a rather quick and boring affair."

Kasik kept an eye on Nina, noting the way she hardly touched her food, and wondered what thoughts ran through her head. She stared at the plate as if considering the effectiveness of using it as a weapon and then seemed to decide against it. He should have looked away instead of allowing himself to soften toward her.

Nothing good could come of it.

It wasn't that she was more desirable like this, in a beautiful blue dress accented with gold that lit up her skin like the sun. It was that she carried herself as if she belonged there. As if she was there by choice.

Nina deserved to know the truth, and he had to be the one to tell her. When the room came into focus again, Chaska and Nina were bent toward each other, Chaska's lips moving quickly and Nina nodding along while the others around him conversed.

The emperor must have noticed because he cleared his throat and addressed them directly. "Chaska," he said. "Did you help our Nina get settled?"

"Yes, my love," Chaska responded, saccharine and direct. "We had a wonderfully enlightening teatime."

Kasik watched as Nina swallowed the bite of food she had finally taken, the delicate line of her throat bobbing slightly before she spoke. "I'm very grateful for the comforting reminder of home."

They spoke as if they shared some secret and he worried whether anyone else heard it. More than that, he worried that Nina seemed to take a liking to Chaska so quickly. The empress was just as calculating as the rest of them. Nina didn't consider him an ally, but neither should she trust Chaska.

The emperor clapped his hands. "Wonderful," he said. The gold of his rings caught the light as he placed a hand on her shoulder, and then he leaned closer and whispered into her ear.

Nina gave in to him willingly, even going so far as to place a hand atop of his. Watching them speak so intimately made Kasik's stomach burn with an unfamiliar emotion. He imagined them speaking like that often, behind closed doors, perhaps with less clothing on, and he was suddenly, loathsomely happy that it would never come to pass. That she wasn't truly meant to marry him, and Maicu would therefore never have the pleasure of knowing what it felt like to be with her in that way.

But her performance was convincing, and Kasik couldn't help but think that she reminded him of his tayta. Obedient but perceptive. Eager but shrewd. Powerful in a way that was threatening if one decided.

"I think our guest must be exhausted from her journey."

Chaska's voice cut through his thoughts. Everyone looked at her, including Maicu, who leaned back from Nina. It felt as though a fist loosened from around Kasik's heart.

"Yes, of course," he said. "Kasik."

Kasik whipped his head toward Maicu, his heart in his throat as if he had been caught. Again. "Please see that Nina finds her rooms."

"Thank you, Emperor Maicu." Nina stood quickly and smiled, the sweetest smile he had ever seen on her face, and Kasik finally placed the nameless emotion burning in his chest. It was jealousy, because Kasik had never gotten that kind of smile. There had never been the time, he knew that, but she had just met Maicu, and he was lying to her even then. He planned to make it so she never smiled again. He didn't deserve a single one of them.

Kasik knew he didn't, either, but perhaps that could change.

The conversation picked up again as Kasik stood. They had all dismissed him, his tayta especially, but still he held himself rigid, forcing his hands to open the door, his feet to carry him out, his eyes to stay straight ahead.

The door snicked closed and he took a deep breath, turned to ask Nina if she was all right, and found her halfway down the hall, her slippered feet nearly silent on the stone floor.

"Nina," he called, but she kept walking. When he tried to grab her arm, she dodged away from his touch and walked faster. There was no reason to stop her, not when she was heading in the correct direction, and he couldn't do what needed to be done in these halls where there were no secrets kept.

The urge to comfort her made his chest hurt.

"Nina, please," he said again, following as closely as he could without seeming too eager. "Let me help you."

Finally, she whirled around. Her eyes and the tip of her nose were red. When she lifted a hand to wipe at a stray tear, it trembled slightly. She clenched it against her belly. "I think you've done enough, don't you?"

The words rooted him to the spot. The truth of them pierced him as surely as the sharpest blade. Before he could respond, she turned and stormed off, leaving him to stare after her and wonder what he was meant to do next.

33

Nina paced in her room the next morning, waiting for the empress or Kasik to knock on her door. It was difficult to know what time it was due to the overwhelming lack of sunlight, and she had hardly been able to sleep in such a large bed and quiet room. She was used to her sister beside her, the sounds of her parents in the kitchen, the hushed rustle of their fields from outside.

These stone walls were thick and cold and strange. Everything about it and its occupants made her skin crawl, but she was glad to have met the emperor and taken his measure. He was brazen and proud, with his flashy appearance and wandering hands and smug smiles.

Nina knew exactly what she needed to do.

It was in that room that she realized she still had power. Perhaps not the kind she had hoped for, but one that held sway over men, nonetheless. Nina would seduce Emperor Maicu into removing his achilla, and then she would remove his head.

As long as she was able to avoid Kunay Atik's touch and Chaska's meddlesome curiosity and Kasik's overwhelming desire to *help*, then she might get everything she wanted.

Even if it was tempting to accept his hand, Nina could not, because leaning on him would lead her closer to a fall, and she could not afford to fall. Falling meant failure, and failure meant danger for Sacha. The kunay and the emperor had no reason to go back for her so long as she didn't give them one.

Someone knocked. Nina stopped her pacing and ran her hands

down her dress and over her hair. At the last moment, she decided to sit on the bed and affect an air of indifference. "Come in," she sang.

The empress breezed through the door. Today, her dress was the color of the sky right before the sun fully rose during the wet season, an orangey red that was on the border of the emperor's color. "Good," the empress said, stepping aside for an attendant to follow her into the room. "You're awake."

They waited for the food and tea to be placed, and then the empress motioned for Nina to join her at the table. If Empress Chaska insisted upon sharing her time, then Nina would sit and eat and drink and glean as much information from the woman as she possibly could. Who else knew the emperor better than she?

The chair creaked underneath Nina. The steam from the tea caressed her face as she took a sip. It tasted normal again, just like home. The familiarity made her heart ache.

"Are you ready for today? Master Wara is looking forward to meeting you."

Nina swallowed the last of her mouthful. "Mmm, yes," she quickly answered. "I'm curious about what he will teach me."

"Good." Empress Chaska nodded, and Nina could have sworn there was a glint of pride in her eyes. "And the mamakuna is a severe woman, but she is not cruel so long as you comply. You *are* a virgin, yes?"

The question was so forward that it made Nina sputter and choke on a bite of fruit. She wiped her mouth with the back of her hand, and it came away red, much like what she imagined her entire face looked like. "I haven't . . . That is, there's never been . . . I don't . . . Yes," she finally settled on, mortification entirely replacing any confidence she might have successfully portrayed.

"That's good." The empress grabbed a piece of pitahaya, a white fruit that was better suited to her elegance, and took a demure bite. “There must have been plenty of opportunity while traveling with Kasik. He is a handsome man, and he seems to care for you very much.”

Nina snorted indelicately. “He only cares about his honor,” she said, completely ignoring the *handsome* part. The way he looked was of no consequence to the feelings she didn’t have for him.

“That is truer than you know,” the empress said with a smile. “I have known him for as long as I’ve been at the kancha, and he has never treated me as anything other than what I am to the emperor. I thought perhaps he wasn’t capable of it, but he seems to be different with you.”

“I can assure you he is not,” Nina said, averting her eyes and fidgeting with the cup of tea to keep her hands busy. “His loyalty is unshakable.”

The lie slipped past the memory of Kasik’s words outside Qorikancha. *Ask me to forsake every vow I’ve ever made.* But that had been before he believed her capable of controlling his desires. Before he had watched as they dragged her away with nothing but betrayal in his heated eyes.

“In any case,” the empress said, a hand brushing aside an errant piece of hair over her shoulder. “It’s best to leave all of that behind. You are meant for so much more than these men can comprehend.”

The sentiment reeked of ambitions and expectations, all of which she was currently desperate to sidestep, and was eerily similar to the words Shayim had told her before she had departed the ayllu.

“Did you know that Master Wara served alongside Emperor Yachua? He taught Emperor Maicu all he knows, and he knows *many* things. Be sure to ask him all your questions and give him your ear.”

The empress’s words were innocent enough, but Nina couldn’t help but feel like there was something the woman was implying. Something she wasn’t saying. “I understand,” Nina said, though she felt like she might not.

"Very good," Empress Chaska said, rising. "Then I shall see you at dinner."

Nina watched her walk toward the door and pull it open, but the empress turned at the last minute. "Just remember, he sees everything." To Kasik, she said roughly, "Temple, then tutor."

Kasik bowed and waited until Chaska was gone to step into the room. His eyes flicked to Nina's feet. "Shoes" was all he said, and then he bent down to reach beneath her bed for the pair of slippers she had carelessly tossed aside after dinner.

"Nina, I—" he started, holding out her slippers as if to help her put them on.

But Nina snatched the shoes from him. "Do not," she said, trying and failing to keep her balance as she shoved her feet into them.

"That's not fair," he said, stepping closer to brace her before she lost her balance.

"Life isn't fair, Kasik," she said aloud. *Distance*, her mind screamed, and she yanked out of his grasp and hopped a step back. The more space between them, the better. "You weren't supposed to be here. We were never supposed to see each other again." With both shoes finally on, Nina gathered herself with a deep breath. "It was much easier to think that I could do this knowing that I wouldn't."

"I am sorry to disappoint." Kasik stared at her, hurt splashed across features that softened in a way that made Nina ache. He ran a hand down his face as if he could wipe it away. "I meant what I said before. This isn't what I wanted, but I—"

"Cannot go against the wishes of your emperor," Nina interrupted. "I am very aware of that. And why would you, when all it took was one word from your tayta to believe that I have manipulated you into feeling anything for me?"

"You do not know me at all if you think I would be so easily persuaded." Kasik stepped forward so quickly that the air left Nina's lungs. His hands went around her arms, gentle but firm. "I am not the enemy, Nina, but there's—"

"You are *all* the enemy." Nina wrenched herself away from him and walked to the door. Her heart beat so wildly that it stole her breath, but it was better to face away from him. To hide how difficult it was to be near but keep him at arm's length. They weren't friends, or allies, or even acquaintances. They were strangers. No one and nothing at all.

"Nina, please," Kasik begged, one hand extended toward her, a tether to ground her in this strange and terrifying world. As always, it was tempting to accept. He was the only person who had seen what she had done and still, he offered his hand. Regardless of her *monstrous power*.

Which was easily contained and not so monstrous, after all. It had taken one touch from Kunay Atik, and she could only feel it like she could feel the warmth of the sun on a cloudy day. There, but hidden behind a haze of white. Near, yet so far.

Like everything else seemed to be, it was entirely beyond her reach.

Nina was aware of the threads of those they walked by. She couldn't touch them, but it was almost as if they were brushing against her, waiting to be seen and cradled and used. The ache of craving was enough to distract her if she let it, but Kasik's presence beside her was steadfast. She focused on the accidental brushes of his arm instead, bent at his side with a hand on the hilt of his blade as if challenging anyone who looked too long. And look, they did.

Attendants in blue flicked their eyes to her and away before she could meet them. The walla were more brazen with their curiosity, stopping to greet Kasik and then letting their eyes trail over her before moving on. There were others milling about who wore darker shades of blue but paid her little mind. Visiting nobility, perhaps, under the protection of the emperor but did not belong to him.

The closer they got to Qorikancha, the quicker Nina's heart beat. She had tried to avoid thinking about what the mamakuna would require of her, but the chunks of gold illuminating the building that flashed in the late-morning light forced her to remember Chaska's words and truly consider them.

A *virgin.*

It seemed that she could not marry Emperor Maicu if she was not one. Perhaps it could be another path to ending this arrangement. A plan, in case murder did not pan out. She only hoped that the gods could not hear her thoughts and strike her down.

A light hand pressed against the small of her back. It was warm and grounding, as always. "Are you all right?" Kasik asked, but his gaze was focused over her head, his eyes darting around as they had in the Tuta Kulla. Even in his own home, he was on watch.

Nina hadn't realized she'd stopped. "I'm fine," she said quickly. Kasik's hand fell away when she resumed walking, and she hated how much she missed the warmth of it.

Until he guided her through a narrow doorway and into the temple of the sun god, and her breath was taken away. It looked entirely different then the first time she had seen it.

The ceilings still soared high above, but the cavernous room was cut with streaks of sunlight that poured in from small pass-throughs interspersed throughout. There was no furniture to sit on, no finery to admire. The beauty was captured in the beams of light and how they illuminated the golden discs bearing the likeness of the sun, the glare so strong that Nina's eyes burned.

On the opposite side of where they stood was a platform, where statues made of gold stood, each in the shape of a man with long hair and a giant headpiece made of glossy black feathers balanced on his crown.

"The past emperors. They are embalmed and then cast in gold to preserve their connection to Inti."

Kasik's voice was little more than a whisper. It sent a shiver down her spine. She took a step closer, was about to ask which one was Emperor Yachua, when a figure walked out of the shadows and into a beam of light.

The mamakuna of Qorikancha. Her elegant purple robes and severely cut features made her seem otherworldly. "You may go," she said to Kasik, who nodded and turned away, barely cutting Nina a glance before he left. She felt betrayed by his hasty retreat, and she hated herself for it.

"Come." The woman beckoned her forward with a hand, but Nina remembered the mamakuna from the acllahuasi, and her animosity that seemed heightened specifically toward Nina. She wasn't sure any of them could be trusted. As if sensing the root of her hesitation, the mamakuna added, "I will not harm you, child. Come closer so that I can fulfill the emperor's request."

Having no other choice, Nina met the woman in the center of the room, underneath a sharp beam of sunlight. The warmth was a much-needed reminder of home. Unexpected that she could find pockets of familiarity among such strangeness.

Up close, Nina could see the woman's eyes weren't black, like she had thought, but a color like the darkened ash that lies at the bottom of the hearth in her kitchen back home. "What you are about to witness is something that no other knows the truth of. Not even the emperor. It is a secret between those of us descended from Pachamama and Killa." She held out her hand, palm up, and Nina thought she was meant to place hers in the mamakuna's, but instead, a burst of flame shot up from the center of it.

Nina stumbled back out of instinct, filled with equal parts awe and terror. *Ikara*, her soul whispered. *She is like me.*

"There is a belief among the men of our land that the fire only presents itself for a girl who has remained untouched. I can see that you have," the mamakuna said, her eyes glittering like two blocks of burning coal. "And I am sure you can see why this must remain between us."

"Of course," Nina breathed. She was entranced by the small fire. It burned in a perfectly contained spiral that tapered to a point at the top. The control it must have taken . . . Nina was envious. And tempted to ask how she could learn to wield her attay so delicately, but it blinked out of sight, plunging the mamakuna's face back into shadows.

"Another one of us at the emperor's side is an opportunity that cannot be mismanaged," she said, but Nina wasn't sure what she meant by *another one of us.* Another woman? Another Ikara? What kind of opportunity? "Be sure to handle the position with care." The mamakuna backed out of the sunlight and into the dark, the shape of her growing smaller and darker until she disappeared entirely, leaving Nina alone and with more questions than she came in with.

Behind her, the golden sarcophagi shone obnoxiously, like small suns set against the night sky. From a near distance, she could hear the sounds of the people of the kancha going about their daily lives.

And within her, Nina's power swirled like the gentle forming of an eddy. A flicker of recognition. A glimpse into the darkness. A reminder of her greatest desire to be free.

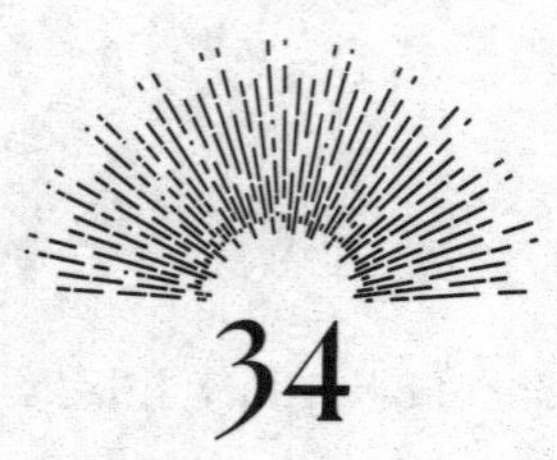

34

Nina was distant when she came out of the temple, eyes unfocused as she walked beside Kasik through the kancha grounds. There were walla and attendants everywhere, all of them eyes and ears for the emperor or Kasik's tayta. Kasik couldn't ask her what had happened inside Qorikancha or what she was thinking. He couldn't share the secret that was eating him up inside. It was torture walking beside her knowing that every single step he took in silence was a betrayal.

Whereas he was laden with worry, Nina's steps were buoyant and hurried. She didn't know where she was going, but it didn't seem to matter. Kasik quickened his pace to keep up.

The path they walked was a bright tan stone, and smoother than even the emperor's road. On either side of them were small buildings where the attendants lived, and larger houses for esteemed guests. To the right, a short wall bordered a ring of bright green grass that was the training grounds, and beside it were the kallankas, crude in their design but no less impressive, that housed the walla.

Kasik missed training with Samaq. A part of him also missed training with Maicu, though those sessions were more of a lesson in restraint. With Samaq, he could let go of the control he spent so much time crafting. His friend had always met him where he was at. Kasik felt a surge of guilt knowing he couldn't do the same for Samaq. Wherever his friend was, he would have to face his troubles without Kasik. And Kasik would face his own alone.

Farther ahead were the steps that led to the main entrance of the kancha. And behind it, imposing and jagged and tipped with snow, set against a gloomy blue sky, was the Rimac mountain range. It was said that the higher one was, the closer to the gods they were, and many people took the risk of climbing those mountains to find them.

Kasik didn't know if they found what they were looking for—most never came back—but he could appreciate the commitment and the unfailing belief. Something he had possessed not so long ago, but not anymore.

They ascended the stone steps and entered the kancha in silence. Nina's attention was pinned to the tapestry as she walked by, but her steps didn't slow. There seemed to be a kind of purpose within her that he had only seen on the road, and he couldn't help but wonder what, exactly, it meant, and what kind of trouble it would invite.

Only when it was time to make a turn did Nina stop.

"This way," Kasik said with a sweep of his hand. Instead of turning right as they would have to reach Nina's room, Kasik veered left, traversing the winding halls by memory, eyes forward and focused on their destination. They passed the walls inlaid with gold, Nina's hands reaching out to brush against them, eyes sparkling with something he could only describe as appreciation. Then the gold was abruptly gone, and so was Nina's confidence as the halls became darker and colder and her pace slowed.

"This is the scholar's wing," Kasik explained. The walls were a dark stone that seemed to absorb whatever dim light the torches provided. As a child, he had hated walking down this hall, but as he had gotten older, he had come to crave the quiet and the cold and the peace he knew could be found at the end of it.

Their steps echoed in the narrow space. Kasik was forced to drop back and walk behind her so that their shoulders didn't bump. He wasn't sure he could handle the contact.

"Tell me about this tutor," Nina said suddenly.

"Well," Kasik started, "the man practically raised me. He's been at the kancha his whole life, first as an apprentice and then as the royal scholar once his mentor died. Then he became my tutor, which I don't think he was fond of at first. But I softened him, so you're welcome for that." Nina glanced over her shoulder, a torch they were passing casting her face in shadow so that he only just caught a glimpse of the hesitant smile she gave him. "He has a sharp mind and a loose tongue. I think you'll like him."

They finally reached a tall, narrow door at the end of the hall. "Ready?" Kasik asked, his hand over the handle, waiting for her to accept this on her own. Nina nodded, and he pushed through without knocking. "Master Wara," he said brightly. "I have brought your next victim."

The man was where he always was—behind a large desk hunched over rows of quipu. Letters from ayllu lords, petitions from commoners, missives from traveling soldiers, records of the Harvest. Master Wara saw it all, and Nina, who had likely never seen anything like this room, was frozen in the doorway, eyes wide and absorbing every detail of it.

The first time Kasik had been invited back was when he was seven years. The same age when he started weapons training. Kasik preferred the chaos of physical strength, of exertion over education, but it was Master Wara who instilled in him the importance of understanding words and holding them true. Man was nothing without words, without story, and Master Wara was filled with and surrounded by them.

The man pushed aside his task and stood, hands behind his back, as he watched Nina take in his small but grand room with a look of pride in his eyes. Nina stepped forward and reached out a hand to run through racks of quipu that hung from the walls. The threads swung soundlessly, and Kasik was reminded of the many days he had spent bent over a table, fingers sore from knotting and unknotting and learning the written language of their people.

"Are you familiar with quipu?" Master Wara asked.

Nina glanced at Kasik before she turned to Master Wara. "No," she said, her voice steady. Kasik was seeing her as he had first seen her, cowed but not defeated, her shoulders rigid and her head held high. The gleam of determination in her eyes. "Our ayllu believes that stories and instruction are best told from the mouth."

"You're not wrong," Master Wara said, coming to stand closer to Nina. "But with the expansion of the empire, physical means of communication became necessary. This is mostly official, of course, but there are some histories recorded as well." He ran his fingers over a particularly dense set of strings. "I've noticed that each ayllu has its own story of how life began. You are from Limac, correct?"

Kasik slowly moved back and out of their periphery. Perhaps they would forget he was there, and he could learn everything there was to know about Nina. Though they had spent so much time together, it had been under duress. Life or death. He wanted to know who she was when she was happy, where she had come from, what she enjoyed.

"Yes," Nina said. "Your creation story is . . . involved."

Master Wara chuckled. It had taken *years* for the man to crack a smile in Kasik's presence. "There are many differing opinions as to the truth of that story."

Kasik snapped his eyes to Master Wara. He had never been told about these *differing opinions*. He had only been told the one story and had taken it as absolute. If Master Wara felt Kasik's incredulity, he ignored it and continued speaking to Nina. "Kunay Atik says that your ayllu is greatly favored by Pachamama."

Nina nodded. "The story is that my mamay made offerings to Pachamama for healthy land and healthy children, and Pachamama was so appreciative of being remembered that she imbued the land with favor. Our crops grew overnight. Our animals strengthened. And my siblings and I . . ."

Her voice trailed off. Kasik hadn't realized he had leaned into the table next to him. It shifted under his weight and both Nina's and Master Wara's attention darted to him. "You may leave now, walla. This is no place for a brute," his teacher said.

Kasik straightened and rolled his eyes. "I'll be back soon," he said to Nina, but her attention was already on the quipu and the stories contained within.

"Now the fun begins," he heard Master Wara say as the door closed behind him.

The last time Kasik had trained was the last day he had seen Samaq. Before that, they had taken every opportunity to spar, not only because it kept them agile and prepared for whatever mission Emperor Maicu sent them on, but because it helped to ground him. To remind Kasik that he was capable and strong, despite what his tayta thought about him.

Atik was not a man easily impressed, but that hadn't stopped Kasik from trying. Then, as he grew older, he realized that his efforts were wasted. Atik was uncompromising and uncaring and incapable of love. If Kasik hadn't been standing there, alive and breathing, he would've questioned if anyone could love such a man.

But somehow, unexplainably, his mamay had. At least enough to create Kasik. Mindlessly, he wrapped a hand around the achilla at his neck. It was always cold even though it sat against the heat of his chest. He remembered when his tayta had tossed it to him after a particularly long day of training. Kasik had only been ten years old at the time, and he had just met Samaq.

Atik had barged into the kallankas and marched to the corner where Kasik's bed was. The achilla had landed on the bed at his feet and stared at him. "Wear this, and don't take it off for anyone. Do you hear?"

Kasik, thinking it meant his tayta cared about him, reached for it with a gentleness that his tayta scoffed at. "It was your mamay's. The rest of her things are being burned, and Emperor Yachua thought this might serve a greater purpose."

Then Kunay Atik left, and Kasik had stared a long time at the space where he no longer stood, the stone pressed so hard into his palm that it drew blood. In his memory, the stone had been warm, but he knew now that it was only childish fondness that gilded the moment, for when Samaq pried the achilla from his hands and slipped it over his head, the sting of cold against his bare chest had brought him back to reality and the truth of his circumstances.

Atik had erased all traces of Aliyma's life and given the only thing left of her to Kasik, the son he had discarded and denied.

Kasik had trained with renewed vigor after that, for no one but himself. To be stronger, faster, *better* than his tayta ever was, and eventually, because it felt like breathing. Like being free. It was the only time that his mind was clear and he didn't have to worry or consider or plan.

After leaving Nina, Kasik took the side exit out of the kancha, the same one he had taken the day he found Samaq and Chaska whispering in the shadows, and paused just outside the door. The training ring was close enough to touch, but between it and him strode Emperor Maicu, his gait relaxed, a curved blade spinning idly in his hands. Kasik was immediately on guard.

"Care for a spar?" Maicu asked. "It's been quite some time since we've had fun."

Kasik couldn't help but think he had manifested this moment with his foolishly reminiscent thoughts. "Of course," he said, because he had no other choice. Nobody said no to the emperor.

"I know I can always count on you." Maicu gripped his shoulder and steered him toward the center of the ring. The walla that were training scampered away with murmured honorifics, but Maicu paid them no mind. All his attention was focused on Kasik.

The brocaded red-and-gold tunic he wore looked out of place, and his blade flashed in the light as it twirled in his hand. Maicu wasn't a strong fighter, but he knew how to distract his opponent and entertain a crowd. One was growing on the other side of the short wall. Walla and attendants alike leaned on their elbows, thirsty for royal intrigue, making guesses behind their hands.

Kasik pulled his blade from the sheath at his hip and spread his feet shoulder-width apart.

"Don't go easy on me, all right?" Maicu flashed a smile. "Just like it used to be."

Like it used to be, when Maicu wasn't the emperor and instead Kasik's friend. When they were just boys without real responsibilities, without the lives of men in their hands, without the burden of failure on their backs.

Maicu made the first move, bringing his blade around and against Kasik's. The sound of metal against metal clanged through the air and vibrated up Kasik's arms and into his jaw and ears. He braced himself for Maicu's next move. They knew each other's dances well enough that the first several moments of the fight were equally matched, Kasik meeting each of Maicu's swings with a perfectly placed one of his own.

"You're not trying, Kasik."

It was true that he was holding back, only meeting Maicu blow for blow, and as his movements increased in speed and pressure, so too did Kasik's.

Maicu brought his blade up and around to the right and Kasik spun away, moving in a circle that had the emperor turning and turning. Kasik lightly kicked the back of Maicu's knees. It had always been his weak spot when they were kids, and Kasik assumed Maicu would have worked on it in the year since he had become emperor. He hadn't done so expecting to fool the emperor.

But that was exactly what happened. By the time Kasik was facing Maicu again, he was on his knees, eyes turned up to Kasik, who towered before him, shock and betrayal screaming from his expression. There was a moment, just a fleeting, whispered heartbeat, where Kasik could see the edge of his blade swiping across Maicu's throat, his eyes widening in surprise, his hands scrabbling for purchase against the blood-soaked skin, trying to hold all of himself in.

The single moment of distraction cost Kasik. Maicu's leg swept him from the side and he landed on his back, all the air in his lungs gone in one *whoosh*.

Maicu stood over him. "You think too much about things that do not concern you." The edge of his blade sank into the dirt a handsbreadth from Kasik's face. "You used to be much more fun."

It took a moment for Kasik to regain his breath and answer the emperor. "I could say the same about you." He took the hand that Maicu offered. "And I am only concerned with your safety."

Maicu grinned, and it immediately reminded Kasik of the friend he once knew. "I am perfectly safe with you, am I not?"

Kasik rolled his eyes and huffed a laugh. "You think too highly of yourself."

"Do I? I'm decent with a blade, deadly handsome, whip-smart, and perceptive." Maicu walked toward the edge of the ring and Kasik followed. "Perceptive enough to see things that others do not see for themselves."

Kasik's steps faltered.

"For example." Maicu inspected his blade before passing it to his guard, who wiped it free of dirt and then gently slid it into the scabbard at Maicu's waist. "I can see that you care for Nina."

Kasik tensed further, mind racing. "I care for her safety," he vehemently stated. "As you have commanded me to."

"Ah." Maicu turned to face him fully. "I think it is more than that."

"You're wrong." Kasik shook his head and held Maicu's eyes, a carefree smile plastered onto his face. "It's not often it happens, but it is possible."

Maicu clamped a hand around the back of Kasik's neck, his long fingers digging into the pulse points on either side, and pulled him closer, until there was only a sliver of space between them. If anyone was watching, they'd think it a friendly conversation. A meaningful touch between men who were like brothers. "Do not insult me, Kasik." He whispered his name like a rebuke. "I see the way you watch her."

Several scenarios ran through Kasik's mind. He could continue to deny it and fuel the emperor's rage, or he could concede and admit he was right. Either way might earn him a dagger in the belly. He never remembered Maicu being this perceptive. His friend had been raucous and carefree, but this version of him felt unpredictable, lethal.

Suddenly the emperor laughed, his breath tickling Kasik's cheek before he backed away and removed his hand from Kasik's neck. He used that same hand to clap him on the shoulder. "My friend, I only worry. Desire changes people. It can turn the most loyal of us into traitors, the fiercest warriors into softhearted pacifists, and the consequences of that are heavier than you can imagine," Maicu said, eyes narrowed as he inspected Kasik's face. "But you've seen what I am willing to do to protect this land. You understand, don't you?"

Kasik merely nodded, thrown off guard at the slightly crazed look in Maicu's eye, at the way he bounced between friendly laughing and deranged warnings. Maicu continued speaking, lost in his own thoughts, eyes clouded over as if Kasik wasn't there at all.

"The gods," he whispered conspiratorially, as if they were listening. "They demand much of me. Nina will change everything." Then he straightened and wagged a finger between them. "Thank you for this. Same time tomorrow?"

Though Kasik's hands were trembling, he folded into a bow. "As you command it," he said, hoping that it would appease Maicu, that he would leave Kasik to consider what he knew needed to be done.

But Maicu stepped closer and placed a hand on Kasik's chest. Head tilted, he hummed as if understanding something vital. "Be certain that Nina receives plenty of rest tonight. She must be exhausted from your long journey." Maicu gave him a close-lipped smile and then turned away. "Oh, I want you to bring Nina to my rooms for dinner tomorrow night, and leave Taruc to guard. I think you need some rest as well."

"Emperor, I—"

"That was a command, Kasik," Maicu chided quietly. Dangerously. Kasik nodded, and then Maicu smiled wide.

"You're a good friend," he said, patting his chest twice before turning to walk away.

Kasik watched and fought the urge to drive his sword into his emperor's back. Never in his life had he wished to be free of his honor more than he did in that moment.

35

"**Do you know** why you are here?" Master Wara asked from across the room, eyes cast up and fingers running through strands of quipu. "In this room with me?"

Nina marveled at the sheer amount of information. It was an entire world contained within one room. It was overwhelming.

"No," Nina finally admitted. "It seems that I am only meant to obey, not question."

"Mm-hmm," Master Wara hummed, and she lost sight of him for a moment as he dove between the bulk of quipu. They were hung from the walls by small golden hooks, more than she could count, each of them a bundle of varying thickness. She assumed there was some sort of system, but she couldn't begin to imagine how he kept track of it all.

A moment later, he reemerged with a bundle of threads in one fist. "Historically speaking, all acllas are chosen ones—for their beauty or their talent—and are taken to the acllahuasi to be refined and educated so that they can properly serve the gods. But you are joining the emperor in a different kind of bond, and must therefore be educated in the history and customs of Vira, as well as those of the acllahuasi." Master Wara spread the threads over the table and dropped into a seat. "Please," he said, gesturing at the seat across from him.

With a sigh, Nina lowered herself. Before she could ask a question, Master Wara leaned forward, his eyes capturing hers with such sincerity that her palms tingled with anticipation. "Today, I am going to tell you the story of how we arrived at this moment, but it will only be half of the story, as all stories are, and I hope that, by the end, you will feel compelled to share yours."

All the moments that led her there flashed before her eyes. The fear, the uncertainty, the determination, the desire, the regret, the acceptance. The acknowledgment of who she was and what she was capable of. The things she was willing to sacrifice to keep her family safe. She wasn't sure if she could share her story aloud without giving away all her secrets and damning herself in the process.

Master Wara didn't wait for a response before he plucked up a string and began running his fingers over it, the bundled end in front of her and the rest of the threads fanned out in a curve. The chair creaked as she leaned forward. "Long ago, there was an Emperor and an Adviser, a Girl and her Sister, and a Scholar." Master Wara's eyes focused forward on a spot past Nina as if he was seeing into the past.

There was a chill in the room, and Nina shivered. The light from the torches danced on the walls, and the shadows shifted. She closed her eyes and listened.

"One day, the Adviser goes to the Emperor, who has just lost his tayta to an unexplainable sickness, and tells him of the strange dreams he is having about a girl with unimaginable attay. The Emperor, remembering old myths of madness and favor, sends the Adviser to find the girl. He will bind himself to her, and together they will usher in an era of prosperity for their people.

"The Adviser agrees and sets out that very day, traveling far into Icosa where he finally finds the girl in a small ayllu. The Girl, having never left home, is afraid to journey alone with strangers and makes one request—that her Sister be permitted to accompany them."

The softness of Master Wara's voice drew Nina into a deep lull. His words played behind her eyelids as if she was dreaming. Or remembering.

"On the journey, the three become fast friends, and when they finally arrive at Amaru Kancha, the young Emperor is filled with jealousy and eager to keep them all close. He creates a circle of elders—the Emperor, the Adviser, the Girl, the Sister, and the Scholar—even though they are all children themselves, and together, they form grand plans for their people and their lands. Ideas to unite under a single banner. Tawantinsuyu, they will call it.

"The Emperor will become more powerful than his tayta, and he will please the gods so that they will gift him a long, fruitful life. But with all this pressure, cracks begin to form. The Girl is not eager to marry the Emperor, and he notices that his Adviser is overtly friendly with her. And the Sister is distant even when she's near. Absent in a way that makes the Emperor wary of her. Because the two seem close, the Emperor asks the Scholar to speak to the Sister and find out her intentions.

"That's when the Scholar learns her secret—the Girl is not the only one with unimaginable attay. The Sister can see the threads of life, both past and future, and she knows a blight is coming for their lands."

A sound pulled Nina back to the present, and she opened her eyes to see Master Wara hesitating, hands hovering over a thread. She said nothing, only watched as he placed the tips of his fingers on a knot and then shook his head.

"The Scholar encourages the Sister to tell the Emperor. She does, and the five discuss how trustworthy the Sister's foretelling can be when all she knows is that a white man will come to destroy them all. The Adviser thinks it is ridiculous. The Scholar stays quiet. The Girl holds the Sister's hand with a look of panic in her eyes. Finally, the Emperor says they will take action. They will build an army to fight the kukuchi.

"And so begins the Harvest, where families are required to provide the chani—children, crops, textiles, and whatever else the Emperor asks of them—to belong to Tawantinsuyu. But it is only the Emperor who wants this, and the other four make their disagreement known. Their circle is fractured. The Sister decides she will not be a part of it any longer, and begs the Girl to leave with her, but the Girl has a secret of her own—she is with child, and it is the Adviser's.

"But the Adviser is willing to forsake all he knows for the Girl. He loves her more than he loves his duty. The night before they are due to leave, the Emperor demands an audience with the Adviser and the Scholar. It is there that the Scholar is forced to reveal to the Adviser that the Girl's attay can be used to *influence*. That the love the Adviser feels for the Girl is a show of control over his will.

"The Adviser, at first, is in denial, but the Emperor tells him the true story of how the Ikara were formed, and the destruction they wrought on the land. The same destruction that will greet them if they fall into the trap once again. The Emperor pleads with his Adviser to heed his word and join hands, and finally, devastated and heartbroken, the Adviser relents."

A knock on the door startled Nina, and she jumped in her seat. Master Wara brushed his hand over the table and collected the strands in a white-knuckled fist. "Come in," he said brightly, as if he hadn't just hypnotized Nina into envisioning a past life.

Kasik's face slid into view. "The emperor is insisting that Nina needs rest."

For some reason, Nina was half expecting Master Wara to laugh and brush him off. Instead, the man stood and gave Nina a shallow bow. "Until next time," he said pointedly.

Nina had no choice but to leave the room and his unfinished story behind.

* * *

There was no rest to be had that night. Despite the exhaustion that blurred her vision and cast a haze over her mind, Nina lay in bed and thought of every worst-case scenario.

Nina would try to kill the emperor and fail. They would go back for Sacha and imprison her for Nina's crimes. They would strip her family of their land and force them into servitude, and then they would execute Nina for all to see, as an example of what happens when someone dares to defy the emperor.

If Nina was truly doing all this to maintain the peace, then she would simply marry Emperor Maicu. Chaska seemed content enough, with her gowns and gold and freedom to move about. But there was a glint in the empress's eyes that spoke of secrets and facades.

Nina knew there was something she wasn't seeing, and she intended to dig deeper the next morning at tea, but Chaska never came. The same stony-faced attendant who brought their tray every morning delivered it alone and without explanation. Nina drank and ate and spiraled further.

Even Kasik seemed to keep his distance. He was quiet as they walked to the scholar's wing and Nina had to quicken her steps to keep close. Even then, the space between them was an ocean. Kasik finally acknowledged her right before he opened Master Wara's door. With his hand still on the latch, he turned to her and said, "The emperor has requested that you dine with him tonight." He paused, and then added, "In his rooms."

Nina frowned. "Alone?"

"Yes, alone." The muscles in Kasik's jaw twitched. Nina wondered if he felt a certain way about the emperor's request, or her naive question. Of *course* they'd be alone. He was the emperor—he didn't need to follow rules of propriety with his future wife, but it also meant that Nina might get the opportunity she had been hoping for. A chance to try and free Emperor Maicu of his achilla. It was exactly what she wanted, and yet the burn of nerves spread through her like a wildfire.

It was all she could focus on as Master Wara droned on about the quipu and how to interpret the knots. There were sequences for each word and number, one string versus two or ten, the length of spaces and the string itself. Her mind was in no position to pay attention, much less understand. Distractedly, she thought about the story he had told her the previous day and whether he would finish it, but when she asked, he gave her a noncommittal answer that left her more uncertain than before.

An unfamiliar guard came to collect her from her lessons. "Where's Kasik?" Nina asked, looking both ways down the hall.

"I have been tasked with escorting you this evening" was all the walla said. Another nonanswer, another stony silence down another long corridor.

This would be the rest of my life if I stayed, she thought. Nina shuddered.

The benefit of being left mostly alone was the time to consider her course of action. Back in her rooms once again, she spent time on her hair, purposely arranging each strand so that it fell perfectly across her shoulders and forehead. She picked out a dress that was a deep red and thin, the fabric settling over her body with barely a whisper.

The hem and sleeves were embroidered with birds and trees in varying shades of green and gold that reminded her of the Tuta Kulla in the early hours of the morning, when the dew that covered the leaves sparkled like stars fallen to earth. She fingered the gold band around her wrist and remembered what it felt like to be surrounded by so much life and love. It made the loss of it that much keener.

Nina pushed the band up onto her arm and arranged her sleeve over it—something to keep her grounded—and then she waited.

By the time there was a knock, Nina had considered whether becoming a wife meant she could request a window in her room. The lack of sunlight and the inability to gauge time would drive her to insanity, but if all went according to plan tonight, there would be no need to ask.

The strange guard swooped an arm into the hall, and Nina obliged with a sigh. It was better that Kasik wasn't the one to guide her. Once she killed the emperor, she would have to navigate the maze of halls to find the receiving room and hope that none of the walla stopped her once outside the kancha.

Past the walls, she could find the achipuma enclosure and hope Illari was there to steal, or she could continue on her own two feet. Whatever was necessary. Kasik would have only become another obstacle to overcome. This way, she wouldn't have to kill him if he tried to stop her.

Because she knew he would. Kasik was rational and intentional, each of his actions and words calculated and carefully construed, and he had proven, time and again, that his loyalties were with his emperor. But then she remembered the feel of his hands pressing into her hips, the way he had whispered into her ear, the words tender yet frantic.

Ask me to forsake every vow I've ever made.

Then the kunay had whispered into Kasik's ear, and for the first time, Nina hoped Kunay Atik was right. She was counting on that power of influence to aid her in convincing Emperor Maicu to remove his achilla. She would keep her thoughts free of harm and focus only on pleasing him until he was stripped of every barrier of protection.

Then she would guide her attay to silently and quickly break his body. With any luck, he wouldn't be found until morning, and she would be long gone.

The walla guided her through one hall after another, all of them the same color, lit with the same number of torches and dotted with the same specks of gold. The monotony was maddening, but she used the time to clear her mind, to empty herself of thoughts and plans and desires, until finally the walla stopped at a nondescript wooden door and knocked.

Three heartbeats later, the emperor himself opened the door.

Nina barely had time to consider him before the walla was bowing and stepping aside and the emperor's hand was extended, waiting for her to accept and be pulled into his room.

She did, with a shaky hand that he soothed with a squeeze.

"Thank you, Taruc," he said, and then the door closed behind her, and it was just the two of them in a firelit room, the cool air a stark contrast to the warm light.

His room was plainer than she would have imagined. A large canopied bed sat to her right, and directly in front of the door was a sitting area where a cushioned seat large enough for two faced the roaring hearth.

The rug beneath her feet was plush, each of Emperor Maicu's steps muffled as he led her to sit. A low table laden with food filled the space between the chair and the hearth, and the emperor's movements were careful when he lifted a golden cup to her.

"Thank you," Nina said. She accepted the cup but didn't drink. Emperor Maicu smirked and took a small sip, his eyes on her over the rim of his cup, watching her as if he knew something she did not. A future for her that she could not fathom.

Nina knew what being a wife looked like in the constraints of her own family, and the families in her ayllu. She had attended the ceremonies, had seen the families grow, had witnessed the partnership her mamay and tayta had.

But this was a *binding* to an emperor. A descendant of a god. A powerful man.

It was too easy to falter under the immensity of that, and Nina had to remind herself that she was powerful as well.

"Are you hungry?" he asked, leaning forward to pluck a juicy chunk of pitahaya from a plate.

Nina was grateful to have his eyes off her for a moment so she could collect herself. "No, thank you," she lied. Her mouth watered at the sight of all the food, fruits and stewed vegetables and slices of a meat she had never seen before, but it was the emperor himself who made her swallow hesitantly.

It was his bare feet, his breezy pants and loose white tunic, the way his long, dark hair splayed freely over his back and shoulders. His head was free of the extravagant circlet he had worn at dinner, but she saw the outline of a dark cord around his neck and the attached achilla pressed against his chest. He reclined and slung an arm over the back of the seat so that the heat of his hand seeped through the thin fabric covering her shoulder.

Nina had his full attention, and her heart thudded under the weight of it as he swept his gaze first over her features, then over her body. She tried to give the impression that she was comfortable but shy, hoping that she could persuade the emperor to lean closer and let down his guard. That she was nothing but an innocent farm girl enamored with the luxury of all that he was.

Buried deep, her power stirred as if hearing a challenge.

"Thank you for having me, Emperor Maicu." Nina shifted to face him and tucked a foot beneath her leg, the cup of chicha gripped tight in one hand. Maicu's fiery eyes watched her every movement.

"Please," he said, placing the tips of his fingers firmly against her neck. "No need for formalities. Call me Maicu."

"Are we so familiar with each other?" She kept her eyes on his and breathed evenly, lest he feel the way her pulse skittered from his touch. Everything was going exactly how she had hoped, and yet she was terrified.

Maicu threw back his head with a soft laugh, his bright white teeth flashing in the dimness. "We are going to become more familiar with each other soon enough. Names are a good place to start."

Nina watched him lean forward and pluck a dark yellow slice of lucuma from a bowl. He handed it to her, and she accepted. She thought the familiar fruit would help to settle her nerves, but they only fluttered under Maicu's heavy gaze.

A spark at the center of his chest caught her eye. There and gone in a blink, but threads of life and will, nonetheless. She focused on them, her eyes narrowed in concentration.

Maicu thought she was staring at his achilla. "Atik tells me that the people of Limac do not wear the achilla," he said, tugging on the leather cord so that the stone was on the outside of his tunic.

Well, that was easy, Nina thought. "No. We believe the gods' protection isn't ours to command. If they offer it, it is because we have earned it."

The words tasted like ash on her tongue. Nina's family had done everything right, had paid every price asked of them, and still they had been torn apart. Maicu's threads dimmed, and Nina shook free of her anger. How attuned the stone was to her intent.

It would be doing Maicu a favor to remove it from around his neck. It would be a display of his power, of his *faith* in the gods. That was what she told herself as she moved closer and stretched a hand toward the stone. The air near it was colder and it seemed to pulse. Nina suppressed a shiver and glanced at Maicu.

"May I?" she asked demurely. Maicu hummed his permission, and Nina placed one finger on the stone. "It's beautiful."

"As are you," Maicu said, his breath tickling the top of her head.

Nina's heart was pounding so loud she could barely hear his murmured words. She slipped her finger from the stone to the cord and followed the path of it up to the bit of chest that was exposed by his tunic. In contrast to the stone, his skin was shockingly warm. Nina swore she could sense the blood traveling beneath. With another subtle prod, she could once again see his golden threads.

With a shaky breath, she met Maicu's eyes and asked, "May I try it on?"

36

Kasik had been instructed to rest, but his body had no intention of letting him do that. Mind racing, he made his way through the kancha and out a side door that let into the royal gardens. They were shrouded in darkness, the moon half hidden by a sea of ashen clouds, and mostly dead. Winter was quickly approaching, and with it, Inti Raymi.

Soon, the kancha grounds would be full of esteemed guests invited to celebrate the winter solstice and the end of the Harvest with the emperor. It made his skin crawl to think of it.

He had no plans when he left the kancha, only that he could not be within it while Nina was alone in Maicu's bedrooms. It was selfish, but he was glad to be given the night off. Glad to be away from them before he did something foolish. The only thing that kept him from running back inside was the knowledge that Maicu would not touch her.

His plan involved Nina remaining *untouched.*

A rock skittered across the stone path. Kasik immediately ducked and then cursed himself for being so skittish. It wasn't as if he was doing anything he wasn't supposed to, but he was thinking about something forbidden and the evidence of that was clear in the lines of his body now hidden behind the half-dead foliage. His breath puffed in front of him. It was chillier than he thought; it would be full winter any day.

All that was forgotten when he saw a body-shaped shadow dart from one side of the path to the other, toward the backside of the kancha where he knew there to be nothing but forgotten trees and the outer wall. Quietly, he unfolded into a running crouch, careful to lift his feet and avoid kicking loose stones. The shape did the same. It was as if they were floating over the ground.

He thought of the kukuchi that Shayim warned about, and the brevity in her voice when she spoke of them. The shadow moved like a wraith, silent and deadly. It made Kasik consider the possibility of there being one behind their walls without anyone knowing.

Kasik hid behind a wide stout bush, peering through the skeletal branches and hoping the shape didn't see him. But they were preoccupied with skimming their hands along the outer wall, wasting their time looking for something that he knew was not there.

Then, suddenly, the wall shifted, and Kasik clamped his hand over his mouth to cover his shocked inhale.

A space large enough for a body opened up. On the other side, Kasik saw trees and the distant, almost undetectable flicker of a torch. The body slipped through and turned back to place their hand against the wall again.

It was then that Chaska's face flashed in the moonlight before she disappeared behind the stone.

After pushing every stone and shoving his fingers into every crevice of the wall, Kasik found nothing that explained the way it had slid open beneath Chaska's touch. He could think of no other explanation except that Chaska was the same as Nina: an Ikara, a descendant of Killa and Pachamama. A being he had been taught no longer existed. He'd encountered three of them now in such a short span of time, including Shayim, and he was beginning to understand that there were likely more of them.

Eventually, Kasik gave up and began the walk back to his room.

He needed to rest, to think, to come to terms with the fact that he knew absolutely nothing at all.

It wasn't as though Chaska was a friend—she seemed to barely tolerate him—but he had known her for more than a year, had seen her day in and day out when he was at the kancha and had dined with her most days. They didn't speak often, but he thought they had spoken enough for him to take her measure.

The empress was aloof. Spoiled. Uninterested in politics, or so it had seemed. Kasik stopped in his tracks, remembering another time when he had seen her sneaking through the kancha grounds. It was a wonder he hadn't recognized her gait. Had Samaq been involved in whatever Chaska was hiding?

Though he could no longer see the wall where she had slipped through, Kasik turned back to stare at it and considered whether he should continue trying to find the hidden door. What if it was Samaq on the other side? He hadn't witnessed his friend leave the kancha or Vira. It was possible that Samaq had defected and was whisking Chaska away as he stood there.

Perhaps I should tell Maicu. The thought was fleeting, but it plagued his every step back into the kancha. Usually, he stayed in the kallankas with Samaq and his men, but without them, the place felt unwelcoming. The men were timid around him, their typically loose lips pressed tight and their eyes surreptitiously sliding to him. He had stepped one foot in only to step back out, the din of conversation continuing the moment the door closed behind him.

But staying in the kancha meant potentially running into his tayta, which was, as luck would have it, exactly what he faced as he turned down the hall that led to the room reserved for him. It was too late to turn around, but Kasik was tempted to regardless.

"It's late," Atik said by way of a greeting. It was unclear what his tayta spent the majority of his time doing. They rarely saw each other outside the evening meals that Maicu insisted he attend, or times like these, when Atik seemed to go out of his way to find Kasik and demonstrate exactly how little he cared for him.

"Hello, Tayta. Is there something you needed?"

Atik pushed off the wall and blocked Kasik's path. In the dark, his eyes looked completely black, like orbs of achilla had replaced them altogether. Kasik wondered if they had always looked like that, or if it was something he was only recently noticing, along with many other things.

"Where have you been?" When Kasik made to walk past him, Atik stepped to the side and blocked him. "Where is Nina?"

The uncertainty in Atik's eyes made Kasik smile smugly "Don't you know?" he asked, pleased that there was something he knew and his tayta did not. "She's with the emperor. Enjoying a cozy, quiet meal. He commanded that I take the night off and have Taruc deliver her to his rooms."

In the shadows of torchlight that shifted over Atik's face, Kasik first saw worry, then frustration. It was unclear who they were for or why he was so invested in Nina's whereabouts, but it left him with a swirling suspicion in his gut.

"You didn't know she went there," Kasik said, almost to himself, his mind combing over the past with a kind of clarity he had not possessed before. "You always know where he is, who he speaks with, what choices he makes. It's almost as though he is a tool. *Your* tool."

"He is young and impetuous," Atik said, eyes hard and voice dangerously sharp. He took a step nearer, and Kasik took a small step back. "I have guided him with a firm hand as the gods have asked me to. I have done *everything* they have asked of me."

"Do they ask so much of you?" Kasik asked carefully. He was trying to glean information, trying to understand the crazed look in his tayta's eyes, the strange words that made it sound as though he communed with the gods themselves. Despite his dislike for the man, Kasik felt a tinge of panic.

Shayim had said Atik was like Dimas hunting Yuri to the ends of the earth, but Kasik had thought she meant it metaphorically. Was it possible that it had been meant very literally?

No, Kasik decided. If his tayta was that powerful, the man would have flaunted it without caution. He would not be stalking down halls in the dead of night and worrying about a capricious emperor.

Atik's face quickly arranged back into its normal affectation of disdain. "It's none of your concern," he spat. "Your priority is to keep Nina alive. Can you manage that? Or should I see to her well-being myself?"

The thought of Atik anywhere near Nina made him want to punch a wall. Or his tayta's face. "Don't go near her," he seethed. And then, because he was stupid and never learned, he added, "It is clear you cannot protect anyone, including my mamay."

Kasik didn't see his tayta's fist heading toward his face until it was too late. It wasn't the first time Atik had hit him, but it was the first time he had done it so aggressively, as if he had lost all control and Kasik, for once, had pressed a nerve.

Kasik doubled over, his hands on his knees, a glob of bloodied spit landing on the floor beneath him, his jaw throbbing and his head spinning. Atik crouched and placed a firm hand on his shoulder. Kasik couldn't tell if he was being held up or down.

"Your mamay thought she could influence me. Thought she had power here, and it was only once my knife was deep in her belly that she realized she had none, and that I was not so weak. Do not tempt me, *Son*, to give you the same lesson."

With a shove, Kasik fell back, the hem of Atik's coat brushing Kasik's cheek as he passed by.

The cold stone seeped into Kasik's body and the nausea grounded him. He was awake, and what he had heard was not part of a nightmare. Atik had just confessed to killing his mamay. All the years believing that she had died during childbirth, too weak to fight an illness, too miserable to stay and fight for Kasik, and she had been *murdered* by the man he called tayta.

If he had known sooner, he would have gutted the man and left his entrails splayed on the floor around him and savored the sounds of his agony. He would have reveled in the irony of it, filling his tayta's belly with his knife only to empty it in betrayal.

Had Aliyma known what was coming? Had she been scared? Had she had the chance to love Kasik at all?

How different his life could have been. How—

"Kasik?"

There was Chaska, the cloak she had been wearing when she disappeared behind the wall still atop her shoulders. There was concern in her eyes as she slowly came closer. He knew he looked weak and pathetic, blood dripping from the corner of his mouth and tears from the corners of his eyes. He hadn't realized he was crying until Chaska had said his name and his heart had frozen in his chest thinking it was Nina. *Hoping*.

But it couldn't have been, because she was with the emperor, and he was alone, as he was *always* alone.

"Come," Chaska said softly, a hand on his arm. "Let's clean you up."

Kasik didn't fight it when she tugged him into his room and sat him on his small bed. Much too small for him. The whole room, really, but he was barely ever there unless he couldn't help it. Like tonight, when he had felt like there was nowhere else to go.

A moment later, Chaska was using a soft, wet cloth to clean the blood from his chin. He winced when she pressed against his jaw with her cold fingers.

Cold, because she had been outside, sneaking out of and back into the kancha she lived in. Perhaps visiting *Samaq*. Perhaps colluding with the kukuchi. Or, perhaps only to escape these walls and these people.

So many secrets. So many enemies. So many weak, spineless culprits.

Including him.

"Why did you offer to help Nina?" he asked quietly.

Chaska dipped the cloth into the bowl of water and then wrung it out. "I know what it's like to be a woman in a world of men who use us to meet their needs. Whatever those may be."

Kasik thought of his mamay and wondered what needs she had met. How had she ended up with a man like Atik? He couldn't imagine there had been any benefit for her, any sacrifice that would have been worth her life in the end.

Unless she *had* loved him, and it was Atik who she had sacrificed herself for.

It was impossible to know the truth, and which version of it to trust. Especially when the person in front of him was lying as she stood there, the fresh air clinging to her cloak.

"And your needs? What are you willing to do to see them met?"

A shadow passed over her eyes. Chaska calmly placed the cloth on the bedside table and took a step back. Her hands disappeared into the sleeves of her cloak. "You forget who it is you speak to."

"I do not, Empress Chaska. I am more aware than ever."

"Now is not the time to waffle, Kasik. If there's something you wish to say, then say it. Otherwise, leave the meeting of needs to those of us who are willing to make the *right* choices."

"I saw you," Kasik spat out. He watched her brow furrow in the dim light and waited to say more. "With Samaq in the yard all those weeks ago. And just now, you moved that wall with a hand. How? Where is it that you were going? Is Samaq out there?" He had halfway risen off his bed, his voice frantic even to his own ears.

Chaska stiffened and took a small step back, her eyes darting between his. "For someone as smart as you are, Kasik, you can be very, very foolish."

Then she took off, flinging the door open on her way out. Kasik caught it before it hit the wall and then followed her, ignoring the throbbing in his face. "Explain it to me like I am a foolish boy, then."

Chaska stopped and whirled around so suddenly that Kasik almost ran into her. "Do not do this here. You, of all people, should know that he has eyes and ears *everywhere*."

"I think you give him more credit than he deserves."

Chaska only looked at him strangely, and then she laughed, and it was filled with anything but amusement. "You think I speak of the emperor," she finally said. "It is not him I give the credit."

There was a moment in which Kasik considered turning away and ignoring whatever Chaska was about to say. It was none of his concern, but it was Chaska's hand that guided him back into his room and closed the door so quietly he barely heard it. "When did you start paying attention to anything other than yourself or your emperor?"

"*Our* emperor," Kasik said, the exchange reminding him of those first few days with Nina. "I have always paid attention to anything that might have caused danger or undue harm to—"

"Yes, yes, we all know how loyal you are." Chaska waved her hand in the air and wore a path into the floor in front of him. "It's the girl, isn't it. She has changed you."

"I don't—"

"You don't need to say anything. It wasn't a question." She stopped suddenly and met Kasik's eyes. They were filled with doubt—for herself, or for him, Kasik wasn't sure. "I am not in love with Samaq, if that's what you were wondering. And no, that wasn't him I went to meet. I'm sorry, Kasik. I know how much you care for your friend."

"And the wall?" Kasik asked. He hoped she would appease his attempt to distract himself. "Have you always had the ability to move stone with a touch?"

"I can do so much more than move it," Chaska said quietly. "And if you don't keep that between us, I will show you exactly what I mean."

Chaska turned toward the door before he could say anything else.

"By the way," she said over her shoulder, a flash of something mischievous in her eyes. "Samaq isn't dead. And I hope that one day, Nina can see her brother again."

Then she flounced out of the room as quietly as she snuck through the grounds, leaving Kasik at the tip of a very long downward spiral.

37

The tremble in Nina's hands was soul deep, a tremor of doubt that always existed within her no matter how confident she felt. But right then, she didn't feel confident at all. She felt entirely out of her depth. Inexperienced. Like a child playing at a grown-up game while the adults looked on with amusement.

Maicu's eyes had darkened with her touch, and she saw the way his breathing hitched the slightest bit, but the smile on his lips was one of quiet amusement. Nina felt small and foolish beneath it, but still she waited for an answer.

His eyes seemed to memorize her face, and then they dipped to her shoulder and her collarbone before climbing back up to her hand and settling on her wrist. Nina took the opportunity to slip her finger under the cord and began lifting it from his neck, slow and seductive even though her mind was screaming at her to yank it off.

But he was too close, and though his hands were soft and his eyes were amused, she could feel a lethal presence beneath his casual exterior. Nina shifted her hand back, toward his neck, the cord securely in hand, and then Maicu moved.

Quick as a snake, he caught her wrist, halting her movement with a firm grip, and then he lifted her arm to inspect it closer.

No, not her arm; the circlet around it. Nina's pulse pounded in her ears.

"This is beautifully crafted," he said, turning her wrist from side to side. "Someone in your ayllu?"

"Oh," Nina breathed, panicked. "I traded for it on market day. A woman said it had come from here, from Vira. We have nothing so luxurious in Limac."

It was a lie, but Maicu hummed, and then his hand slid from her wrist to her forearm, his long fingers splaying against her trembling skin. "No need to be nervous," he whispered sweetly.

Nina was so nervous she felt sick. She carefully placed her hand back against Maicu's chest to steady herself. His heart beat just as hard as hers. It was difficult to restrain herself, but already his threads were diffusing beneath her careful attention. She had to calm down.

The sleeve of her dress had slipped back, and Maicu's steady hand traced a path until he cupped her elbow. Nina slipped her fingers underneath the cord once again and slowly lifted the stone from his chest. It hung between them, swaying slightly, both their eyes following it for a moment.

Nina could feel its presence, the chill that felt like both life and death. It made her want to drop it and run. She fought against that instinct and pushed closer to Maicu, her body practically covering his, and brought her other hand to slip underneath the leather cord. All she had to do was slip it up and off his head. It was easier than she thought—

The pressure of his hand on her elbow increased, his fingers digging into her skin and holding her in place. "Wait," Maicu said, his breath warm against her cheek. "What is this?"

Nina froze, heart in her throat. She had been caught. Emperor Maicu would have her killed and then he would replace her with sweet Sacha, who would have to navigate this den of secrets and the threat of kukuchi and—

Maicu twisted and lifted her arm so that he was peering closely at her elbow. "What happened?" he asked, his thumb running over her skin.

"What?" she said, confused. She tilted her head to see a jagged scab right above her elbow. "Oh, that's nothing. Just an old wound."

"It will scar." The words were quiet but dangerous, and then his head snapped up to meet her eyes. "Are there others?"

"Other . . . wounds? No," Nina said quickly. "It was a small accident. It's not—"

"Was it Kasik?"

"What? *No*, of course not. Kasik would never—"

"Then who?" Maicu's words were fevered, his eyes hard with determination. He stood and towered over Nina. "The only other walla who have guarded you were Taruc and—" He must have seen the flicker of recognition in her eyes when she finally realized why the walla was familiar. Taruc had been one of the walla to escort her to her room the night she had arrived. They had dragged her down the hall and she had fallen and scratched herself on his scabbard. A small accident that had turned both walla white as smoke.

Maicu stalked past her to the door. Nina scrambled off the chair and reached out to him. "Wait," she said. Her fingers wrapped around his wrist. He whipped around, his eyes on their joined hands before lifting to meet hers. "Where are you going?" she asked frantically.

They'd barely had any time together. The food was still steaming on the table. That stone was still around his neck, mocking her as it soaked in the dim light and winked with every one of the emperor's movements.

"To teach a lesson." His voice was a murmur as he snatched up Nina's arm and tugged her closer. "I should teach you one as well. Make you remove this," he said, plucking at the fabric at her waist, "and inspect every inch of your skin. It's what you wanted, is it not? To *test* me?"

Nina hadn't been testing him, and if he knew her true intentions, he would kill her on the spot, but all she could do was continue the lie. Her attay was useless to her, still cowering in the shadows beneath the weight of uncertainty and the achilla. She had to soothe the manic fervor in Maicu's eyes.

"I'm weak." She lifted her other hand and placed it on his chest, remembering another time when her hand was pressed against another chest in willing defeat. "I was craving your touch, and I let my desires get the better of me. I'm sorry, my Emperor. It will not happen again."

There was a heartbeat of silence as he drew nearer and measured her words. Near enough that she could see the flecks of black swimming in the gold of his eyes. He placed his lips to the corner of her mouth, slid his nose along her cheek and to her ear.

Nina held perfectly still, bile in her throat to be so near and so utterly powerless to do anything about it. "Unfortunately," he whispered. And then he pulled away and smiled, his demeanor softening. "If the mamakuna hadn't assured me of your purity, I would have known by that performance. It was clear you had no idea what you were doing. It's a shame I can't teach you." He reached up and tucked several strands of hair behind her ear. "Come. I will take you back to your rooms."

Burning with insult, Nina nodded and allowed Maicu to tug her out of his room and away from a horribly squandered opportunity. If only she had been more aware of her own body, more careful. If only she had been able to capture his attention better. If only she had thought to grab a utensil from the table and stab it through his oddly bright eyes.

They walked through the halls as if they were on a leisurely stroll through the gardens, but neither of them spoke, and though his pace was normal, Nina could tell his mind was racing.

As was her heart. She had failed. Underestimated the emperor and the strength of his conviction and overestimated her own allure. But she had seen him falter for the slightest moment, his eyes darkened with desire, the stutter in his sharp inhale. It was a kind of power Nina was unfamiliar with, and she was determined to master it and wield it once more.

The night of the ceremony would be the perfect time. Once she was his wife and required to perform her duties, she could convince him to bare himself to her entirely. Then she could use her attay to diminish his will. Grind it to ash beneath her fingers. Take this godly gift and use it to control the men in power, so that she never had to fear them again.

No. The thought almost stopped her, but Maicu's hand in hers was unyielding as it tugged her along. Nina was not interested in that kind of power. She was only intent on returning home. To her family. To freedom.

They turned a corner, and at the end of the short hall was Taruc standing before her door. "Emperor," he said with a deep bow.

Maicu disentangled himself from Nina and stepped forward. "Taruc," the emperor replied. Then he placed a hand on the walla's shoulder and jerked forward.

Everything slowed, as if she were watching from beneath the ocean and the salt was burning her eyes. She heard Taruc grunt and saw the way his eyes went wide with shock. He coughed once and then inhaled sharply. Nina hardly understood what was happening, but her heart fluttered in her chest, and her hands shook as she placed them on the wall at her back.

Again, Maicu's arm pulled back and slammed forward, and Nina finally saw the blood on the floor, drops that seeped and spread and stained. Each one like a drum beat in her chest. A flare of life that illuminated the hallway in a flash of golden light. Taruc's will, there and gone between one blink and the next, brighter and louder than ever before.

Nina watched as that flare of light faded and then winked out entirely.

Taruc's body slumped forward onto Maicu's shoulder, and then Maicu stepped back and let the body fall to the floor. When he turned his attention to her, the black of his eyes almost wholly swallowed the gold, until there was only a ring of it that looked like it was lit from within. In his hand, a small silver blade twinkled ominously in the firelight.

"Nothing"—Maicu stepped closer, until the tips of his toes were touching Nina's—"will come between what the gods have in store for us." He slid his knife beneath his tunic and then brought his bloody hand to her cheek. It was a tender touch, an intimate exploration that made her knees tremble. She could smell the iron tang of blood mixed with the sweet odor of chicha as he pressed his lips to her forehead. "Sleep well, Nina," he murmured in her ear.

And then he turned and strolled down the hall, leaving Taruc's body and Nina behind, the blood he'd smeared on her cheek a reminder of who was to blame.

When he was gone, Nina carefully skirted around the blood that spread from underneath the body, swallowing the stone and crawling closer to her, chest tight with a scream that pressed against her throat and tongue.

Beneath that, there was something else. Something that she refused to identify.

A remembered pressure. A reluctant satisfaction.

Her attay stirred sleepily. It saw the death, the blood, and it smiled.

38

Kasik watched the sunlight fill his room, the thoughts that had kept him awake all night no less agitated than when he lay down, and considered what to do next. He was now in possession of another secret that belonged to Nina. Samaq was her *brother*. His friend who Kasik had known for almost ten years was Nina's flesh and blood. The similarities were there. Their smiles, their desire to trust, their propensity toward affection.

At least he wouldn't have to tell Nina her brother was dead. If only Kasik knew *where* Samaq was, and why. He decided to think on that rather than the devastating news his tayta had delivered. There was nothing he could do about that mess, and wallowing in self-pity didn't help.

Struck with an idea, Kasik threw back the sheets and dressed in training clothes, determined to exert some of his anger in the ring. When he arrived, he found he wasn't the only one up so early. A few of his fellow walla lingered nearby, all of them watching him with wary eyes. He looked behind him, wondering if perhaps Atik was hiding in the shadows, waiting to pounce on him once again.

Then he remembered what his face must have looked like, and thought *that* was why they were staring at him. But nobody said anything, and he was beginning to think he was missing something crucial.

"What's going on?" he asked the walla closest to him. It wasn't someone he knew by name, and that made Kasik feel guilty.

The boy nodded his head in deference and then glanced at the others surrounding them. "Taruc is dead, Kamayuq."

"What?" Kasik whispered the question through clenched teeth. "How do you know this?"

"The emperor tasked those two with cleaning up the body." He nodded over Kasik's shoulder to a couple of men cleaning their hands in a trough of water that they usually used to clean their blades. "He was found stabbed . . . outside Nina's door—"

Kasik was running back into the kancha before the boy finished his sentence.

Everything was a blur as he turned corner after corner, skidding across the stone floors and glancing off stone walls until coming to a stop before Nina's door, where a dark stain had been hastily scrubbed. There were no walla guarding her door. No sign to tell him she was safely inside.

All he could do was imagine the worst. He didn't bother knocking, simply threw himself into the room, chest heaving as his eyes landed on the back of Nina sitting at the small table, the fire in her hearth down to embers. He rounded her small frame and sank to his knees in front of her, relieved to see her beautiful brown eyes open and alert as they traced over him.

"Kasik?" she whispered. She reached out and ran gentle fingertips across his jaw, sending a wave of pinpricks over his entire body. Kasik had forgotten about the run-in with his tayta, the bruise that darkened his jaw, the revelation about his mamay. Nina's fingertips brought awareness to the pain, but also to another feeling, one that eclipsed the pain and made his head spin.

"What—" she started.

"It's nothing," he told her. And it *was*. Nothing but a distant discomfort now that he knew she was alive.

But her fingers didn't leave his skin. They followed the path of his neck, down the slope of his shoulders, her hand coming to rest against his pulse. She moved closer until he was breathing in the scent of her, imagining it everywhere.

Then her forehead dropped against his shoulder and her chest rose and fell with a quiet, deep breath.

"Nina," Kasik started carefully. "What happened?"

He felt her hand curl into a fist. Felt the tremble of clenched fingers and frustration as if they were his own. And then she stood abruptly, pacing the floor in front of him with her hands in her hair.

"It's my fault," Nina said miserably. "I tried to *seduce* him. Gods, I was such a fool. I didn't mean for any of this to happen."

Kasik pushed off the floor and stood. "What are you saying?"

"The achilla, I wondered if I could get him to remove it. And he almost did." She finally looked at Kasik. "I didn't know how else to convince him, but then he found this," she said, thrusting her bent arm at Kasik and showing him the small scab on her elbow. "And he pushed me away. He *denied* me, and then he said he was going to teach me a lesson."

The way she said the word made it sound as though she was hurt by his rejection. A flare of anger pulsed in Kasik's chest. "He was going to deny you regardless." The words were harsher than he meant, and the hurt that passed over Nina's face made him falter. He ran his hands through his hair and cursed. It had to be done. She needed to know the truth.

But he was momentarily distracted by the dress she was wearing, gossamer and gilded, just barely grazing the curves of her body and floating around her bare feet to the floor. She had worn it to see the emperor. To *seduce* him. Gods, he hated that word. Hated himself for the burning rage he felt whenever he imagined the way her hands had touched the emperor.

Even with his achilla around his neck, her attay drew him in and drowned him.

Focus, he told himself. "You could not seduce the emperor because he does not intend to marry you," he stated.

Nina's head snapped back. "Of course he does," she said angrily. "That is the entire reason you forced me here."

He shook his head. "That's only what they told me. You have to understand that I knew nothing of this—"

"Of *what*, Kasik?"

Finally, Kasik faced her fully. "You're here as a sacrifice." The words felt like an omen on his lips, as if saying them aloud would bring them to fruition. He pushed on despite the foreboding in his gut. "They believe the gods offer them favor and protection from the kukuchi in exchange for your life."

Nina scoffed. "A sacrifice?" She searched his face, but when she found no hint of jesting, her brows furrowed. "Why me?" she said slowly, her eyes trailing off to the side, her face shifting from disbelief to disgust in a matter of heartbeats. "Shayim was right, then. About the kukuchi."

"It seems so," Kasik said.

Nina turned sharply and pinned him with her eyes. "When?" she asked, voice dangerously low.

"They only mentioned waiting until Inti Raymi. They didn't tell me—"

"No, Kasik. *When did you know?*"

It was then that he realized he had mistaken the softness of her words and the distance in her eyes for acceptance when truly, it was the feeling that she had been betrayed by him that lined her mouth and tongue and the fires of rage that lit her eyes from within.

Kasik swallowed the lie that sprang to his mind and opted for the truth, consequences be damned. "Maicu told me the night we arrived."

"You've been holding on to this secret for *four days*? All this time, and you knew my fate."

"I wanted to tell you." He took a hesitant step closer, but she moved away, the backs of her knees hitting the bed behind her. "I tried so many times, but there was never a good time and I was afraid of what you would do."

"Because I'm a monster—"

"No, Nina, that's not what I—"

"—and this monstrous attay inside of me is *terrifying*, right? More like *terrifyingly useless.*" She hastily pulled her hair to one side and began braiding it, her movements quick and angry. "I was going to kill him. That's why I threw myself at him. Like a *fool.* I wanted to remove the stone and then rip his will apart."

The jealousy and anger simmering in his chest left with a sigh, replaced instead with a deep, sorrowful remorse. She had been planning this alone for gods knew how long, and he had been selfishly worried about himself.

About a tayta who cared nothing for him.

A mamay who was dead.

A friend he thought was gone, who was also Nina's brother. Kasik was reeling, his mind fractured into a handful of directions, but the clearest path sat before him like a pitahaya ripe for the picking.

"Leave with me," he finally said, striding forward and sliding his hands onto her cheeks, covering the bloody mark that was there with the heat of his own. As he should have the moment he knew the truth of Maicu's plans. The moment his tayta had confessed what he had done. "The first night of Inti Raymi, all the guests will have arrived and there will be plenty of distraction. We can leave this place and never look back."

Nina tore his hands away. He felt the loss of her keenly, knew he was losing her even as he betrayed everything he knew. "You said the emperor would come for me. That he would never stop looking for me until he had me. Did you lie about that as well?"

"I never lied, Nina. He *will* come, but we can prepare. We can go to your family and take them to Shayim's. We can—"

"*We* cannot do that." Her words were like tiny knives that lodged themselves into the soft parts of his body and burrowed with every breath he took. "How can I trust you with that stone around your neck? You fear me. You believed your tayta when he said I manipulated you. You *lied* to me. How do I know that you aren't doing the gods' bidding even now?"

Kasik reached up and tore the achilla from his neck. It fell to the floor with a thud. "Search me, Nina. Reach inside of me and find what you are looking for. I have nothing to hide."

The hunger in her eyes was sharp, its teeth scraping against his mind and soul in a way that took his breath away. The pulse beneath his skin slowed. The room around him narrowed to a point, and at the center was Nina, her soft brown eyes thinned in concentration. Her full lips parted in thought. The tops of her cheeks red with effort. Her chest heaving with the thrill of the hunt.

And then, just as suddenly, he was free. As if a tether holding him up had been cut, Kasik stumbled back, the ground tilting beneath him. He steadied himself with a hand on the small table, which creaked beneath his weight.

Nina bent and scooped the achilla from the floor and shoved it at him. "Put it back on," she said, shaking it for emphasis.

"Nina, I told you that—"

She shook her head. "Nothing can be amiss," she said. "No one can know that you have placed your loyalty elsewhere."

His hands shook as he reached out and took the achilla, Nina's attention on him like a weight rooting him to the spot. The moment it was back in place, that pressure lifted, but it wasn't relief he felt. It was dissatisfaction. As if a hole had been carved into his soul and left empty.

Nina watched him closely, her eyes darting over his features, looking for something he hoped she could find. "You would leave everything you know, everyone you love, risk everything you have"—she gestured to the room and the space beyond—"for a stranger?"

"You are no stranger, Nina" he said gently. The truth of it tasted exquisite on his tongue. He stepped closer. He ached to reach out and press his words into her chest. "My soul recognized yours the moment I laid eyes on you. I don't know what it is, if it's your attay, if it's fate or a cruel joke, but I know that it does not matter. You have become a part of me, and I cannot bear to lose any more pieces as it is."

There was a moment when Nina placed a hand over her mouth and turned away, where Kasik was certain he'd said too much. That everything he felt was his own delusion, a life-altering mutation of his soul that had begun the moment he saw the stubborn set of her jaw and the careful hope in her eyes.

Nina would deny him. She would swallow his words and spit them back out because she didn't need him. She had made a plan that didn't include him. She had found a way to save herself.

Kasik would accept her decision regardless. It wouldn't change the fact that he would help her, that he would rather die than watch *her* die, that he would do anything just to ensure that what had happened to his mamay would *not* happen to her—

"All right." The words were a whisper through her fingers but a knife through his spiraling thoughts. A sliver of hope among a sea of uncertainty, and he held on to it for dear life. "I'll go with you. But you have to promise me that—"

"Anything," he gasped, striding forward, desperately closing the space between them. Thrilled at the way she lifted her head to meet his gaze, her neck exposed to him, the pulse there fluttering quickly. He was glad to know that he was underneath her skin just as much as she was underneath his. "I will make any promises you ask of me. My will is yours." He slid a hand to the back of her neck to support her head, felt the moment she fully let go and saw the way her eyes fluttered with relief. If she let him, he would carry all her burdens, no matter how heavy.

For now, he was grateful for this small measure of concession. The feel of her breath coasting across his lips was like the sweetest surrender he would ever have the privilege of knowing.

"Once you're safe," he murmured into her lips, "I'll find Samaq and my men and—"

"Samaq?" She slipped out of his touch, the loss of her like a bucket of cold water over his head. Her hands were fisted in his tunic as she held him at arm's length. "What do you know of my brother?" she asked sharply, bewilderment lining her brows.

Her question was cut off by knocking at the door. They flung apart just as it opened and Empress Chaska breezed through. The smile on her face fell the moment she laid eyes on them. She looked at Kasik's jaw, then Nina's bloodied cheek and the dress she wore.

"Well," she said after a moment, arms folded against her chest. "If you're going to sneak around, at least wait until the cover of night."

"A lot of good that did you," Kasik replied dryly.

Kasik felt Nina's questioning glance, but Chaska practically rolled her eyes at him. "We have things to do," she said pointedly.

"Right." Kasik reluctantly turned to Nina. "Empress Chaska is going to escort you to Master Wara. I have a few things to attend to, but I'll see you tonight."

It felt wrong to leave her; everything else felt trivial in the wake of what they planned, but it was important to keep up appearances. To continue to be the obedient walla they knew him as.

Soon enough, the bars of his cage would no longer contain him.

39

With the eyes of the empress on her, Nina was acutely aware of her own rage. The injustice of it all was maddening. That she had been brought there against her will, torn from her family and forced to give up everything and everyone she loved, just so that they could build their empire.

And *she* was the monster?

Nina replayed every conversation, every look passed between walla and kunay, kunay and emperor, emperor and empress, empress and mamakuna. Who knew the truth of her fate? Who had been lying directly to her, stuffing her with luxuries while leading her to slaughter?

She had fallen right into their trap. Had been acquiescent and loyal to her vow. As if anyone's vow had ever meant anything at all. Not even the gods had helped her—if anything, they had allowed her to find this place, become this person, succumb to this fate.

And Nina refused.

No longer would she hold herself to their impossible standards. No longer would she try to meet their incredible expectations. Kasik had asked her to leave with him, to wash her hands of murder and revenge and power, and she would do it, if only to take control of her story once again.

Empress Chaska poured their tea while Nina tried not to fidget. Every moment of silence felt like a death knell. The longer they stayed, the more opportunity there was for things to go wrong. But Kasik had been right—if Inti Raymi celebrations at the kancha were anything like they were at home, then there would be plenty of distraction. They could not afford to be reckless in this.

Nina had already seen her impetuousness cause problems. Had she not tried to trick the emperor, Taruc might still be alive. As much as she wanted to be free, she didn't want anyone else to die. She could leave and hide and finally put all this behind her.

"Power is such a fickle thing, don't you think?" Chaska interrupted Nina's thoughts and slid the cup of tea in front of her, head canted subtly in thought. "It can be incredibly deceiving and yet, somehow, we all believe when one claims to have it."

"It isn't difficult to believe when every command is obeyed." Nina sniffed her tea and took a small sip. It was fresh and hot and familiar, just as she liked it, and for a moment, all her worries were soothed.

"Yes, but we never seem to question who *they* answer to."

Confused where this was going, Nina narrowed her eyes. "They answer to no one but themselves. That's the problem."

Chaska leaned back, the steaming cup of tea cradled in her hands, her red dress so dark it almost looked black in the firelight. "Everyone has a master," she casually said. "The most dangerous are the ones who believe they are righteous rulers. That the suffering of some is necessary for the salvation of all."

"And you disagree with that?"

"No," Chaska said quickly. "I only believe that we should have the right to choose our suffering. If someone is forced, then we cannot blame them when they fight against it." Her sharp umber eyes met Nina's, and though the room was dim, they were filled with light. "We cannot run from suffering, just as we cannot escape death. But we can rise up against those who demand our blind faith."

Chaska's words were inspiring, but the weight of them was lost underneath their circumstances. "But you are here," Nina said, gesturing to the room, to Chaska's clothing and jewelry and general ease. She was speaking of resistance while she sat comfortably in the lap of luxury. "You are not rising up against anything."

"Am I not?" Chaska leaned forward and placed her cup on the table. "*Here* is where I belong. *This* is my seat of resistance, and there is much you do not see because you are not willing to look."

The word *resistance* echoed in Nina's mind, and Chaska's voice slowly morphed into Shayim's.

We are a resistance, the Seer had said.

"You cannot hide from this, Nina," Chaska said softly. "The future is uncertain, but your part in it is not."

Nina opened her mouth to ask what she knew. Was Chaska aware of her true fate? Did she still think Nina was there to marry the emperor? Did she somehow know what Nina intended to do last night? But Chaska held up a sharp hand. "I cannot say more than that, but I can tell you that I am *not* your enemy, Nina."

"You are all my enemy," Nina said, but the venom with which she had said it to Kasik was gone.

Chaska lightly laughed and shifted back in her chair. "You remind me so much of your brother." She said the words casually, as if Nina could have known, if only she had thought to ask.

"Is he here?" Nina leaned forward and gripped the small table, hands trembling and heart racing. "Is he safe? Can I—"

"He is not here," Chaska interrupted. "And you can rest knowing he is safe with my people. For now. But Nina, the tides are rising, and no one will be safe much longer. One day soon, you will have to make a choice."

But Nina had made her choice, and she would not share it with Chaska, no matter how adamant the empress was. They may not be enemies, but neither were they allies.

They finished their tea and then Nina was escorted to Master Wara's room. Unlike Kasik, Chaska politely knocked on the door. It was opened a few moments later by a harried-looking Master Wara, who took one look at Empress Chaska and gave a small bow. "Empress," he said breathlessly. "What a surprise to see you. Will you be joining us for today's story?"

"Not today, Master Wara. I have many things to attend to before the festivities begin."

"Of course," Master Wara said. "Another time, then."

"Yes, another time," Chaska replied. Then she turned to Nina. "Remember what we spoke about. It's never too late to change your mind."

Nina watched the empress leave and ignored the urge to chase after her and demand to know more about her brother. Whatever the reason, she knew Chaska would not give her answers. Perhaps Kasik would explain once they were free of this place.

Master Wara opened the door wider, and Nina entered. Just as before, she was struck with an overwhelming sense of awe the moment she stepped over the threshold. The amount of information hanging from every available space made her feel insignificant. Her fate inevitable. She imagined her story hanging from one of those hooks and what, exactly, it would say about her.

"There we go." Master Wara extricated himself from a tangle of threads. One caught in his hair and he plucked at it absentmindedly. "Come—sit. If I remember correctly, we left off right about here." The threads were fanned out on the table in front of him, and Master Wara ran his fingers over one with many knots.

In fact, the last several threads were thick with them. Nina eagerly sat across from the teacher. Finally, she would hear the rest of the story.

"As I said, the Emperor pleads for the Adviser to heed his words, and the Adviser relents. That night, he goes to confront the Girl that he loves and she denies using her attay to influence him. She tells him that she is with child, *his* child, and begs him to leave with them. The Sister and the Scholar are waiting for them just outside the kancha grounds."

Nina settled into her chair, once again pulled into a story so rich that she could almost see it. She watched Master Wara's gaze go distant as if he, too, could feel everything.

"But the Adviser has changed. The Girl cannot find his threads, and the Sister cannot See them as before. He is no longer filled with love or free will, and not only does he refuse to go with the Girl, but he drags her to the lowest levels of the kancha, where he keeps her imprisoned until she gives birth. The Sister waits for the Girl and watches, devastated, as the Scholar's threads change before her very eyes. She tells him he must go back, that it is his fate to accompany the Girl in her final days of life, and then to teach and love her Son like his tayta will not."

No longer was Master Wara's gaze distant. He was staring right at Nina, his words like arrows through the fog of denial and refusal that she had surrounded herself with.

"The Scholar agrees, because he loves the Sister more than anything. When he goes, he leaves a piece of his heart with her, and when the Adviser kills the Girl after her Son is born, the Scholar loses another piece of his heart. But slowly, the Son mends the holes left behind. The Scholar's purpose has never been clearer.

"Until ten years later," Master Wara said, his voice so low that Nina had to lean forward to hear him, "when the Adviser has another dream of another girl with attay like he has never seen in a place far from Vira. He goes to collect the girl, but comes back without her. She was hidden from him, somehow, but the Emperor has collected many boys to fight for his cause, and he is very pleased."

Nina's breath caught in her throat. She felt tears on her cheeks but didn't bother to wipe them away. She was afraid to move, afraid to break the surface of truth she was walking toward.

"As predicted, the Adviser has been cruel to his Son, but he has been very careful to groom the Emperor's youngest son for service. When the Emperor dies from the same illness that stole his tayta's life, we are told that the eldest son takes his own life in misery." Master Wara paused, as if to give Nina time to contemplate the blatant lie. "It is the Adviser who places the youngest son on the royal seat. And it is one year later that the Adviser dreams again."

"I think I know how this story ends," Nina whispered past the lump in her throat. Master Wara's hands found hers on the table. They were rough from years of knotting and interpreting threads, and they reminded her of her tayta. Warm, and steady, and strong. It only served to deepen the ache that the absence of her family left behind.

"This is not the end." He emphasized the last word with a squeeze. "But you are not alone, and you are not so easily defeated. Now, listen closely. There is—"

A knock on the door forced Nina back into her seat, fingers tingling with dread. Master Wara stood so quickly that his chair almost toppled over. "Come in," he said, and then he shot Nina a look. *Stay quiet.*

She didn't turn when the door opened, and it only took one heartbeat to know who it was. Nina felt Kunay Atik's presence before she saw him. The room grew colder and her power stirred angrily within her.

"Kunay Atik," Master Wara greeted. "To what do we owe the pleasure?"

"Can't a man visit his favorite scholar?"

Nina still hadn't turned to face him. Was hoping he would ignore her as he had done thus far.

But she wasn't so lucky. She could feel his presence like a harbinger of death, and it was like a blade through flesh when his hand settled on her shoulder. If she wasn't aware of her own power, she would have thought she was dying right then. That her innards were being torn out and twisted.

Except, there was no blade and no blood. It was only her attay being stolen right from underneath her beating heart.

Master Wara's eyes didn't so much as drift toward her as he spoke to the kunay. Nina wasn't sure what else was said, only that Master Wara's movements were stilted, and he came around the table as if to hide what was on it.

But Nina was drowning in a sea of nothing. She was searching for air only to find that she had ceased to exist, and though the pressure from Kunay Atik's hand disappeared, the presence his touch left behind was a bloody wound that only time could heal.

Each heartbeat that pounded as he stood there was a moment lost. A step closer to an undesirable end to her story.

"Nina? *Nina?*" Master Wara was bent in front of her, his eyes peering worriedly into hers. "Breathe, Nina," he said, and Nina obeyed, sucking down air as if she had been without for too long. "Good. Now, listen carefully. You must remember that even when you feel powerless, within you is the ability to choose love. *That* is the greatest power there is."

Nina heard his words but did not understand them. She was only capable of nodding, of offering a quiet "yes" when he asked if she could find her way back, even though it felt like a lie. The halls were unfamiliar, and Nina's body felt unlike her own. She stumbled away from Master Wara's until she found a walla who carefully guided her back to her room.

There, she collapsed onto her bed and curled into a ball, as if she could hold the pieces of herself together that had been exposed. She fell asleep with Master Wara's story in her mind, and she dreamed that she was the Girl, and it was the Adviser's blade in her belly, and she was powerless to stop him.

40

It had been one week since Kasik asked Nina to leave with him, and each day that passed left him raw with uncertainty. Nina was withdrawn, but the emperor had assigned a second guard to her, so they didn't have a moment alone. Kasik had been instructed to leave at night so that he could go back to his room and rest, which consisted of tossing and turning until the sun rose. As much as he wanted to disobey, he remembered Nina's words. *Nothing can be amiss.*

It was unexpected when a knock came at his door late that morning. He opened it to find the emperor's errand boy, disheveled and breathing hard as if he had run the whole way there. "Emperor Maicu would like to inform you that the celebrations have been moved up. Our guests will begin arriving today."

Kasik looked at the boy as if he was mad. "Inti Raymi?" he asked. The boy nodded. *"Today?"*

"Yes, Kamayuq. You must dress and receive them as soon as possible."

Kasik slammed the door, his mind fractured as he dressed in his ceremonial uniform. How had Maicu managed to move an entire festival that happened at the same time every year for centuries? If it was true, it would have been planned weeks ago to give guests time to make their way to Vira. There would have been early collections and extensive rearranging.

Kasik paused. Weeks before he had been told he was going to Taqsay to collect Nina, his tayta had disappeared. Which wasn't strange in and of itself, but he had been gone for longer than usual, and when he had returned, he had brushed by Kasik without a word and then sealed himself with Maicu in his rooms. A few days later, Kasik had received his mission.

Maicu had planned this long before today. He had purposely kept it from Kasik, and Kasik got the sense that it was because Maicu did not trust him.

He had to tell Nina, but first, he had to greet their guests.

Typically, the three days before Inti Raymi were spent fasting and preparing for the grand feast, which was followed by a parade through the streets of Vira the next morning, and performances and dancing into the night. But he and Nina would sneak away during the chaos of the feast, when their guests—nobles from the absorbed ayllus spread across Icosa and Amaru—were drunk off chicha and stuffed with rich foods.

Before that, he would have to stand shoulder to shoulder with his tayta on the steps of Amaru Kancha and welcome their guests. His first year doing so as a kamayuq. Kasik rushed through the halls and made it just in time, nostrils flaring with heavy breaths. The kunay gave him a sideways glare but said nothing.

The golden temple twinkled dimly in the cloudy late morning. Around them, attendants in blue saw to last minute preparations. Houses were aired out. Hearths were stirred. The baths were perfumed for the wives, some of them girls from the acllahuasi.

Kasik wondered how many of them held attay in their meek and pious hands, but it was the mamakuna and Empress Chaska who would greet them. His job was to stand still, to represent Kunay Atik and Emperor Maicu, to avoid murdering his tayta in a fit of rage and evade all suspicion.

His ceremonial uniform was an exact replica of the kunay's, a deep red tunic with a scene stitched into the body in a slightly darker shade. There were wings and waves and suns shaped like eyes to represent the all-powerful and all-knowing sun god, Inti.

Hopefully the sun god had no interest in knowing him and his plans.

Beyond the kancha grounds, farther down into Vira, plumes of smoke curled into the sky, their people readying for their own celebrations of a successful harvest and the winter solstice. They would leave offerings at Qorikancha and drink chicha with their neighbors and dance until the sun came up.

With the first light of day, Emperor Maicu and his closest allies would march past the kancha walls and Qorikancha, down the emperor's road and into the city, but Kasik would not be among them. If all went according to plan, he and Nina would be long gone.

"You seem to have healed well." Atik's voice was formal, as if it hadn't been his fist that had harmed Kasik in the first place. As if he hadn't admitted to murdering his mamay in cold blood.

"It wasn't much to heal from. You seem to have gotten soft in your old age. Or is it only women you are used to hunting and killing?" Kasik could feel the heat of Atik's gaze on him, but he ignored it. "Ah, here comes our first guest."

It was Lord Anri approaching, regal in bright red, his dark skin vibrant despite the creeping cold and lack of sun. At first glance, it was impossible to tell that they had traveled for several weeks from the northern tip of Icosa to get there. He knew they weren't used to the climate, as the temperatures in Tullumay tended to stay warmer. It was a beautiful place. One he had been looking forward to visiting with Samaq by his side.

Kasik swallowed the urge to ask after his men. To know if Lord Anri had laid eyes on them after all, but then he would give away the fact that he knew Samaq was not gone, as Emperor Maicu had said.

"Kunay Atik. Kamayuq Kasik. As always, it is an honor to be here." Lord Anri placed a hand over his heart. "Emperor Maicu and Empress Chaska, are they well?"

"They are well. Your daughter is a loyal empress." Atik gestured toward the walla beside him. "Kinto will escort you to your house so that you may rest before the festivities begin."

Lord Anri bowed and stepped aside, the rest of his party, all men in shades of red, moving with him.

Kasik remembered the last time he saw Nina in red, the way it had made the flush of her cheeks stand out. How it had matched the bloody handprint on her cheek.

"Your thoughts run away with you."

He glanced at his tayta, careful not to take his full attention off the commotion surrounding them. "My thoughts are exactly where they are supposed to be."

"You may have the emperor fooled, but I am not so easily misled." Atik faced forward as he spoke, his voice low enough so that only Kasik knew he was speaking. "Look what happened to your mamay. Rumi. The moment Emperor Maicu allows it, your life will be forfeit."

"How it must pain you to be under the thumb of a child." Kasik smiled and nodded at an older man who passed by. "To know that your power is so limited."

"You know *nothing* of power," Atik spat. "But you will soon understand exactly what it looks like, and what it costs."

A group of men emerged from Qorikancha, and all Kasik's rebuttals were swept away. They were large men, with their long hair loose around their shoulders, and the beasts they rode larger than any he had ever seen, all of them covered head to toe in the deepest, darkest black.

It was a refusal to acknowledge Maicu as their emperor. A rejection of his invitation to join Tawantinsuyu. A line drawn between their territories.

They walked down the road through the kancha grounds very carefully, as if one wrong step would end in their deaths. The way that the walla and attendants were staring, Kasik didn't blame them. They were only safe as long as they didn't present a threat, but their very existence was one, and the man leading them was a force all on his own. Juac, the lord of Karu, the farthest and wildest ayllu in Uwaco, stopped before an attendant several lengths away and shed himself of weapons. He was an imposing man, large shouldered and broad chested, his skin full of scars.

Uwaco did not keep an acllahuasi as Amaru and Icosa did, nor did they serve the gods in the same way as those from Vira. It was unclear why Juac was there at all, if Kasik thought about it long enough. But he didn't have the time. Juac easily freed himself of all his weapons and then strode forward alone.

Kasik couldn't help but admire his audacity, though his decision would only serve to make the emperor more eager to win them over. He would offer Juac all the wealth and benefits that he offered all the lords of the ayllus he absorbed. Wives and servants from the acllahuasi. Gold from the empire's coffers. Achillas for protection.

Most of the ayllus gladly accepted. They were able to keep their positions of notoriety and their customs and only required to offer up their harvest and their children. Such a small price to pay for stability.

But Juac gave the impression that he would not be so easily convinced.

"My men and I will stay outside of the kancha, in the city." Juac pointed down the mountain and toward the east, where the sky was a dark purple. "If we do not return to Karu unharmed in six weeks' time, they will bring the force of our army against you."

"You dare come and make threats," Atik seethed. Kasik saw his tayta's knuckles blanch around the hilt of his blade. "We should cut you down where you stand."

Juac shook his head. "But you will not, because it is Emperor Maicu who has invited us, and you bow to his every command." Juac stepped closer and lowered his voice. "We know the kukuchi come. We have heard whispers of their might, and we are prepared to fight against them. Are you?"

At the mention of the familiar word, Kasik's spine stiffened. Atik's nostrils flared as he tried to temper his anger. "You are making a grave mistake."

Juac shrugged. "I do not believe so. It is *you* who need our warriors. If Emperor Maicu cannot convince us to join, then the mistake will be yours alone." Juac turned away without bowing and walked back to his men.

As soon as he was far enough away, Atik whirled around and strode up the steps to the kancha doors, leaving Kasik behind to consider just how tenuous Emperor Maicu's hold on power seemed to be, and if it had always been this way, or if he was finally seeing the truth.

41

Nina had become accustomed to her routine. A tray of food and tea would arrive in the morning, sometimes with the empress, sometimes not, and then Kasik would escort her to Master Wara's, where he would flutter nervously around the room and explain to her the useless history of Vira and the emperors who have ruled it. He did not tell her any more cryptic stories, and she did not ask for them.

Sometimes, Kunay Atik would show up unannounced and watch her learn. Always, he would place a hand on her shoulder so that the touch of his power never left her. She was a shadow of the girl who had been so determined and optimistic in the Tuta Kulla, and her attay was a distant memory.

That morning, Empress Chaska found her in bed and forced her out. "Up, up, plans have changed," she said, her voice bright enough that Nina shrunk away from it. Chaska threw her slippers at her and then dragged Nina through the halls, her guard following close behind. Nina was too tired and hollow to ask questions, and she knew Chaska would not answer them, anyway.

The bathhouse was empty when they arrived. Nina undressed and gladly followed Chaska into the water with every intention of sinking to the bottom until all her thoughts were clouded with pressure. But Chaska grabbed her arm and tugged her up. "We don't have time for that," she said, shooting a glance behind her. "The ceremony has been moved up. You're to marry the emperor in three days' time."

At that, Nina straightened. "But Kasik said—"

"Kasik didn't know until this morning. Listen to me very carefully."

Somewhere in the bathhouse, a reed door opened and closed. Quiet voices filtered in through the fog. "The performances during the day are for the citizens of Vira, and the emperor will not join until the grand feast begins. Only then will the doors of Amaru Kancha open. There will be many people and much commotion. It will be easy for things to get out of hand."

The words were nonchalant. Chaska did not look at her as she said them, and her hand gently ran over the surface of the water, sending small waves of ripples that lapped Nina's skin.

"You should be prepared," she calmly added, "in the event that we must make a quick escape. Wear something warm, and perhaps find a blade to hide under your dress. Most everyone will be wearing achillas, but a stone can't protect you from the cold, or falling rocks, or a knife in the throat." Chaska shrugged innocently. "You never know when you might need to defend yourself."

Then she stood and stepped out of the tub. Once wrapped in a drying cloth, she turned to Nina again. "The walla are occupied today, so an attendant will escort you to the seamstress where they will fit you for your ceremony dress. Be sure to ask for a coat while you're there. And Nina," she said, forcing Nina to meet her shrewd stare. "Remember what I said. No one is safe so long as one of us is threatened."

It was clear that Chaska had something planned and wanted Nina to join the fight, but the emperor was not a force they could fight against, not with every strength at his disposal and the gods at his back.

Leaving was rational, not cowardly.

It was what she told herself as the seamstress and attendants tugged a crimson dress down her body and then stepped back to marvel at it. The room was large and brightly lit, with changing screens blocking off one corner, tables full of textiles and tools across from it, and a dais in the middle, which she stood upon. Directly in front of her was a large piece of reflective glass like nothing she had seen before.

Nina saw her dark eyes that reminded her of the soil of her family's fields, and her long hair that escaped from its plait, and her brown skin that had lost some of its richness from being behind stone walls for so many weeks. The red of the dress was a stark contrast against her skin. Garish, almost. If she squinted, it looked like she was swathed in blood.

It was a dress fit for killing an emperor. Her power flickered in her chest at the thought, and she pressed a hand to it in surprise. It had been a week since she felt it, and only one day since Kunay Atik had last touched her. If she could, she would shred his soul apart with her bare hands. She would—

Nina gasped, pieces of stories and truths falling into place like the click of a latch. There was something in Master Wara's story that he had gotten wrong. Something that would change everything. She had to tell him.

But first, she waited for the seamstress to finish her final alterations and then changed back into her clothes. The seamstress gave the dress to the attendant who had accompanied Nina with strict instruction to not let it drag on the ground. Nina didn't offer to help. Instead, she took advantage of the opportunity.

"I need to see Master Wara," Nina told the woman.

The attendant shifted the bundle higher in her arms. "I was told to escort you to the seamstress and back. Nowhere else. I cannot disobey the emperor."

Nina was compelled to step forward and place a hand on the woman's arm. There was a vibration in the tips of her fingers. A slight tingle that made her heart race. The attendant glanced at her hand, then back at Nina with a crease between her brow. "It'll just take a moment. You won't even notice I'm gone."

The woman's usually stony face softened into a daze, and then she sighed. "Just a moment," she agreed.

Without taking a breath to think about what she had just done, Nina turned and sped toward the scholar's wing. The cold of the hall crawled up her arms and into her chest, replacing the burning sensation that had come with that small touch and simple command. Nerves fluttered in her belly.

Nina easily found Master Wara's door. The kancha was no longer a mystery to navigate. She knocked and waited.

There was no sound from the other side. Nina knocked again, but the unnatural quiet continued, her quick breaths the only noise to be heard. She glanced both ways down the hall, then pressed the latch. The door opened easily, creaking as it revealed the room beyond.

Master Wara's space had always looked like controlled chaos. She might not have known where anything was, but she was certain that he did. What she found now was *not* his mess.

Quipu were strewn across the floor, their strands tangled, their knots undone. The two chairs that Nina and Master Wara typically sat in were overturned, and on the corner of the table were splashes of something dark. *Blood?* Nina stepped closer and ran her finger through a spot. It smeared across the stone like paint.

Heart thundering, Nina slowly backed out of the room, careful to leave everything just the way it was. Her mind raced as she hurried away, and the disquiet of her soul warned that fate would have her next.

42

From the top of the kancha steps, Kasik surveyed the grounds once more, taking note of where the walla stood guard, most of them strategically placed by himself to allow for a quick escape. The path to the achipumas' enclosure was mostly clear, with the majority of the security focused on the kancha where the emperor would be. The plan was for Nina and Kasik to walk straight out the main doors and retrieve Capac, if they had the chance. If not, the other walla would take good care of the achipuma in his absence. It was the best he could do, given the circumstances.

The doors to the receiving room were wide open, the din of conversation and music joined by the commotion outside the room, where tables were set up underneath the stars for those who hadn't been invited inside. Master Wara wasn't there, which was not unlike him. The man hated crowds more than anyone he knew.

Atik was also nowhere to be found. His tayta was known for disappearing and reappearing only when he was most needed, but he never missed an opportunity to flash his status in public.

The murmur of conversation quieted, and Kasik knew why before he walked the few steps to the open doors. The wind blew over him, icier than normal for this time of year, and the fur on his shoulders tickled his neck. A chill went down his spine, but it was Nina in the torchlight, all eyes on her, who did it.

The dress she wore was molded to her body, encasing her like a living statue that had been dipped in blood and hung to dry.

It wasn't the dress that made him shiver. It was the look in her eyes as she beheld the room. It had been three days since he had last seen her, and he barely recognized her.

Kasik watched her smile transform the shape of her face and the set of her shoulders. Her eyes were ringed in darkness, and her lips were bright red and glistening. The last time she had looked so full of life was when she was with Shayim, dancing under the moon with the fire at her back.

From across the room, she was an entirely different person, one who was powerful and deadly. He had seen it before, but it was easy to forget the two personas coexisted. The Nina he knew who wanted nothing but to be free of these people and find her family, and this Nina who held power within her that could shatter a person's body and mind.

He kept one hand on the hilt of his blade at all times, watching as Nina was led along the edges of the room to sit beneath the bloodred tapestry at Emperor Maicu's table. Maicu stood when he saw her, the appreciative glint in his eyes clear enough for Kasik to see. The man knew of his plans, and still he wanted her.

Nina bowed, and then she sat to his left. Chaska and the mamakuna were on his right. Atik and Master Wara *should* have been beside Nina, but those seats remained empty. Kasik had refused a seat with the excuse of keeping a closer eye on the crowd, and now he was grateful for the foresight.

It was easy to lose track of time in the receiving room; there were no windows, just like most of the kancha, and the torchlight never ran down. A trick of the Ikara, he assumed, which he had never questioned before, but it made it so that the revelries began and ended only when the emperor decreed it so.

One hour passed, then two. Kasik walked the length of the room, his eyes never straying too far from Nina, even as he searched for Lord Anri.

He hadn't been able to ask about Samaq with his tayta nearby, but with Atik not there, Kasik was desperate to know more than what Chaska had told him.

Of all the faces Kasik searched, none belonged to Lord Anri. Eventually, he gave up and returned to watching Nina. Remembering, hoping, fearing. There was doubt in him, somewhere beneath the certainty he felt when imagining their future, but he couldn't tell if it was because of his own insecurities or her total and utter comfort with the lie she was wearing like an old cloak that threatened him.

She sat as if she were made from stone, fearless and unflappable and unfamiliar. As if she had planted roots and intended to stay and rule.

A flash of movement from the emperor's table made him turn. Nina's hand had moved from the arm of her chair to her forehead, a light touch with furrowed brows that made Kasik's heart pound harder. He was at the farthest edge of the room and still he could see a look of confusion cross her face.

Something isn't right. He began making his way toward the front, navigating the long tables set in rows, the chairs that were pushed back to allow clear lines of sight for rowdy conversations.

This time, when he sought Nina's eyes, he found her staring back at him.

Emperor Maicu bent to whisper in Nina's ear. Kasik tried to read his lips, but his head was turned away and Kasik could only see red as he watched Maicu's hand land on Nina's thigh.

A resonant chime cut through the air. What followed was a silence thick enough to cut, until the emperor rose from his seat to face the crowd.

Kasik was forced to stop. He held his breath lest he scream Nina's name.

"My friends." Emperor Maicu's voice was profound in the quiet.

"Before we continue the festivities, I wanted to present to you three gifts." He held up a hand with three fingers, gold rings flashing as he swept them through the air.

The crowd roared with applause. Kasik could have sworn the torches burned brighter in response. A thin film of panic crawled over his skin—this hadn't been a part of the plan.

"This first gift," the emperor continued. He paused dramatically, and then he flourished his hand to his left.

Kunay Atik appeared from a small door set into the stone wall. In front of him was a hooded and hunched figure. Unrecognizable, and yet Kasik's heart squeezed at the sight of them walking toward the center of the room.

Emperor Maicu rounded the table to meet them. They were directly in Kasik's line of sight, but there was no clear path forward. Atik kicked one of the figure's knees, and they hit the floor with a painful thud.

The room leaned forward in anticipation. With *hunger*. Kasik swallowed the urge to vomit and slowly crept closer.

"This gift is for those who would think to betray me. May it serve as a reminder of the might of the gods."

Atik yanked the hood off, and it was as if the air had been sucked from the room.

Before him was a face he had come to know better than his own tayta's. A man who had spent hours teaching him how to read quipu and social situations. Raised him when his tayta had no interest. Loved him when nobody else seemed capable of it. His eyes burned as he refused to blink or look elsewhere. Kasik forced himself to stay where he was, to witness Master Wara's fate, even as every fiber of his being screamed in agonizing protest.

Distantly, he heard the gasps of the crowd. He looked at the table behind Emperor Maicu. Surely, someone would stop this. Whatever was happening could not be allowed to continue. But Nina was barely propped up over the table, her eyes cloudy and distant, and Chaska was frozen in her seat.

Despite the blood on his face and the submissive position, Master Wara sat tall and unbothered, back and shoulders straighter than Kasik had ever seen them. Usually, they were curled over a table and rows of quipu, or curled over Kasik as he taught him to transcribe their knowledge, or curled over a cup of tea before a fire.

Everyone who knew Master Wara loved him. There was always a word of encouragement from his lips, a look of pride in his eyes, a helping hand. Those same qualities shone through him even then, bloodied and on display. It was clear the emperor meant to humiliate him, but Master Wara looked like a pillar of hope and rebellion before them all.

"Observe what happens to those of you who would dare to plot against me and my people."

As if knowing what was coming next, Master Wara lifted his eyes to the heavens and exposed his neck. There was a scream of metal cutting the air, and then a flash of light as the blade sliced across bare flesh. Bursts of startled gasps and screams rose like a wave.

Kasik hadn't seen Maicu draw his blade, nor had he expected such a vicious killing. He grasped on to a chair to avoid collapsing, unclear where his dread began and his body ended. But through it all, Kasik kept his eyes on Master Wara. The blood pouring from his neck. The way his head fell back and almost tore off from the depth of the cut. The slack in his hands that had always been filled with the weight of the world.

Finally, his body gave up and listed to the side, falling into a heap at the feet of the emperor who didn't care to spare a glance.

Such little regard for the man who had taught him, who had served his tayta before him and his empire proudly and boldly for so many years.

Kasik stared at his mentor, his teacher, his *friend* and he held himself together with the barest of threads that reminded him of why they needed to run, to leave and never look back. If Maicu had his way, it would be Nina's blood covering the floor. Nina's unblinking eyes devoid of life. Nina's body tossed aside so carelessly.

It was meant to be a warning, but it was only a reminder. A catalyst. An affirmation of all the choices Kasik had made, and all the things he knew to be true.

More than ever, Kasik wanted Nina to use her attay to rip the entire room to shreds. He would climb over tables and bodies to get to her if he had to. He would—

"The next gift," Maicu proclaimed loudly for all to hear, and then he pointed a hand at Nina, "is for my betrothed."

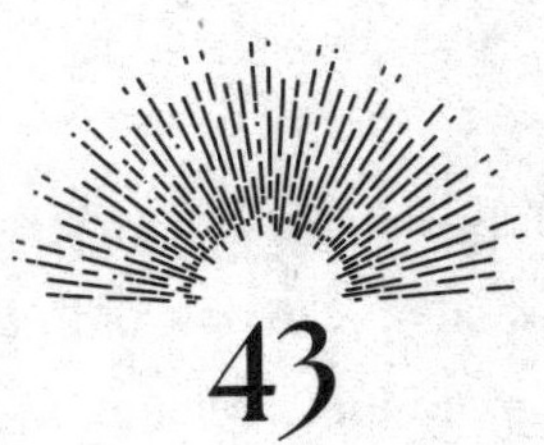

43

Nina was barely aware of her surroundings. The blood coating the floor was obscenely garish, and the *smell. Gods.* It permeated the room and clogged her nostrils until she was sure she would vomit.

Tears blurred her vision, making it so the faces of shock surrounding her were terribly softened into nightmarish visages of wide eyes and down-turned mouths. Kasik was across from her, so close but so far, and between them were endless stretches of tables and unfamiliar faces. Everything seemed to tilt and list until Nina was unsure which way was up.

They had put something in her drink. Something that made her own body feel foreign. Frantically, she searched for her attay, trying and failing to reach beneath the fog of terror and probe for threads of life and will, but the icy hand of the achilla was all she could feel.

Except for Master Wara, whose gold threads faded to a pinprick until winking out of existence forever. She should have escaped while she still had the chance. Would have, if it wasn't for a thick and pressing foreboding that rooted her to the spot.

Eyes glued to him, Nina watched as Maicu motioned to the side again. Atik appeared with another hooded figure, this one frail and stumbling toward the center of the room, their head barely above their shoulders as it rolled this way and that. Atik moved them slowly, carefully. With much more care than he had shown Master Wara. Whoever it was, they were important. Nina felt it in her bones.

She tried to stand but lost her footing. She refused to sit and watch Maicu kill another innocent person while Master Wara's body was still warm at his feet.

Walk away, her mind screamed at her. *Save yourself.* But she could do no such thing. She would have to wait and watch and prepare.

"May I present to you," Emperor Maicu announced, the weight of his words softened by the shifting of bodies and chairs. The crowd seemed interested and uncomfortable, not quite sure what was happening but enjoying it, nonetheless. Nina didn't understand what was happening, either, but she braced herself against some unforeseen enemy when she heard blades being freed from their sheaths.

Directly across the room, several tables filled with captivated people between them, stood Kasik, and on either side of him was a walla with a blade held to his neck. Kasik's hands were in the air, palms out, and his eyes were pinned to hers. A yawning pit opened in Nina's stomach. Whatever they had given her made everything feel dampened and slow, but the dread pooling beneath her skin was visceral enough to pierce the fog.

Movement stole her attention. Maicu reached for the hooded figure, his fingers curling around the edge of the cloth bag. In his right hand was the blade he had used to slaughter Master Wara. Blood still dripping from the edge and landing on the floor with a *plop*.

Nina couldn't have moved even if she tried. Anticipation tingled in her fingers, and her attay swirled and eddied with nowhere to go.

Then the bag was off, and the head was free, and Maicu's words were little more than a whisper among the screaming in her mind. "Sacha the Seer, from the far reaches of Limac. Sister to my betrothed."

All at once, Nina moved, a force of fury propelling her out of her seat and over the table. Her attay clawed at her insides, clawed at the emperor, only to meet wall after impenetrable wall. There was an achilla on each of his limbs, in the circlet on his head, hanging from his neck. Only then did she notice them. Only then did a firm hand wrap around her shoulder and quiet the screaming of her power.

"No!" Nina screamed over and over as walla moved in to hold her down. She thrashed and kicked against the hands that tore her from her mission. No longer was she poised and powerful. She was the wild animal they had feared, screams of rage echoing up to the ceiling and beyond to the stars, the gods, the whole of the upper realm.

From a distance, she heard Kasik scream her name, his voice broken and beaten. She mourned him already, mourned their freedom, the plans they had built and the secrets they had kept. They would die with them. But Nina would do anything, sacrifice everything, to reach her sister's side. There had never been a question about that. She would throw herself at the feet of the emperor again and again if it meant saving Sacha.

An arm wrapped around her waist and pulled her against warm flesh. With it, everything went eerily, agonizingly quiet. Her rage cooled into a low fire. Her mind slowed to the pace of a sea slug crawling over the bottom of the silty ocean.

The lack of Atik's threads filled her mind. It subdued her agony enough so that she could *see* her sister, so far from her reach. Stringy brown hair loose around her chin. Too-big dress hanging from her too-thin frame. Her eyes half opened; a small hand extended toward Nina.

"Sacha," Nina cried. She would have fallen if it wasn't for Atik's arm holding her up. His other hand wrapped around her chin and forced her to watch. As if she would turn her eyes away.

The people surrounding her had turned over chairs in their haste to retreat from her wildness. They watched her with shades of guilt and remorse, sorrow and pleasure, fear and curiosity. So much, yet nothing all at the same time.

Even Empress Chaska, sitting just a few seats away, did nothing. For all she had beseeched Nina to be courageous, she was sitting like a coward, mouth agape, waiting to watch the show.

No one stepped forward to intervene, to hold Sacha's hand when Nina could not. No one spoke a whisper of a word.

No one except Kasik, who struggled against the hands that held him, Nina's name a chanted plea on his lips. One of the walla dug his blade deeper into Kasik's throat, and Nina tracked a drop of blood as it carved a path down his neck.

"Tell me, Sacha," Emperor Maicu said. Nina flicked her eyes back to him, to Sacha who swayed on her feet. "Can you See Nina's future? Can you *See* how her life will enrich Tawantinsuyu?"

Sacha's mouth worked to form a word, but her voice was little more than the rustle of a solitary leaf as she said, "Yes." Her eyes, however, said so much more. They were narrowed in ire, burning from within. They glittered in promise even as the emperor's smile was sharp with wicked delight and cunning victory.

Behind her, Atik's chuckle filled Nina with such a murderous rage that she felt like a hapless creature caged beneath his touch.

All the pieces she had been haphazardly collecting fell into place.

Nina had used her power, and they had come for her and found Sacha. She had brought their enemies straight to their door. Kunay Atik had used her love for her sister against her. They were the Girl and the Sister. An Ikara and a Seer.

One as collateral. A pawn.

The other, a spare. A sacrifice.

Nina had been utterly and thoroughly fooled.

The rage came rushing back in like a tidal wave, building up slowly before it reached a crest and broke upon a shore of desperation. She lunged forward with a roar, hair tearing from her scalp, the pain ignored as she reached deep beneath the blanket of Atik's attay to grasp at her own, willing to tear it from her insides and let it shred her soul if it meant shredding everyone else in this room. She would have them beg. She would make them regret ever having set eyes upon her, for *craving* her—

"*Aht, aht,*" Maicu tsked, his eerily calm voice breaking through the fog of her wrath enough to clear her mind and see the knife he held at Sacha's throat. "We're not finished yet."

Sacha was limp in the emperor's arms, her body fully leaning on Maicu. Her beautiful baby sister with the purest heart, reduced to a prisoner for the sake of Nina's cooperation. She simply could not comprehend it. Refused to imagine a scenario in which that knife went through her sister's throat.

"There is one more gift."

The crowd was nonexistent, as far as Nina was concerned. She had eyes and ears only for her sister, whose name she whispered over and over, a desperate plea for her to open her eyes, to see. They had called her a Seer, and Nina knew the truth of that word as she knew the truth of her name. Memories of her sister came unbidden, the dreams she had shared with Nina, the strange conversations and the things Sacha had known that couldn't be explained. They had always thought her ill and strange. Weak. But all Nina saw when she looked at her now was the strength of her love.

"This one is for all the citizens of Tawantinsuyu."

Silence fell as the emperor took slow, measured steps down the length of the room, dragging Sacha along in his arms. Nina was hoping he would bring her close enough to touch, but he gently let her go into the arms of a walla before walking back to her.

Behind her, Atik shifted away, and Nina almost collapsed from the loss of his touch. She heard Kasik say her name again, and she heard a chair shift down the table, but she focused solely on Maicu. "If you so much as lift a hand against me, your sister's life will be forfeit," he whispered, his lips close enough that she could feel them against her ear. Then he turned back to the gathered crowd. "Nina of Limac, an Ikara with attay the likes of myth, will usher in the favor of the gods in its full glory, through an honored sacrifice."

Maicu's extended hand slid around her neck and settled at the back of her head, replacing Atik's touch. But the damage had been done. His power had seeped into every crevice of her and filled it with an emptiness that left her hollow. "The gods have chosen her for their service, and it is her blood that will grant Tawantinsuyu strength and longevity as we face down those who decide to form against us."

Whispered confusion erupted from the crowd and melded with the whispered dread of Nina's heart.

She heard words like *archaic* and *savage*. But she also heard words like *deserved* and *necessary*. The people were greedy; they would accept whatever gifts they knew would ultimately benefit them, evident in the way the whispers turned into an excited roar. The sound of it bounced around the room, inside Nina's skull, rattled her very bones, and it was a sound of triumph. Of celebration. Their faces had been transformed from shock to victory, sharp smiles and deadly eyes and hawkish greed.

Nina's strength was failing. She tipped into the table and braced herself against it. "The Mamacoca leaf, when mixed with ground achilla, is the perfect substance to quell your powers. With enough of it, we can keep you subdued for weeks."

As he spoke, chaos erupted in the room. Nina dared to glance away from Maicu and saw Kasik break free of the walla holding him. His blade swung through the air. Blood splattered the tables. Bystanders scrambled out of the way. Bodies fell to the floor.

"Take Empress Chaska to her rooms," Maicu yelled at the same time Atik called out in panic, "For the gods' sakes, someone *stop* him!"

People screamed and ran for the doors, a sea of red and gold passing by, cutting off her sight of Kasik. She saw flashes of Chaska's long, dark hair in her periphery, but it was Sacha's small body curled in a walla's arms that she kept her eyes pinned to.

"Sacha!" Nina yelled, her sister's name searing her throat. Her tongue felt numb in her mouth. "Do not harm her! *I will kill all of you.*"

But her threats fell on deaf ears. Atik only smiled and stepped closer. Nina pushed away from the table and collapsed. She heard Kasik scream her name and then his voice cut off. It had never been clearer just how useless, how *powerless*, she was.

"She makes a fool of us with her words," Atik said mildly.

Maicu sighed, and then his hand wrapped around the back of Nina's neck. There was a tiny prick of pain, and the world around her began to soften. Her body grew heavier, her arms weaker. They barely held her up as Maicu grasped her chin and spoke. "Soon, you will be free of this world's worries, my love. With the gods' favor and Sacha's Seeing, our enemies will be defeated. She will be a savior to our people."

And then he let her go. Nina fell to the floor and it seemed to swallow her, to pull her down as she tried in vain to crawl to her sister. She heard the clang of metal, the scuff of boots against stone. Master Wara's body was being dragged away.

No, not Master Wara, she realized. *Kasik.* A trail of blood was left in his wake. Nina screamed his name, then Sacha's. Her fingernails bent back and snapped as she dug them into the stone.

The room had fallen quiet enough that she heard more than saw Kunay Atik crouch before her. "You have lost," he whispered through the havoc of her mind. His eyes were wide, wild, the whites even darker than she remembered, as if he was being consumed by the void of his soul from the inside out.

"I am still alive," she spat at him. "It is not done until my soul has left this realm, and even then, I will hunt . . . you . . . down."

Atik searched her eyes for truth. Nina wondered what he saw and if it worried him. Firm hands slid under her arms and scooped her up. She hung suspended between them, much like that first day they had dragged her through the halls.

She was weak. Powerless. Consumed with thoughts of Sacha and slaughter.

"I will hunt *all of you*," Nina screamed into the quiet.

She heard Maicu's nervous laughter, and then she finally lost her fight to the darkness.

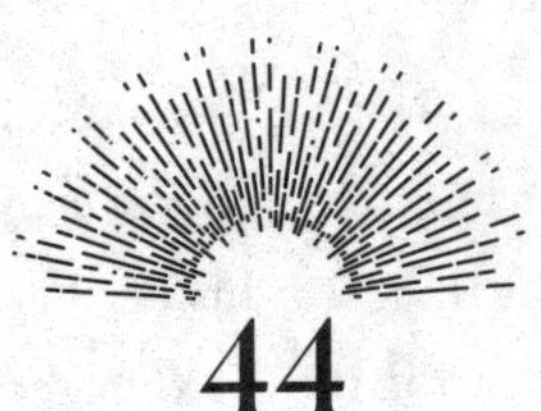

44

Kasik was made of agony and sorrow. Failure flowed beneath his skin. His bones screamed and his heart ached and there was nothing else as he lay in the dark and dank cell in the dungeon beneath the earth.

"Fitting," a voice said from the other side of the barred cell, "that this is where you should die. It's where your mamay brought you into this world."

What heinous thing had he done to deserve this kind of torture, that his last living moments would be filled with the face of his tayta smiling with smug satisfaction, and the vision of his mamay suffering alone? It appeared the gods wouldn't allow him to slip into a peaceful death. He might as well indulge in the pain.

"For someone who claims to want nothing to do with me," Kasik rasped, "you spend a lot of time seeking me out."

The shadow of his tayta chuckled darkly. "I've only come to see how far the mighty fall. It's a long way down for you."

The bars clanked open and then bootsteps echoed closer. Kasik opened his eyes, unaware that they had drifted shut, to find Atik crouched and peering at him through strangely dark eyes. A hand pushed his hair back, and Kasik thought his tayta meant to offer a comforting hand in his last moments of life.

But then that hand tightened into a fist at his scalp, making his eyes water with the sting of it, and he realized there would be no comfort. Only gloating and suffering.

"My tayta died when I was young. He was gods-touched. Did you know?" Atik continued, voice low, barely a murmur. "They had bestowed their will upon him, and his tayta before him, all the way back to Dimas himself. So much of that history has been lost, but not this gift. I inherited it when he died, and I thought it would change everything. I was *good* and *obedient*, just like you. But I spent my life serving others—the gods, Emperor Yachua, his pathetic sons—as if it wasn't *me* with the power. Yachua was a man felled by a mortal man's disease. But me? I am blessed by the gods. I am *invincible*." Atik released Kasik's hair with a shove.

"You killed a woman," Kasik paused to cough, "because you were afraid of your *feelings*. You are nothing . . . but a *coward*."

Whatever strength Kasik had been able to muster to throw that insult was stolen by Atik's boot. It flew into his stomach, the force of it enough to make Kasik's vision blur even further, but the pain was already there. It was like adding water to a full cup.

"And look where bravery has gotten you," Atik said. "I knew Maicu's love for you was conditional. I knew it would take only the smallest amount of pressure for him to turn against you, just as he did his brother. Just as he believes that sacrificing Nina will save our people. He is a *fool*, as are you." Atik grabbed the cord around Kasik's neck and twisted. It bit against Kasik's skin. "This stone you wear wasn't even hers. You are so desperate to be loved that you convinced yourself she would leave something behind for you."

There was physical pain, and then there was emotional pain, and Kasik hadn't known until that moment how different the two were. One was manageable while the other was not, but they heaped atop one another, driving him deeper into a dark pit of despair.

"And Master Wara? What was it he was guilty of?"

"Getting in the way," Atik spat. "But everything is falling perfectly into place. A few more steps, and it is *I* who will rule Tawantinsuyu with the favor and power of the gods at my side." His voice floated in the darkness, surrounding him like a vengeful spirit, and then Atik was whispering in his ear, a detached voice that he knew would follow him for eternity. "But *you* have been measured, and you have been found entirely lacking."

The next time Kasik opened his eyes, he was alone.

"Well, this is pathetic," intoned a voice from the depths of the dungeon. Perhaps it was his tayta coming back to mock him some more.

Keys rattled, followed by the clank of metal.

Another prisoner, come to keep him company?

A hand on his shoulder, firm yet gentle. "Drink this," the voice said.

Kasik obeyed; what else was there to do when a god commanded you?

The liquid was earthy and strong enough that it sent a jolt of numb awareness through him. He realized he wasn't dead. There was no god with him in the cell, and he was being freed.

"What was this?" Kasik peered into the empty cup as if the answer was at the bottom.

Chaska laughed. "Master Wara's tea. You aren't healed, but it should help strengthen you long enough to get out of here." She smiled a lopsided smile as she undid his shackles. "If we leave now and ride hard, you might be able to catch them before they reach the mountaintop."

Kasik's mind raced. "The mountaintop," he repeated slowly. "Mount Rimac. That's where they are taking Nina?" Hands suddenly free, he pushed himself to his knees with a grunt. "How are you here?" he asked roughly, a hand pressed to his ribs where they screamed in protest. "Did you know what they had planned?"

"I didn't," Chaska answered, and Kasik believed her. There were circles under her eyes, and her hand shook lightly as she pushed a clump of hair behind an ear. "And neither did they know about my attay, or *my* plans. My tayta and his men surround Amaru Kancha. Maicu and Atik will have no royal seat to return to. But you have to help Nina." Chaska stood and pulled Kasik to his feet. "The only thing Shayim is sure of is that Nina must survive."

"Why wouldn't I help her?" he asked sharply. "Everything I have done has been for her."

"Because she was powerless here, but she will not be powerless any longer. She will be angry and dangerous."

"She's not dangerous," Kasik said softly. "She only wants to protect her family."

"And when she is full of wrath and no purpose? When she is unrecognizable? Will you stand by her even then?" Chaska stepped closer, her dark eyes flashing in the dim light. "There will come a time when you must choose a side. Will you choose wisely?"

Kasik opened his mouth to answer, and then closed it. His whole body ached and blood leaked between the fingers he held at his side. A stab wound, he vaguely remembered.

"Come. We'll have time for answers later, as long as you live."

Kasik moved more quickly with her help, and though each step was a struggle, the fact that he was upright at all was a feat.

Chaska led them through the maze of the dungeon and the kancha hallways. There was no one left within the walls, and outside was even quieter. Kasik wondered if they would continue with the processions and offerings, or if they thought Nina's blood was enough to suffice.

They had all stood there without raising a finger to help or a word of dissent. The way they had *cheered* as the emperor proclaimed Nina's fate. He would have cut them all down, if he could. But he was only one man.

Kasik assumed Maicu had taken his most trusted walla with him. It would be almost impossible to get to him, but Atik only guarded himself.

He was too proud to have a contingent surrounding him. If Kasik had the element of surprise on his side, then he might see a victory.

Capac was already roused and waiting when they arrived at the achipuma enclosure. Illari was beside him, tiny flakes of snow collecting on both of their heads. Once seated, Kasik leaned over Capac and wrapped his arounds around the achipuma's neck. His fur was warm and comforting. "We must be swift, my friend," Kasik whispered into his ear. "We must save Nina."

Illari took off on a bounding leap, Chaska seated proudly on her back. They rode down the path and through Qorikancha where a line of men in green guarded the outer doors. Kasik spotted Lord Anri, who lifted an arm in greeting to Chaska before placing it over his heart, and then the city was a blur as the achipumas tore off to the side and up the mountainous path that led to Mount Rimac.

Kasik lowered his body and held on with what little life he had left.

45

The absence of Nina's attay felt like swimming through the ocean at night. It was endless darkness. It was fear and hopelessness. It was being back in the cell deep below the acllahuasi where she had convinced herself that she was nobody. That her life meant nothing.

There was no end to it. Nothing to grab on to. As she waded through the brackish waters, she heard snippets of conversation and saw flashes of images.

Atik's face above hers, soothing words, and evil eyes.

Sacha, limp and pliant in her arms, words spoken but left unsaid.

Nina tumbled through the darkness, and she wondered and waited. She felt hopelessly afraid and relentlessly vengeful. A fire burned in her belly and threatened to destroy everything she was, everything she hoped to be.

Her mamay's voice spoke to her. *Be cunning. Be fast. Be strong.* Her tayta's eyes pleaded with her. Lali's cries could be heard in the distance. Sacha's hand was in her own. Samaq's blood soaked the ground at her feet.

Spare no one, Nina. Kill them all.

Their lifeless eyes stared at the sky and Nina's hands were slick with their blood. *You've failed*, the gods said, and then they took her attay.

Nina was the Girl from Master Wara's story. She was Pachamama. She was herself and nobody and everybody who had ever dreamed and wanted for more. Was she supposed to love or kill? Hope or hate? They filled her equally, warred for space within her, thrashed against each other until she felt full to the brim, ready to implode.

Nina didn't know what was said and what was remembered and

what was fabricated by the terrors in her mind. There was no way to tell how much time had passed, but she knew the ground beneath her rocked, that they moved ever forward toward a bloody end. She saw herself in the reflection, dipped in red. Voices mocked her for believing she was powerful enough to stop this, to stop *them*.

The gods laughed at the emperor's efforts to please them. They spoke to Nina of her purpose. *You will change the world*, she heard them say, but it was Shayim's voice, and then it was Chaska's, and then it was her own.

All the while, Nina poked and prodded. She found the holes in her memory where the light did not shine. She brought them to the surface and let the hurt of betrayal remind her of who she was.

The betrayal of the gods for using her to suit their needs.

The betrayal of her parents for not preparing her for this power.

The betrayal of Kasik, a man who confused honor with cowardice.

The betrayal of herself, to have ever believed she was no one to anyone.

Because she was someone. The emperor had chosen her. The *gods* had chosen her, and she had wished for nothing more than for them to forget her.

But they refused, and she would make it so they could never know anything else but her rage, never speak any other name than hers, never feel any other warmth but her fire.

She would become their greatest enemy, and she would destroy their world to remind them of what they made.

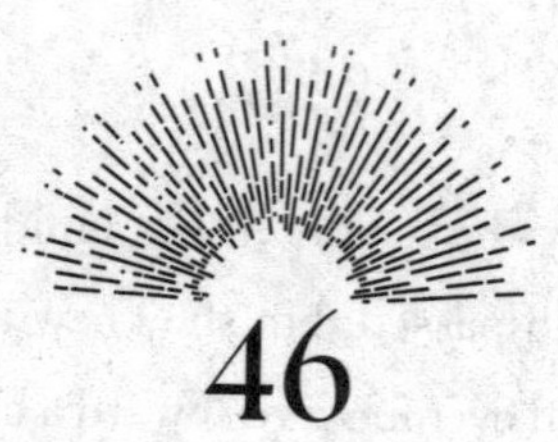

46

Snow soaked into the fur around Kasik's neck and weighed him down as he pressed himself against Capac, urged him to go faster. It was only when he slipped from his seat that he realized his body was failing him, that the tea Chaska had given him was not enough. He landed on the cold earth with a thud and a groan. Capac, breathing heavily above him, nosed Kasik's head worriedly.

"We cannot stop. We cannot let them win," Chaska said as she attempted to lift him from the ground. Together, they slipped in the freshly fallen snow and got him to his knees, where he took a moment to breathe away the dizziness, and then to his feet, where he leaned heavily against Chaska for support.

Then he lifted a leg to mount Capac, and the achipuma, better than any achipuma there had ever been, lowered his body to accommodate Kasik's weakness.

"Good boy," Kasik whispered into his ear as he slowly, painfully, slid onto his back. This time, Chaska tied a rope around his and Capac's bodies, so that Kasik could not fall off. He trusted Capac to follow Chaska.

The skin on his ribs and stomach was tender to the touch. He noticed the purpling when he finally got the courage to look and regretted it immediately, intimately aware of all the ways a man could die, ways that he himself had inflicted on others. Perhaps this was his penance, to die as he had killed, as he was meant to die before Nina had healed him.

When his vision began to blur, he knew he didn't have much time. And yet Chaska was there, pushing him, encouraging him, reminding him to keep going. She spoke to him to keep him awake, told him of her home, of the way she had wormed her way into the position she was in by convincing everyone that she was vain and unbothered and distracted. All while sneaking and learning and telling.

And she told him about that night, finding the door within the wall. It was Lord Anri she had met outside. The resistance belonged to them, and she was their ñusta. Maicu was nothing but a tool. A pawn that had delivered their greatest asset right to their doorstep.

"He has been convinced that giving Nina to the gods will earn him their favor, but it is Atik's voice that whispers in his ear—not the gods. The sacrifice of her power will usher in the pachakuti. It will bring the gods back to the mortal realm. They believe it is their time to rule once again."

For a moment, Kasik was back in the tent beneath Shayim's cunning attention.

They yearn for the pachakuti—the turnover of time—to return them to power, and they use mortals like Maicu to do it.

Snow began to fall in earnest as they rode, a sheet of cold that blurred the edges of Kasik's vision even further. He couldn't feel his hands or his face.

It felt like he was floating. Like his body would be swept away into obscurity, like there would be nothing left of him but a memory. He hoped Nina would remember him. That his death would not be in vain. All he had to do was hold on.

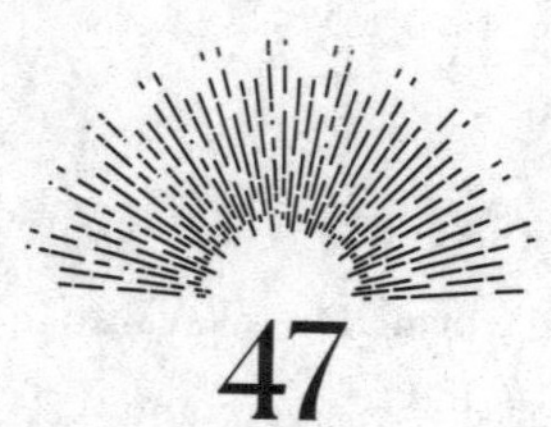

47

The gods shoved Nina back into her body, forcing her to hear and see and think. Up ahead, their party had come to a stop, their bodies hardly visible through the falling snow. She could feel that Sacha was nearby, that tug in her chest relentlessly pulsing and pushing and begging Nina to come closer. She thought her sister safe, and now there she was, so close but so far.

Sluggishly, she turned her head to peer at Atik's face and found him looking at the mountaintop with determination in his eyes. The achilla around his neck swirled as if full of life.

Nina stared at it, transfixed, until the kunay swung his body out of their seat and then reached out his hands to grasp Nina's hips. Unable to feel her legs, she fell into him. Could do nothing as he picked her up and threw her over his shoulder.

"Careful, Atik," Maicu hissed at him. She could feel his heart underneath the layers of his cloak and tunic, the way it beat frenzied and erratic.

Nina's head throbbed as they trekked up a steep incline. Just when she thought they would tumble backward, fall all the way down to the bottom of the mountain, the ground leveled, and she was being placed on her own two feet.

The world tilted, and then it settled.

The sight took her breath away.

All around them, jagged mountain peaks stabbed into an endlessly steely gray and somber sky. Snow swirled, softening their voices and footsteps. Ice covered thin branches and hung off in weapon-like shards. Below her feet was a circle of dark stone.

Achilla, she realized as a chill worked up her spine that had nothing to do with the temperature and everything to do with the gods' *protection* eager to seep into her skin. It was the same feeling Atik's touch gave her. A bone-chilling emptiness. A thief of her soul.

"Remember what happens if you disobey," Atik told her.

Nina turned slowly to meet his eyes. "All I have been is obedient, and yet here we are."

"Patience, Nina. Your reward is coming."

He left her standing in the center of the flat expanse. Nina's legs were desperate to carry her to Sacha, but Atik got to her first, and then Maicu was blocking them from sight.

The snow gave everything a hazy, dreamlike quality. She was having trouble discerning what was real, and what was merely in her mind, which told her she was in danger, but her body wasn't responding. Maicu was moving in spurts. Beside her one moment, then in front of her the next. When she blinked, a circle of people surrounded them.

They were pillars of flesh in the middle of the barren mountaintop. Walla in red, curved blades at their waists and hands folded in front of them. Atik and Sacha directly behind Maicu, the hem of Sacha's blue dress fluttering in the wind. Nina couldn't help but worry that her sister was cold. That the longer this took, the more danger she was in.

Unwittingly, she sought Kasik. He had always been there when she was in danger, but not this time.

Maicu took Nina's hands in his. She looked down at the rings on his fingers, the achillas on each of his wrists.

"Do you understand why this must be done?" he beseeched her.

She looked up at him, at the eagerness in his eyes and the slight tremor in his hands. The only thing she understood was that she was willing to do whatever it took to ensure her sister was safe. Even if that meant exposing her throat and letting the gods have her blood.

"Your sacrifice will not be in vain." Maicu dropped one of her hands and produced a small blade from the folds of his cloak. Nina glanced over his shoulder toward Atik and Sacha, heart in her throat. "There are those who seek to destroy this empire, to take our people and kill and convert and conquer. We *must* prevail, and we shall with the blessing of the gods."

The tip of the blade was placed right over her heart. Maicu's right hand joined the left on the hilt. "It will be fast," he said. "You will feel no pain."

But Nina knew it was a lie. Every sacrifice she had made thus far was painful, a sunderance that stole pieces of her soul. This would be the greatest one. Her final stand. Nina's hands fell loose to her sides. They had been balled up and fisted so long, holding on first to her old life, then to her old self, then to the idea of Kasik and his promises. She was exhausted beyond measure.

"Keep her safe," Nina whispered, eyes closed and tilted to the sky. "Make sure she—"

There was a strange sound. A deep inhale that might've been the wind, and a sputter of life that might have been the cracking of earth. Nina opened her eyes.

Maicu's brow was furrowed, his golden eyes wet with unshed tears, his mouth opened in a silent circle. There was a look of betrayal so deeply etched onto his features that Nina thought she had accidently grabbed on to his threads, but when she looked to find them, they were there, a brilliant flare of gold that pulsed like a heart.

And beside the center of Maicu's chest, where those threads began to dim, was the blood-soaked tip of a long blade right through his heart.

Nina's attay surged in defiance. She stepped back, and Maicu's hands fell. The small blade he had been holding to her heart clattered to the ground. The blade in his chest disappeared, and then Maicu fell to his knees. A shudder ran through the black stone. Blood formed a circle around Maicu.

The earth shifted beneath their feet, and then the world fell silent.

Nina looked up into Atik's eyes, the blade he had used to kill Maicu dripping blood onto the ground at his feet.

"What have you done?" she whispered.

Atik smiled, a wicked tilt of his lips that was sharpened by the dark glint of his eyes. For a moment, she could see a flash of gold light at his chest. But it was gone with the wind and in its place was a hole devoid of life.

She remembered what she went to tell Master Wara the day she found his room in disarray. A part of his story that had not been right.

"I have finally taken what is rightfully mine," Atik said. He stepped over Maicu's body without a glance and prowled closer. Nina backed away. "*Aht, aht*, stop right there. Any farther, and he'll bring her closer."

Nina followed the line of Atik's pointed finger to find a broad-chested walla holding Sacha, her head resting on his shoulder and a knife glinting at her throat.

Nina laughed. She couldn't help it. "How can I believe anything you say when you've already broken your word? She isn't supposed to be here. She was supposed to be *safe*."

"And she will be," Atik answered. "So long as you comply."

"Just as Kasik complied. Just as Maicu *complied*. We have all been *complying*, Kunay Atik." Nina's chest was heaving, her words echoing across the mountaintop. She saw men in red on the outskirts of her vision, their tunics like gashes of blood against the snow. She felt them lean closer. "What is it that you want from me?"

At this, Atik spread his hands. "I only want what I have been promised." He spun the blade from one hand to the other. "We are gods-touched, you and I. *Ikara.* We are meant to *rule*, not *serve*. I have given the gods their sacrifice, and so I will have their favor and rule over Tawantinsuyu."

Again, Atik's threads sputtered. "You are no Ikara," Nina said. "We are descended from Pachamama and Killa. We are powerful, and you are *powerless*." She dropped her voice and took a small step closer. "Do you know that you have no threads of life, no free will? You have been consumed by the gods, and soon, they will spit you out—"

Atik's hand whipped out and wrapped around Nina's throat, cutting off her words and her air and her attay. She scrabbled for purchase against his wrist, but he was too strong. He pulled her close enough that she could see herself reflected in the black pit of his eyes.

"Do as I say, and she lives. Refuse, and you both die. It is that simple, Nina. I will wield you as a weapon against our enemies, and I will rule over Tawantinsuyu without opposition."

Her heart was galloping in earnest. Rage and defeat warred within her.

Over Atik's shoulder, Nina saw her sister stir. Their eyes met, and Sacha's filled with the softest of reliefs that made Nina's heart stutter and her eyes burn.

She looked half dead already. The sister she remembered was buried deep beneath sallow skin and protruding bones and cracked lips. Nina wanted to scream at the stars, for her voice to rattle the mountains and bury them all beneath the snow. But the only reason she would open her mouth was to surrender.

It was in that moment Nina realized it was never a question. If she could go back, she would do it all over again. Give her life for Sacha's as many times as it took. She had been willing to become a bride, and now she was willing to become a weapon.

Sacha's small hands came up to wrap around the arm of the man that held her. "Nina," she called, "Don't. Please." Her voice was tender, soft and sweet as Nina had always remembered it. It would stay that way. Nina would keep her safe from the world, from the atrocities she knew she would commit.

There was no length she wouldn't walk. No height she wouldn't climb.

This time, Nina did not hope for a savior. She did not pray to the gods to rescue her or look in the distance for the faces of her mamay and tayta. She made this choice willingly, out of the strength of her love.

". . . have to do this," she heard Sacha whisper. The words carried on a gust of wind that blew the thin hairs away from Nina's face like a gentle caress, but Nina had already looked away and resigned herself to her fate.

Atik held her by the throat, waiting for her answer, the one he knew she would give. She had shown him what she loved, and he would use it against her until the end of time. There was no other choice to be made.

"I'll do whatever you ask of me," Nina said, her voice thin but the words heavy with promise.

Atik smiled, and deep from within the pits of his blackened soul, his threads flared to life.

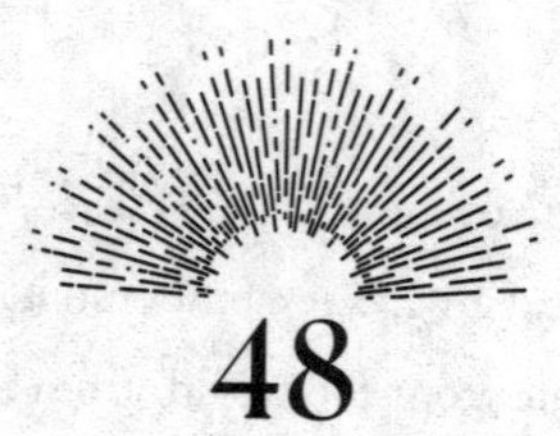

48

They didn't hear Kasik approach their circle. He didn't know what he would find, but he hadn't anticipated the utter stillness on the top of that mountain, or the way Atik held Nina so close, his hand wrapped around her throat, a barbaric smile on his face. Nina smiled as well, but hers was something different altogether. A wicked vow carved in blood.

He couldn't hear their words, but it didn't matter. He didn't need to.

Kasik's only plan was to kill his tayta. He didn't intend to live, didn't care that his tayta would still win, in the end, because Kasik would be dead at his feet. He used the last of his strength to pull himself closer, gathered his final breath and—

Coughed.

Blood spurted from his mouth, stained the pure-white snow in front of him a garish red as he fell to his knees. In his last moment of lucidity, he looked up to find Sacha's eyes wide open and staring straight at him. *Through* him.

"I have to do this," she whispered. And Kasik understood the moment the last word left her mouth what *this* was. It was in the way she tilted her head ever so slightly to give the blade at her throat more space. It was in the way she curled her small hands over the walla's large arm as if bracing herself. It was in the way her nostrils flared, with one final, deep inhale, as if she was gathering the courage she needed.

Kasik tried to scream his dissent. Nina would never forgive her for this. It would be the thing that would break her. But he could do nothing, say nothing, as Sacha pushed herself forward against the edge of the blade, as it sliced into her delicate skin, as it painted her hands and the earth a blinding, bloody red.

49

Nina screamed. She screamed until the mountains trembled and the shards of ice on the trees shook free and speared the ground. Atik dropped her and whirled around, an agonized scream leaving his mouth as Sacha fell to her knees. A tide of blood poured from her neck. All Nina saw was red. All she felt was the indescribable need to reach out, to heal, to *fix*.

Nina could do it. The power of Atik's touch had died the moment his threads had appeared, and they still burned brightly in her mind's eye. The achillas around his neck kept him safe for the moment, but her priority was Sacha. She dove for her sister, soaring over Maicu's body, and caught her before her head could hit the ground.

Sacha's mouth opened and closed with gurgled words. Nina pulled her close and pushed the hair back from her face, shushing her, soothing her, trying with all her might to ignore the river of blood that pooled around them.

"I'm here, Sacha. I'm here," she whispered.

"I will not let them turn you into a monster." Sacha's voice was barely there. A thin strand of life like the threads in her chest. Nina closed her eyes and reached as deep as she could, but Sacha's threads were a tangle of possibilities. Endlessly overwhelming. Nina couldn't determine what was Sacha's will and what was her own, couldn't find the strength to tie together flesh and sinew like she had for Kasik.

Kasik. In the distance, she thought she heard his voice. It distracted her, and Sacha's threads grew thinner and lighter until there wasn't enough left to grasp. Nina poured herself into Sacha, gave her as much of her will as she could. The mending was done, Sacha's wound had closed, but her body couldn't replenish her blood. Nina's will wasn't enough.

When she opened her eyes, Sacha watched her with a small smile. Her fingers brushed against Nina's cheek. "It was always you," she whispered. "You are all I See."

"Sacha, please," Nina cried. "Please don't leave me."

But Sacha was gone. Her eyes stared blankly above, her chest still, her arms limp in the snow. Nina screamed until her throat was raw. Tears fell and froze to her face and cracked her skin open until she was sure that everything she had ever been was gone.

She gnashed her teeth at the gods, cursed their names, collected the threads of those around her who watched the scene unfold before them with confusion, their hands on their blades, ready to fight despite the uncertainty brimming in their eyes. She couldn't distinguish one from the other, knew only that they were nothing but clay in her hands.

She began to squeeze, intent on bringing everyone to their knees.

And then: *"Nina!"*

Her head snapped toward the voice, the essence of vengeance on the tip of her tongue and tingling in her palms. But there was Kasik, on hands and knees, crawling to her. Her rage stuttered. Somehow, he was there, and he was fighting, and his voice centered her, reminded her, for a moment, of the person she could have been.

But half her soul was gone. She had given it all to Sacha, and there was space for more purpose than ever before. More awareness. More power. The men surrounding them dropped to their knees, their hands cradling their heads. If they wore achillas, it did not matter. Her wrath was righteous and undetectable by their measly stones.

Their voices rose in a chorus of screams, a symphony of pain unending that made her soul hum with pleasure and her power vibrate with joy. In her delight, and the clarity it provided, her eyes found Atik, a beacon in the middle of the melee, a knife poised above Kasik.

Kasik was speaking, but she couldn't hear him.

All she could see was his hand reached out for her. The revenge to be had.

Atik, with his threads fully restored. The achilla that hung from his neck and swung from side to side as he lunged forward. The blade in his hand as he plunged it into Kasik's back.

More blood on the achilla altar. Another offering to bring the gods closer than before.

More power for Nina to tear them all down.

Nina slipped out from underneath Sacha's body and lunged for Kasik at the same time the blade landed a second blow in his side. He screamed, but he left his hand open for her, where, in the center of his palm, was a small blade.

It didn't matter that she couldn't use her power against Atik. He was a man, a mortal, and he would bleed like one. Nina scooped up the knife and swung wildly at him.

But he was fast. He twirled out of the way of her arc, dancing lithely between the bodies of his emperor and his son. Nina was forced to follow, to crouch as he stabbed at her.

"You are no match for me," Atik said. His eyes swirled from black to brown, and Nina laughed.

"The gods abandoned you." She pointed her blade at his chest. "They've removed their will from you because you are not *worthy*. They know you will fail."

"*I will not*," Atik said, and he charged.

Nina braced for the impact, but she was weak, her attay and her mind shattered and scrabbling to fit the pieces back together. Her back hit the achilla altar with a crack that stole her breath. Black spots appeared in her vision, along with Atik's face. His legs were a cage around her body. His hands pinned her arms to the ground.

But he was just where she wanted him. Atik's achilla swung back and forth, suspended in the air between them like unsuspecting prey waiting to be snatched. "You are a *fool*," she spat. Little droplets of blood landed on his cheek, and she could only imagine he thought her crazed. "The gods laugh at how easily they have been able to manipulate you."

"*Nobody* manipulates me." Atik leaned even closer, his voice low like a secret. "The one who tried got my knife in her belly, just as you will."

He was squeezing her to death and all Nina could do was laugh. "Aliyma couldn't use her attay against you and still she was able to wrap you around her finger. Just as the gods do. *You have no will*, Atik. Her attay could not influence you."

It was what she had wanted to tell Master Wara. The part of his story that made no sense. If Aliyma's power was like hers, then Atik's power would have silenced it. She wouldn't have been able to hurt or control him even if she had tried. She had truly loved him, but he hadn't truly loved her. He wasn't capable of it.

"Yachua *lied*, and you willingly killed the only person who had ever loved you."

It was only a moment, but Atik faltered. His bruising grip on her arms lightened. A flash of doubt and fear passed over his face. And then he moved, so suddenly that Nina flinched away, but his hands wrapped around her throat and held her down while his elbows pinned her arms and his achilla settled into the middle of her chest, its icy fingers sinking beneath her skin.

"You lie," he seethed, and it was truly pathetic how easily he had unraveled. How blind he had been to it all.

"I do not," Nina rasped. Her vision pulsed with every beat of her heart. She pushed her arms against his, wiggled her fingers closer. All she had to do was rip the achilla from his throat and then she could use her attay to tear his soul to shreds. "You are nothing but an empty vessel to be used however the gods see fit, and they *tire* of you."

Atik's fist slammed into her face, knocking her head to the side and stealing her vision for several terrifying moments. It came back in spurts and spots, and she saw a hand that was not hers. A hand that she was sure was a figment of her imagination.

A hand that reached out and snatched the achilla from around Atik's throat.

50

It was the last of his strength. Kasik fell to the ground next to Nina, his tayta's achilla wrapped in a fist. He watched through sideways eyes and a fog of near death as Nina slowly rose, her eyes alight with the fire of a thousand suns. Her hair had come free from its pins and plaits and it billowed on a phantom breeze.

She was a vengeful god. Retribution and rage.

Kasik shivered with cold and fear. No more than an arm's length away, Atik sat on his knees, his arms spread wide and his mouth open in a silent scream. The tendons in his neck protruded grotesquely, the blood close enough to the skin that he looked like he might burst. Blood leaked from his eyes and ears and mouth, and Kasik knew that there would be nothing left of his tayta very soon.

Time seemed to slow. He turned to Nina so that her face would be the last thing he saw. A measure of comfort in the cold.

But she was unrecognizable. She towered over them both, a god among mere mortals, and she bared her teeth in a nightmarish grin.

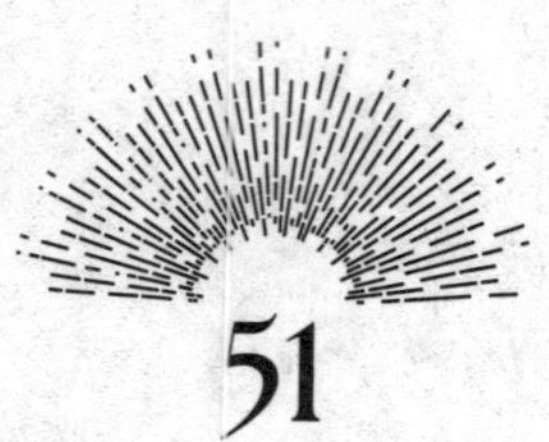

51

Nina became pure retribution. Vengeance coursed through her as Atik's threads thrummed in her hands, his body skewered on the end of her control.

Attay flooded her once again, and she gasped with the strength of it, fueled by Atik's life so that every will within range glowed like an exploding star.

Nina used all her strength to lean forward and place her cheek against Atik's. "You have failed," she breathed into his ear. "And you will suffer the gods' wrath for it. I hope you burn in their displeasure, that the faces of those you've murdered are all you can see. I hope you never forget that you were defeated by me, that my name rolls off your tongue with every breath you take in eternal misery."

She placed her hands on his shoulders, felt them tremble beneath her touch. At last, she was able to feel his will buried deeply beneath the darkness of his soul. "The gods have used you, and now they forsake you." Then she grasped his will, and she twisted. His eyes opened wide in terror. Streaks of red joined the black, and then he crumpled backward, legs folded unnaturally, unseeing eyes staring up at a sky full of betrayal.

Nina pulled free from Atik and surveyed the mountaintop. Her attay began reaching, grasping at the golden threads surrounding her that had scattered to the wind, men running for their lives, scrabbling down the mountainside like ants fleeing from their predator. She began pulling indiscriminately, uncaring who died and who lived, felt their lives drain from their bodies as they burst like overripe fruit, blood leaking from their eyes and mouths and ears and nose, feeding the earth her revenge that, in turn, fed her attay twenty times over.

And yet, it wasn't sated. It hungered for more.

These people had turned her into this, had forced her to become their worst nightmare. Was she to blame for taking pleasure in their demise? For accepting the role they had forced onto her?

Nina found Maicu on his side just past the ring of the achilla altar. Somehow, he was still alive, and his fingers twitched as she approached. She imagined how she looked, bloody and half broken but filled with power. With *purpose*.

What a treat the gods had given her that it would be her hand to take his life.

She fell to her knees before him, the blade held between two fists.

"Can you hear me?" she asked calmly.

Maicu took a shallow breath, and then whispered, "Yes."

"The rest of my family. Are they alive?"

An almost imperceptible shake of his head. His lips parted, and Nina had to put her ear to his lips to hear him over the screaming wind. "Ask . . . Kasik."

The blood beneath her skin froze with those two small words, but her will exulted in the weakness of this once-great emperor. She was blind to the faces of those she had killed, blind to the destruction she was wreaking on behalf of the gods. She was playing into their hands, and she was enjoying every moment of it.

Slowly, she reached out to grab Maicu's golden circlet lying discarded above his head. He watched with unblinking eyes as she wrenched the achilla from the center and held it up to the light. It swirled with life, with knowing. The gods' will beat at the center of it, and she squeezed it in her fist and turned it to dust. It shimmered on the breeze as it floated free. And then she reached for his threads, fully pliant in her hands.

Pleasure thrummed through her at his wide, panicked eyes. It was tempting to hold him there forever, to revel in his vulnerability and pain until the end of time. Perhaps she could keep him alive and control his every move, his every thought.

Nina reached for the emperor slowly, gently, as she had once in his rooms when she was weak and afraid. She delicately ran her hand across his head, combed her fingers through his thick hair, then grabbed it into a fist and pulled. His head sprang upward, eyes to the sky, and Nina moved closer. "You made the wrong choices, Maicu. You will pay for the gods' greed. It's a shame that you won't be here to witness as I destroy them."

The emperor shook his head. His eyes were different now, lighter. Less burdened without the crown on his head. "The gods fear nothing, not even you."

"We'll find out soon enough," she whispered gently as she slid her hand over his chest.

Nina was finally completely attuned with the strength of her attay. She saw how easy it would be to destroy Maicu's body from the inside out until he was a puddle of gore and grit. How the pain would drive him into madness. How the blood would feed her appetite.

She saw it all, and yet she fought against that pull.

This is not who you are, she heard her sister whisper.

With a squeeze of her mind, Maicu's last breath left his lips. His heart fell silent beneath her hand.

All across the mountain, there was quiet.

The tang of blood carried on the wind. Small flakes of snow melted against her overheated cheeks. Nina raised her eyes to the sky, and she screamed. It echoed back to her in a mockery of her pain.

On hands and knees, she crawled first to Sacha. Her body was too light as she collected it in her arms. Too cold. Too still. In life, Sacha had been warm and soothing and good. She was the only part of Nina that forced her to be better.

Now she was gone, and it was Nina who had failed. She pressed her forehead into her baby sister's chest and murmured the same three words over and over, as if she could press them into Sacha even in death.

I'm so sorry. I'm so sorry. I'm so sorry.

It would never be enough, and Nina would spend the rest of her life demanding penance.

Several arm's lengths away, she saw the fur of Kasik's coat dancing in the breeze. He was face down in the snow, his pulse entirely still beneath her hand once she reached him, his once vibrant and responsive threads absent in her mind.

Gone, just like the answers the emperor said he had.

Perhaps this had been her fate all along. To be betrayed, to lose those she loved, to become an instrument of death and destruction. A pawn in a long and twisted game.

A monster of their making.

Nina accepted their invitation, and she was not afraid.

EPILOGUE

Kasik stood over the devastation at the top of the mountain, the jagged shards of the achilla altar at his feet and the gods' will filling his head.

He had died, and they had revived his soul, sliced him apart, searing and demanding, until he was cold and empty.

A vessel waiting to be filled.

Time had no meaning. Bodies covered in snow littered the ground, blood frozen beneath them. One by one, he wiped their faces. He saw the victims of Nina's wrath. The victims of his tayta's failure, but the man was nowhere to be found.

It mattered little now. Nothing had ever been so clear.

There was who he was *before*, a mortal filled with mortal longings that weakened him to the truth of the world. The insignificance of their lives was like a weight lifted from his shoulders. No longer was he concerned about his own desires. No longer did they cloud his judgment.

And there was who he was *now*, remade in the gods' image. Filled to bursting with their will, until his own ceased to exist. Finally, he was who he was always meant to be. All he could see was the gods' plan for his life, *all* their lives, and it was good.

Nina would destroy their world. She would usher them into chaos and destruction, and it was Kasik who would stop her. Through him, the people of Tawantinsuyu would be led to victory.

And the gods would finally return home.

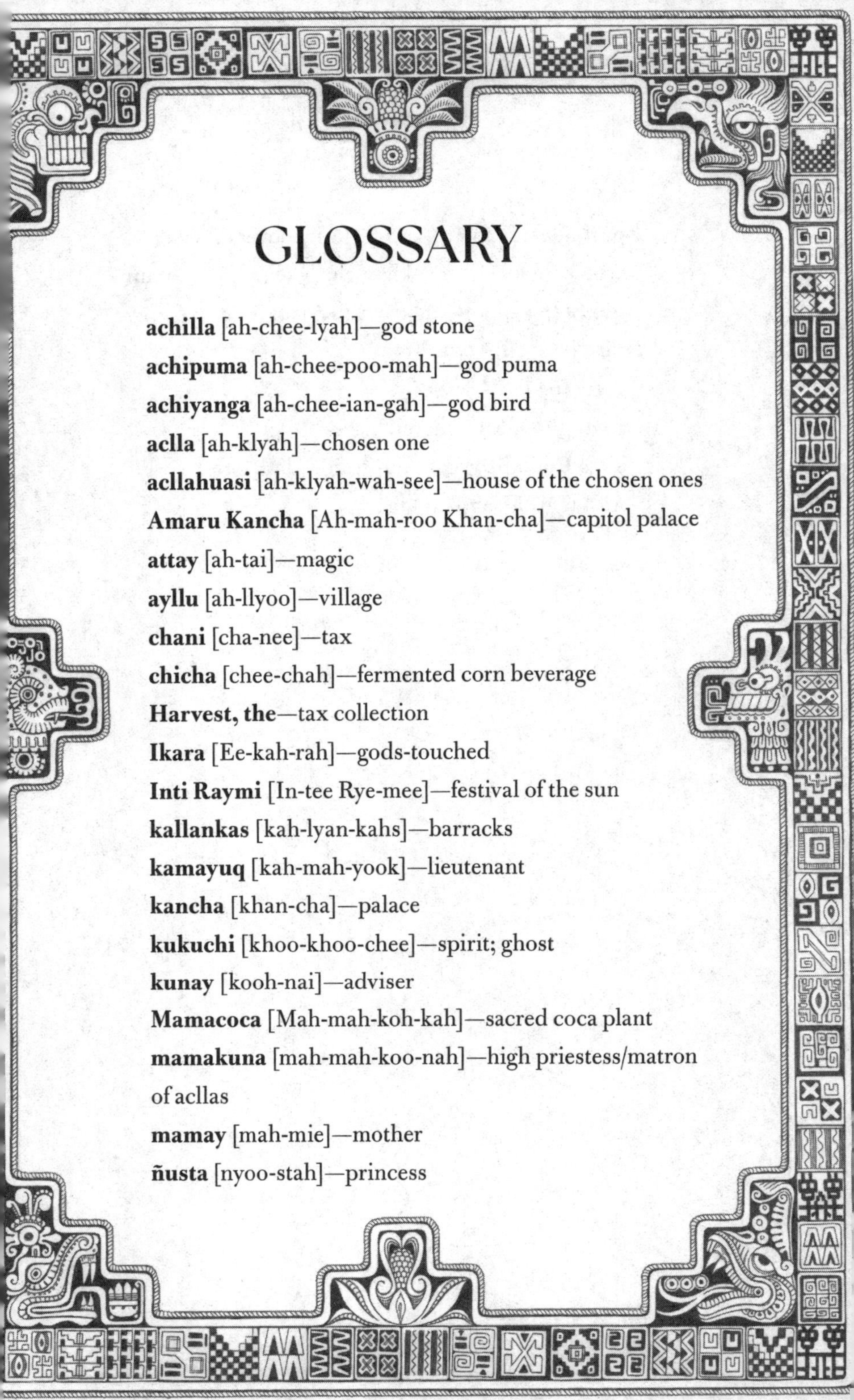

GLOSSARY

achilla [ah-chee-lyah]—god stone

achipuma [ah-chee-poo-mah]—god puma

achiyanga [ah-chee-ian-gah]—god bird

aclla [ah-klyah]—chosen one

acllahuasi [ah-klyah-wah-see]—house of the chosen ones

Amaru Kancha [Ah-mah-roo Khan-cha]—capitol palace

attay [ah-tai]—magic

ayllu [ah-llyoo]—village

chani [cha-nee]—tax

chicha [chee-chah]—fermented corn beverage

Harvest, the—tax collection

Ikara [Ee-kah-rah]—gods-touched

Inti Raymi [In-tee Rye-mee]—festival of the sun

kallankas [kah-lyan-kahs]—barracks

kamayuq [kah-mah-yook]—lieutenant

kancha [khan-cha]—palace

kukuchi [khoo-khoo-chee]—spirit; ghost

kunay [kooh-nai]—adviser

Mamacoca [Mah-mah-koh-kah]—sacred coca plant

mamakuna [mah-mah-koo-nah]—high priestess/matron of acllas

mamay [mah-mie]—mother

ñusta [nyoo-stah]—princess

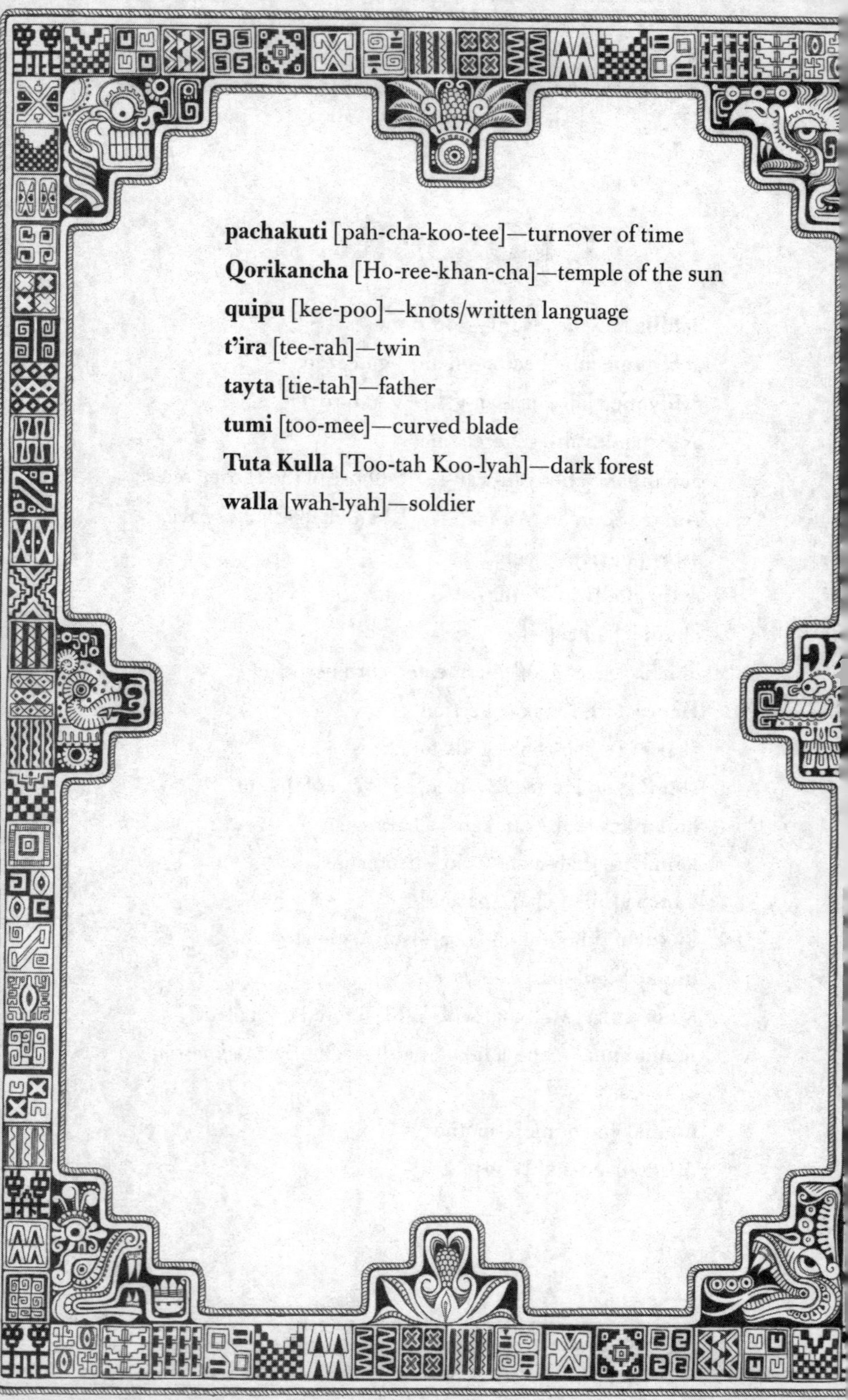

pachakuti [pah-cha-koo-tee]—turnover of time

Qorikancha [Ho-ree-khan-cha]—temple of the sun

quipu [kee-poo]—knots/written language

t'ira [tee-rah]—twin

tayta [tie-tah]—father

tumi [too-mee]—curved blade

Tuta Kulla [Too-tah Koo-lyah]—dark forest

walla [wah-lyah]—soldier

ACKNOWLEDGMENTS

In the words of Snoop Dogg, "I wanna thank me for believing in me. I wanna thank me for doing all this hard work." But so much of this would not have been possible without certain people who deserve effusive thanks.

My agent, Melanie Figueroa: I knew the moment we spoke that you were going to change my life. That your faith in me and this story was going to take us to places I couldn't have imagined. And I was so right. *Thank you* will never be enough.

My editor, Karen Chaplin, for pushing me to become the best storyteller I could be. My copyeditor, Sarah Mondello, for keeping my horrendous timeline on track. My publishing team and everyone working behind the scenes in making this dream a reality: I see you, and I'm so grateful for your hard work and consideration. Sisa Quispe, who served as a culture consultant and sensitivity reader: your feedback and encouragement were invaluable during the process of shaping *Their Will Undone*. My cover artist, Steph C, for beautifully bringing my book to life.

The authors that took time out of their busy schedules to read and blurb: you inspire me every single day. (A special shout-out to Angela Montoya for reading and critiquing my query letter back when I was a nobody with audacity.)

To the friends that have come alongside me—Taylor, for always excitedly reading my dumpster fire of a first draft. Kelly, Ayngelea and Alexis; for listening to me rant and reminding me that I am strong enough to keep going. Sydney, for being a voice of reason and for explaining a high-yield savings account. It's been a privilege being just a girl alongside you in this crazy career. Megan and Kelsie: there would have been absolute devastation and chaos without you two by my side (and significantly less texts and tea). To my book club girlies: thank you for letting me force you through my TBR, which was mostly just research for whatever book I was working on at the moment; and Meg, for letting me convince you to abandon your real life and join me in fictional worlds, and for generally being the best friend a girl could ask for. To every single person on Instagram and TikTok that liked, commented, shared, and generally hyped this book: your support means the world.

To my family—Elisa, for telling me, "Don't die, just cry and keep writing," when I said this book was going to kill me. Mom, for convincing me that this was not a pipe dream and it was worth the sacrifices. (You were right.) Dad, for being calm and steady and proud of me, no matter what. Adrian, for every celebration you've hosted at your house and the bottles of tequila you drank in my honor.

To God, for giving me this brain that never shuts up but is apparently pretty good at writing stories.

And last but certainly not least, to my kids: I am who I am because of you; and to my husband: thank you for being so competent and capable, for feeding me, for being both mom and dad while my brain was in a different world, for letting me yap your ear off about plot holes and magic systems and never once batting an eye, and for loving all parts of me always.

AUTHOR'S NOTE

This story was inspired by the Maiden of Llullaillaco, an adolescent girl found mummified on the top of the Andes Mountains. In my research of South American history, I kept getting pulled back to her story and the circumstances surrounding her life and death. I couldn't help but daydream and ask myself, *What could have happened if she'd had the power to save herself?*

Though I researched for years and worked closely with a culture and language consultant, I've taken many creative liberties to tell Nina's story while also reflecting my own life experiences with power and religion. Inspiration was taken from Inca history, languages such as Quechua and Aymara, and Andean Cosmovision, but this specific story is not meant to be historically or linguistically accurate. A glossary with pronunciation has been included, but I encourage you to seek out nonfiction sources for the most authentic information and to learn more about the beautiful cultures and peoples of the Andes.